THE GHOST AND THE FALLEN

LANA J. PRINCE

Book Cover by David Gardias

Illustrations by Júlia Plasse da Silvia, @_julpers

Map illustration by Virginia Allyn

Developmental Editing by Noah Sky

Copyediting by Carrie Napolitano

Line Editing by Dylan Jones Gosselin

First edition 2023

ISBN-13, ebook: 979-8-9884708-1-6

ISBN-13, Paperback: 979-8-9884708-0-9

ISBN-13, Hardcover: 979-8-218-21720-4

To my first readers,
Not everyone can be saved

SOMNIUM

THE DREADLANDS

SOUNDLESS STREAM

THE SLUMS

THE WOODLANDS

NORTHERN SUMMIT

VOCLAINE MANOR

AMPITHEATER

HOUSE OF LORDS

EASTERN HEIGHTS

KOVANS FOXHOLE

SOMNIUM UNIVERSITY

THE DOME

CROSSPOINT YARD

BOTANIC PLAZA

TERTAIN MANOR

THE TENTS

WATEREDGE

MOMENTUM MUSEUM

N

W   E

S

CHARMED BAY

THE MAGICIAN

Jinx

Two weeks prior

The creature visited her in a nightmare. Holding up a single murky finger, he smiled behind that skeletal mask of a deer with high branch-like antlers and hazy silhouette. Predatory stillness kept it at bay, like watching a frame stuck in time. Its treelike horns reached up toward the leaves of the mountainous trees looming above. The demon's overwhelming presence accelerated her already thrumming heart. She strained her neck upward to meet it as trickles of sweat snaked down her spine.

The bargain she had made—the magic tying it together—pressed against her skull. It was as if it were tugging on that bargain, pulling her toward the creature. But what truly made her nauseous was thinking about that damned finger.

It was a reminder of what she had done, what it had cost her.

One finger.

And one year was all she had left.

Jinx's clock was ticking, the hands of time rhythmically tapping out each and every second. The demon did not sing the vexing riddle or speak his dreadful voice that burned her ears.

The organ in her chest beat against her ribcage, pulsating vibrations through her veins.

The depths of darkness within his murky eyes flashed red. Air died in her lungs. Her heartbeat sped up. Tendrils of sweat beaded across her forehead.

Though her skin was cool to the touch, her muscles beneath felt like they'd been set aflame. The increasing tick of the clock matched the cadence of her heart's sprinting pace.

Her eyes split open. Sickness rolled up her throat, acid scorching her insides.

Jinx twisted to one side, releasing her dinner. Wiping off her mouth with the back of her hand, she panted heavily, erasing the nightmare with a series of blinks.

She stared at the four plain walls around her. The wallpaper was peeling away, the splintery wooden floor waiting and eager to pierce flesh. Moonlight poured in through the cracks of the abandoned building's boarded windows. Her temporary home.

Reality.

Jinx finally took a deep breath. Resting her head back onto the pillow and pulling the blanket tighter around her, she tucked herself into the fetal position of a newborn. Shivers twitched throughout her body, from her spine to her stomach.

She forced herself to go back to sleep, squeezing her lids shut.

But Jinx could not ignore the fear embedded in her heart and the image of that creature rooted in her brain. As she re-entered the world of slumber, the demon returned, relaying the same message. The one she received every year previous, counting down to her final one.

One year left.

Once awake, Jinx navigated herself through the steam-infused industrial zone of Crosspoint Yard, over to the high-rise riches of Eastern Heights via rooftop. She jumped and skidded over the oily red brick buildings until her feet finally met the green tiles of gold-crusted roofs lingering above limestone walls.

As she reached her destination, she caught sight of one woman threading through the speckled masses of ladies passing with and without chaperones, depending on the progressiveness of the family. The woman wore a yellow dress, her corset beaded with pearls arranged in a specific crossed pattern. Her laced skirt rounded out at the bottom due to the bustle underneath. On her head laid a tilted hat with feathers and flowers blossoming atop. Matching lace gloves wrapped around the doorknob of the store she was entering.

Her mother.

Jinx's throat tightened. She was a replica of her mother, with long obsidian hair and brown silky skin. The only slight difference rested in their eyes. Her mother's were honey brown, Jinx's emerald green—a gift from her dead father.

Jinx lowered her chest down to the roof, her eyes trailing her mother as she stepped into a bookstore.

Hugo's Hearty House: the printing press Jinx's uncle had been trying to start for ages.

Her mother hugged her brother, and he took her to his office. Jinx crawled toward the window in the back, where she could gain a clear view of her family.

Her uncle, Hugo, offered Jinx's mother a chair and went to open the back door, returning with a cake. White frosting coated the delicious delicacy. He inserted candles and lit the tip with a match. Her mother's cheeks reddened, tears strolling down, and her uncle wrapped her in a bearlike embrace.

Jinx breathed in, fighting the swell of emotions she let herself feel for only a moment.

Her mother stood and blew the candles, wisps of smoke curling out.

"Happy Birthday to me." Jinx whispered, pressing her lips together.

A flash of a memory crossed her mind: the day she'd left her home in the Slums. She watched from afar when her uncle had come home that day. Rejoicing with crumpled letters in hand. Elated an investor had taken an interest in the press, changing their lives forever. She relaxed, seeing her bargain in effect.

However, since she shook hands with the creature, she'd become a monster. Transforming into the Ghost of Somnium—the legendary beast that every citizen in Somnium feared. They feared her even more than they feared the Cursed, a people with magic flowing through their bloodstream. Infected by a plague that had struck Somnium twenty years ago.

Through the window, her mother collapsed onto her knees, burying her face into her laced palms.

Jinx had given up once she turned fourteen, feeling hopeless to solve that riddle, thinking it was for the best. But she was twenty now. The creature had started visiting her in her dreams again, and her one-year deadline to break the curse loomed, striking her with renewed motivation. It was her last chance to go home.

Ambling along the cobblestone streets below, cutting in ahead of a horse-hauled stage-coach, Apollo Voclaine was returning from the House of Lords. A Son of the Seven—the Seven aristocratic families that ruled Somnium.

A merciless grin spread her lips as an idea formulated in her mind.

It was her last chance.

One more year was all she had.

And damn the Virtues if they tried to stop her.

By the seventh day of trailing Apollo, Jinx had come to realize his days were rather repetitive. In the mornings, he would wake early, open his curtains, and write in a notebook while looking out the window. He'd then work on his desk, penning papers and flipping through files. Then he'd paced around the room and return to work again, pushing his reading glasses back up his nose every few seconds. Afterward, he'd go on to do more tedious activities. Jinx shuddered just thinking about it.

Jinx thanked the Virtues that she was never forced to do a job like his. Stuck in a room all day, reviewing stacks of paperwork for his father.

Today, at least, was slightly different compared to the rest. The four Voclaine siblings sauntered over to the Dome, a glass orb that covered an intersection of four grand buildings housing hundreds of small high-end shops.

The youngest of the Voclaine siblings was a girl that went by the name of Fey, a ballerina in spirit and sport and twin to the boy beside her, Thatcher. She walked faster than the rest of them, ticking off what Jinx could imagine was likely a list of things to buy at the market.

Her twin, Thatcher, rolled his eyes at his sister's antics, falling into step beside Apollo. Thatcher rambled on about something that Jinx was too far to overhear. Apollo's complexion softened at his brothers' words; as he responded, Thatcher gave a bellied laugh.

Apollo jerked his chin for his brother to move along forward; Thatcher waved a hand before hurrying up to accompany his twin ahead, securing the strap of his brown satchel across his back.

Another sister, Arya—the second oldest, dressed in lavender—cooled herself with a folding fan. She, too, was an interesting Voclaine child. Jinx picked up two odd traits from her, characteristics she'd dig deeper into if Arya had been Jinx's individual of interest. She snuck off at night and guarded her collection of fans as a dragon would protect its gold. Arya, however, was not Jinx's target.

Apollo merely glanced at Arya, who stepped ahead of him. Placing his hands in his pockets, he watched over his siblings. He was their protector and the head of the quartet.

The glass Dome glittered before them, reflecting shimmers of sunlight off its golden skeleton.

Apollo crossed an invisible boundary, a single foot passing the threshold. Movement ceased to exist. Jinx blinked twice.

What she witnessed before her was unlike anything she'd ever seen. There were rumors about how Apollo was able to control a crowd of citizens. But this...this was unheard of.

People did not dare to blink. Movement outlawed, banned for the seconds he held. Apollo dipped his chin, and life returned as if it had never been halted.

Jinx's mouth dried. People parted, creating a walkway for him and the other siblings. The Voclaines strolled past these watchful eyes as if they were not even there. Apollo continued on through the Dome, ending conversations with a single word, a single uncaring stare, a single brush of a hand. Mothers and daughters threw themselves at him, though he barely cast a glance in their direction; still, Jinx watched as the women audibly swooned.

Apollo stayed behind his brothers and sisters, trailing them as they bought trinkets, shoes, and food. Occasionally, he twisted the ring on his finger, a habit of his that Jinx had picked up on more than once.

THE CHARIOT

Chapter 1

Apollo

This was Apollo's fourth glass of wine, though his only reason for indulgence was that he was hoping it would drown out the noisy soiree of his twenty-third birthday, which was orchestrated by his mother. The Momento Museum had been bustling for two hours now. A wailing quartet of violinists played alongside a pianist in the far corner of the room. Relics and ancient artifacts had been set carefully aside, opening up the floor for those wishing to take part in a dance. The Seven Aristocratic families were all in attendance—including his own— as well as some other lords and ladies of high society.

Apollo set down the empty glass atop a waiter's passing tray, lazily picking on another. He swirled the crimson liquor, watching the remnants cry as they fell down the sides of the cup.

"It is a marvel watching you brood at your own gathering, Pol," Thatcher commented.

Apollo ignored the uncalled-for statement, keeping his thoughts to himself. If Mother had forced his brother to celebrate something he was not keen to commemorate, Apollo could only assume Thatcher would have acted the same way. However, it wasn't totally different from his normal demeanor, as Apollo always seemed expressionless.

Apollo had always been aware of his reputation, the man that society painted him out to be. Vile, reserved, insensitive. He simply preferred being truthful. To him, a fake smile was always too much work.

He let the dry, bitter wine sting his tongue, his gaze fixed on the dancing throng before him.

Lords had dressed up in their finest suits and ladies donned their finest silks, gloves reaching the ends of their elbows, corsets pinching their lungs, breasts hovering near the edge of their bodices. The collective smoke from their cigarettes puffed above them, forming a heavy cloud which lingered above the heads of those lost in music.

"How can you tell he is brooding? I would have pinned him as bothered," Kovan wondered aloud, tentatively combing his fingers through his swift silver hair, his brow beaded with sweat from a previous dance.

Agitation pricked at Apollo's neck. "While you two stay here obsessing over me and my state of mind like two hungry ladies in wait, I will take a walk around the museum. Enjoy yourselves." Apollo offered a curt nod and a minimal grin before peeling himself away from his younger brother and their friend.

A twinge of guilt wrapped itself delicately around his gut as he reflected on his word choice. Apollo only wished to retreat into the Voclaine home. He sauntered on, weaving between bodies lost in their own buzzed trance.

Large assemblages like this sometimes tipped his senses into overload, antagonizing that thing trapped inside of him, that nightmare entwined within his soul.

Apollo drained the rest of his wine, carefully holding back the anxiety that was boiling in his stomach. Gooseflesh peppered his skin, the hair on his neck standing on edge.

Above him, the highly detailed arches and painted ceiling of the museum felt like they were caving in. The illustration of the four Virtues hovering above him weighed heavily on Apollo's chest. It was like they were scrutinizing him through their dead stares as if they knew the genuine horror he was.

Apollo tried his best to keep breathing, grasping at any attempt to dampen the rising emotion of fear.

Apollo Voclaine knew, however, that as long as the ring remained on his long, slim fingers, he would prevail. Or so he hoped.

The liquor finally had invaded his system, easing his anxious insides. His vision gradually turned sluggish, his eyelids drooping.

Apollo wiggled his fingers, eager to control something within his own body. He wiped away the faint moisture of his clammy hands on his white pants and straightened the lapels of his light gray tailcoat before fishing around in his pocket for his gold watch.

All of a sudden, two ladies in wait latched themselves onto Apollo's arms. They begged him to dance, flaunting offers of debauchery, whining to bring him closer. A bitter taste coated his tongue. He shrugged off their digging nails. "Do not touch me."

One more hour. He just needed to survive one more goddamn hour of these artificial people. Finally, Apollo found himself spit out from the throng, entering the uninhabited area of the museum.

Positioned on the wall in front of him was a brilliant portrait of the four Virtues.

Fortuna, the Virtue of Wealth and Bravery. She walked along the valley, holding a wealth of golden coins in one hand and a spear in the other, providing for and protecting the families next to her.

Elu, the Virtue of Life and Nature. She rested atop the cushion of thick, white clouds. A careless hand swiped the sky below, nurturing the blooming fauna below with fluttering speckles of gold.

Esme, the Virtue of Love and Fertility. Sitting beside Elu, there was a harp in her hand, playing the strings of desire. A flock of doves soared overhead.

And below the other three, swathed in shadows, lurked Akuji, the Virtue of Death and Fear. His black wings—those of a fallen angel—splayed out across the depths of obscurity.

Behind him rested a silver balance scale, prepared to measure the purity of the soul, and in his hands were two sickles, ready to pry the core spirit from a being.

Far behind these Virtues, hiding behind a gathering of people, something greater lay in wait. It appeared as if someone had almost tried to wash it away, scratching with a rough rag, as if the artist regretted even mentioning its existence. Pain infused within those thick strokes, the being was hard to see but was still there, its long fingers puppeteering the minds of mortals.

A force pushed Apollo's slender body back as a blotch of cold kissed his midsection. He withdrew, staring down at his clothes. Red wine bled down his white attire.

"Your Grace!" A female gasped, drawing Apollo's attention. "My deepest apologies."

A head of thick white curls bobbed down before him as she lowered her head. The lady shuffled over to a passing server, plucking a handful of napkins from his tray. She pressed them against his stomach, blotting away what she could.

Apollo stepped back, hoping to avoid any more physical contact. "It is fine. It is truly nothing to worry about."

At that, her eyes dared to meet his gaze. Her ebony skin reminded him of luminous silk under the orange glow of candlelight. Big doe eyes of innocence fluttered beneath thick lashes.

"No, I insist," she said. "It is awfully rude of me to not pick up after my mess. Especially since it is your birthday."

Apollo raised a hand to stop her. "Lady...?"

"Lady Hunt." She performed the most calculated curtsy. If it wasn't Apollo's honed eye taking her in, it could have fooled anybody. Though it seemed not entirely natural, anyone born in a house of wealth would have been flush. This lady was fraught for a mere second.

Despite her almost flawless curtsy, Apollo had not heard of a so-called Lady Hunt. Part of his job as a Son of the Seven was to know the name of every person who habituated in Somnium. This interaction lacked an important puzzle piece.

"Lady Hunt," Apollo repeated, "I urge you to enjoy your night. A suit isn't anything of importance."

Lady Hunt curtsied once more and departed. Apollo watched her curvy figure disappear within the bustling crowd. She struck him as odd.

Not only had he not known that the Hunts had a daughter, but in his core, there was something else he could not pinpoint. A familiarity of sorts.

"Wait, Lady Hunt," Apollo said. "Have we met prior to this encounter?"

She pivoted, offering a smile. "I do not believe so. Those drinks are getting to you. I must be off, Your Grace."

He gave her another once over, boring his gaze deep into her eyes, attempting to trace a moment where they possibly could have crossed.

The intensity caused a hitch in her breath. There was a wavering in her eyes, a faint echo of silver and green lining outside the brown iris. It disappeared as quickly as it had arrived.

"Certainly." Apollo watched Lady Hunt walk away, deciding to leave well enough alone. Her steps are unannounced. Unlike the rest of the females, the sound ceased at her departure. As if noise were an enemy.

What a strange woman.

An instinctual call summoned Apollo to the next relic—an artifact known as the "Vessel." It was a simple wooden box, dark and inscribed with runes unknown that no scientist or priest could decipher. It was also impossible to open, lacking any obvious indications of ownership or history.

A golden plate was situated right below it, with all existing information etched into the material. According to the engraving, the Vessel had been found in the Woodlands by a headmaster of Somnium University—who'd died three years prior—on an excursion with his fellow students. A tree had grown around it, hugging the box, shielding it from the rest of the world. It seemed almost like a message from nature, who'd wanted to keep it a secret.

A buzz skidded across his shoulders. A sour tang spread across his tongue as a foul, rotten scent reached his nose. A warning.

Take it.

There it was. The maddening, dark, and rasping voice resounded at the back of Apollo's skull.

A dry swallow.

He hadn't heard that voice in years. Why was it suddenly speaking to him now? When Apollo had tried so hard to get rid of it?

Take it. Destroy it.

Sweat licked the edges of Apollo's raven hair. He felt his hands begin to tremble in that uncontrollable way that hinted at devastating destruction.

Do you want to get rid of me? Destroy the Vessel. It had taken years for Apollo to forget that horrible sound, that sensation of someone shoveling through his mind, trying to make it their own. There was no purpose of it speaking again. There was little possibility of that piece of him becoming stronger. That voice. That thing.

Yes, Apollo did want to erase that demon from his soul. It reminded him that his body would never truly be his, his mind chronically shared.

Apollo wielded his best mask, hoping to appear calm and unbothered. He took another glass of wine from a nearby table and finished it in one sip.

A disarming surge of chills wretched Apollo's spine as frigid pressure built up in the back of his eyes.

"Darling." His mother's voice cut through the pain, joyous above the shrill of the music.

His vision sharpened, colors becoming more enhanced. His ears crying over the music increasing in sound.

"Darling."

Apollo clenched his jaw, desperate to hold himself together, even if the threads of his sanity were wearing down to a single string.

"Are you alright?" A scorching, feverish hand grasped his glacial skin. His mother had been closer than he expected; Apollo had to get away. "You're freezing."

"I must use the restroom. Mother, if you'll excuse me." Apollo beelined for the lavatory.

Locking himself inside the room, Apollo shifted all of his weight to his hands, holding the edges of the porcelain white sink. His lean fingers dug into the sides as he stared at his reflection.

His normally creamy skin had gone a shade even paler. Soft raven hair that had once appeared neat and parted down the middle was now disheveled. Apollo's winter gray eyes started to change their color. His reflection grinned back at him, revealing pointed teeth.

His mouth moved, speaking in a voice that was not his own.

Come on, Voclaine. You've wanted me gone for years. Take the damn Vessel and destroy it.

Apollo's face fell into his hands as he tried to smear away the image infiltrating his mind.

Looking back again in the mirror, Apollo now only saw his true form before him.

His heart settled, vision returning to normal. Every trace of that demon was gone.

Only then, staring at his hands to assure himself of reality, did Apollo notice that his ring was missing.

The voice had only spoken to him after he had that exchange with Lady Hunt. It was unlikely that the ring had simply fallen or slipped off his finger, so there was only one correct answer.

The dire ring must have been stolen–keeping him mentally balanced since he'd been in the Woodlands. He thought back to the woman who'd called herself Lady Hunt, the silver and green behind the brown eyes. It must have been a false identity. There was only one person in Somnium who was known to fabricate identities. What were the statistical chances of encountering such a person? Slim, but still possible.

Valuable people lingered across every inch of the floor, setting themselves up as perfect marks for a criminal. And it was a perfect environment for pillaging.

The number of guards posted at the entrance wouldn't matter for one specific thief.

He had just encountered the most wanted criminal in all of Somnium City: Jinx.

Chapter 2

Jinx

Jinx smiled. She had gotten what she came for, though it was hard to tell how the ring benefited her. The silver ring of Apollo Voclaine held significant value to him, something that had been glaringly apparent as she watched him over the past two weeks. That ring never once left his finger.

Another thing she'd discovered over the past two weeks was that Apollo didn't often reveal his true feelings, his features frozen in a bored stare. It nearly frightened Jinx how calculated and composed the man was. And yet, as exhausted as he often sounded when speaking with others, there leaked a certain charm that encaptivated those who listened.

Apollo Voclaine was a human that Jinx would have liked to study more in-depth—if time hadn't been of the essence. If she couldn't answer the riddle by the end of the final year, Jinx would never be with her mother again. Separated forever. Eternally forgotten, never existing to begin with. Jinx was down to her last resort. Stealing from the first son of one of the most powerful families in all of Somnium City was desperation personified.

Jinx tucked the ring away in the pocket of her dress, securing its safety. She could not afford to leave immediately without appearing too suspicious. In swift calculation, Jinx decided to linger just a few minutes longer.

The red stain spreading across his white ensemble would hopefully distract Apollo enough to allow Jinx to take her exit. She noticed how indifferent he had been about the encounter, wanting only to get away from her and the crowds. The rigidity in his shoulders conveyed hints of his concealed stress. And she could tell by the glint in his winter gray eyes that he was intelligent. Perhaps even brilliant if Jinx wanted to extend him any credit.

Jinx had studied human interaction intensely for most of her life. Understanding people by their slightest movements and facial expressions helped ensure her survival. She could often tell what they were thinking by reading their body language. She'd become enough people using her illusions, manipulating their perception of her. It'd become second nature.

In large part due to this wealth of prior experience, Jinx had estimated that Apollo's stress over the stain would grant her a bit more time to make her getaway.

Footsteps drew near, hurried and weary. A server. Jinx looked over her shoulder and confirmed her guess. She pinched a wineglass from the server's tray, held it up by the stem, and took a slow sip before proceeding.

Upon entering the gala, getting her eyes checked at the entrance—a protocol that'd gained prominence due to the mass enigma of the Cursed—guards drew a lit torch up next to her face. As the flame almost seared her skin, Jinx analyzed the environment before her—assessing who was in attendance, who was a threat, where Apollo was, and where the best area would be for her to fit in. She eyed a spot over by the appetizer table that looked like it would fit the bill.

Jinx had already noticed that a bright blonde woman kept approaching the table to grab a snack every couple of minutes. Her hair was crafted into an elegant updo, twined with peppers of gold. Jinx quickly adjusted her position to enable easy interaction with the woman. Once engaged in friendly conversation, no one at the party would suspect Jinx was out of place.

Suddenly, the beautiful violins sounded their emotion-laden call. The dancers swirled, changing their partners, with the ladies' skirts blooming throughout their pivots. Jealousy left a bitter taste in Jinx's mouth.

If the Virtues hadn't gambled with her life, if she hadn't been so stubborn when striking that deal, would she be dancing alongside them now, as carefree as her fellow gentry? Her peers drunkenly smashed their glasses together, spilling liquor to the floor that, on its own, could easily buy a manor. Would her mother still be with her, sewing gorgeous dresses for Jinx to wear to these events?

She shoved the idea away; it was useless to think about what could have been. Those were thoughts that would only infiltrate her mind before bed when she could let her guard down.

She could not afford to do so now.

Jinx was standing on risky ground. One minute mistake could send her to the guillotine. Not only was she the most wanted criminal in all of Somnium—she was also a Cursed.

Twenty years ago, in the city of Somnium, a plague hit, killing thousands of people. How the plague began was still a mystery, but fear terrorized the minds of humans ever since. Those who survived had the chance of obtaining unnatural abilities. Humans turned to the Virtues for answers, who then created and perpetuated a false rumor that those contaminated had been transformed into fiends. They were Cursed.

Magic users.

Shunned from society, forced to live in hiding.

The Cursed looked as regular as any other walking pedestrians except for the traces of silver in their irises.

Jinx, in particular, was an illusionist, able to mimic and "wear" faces that were never her own. A moldable mirror to those around her.

Not a soul knew her true face, for that was a secret she'd kept to herself.

Her true skin was a caramel brown. Her thick hair was not a curled mass of white hair but slick obsidian that scraped down to her hips. Fighting leathers hid beneath her miraged dress.

She also had piercing emerald eyes streaked with silver.

It was the one giveaway of what she really was beneath the facade she put on for everyone else.

Every Cursed being had silver in their eyes. Those who survived the plague had to develop savvy ways to live, hiding them behind colored contacts.

A gentle hum trembled the hefty folds of her blue dress. Jinx snaked a swift hand to the pocket where the ring was. The jewelry had indeed been vibrating, emitting energy so hot it almost burned.

Jinx visibly flinched. What was Lord Voclaine hiding? Why did this inanimate piece of jewelry feel so alive?

"Pardon," Jinx was tugged from her thoughts by a soft, gentle voice accompanied by rich red lips, "could you pass me that square of cheese over there?"

Jinx nodded, handing over the entire tray.

"I'm afraid you misunderstood." Her blonde tablemate snorted, grabbing the tray any-way. "I meant a single square, not the entire block." The lady tucked a short strand of blond hair behind her ear, the shoulder-length waves swaying. Her amber eyes warmed into liquid as she took a bite.

"I did not. You've been eating a different piece every five minutes. Might as well take the whole thing," Jinx explained, glancing at the blonde through the corner of her eye.

The lady's cheeks flushed a shy pink, as if she'd been confident beforehand that no one had noticed her appetite. Her lips kicked up into a charming grin. "I'm afraid we haven't met. Lady Camilla Tertain." She reached out a laced, gloved hand.

Jinx delicately took it and offered her own in exchange. "Lady Hunt."

"A pleasure."

"Likewise." Jinx studied her. Camilla's sight jumped from person to person, hyperaware. Nibbling on the piece of cheese, she seemed like a tense mouse amongst a party of wolves. "You don't come to these functions often, do you?"

"Afraid not. Can you tell?" Camilla asked.

"Slightly."

A man with features resembling Apollo's approached. The second son of the Voclaine family, Thatcher Voclaine, was the more beautiful of the two brothers. Thatcher's ice-blue eyes, raven hair, and soft nose offered him a youthful, fetching allure, while Apollo's aura had always seemed darker, however charismatic. Both brothers were slender and tall, around six-foot-one.

"Thatcher," Camilla happily greeted him.

"Camilla." He bowed deep at the waist. His eyes came alight at the sight of the blonde.

If Jinx had to guess from Camilla's relaxed body language, she was not aware of Thatcher's intrigue.

Thatcher then turned his attention to Jinx, her knowing stare earning a tiny twitch of his brow. It seemed both brothers were insightful. "And who might this be?"

"Lady Hunt." Jinx curtsied. "Though, if I may, I must excuse myself. It appears I have reached the end of my night."

"One dance, Lady Hunt." Thatcher's tone was so alluring and convincing that it could've drawn in even the purest of souls.

"I'm afraid I must decline," Jinx tipped her chin, adamant, "Goodnight."

Before she could take one step across the floor, her eyes met Apollo Voclaine's wintry stare. A cigarette flicked between his fingers, with a match sparked alight at the end. Drawing in a deep breath, his chest expanded as the smoke curled out of his lips and back into his nose.

He moved with trained, careful grace.

Unease pooled deep in Jinx's belly, her complexion revealing none of the fear that was now brewing in her veins.

"Is everything alright, Lady Hunt?" Thatcher followed her line of sight. "Ah, pay him no mind."

Jinx laid a hand on Thatcher's arm, finding more muscle than she'd originally expected. "Do me a favor, Mr. Voclaine."

"Please, call me Thatcher."

"Thatcher," Jinx echoed his drawl. "Do me a favor and wish your brother a happy birthday for me. My departure is urgent." She batted her lashes innocently before handing over a replica ring, one that she had conjured discretely in the hiding hand between the folds of her dress. "He seemed to have dropped this when I crashed into him earlier. Do give it to him."

"Of course, Lady Hunt." Thatcher took the ring and, in return, placed a gentle kiss on Jinx's knuckles.

Jinx leisurely wandered outside. Swiftly feeling a tug on her senses, her attention turned toward the box, the Vessel, in the museum. She shrugged off the dark, pulling sensation, finally stepping out into the night. The salty aroma of the ocean greeted her as she stepped into the darkness. Lamp posts illuminated the Main Street before her, its stone walls barricading the land against the charmed bay. Jinx walked deeper into the alleys of the cream granite buildings until she completely lost those in attendance at the party.

The ring she had illusioned would last until she was far enough away for anyone to notice otherwise.

Alone at last, Jinx lowered her illusion, exposing her true form and the black leathers beneath, Lady Hunt's dress vanishing from the material world. There were throwing knives hiding in every crevice of her body, with a dagger strapped to each leg.

Jinx pulled her hood over her braided hair, obscuring the light of her eyes.

At the end of the alley, Jinx fiddled her ebony gloved fingers into the cracks of the wall, scaling the granite before ultimately hauling herself onto the roof of the Moment Museum. The inclined tiles tested her balance.

"What's wrong with you?"

Jinx's heart reached her throat. The voice came from behind the building, the speaker furious at another person whose voice was hushed.

Jinx crawled across the tiles with spider-like agility, her lithe limbs not emitting a sound. She peeked over the ledge, nose barely hidden.

Below, two men in brown cloaks quietly argued between themselves. Their movements were firm and tense, their nervousness rippling out from their murky silhouettes. It was difficult to pick up their aggressively hushed tones.

"You nearly compromised us."

"I didn't. Now sit and wait. Patience..."

The timbres of their voices lowered with each passing word. They shifted into the shadows, obscuring their bodies to the point where Jinx could no longer see them.

An urge to chase after them clawed at her muscles, but she resisted. She would do no such thing. She had her own agenda. Her curiosity had always led her down the wrong path in the past. She would not make the same mistake now.

Jinx rested on her back, lazily crossing a knee above the other and putting a hand behind her head as a cushion. She deeply inhaled the fresh ocean air, listening to the waves crashing against the rocks.

The stars above twinkled, the full moon flooding the rocky Wateredge in its light.

It reminded Jinx of a night where the moon held an identical visage, one she had once spent with her mother and uncle, only her family had been much poorer then and was living in the Slums, which was inland and closer to the woods. Her nostalgia played with her mind; it was as if she could almost feel her mother's phantom touch.

If her mother and uncle had died, Jinx would have suffered plenty less. But no, they were alive and well, living in the same area she was currently ruminating in. Wateredge was the second wealthiest district in Somnium; her family had thrived off the sacrifices she had made.

Every week, Jinx would linger in the shadows, checking in on them and their safety and well-being. She'd read the newspaper in front of her uncle's printing store, then linger outside of her mother's home, watching her sew lavish dresses through the window. Sometimes,

Jinx would even imagine herself running back to them, her mother's or uncle's arms encasing her, never letting go.

But then again, she was Cursed. The farther she stood from them, the better. It was part of the deal's parameters. Unlike the rest of the magic users in Somnium, Jinx had never been infected, rather hexed.

Jinx's skin warmed near the pocket that contained the silver ring. It hummed once more.

She could feel her everything in her core urging to answer the summons.

Jinx fished the jewelry out from her pocket, exposing it to the passing sea breeze.

She examined the silver ring resting in the center of her palm, wondering how the son of a duke wound up with an ancient rune-engraved ring, a singular crack webbing across the band.

The narrow area bordering Crosspoint Yard and the Slums was the hub of the Cursed. There, they hovered in the dim shadows like rats, scurrying and scavenging for scraps. Barely living. Barefoot children padded across the dirt-packed road, their frames rawboned and cheeks sunken. Men and women fended for what they could to survive, hoping to make it to the next day. The smell of dung rotted the air.

Jinx was no stranger to this area; much of her childhood consisted of these paint-peeled walls and stale bread. Now she walked the very ground that she had clawed her way out of eleven years ago. She returned whenever she could; Jinx always gave a percentage of what she took to the Cursed. All for a price, of course. She'd help them only if they helped themselves. For some of them, it meant spending hours trying to find a low-wage job, either selling what they would bring back or stealing from others. And taking other, more extreme measures.

When desperation bleeds into the mind, a person will do anything just to survive.

Jinx shrugged her shoulder, readjusting the light sack of trinkets and fruit that dangled to her side. Her hood covered up to the tip of her nose, her magic masking her true face. She felt around for the crack in the cement walls, a concealed door that led to the very center of the Cursed network.

Locating it at last, her forefinger dipped into the crack, pushing into it. A door opened ajar, and grime and pebbles crumbled, floating down around her. Jinx summoned the organ containing her magic by her belly. Willowy green flames and smoke encompassed her. Power thrummed across her skin, glossing over her with a veil-like wave of heat. She envisioned a hunchbacked grandmother with a cane, white lanky hair wrapped up in a scarf, carrying a basket—and fully transformed into the disguise.

This was the beldam that the residents knew as Jinx's runner. Whenever the old woman appeared, the residents of the Netherwen knew Jinx had brought gifts.

She descended down the darkened stairs that waited just beyond the door, forcefully stomping her footfalls, really selling herself in the role she'd assumed. Torches illuminated the pathway, leading into the Netherwen district of the Cursed.

Houses were built into the walls of the cave, toppling toward the center of the district, and small red mudbrick houses built up on top of each other. Wet rock maintained the cool temperatures. Prospectors venturing to Somnium above returned with whatever they could find. It was a safe haven for the small, vulnerable population that resided there.

Whispers rumbled across the city streets, wary looks pinning her down. Civilians crept back as she approached.

"She's returned."

"The crone returned?"

"Is it Jinx's messenger?"

Hundreds of similar murmurs peppered the expanse she crossed. Jinx found her way to the food bank and drew her lips into a sugary, wrinkled smile. Silver-eyed Cursed were all around her, scooping up molded bread, brown apples, and overdue porridge that had already been swarmed by whirring flies. The mutterings ceased once she approached the administrator, Harrison, a gray-haired, middle-aged male who'd taken the initiative to begin the Netherwen. A sanctuary for the Cursed to live worry-free.

Jinx dropped her heavy basket on the table, announcing, "This is what Jinx was able to bring this month."

Harrison pinched at the cloth of the basket, peeking in. "It's less than last month."

"Be grateful the face stealer brings anything at all," she hissed back.

"*We are*," he said, lifting his gaze to the mass of hungry citizens around him with thin lips and cratered stomachs. "It's been getting harder down here."

"As it is up there." Jinx dumped the contents on the table. "Divide it as you will. I don't have the time today to assist. The next months may become more complicated as well."

A child yanked on the hem of Jinx's illusioned dress, asking to be picked up. She gave in, bracing the child on her hip. The little girl stretched her arm to caress Jinx's face.

"No touching, girl." Jinx gave her a light smack across the knuckles. "I don't want more wrinkles." She then reached behind the child's ear and swiped a copper coin she had hidden in her sleeve. The child gasped and reached for it as Jinx moved her hand back.

Harrison inspected each item, sorting them into piles. "How come?"

"I cannot say. Jinx simply informed me that the next few months will be unpredictable." She turned her attention back to the girl. "Give me a good reason to give you this?"

The child squeaked. "I've been working on my magic. See?" Opening her palm, tiny bubbles rose to the tips of her fingers. She blew them bigger and smaller, playing with the size.

Jinx peered at her, judging her performance, before ultimately giving her the coin. "Alright, here you go. Run along. Don't go doing that above."

"Thank you for telling me ahead of time," Harrison said gratefully. "I'll plan accordingly. Please tell your employer to try their best. Jinx's help is all we have."

Jinx turned over her shoulder, glancing at the slender faces—pleading and ill—that she knew too well. If she'd had time on her side, she would have tried to help them learn how to channel their powers. The Cursed had the potential to be strong, overpowering humans with their unnatural abilities. If they'd wanted to, they could've taken the city on their own.

The Cursed may have magic coursing through their systems, yet there was panic within their hearts to fight back. A monkey who was told could not climb a tree for all its life would not climb a tree. Exactly why, instead of rebelling, they'd been so hunted and beaten down by society that they'd fled down to the Netherwen. They'd grown tired, while those remaining Cursed above still contained the will to fight back every day.

But there were more selfish matters for Jinx to attend to. She rubbed her hands together.

"If you want to repay Jinx, she does need something."

Harrison's facial expression piqued his interest.

"Do you know of a person who studies potentially magic-embedded objects?"

"Above ground, there is one man..." Harrison leaned over the table and told her how to find the one she sought. Jinx headed over to Crosspoint Yard.

A bell chimed overhead as Jinx entered a jewelry store owned by the Cursed in the depths of the Crosspoint Yard alleyways. She was currently pretending to be a broken-down woman from the Slums–separate from the beldam. The Cursed were treated the same as the penniless from the Slums by the well-off Easterners.

"How may I help you, ma'am?" the jeweler asked.

Jinx shuffled across the store, fetching the ring from her wooden basket.

"Hello, good sir. I've come for your knowledge." Jinx placed the ring on the wooden table. "Have you seen anything like this? I found it on the floor last night. Curious...I've never seen runes such as it."

He plucked the band, scrutinizing the piece at eye level. "Can't say I know the language, unfortunately." He put the ring back down, dismissing her.

"Oh, come on. You won't help an old woman? Harrison sent me over," Jinx said.

The man still appeared unfazed.

"This is an errand for Jinx," she added.

The jeweler examined his surroundings, tight-lipped. It was as if she herself were a trap laid by members of high society, ready to drag him out of his shop and gut him on the spot. She flashed the silver lines of her eyes. He flashed his own, recognizing her as distant kin.

The jeweler picked up the metal band and inspected it once more. His brows pinched, wrinkles scrunching as he took a closer look. "You work for the Ghost?"

"Dispatched me herself." She smacked the table as a crazy crone would. "What are you?"

"My magic lets me identify the pure material of objects. Comes in handy when running my business." He closed the blinds to his store and released his magic on the band. Sweet-smelling magic filled the store, tickling the tip of Jinx's nose. She sneezed and sniffled back.

The jeweler's eyes popped open, his body trembling viciously. Unable to release the band, whimpers of pain flooded the store. Veins separated from his skin, and black ink swamped his fingers, slowly beginning to take over the whole hand.

Jinx hooked her finger around the ring, tugging it away from him until the jeweler was finally released. He fell back against the wall of trinkets, which then crashed onto the floor, shattering into a sea of glass.

The two stared at each other, panting.

"*Where did you find that?*" he asked.

"What did you see?" Jinx persisted, more interested than ever.

"Nothing," he said. "I saw darkness. It fought against me, pushed me out. Whoever owns that doesn't want anyone to see their truth. You're better off throwing it in the Charmed Bay." He stuck to the wall, keeping his distance from the object.

The sound of rushed footsteps trampled closer before the door opened.

"Father, are you alright?" A teenage boy hurtled to the man's side before spotting Jinx across the table.

"Yes, my boy," the jeweler responded. Using the help of his son to stand back up on his own feet, he nestled himself closer to his son, away from Jinx and the ring.

The teenager looked at Jinx, closing the space between them. He recognized that she was one of them. "There's been a shift in the air. I don't know what it is, but danger is here."

"What sort of danger?" She stuffed the ring back in her pocket, nerves keeping the band close at her side.

The teenager ruffled his ginger hair. "I'm not sure, but the winds shifted. It speaks of an awakening. Primordial, chaotic."

"Evil?"

He shrugged. "Perhaps. That is all I know."

Unsure of how to handle that information, let alone process it, Jinx shook their hands. "Thank you. I apologize for the inconvenience. Be careful out there. The authorities are checking eyes now."

Jinx dipped her head and walked out.

For two nights, Jinx met with all kinds of Cursed, asking all of them about the ring and urging them to use their abilities on the object. She was curious to know if anyone could figure out its history or inscriptions. Alas, each attempt ended the same way. A horrible ache accompanied by a burst, propelling someone across the room. Some left burned, others delirious, most terrified.

Jinx then turned to the public library, which was broken up into houses owned by politicians. Her research told her that the ring was a myth. The problem with myths, however, was that there was always a dose of reality behind it. Jinx herself embodied this phenomenon.

The ring also failed to have a manufacturing number or anything to distinguish it as a series. Its material was unlike anything she'd encountered, its components otherworldly and its runes untraceable. It was as mysterious as the Vessel itself.

Through no fault of her own, Jinx lacked all answers to the growing list of questions she had, like how Apollo came to possess such a ring and why he never took it off. Where had he gotten it from? She doubted it was a family heirloom. The Voclaine family had a reputation to maintain. Apollo's ring had to be a secret from the rest of his kin. He couldn't risk anyone knowing that he carried around a ring that was imbued with magic.

Jinx circled back to the only possibility that remained. Apollo Voclaine was a Cursed; he *had* to be one.

She braided her hair as she strolled across the flat rooftops of Crosspoint Yard. The moonlight drenched the district in pale blue colors. Streetlamps highlighted the avenues as people wandered the streets, many of them workers exiting their factory jobs. Smoke would soon evaporate for a few hours before laborers returned to their positions at the crack of dawn.

She inhaled the fresh summer breeze, cooled off by the night. Stars twinkled overhead, and silence drifted in.

Jinx was still curious about Apollo Voclaine: society's greatest mystery. But she now had an advantage. This ring clearly concealed something Apollo wanted to keep hidden, and if her guess was correct, it was his magic. Knowing this would give her the upper hand if she wanted to strike a deal with him.

If Jinx were Apollo, she knew she'd been trying to get as much information as she could about her attacker, trying to secure the best outcome. She had to formulate every possibility for her conversation with him tomorrow, consider how best to approach the interaction, and anticipate things he could use against her.

A shriek tore Jinx from her thoughts. Instinctively, she hauled her hood over her face again and crouched near the ground in spiderlike grace.

Below, a woman yelled out again and launched out the side door of a building, her body crashing to the floor, a bag of fruit and bread spilling all over the ground. Three men closed in on her, stepping on the food. "Fiend whore," one man spit. Dragging her by the collar, they thrust her limp frame against the wall.

Another man smashed a half-drunken bottle of beer, glass splintering all around them.

The woman wailed. "Please, I have a family. I need to feed them. I bought this with my own money." She scratched her nails against their grip, choking on her own breath. "I'll do anything. Just please let me help them."

The third man flicked his wrist, revealing a small blade. "Should have thought of that before you let Akuji's demons infect you."

Human bastards.

Jinx blended into the shadows, climbing down the building, using the brick walls as her ladder. She wanted to get as close to the group as possible without alerting any of the woman's attackers. Jinx willed her illusion to mask her face in a shroud of darkness.

Nimble footfalls keeping her silent, Jinx stepped mere centimeters from the man with a broken beer bottle before snapping his neck in a single movement. He plummeted.

Jinx ripped the woman free, placing her behind her back. "When I tell you to run, you flee and go straight home." The woman nodded, trembling.

She threw away every thought, every chatter in her skull. Her heart slowed down as a sensation of hot muscles trickled across her frigid skin.

"Now!" Jinx whispered, and the woman took off.

The man with the blade jumped toward the woman escaping, while another threw a jab at Jinx. She breathed in, her vision slowing. Jinx averted the punch, gripping his arm and wrist instead.

Using his weight against him, she twisted his arm, dislocating his shoulder. He yelped. Jinx trapped him between her and the grime-covered floor. She then turned toward his co-assailant.

The woman screeched as the man with the blade tripped her. Jinx plucked a throwing knife from one of the hidden pockets of her leather suit. Angling her elbow and closing one eye, she hurled it toward him, striking the center of his neck. He tripped on his knees and was gone. The woman shouted and fled into the distance.

Jinx dug her boot into the back of the man's skull. A crack. She grinned mercilessly. "Doesn't feel too nice, does it?"

"Please." He was starting to turn red, then purple. Jinx pressed down harder.

"Why did you attack her?" She knew the answer; she just wanted to hear it from his own lips. Unsheathing the dagger at her side, she nudged the tip of the blade to his Adam's apple.

"Because…" He groaned. "She's a silver-eyed monster. *Devil-filled.*"

Hatred burned in her throat. The Cursed were not monsters, but perhaps Jinx was, and that could have been the misunderstanding beginning a trail of rumors. The Cursed were biologically different from their human neighbors in some ways. A separate muscle somewhere in their torso held the fuel of their magic. Females bled only twice a year. And the Cursed had six senses instead of just five.

But they all still breathed, slept, and ate. They all had a heart flooded with emotions, feelings, and sensations. The Cursed had human qualities, too. After all, just twenty years ago, *everyone* had been human. The Cursed hadn't chosen to be infected.

Jinx snorted, cocking her head to the side. Flipping him over, she clutched the man by the collar, his head bobbing back.

"Look at me." She hissed. Calling on her power, she swiped a hand over her face, transforming her own to match his. Stubble-bearded, mid-fifties, brown-eyed, and pathetic.

Fear encompassed the man, his teeth clattering. "I-I-It's *you.*"

She mimicked his tone, "S-s-say my name. Let it be your last word."

"Jinx."

She sliced across his neck; crimson poured out. Jinx wiped the wet blade on his shirt before sheathing it. She then left him to bleed out, the moon and Akuji as her witness.

Chapter 3

Apollo

"According to studies conducted by statisticians of the University of Somnium, there seems to be more of the Cursed appearing these days, becoming more noticeable in the streets, uncaring of their appearance," the Duke of Kami explained. The Seven Dukes of Somnium and their offspring were listening attentively to the new information that Duke Kami had brought to light. For years, the House of Lords held meetings at the end of every week to discuss matters of the city and how they could approach these situations, good and bad.

Apollo had been attending these meetings with his father since he turned fifteen years old. At that point, Father had deemed that it was time for him to learn about what it meant to be both one of the Seven and the firstborn, which would require him to take on responsibility for the future of the family. Ever since, he'd spent every Sunday in the golden courtroom for hours on end. Since Apollo comprehended the various matters easily, all of his unaccounted went into reading any sort of book: educational, non-fiction, fantasy, mystery, romance, and so forth. He was also fascinated by studying human behaviors, eager to obtain the ability to understand someone with no words involved.

"It turns out that our original theory of these creatures was incorrect. Some of their Cursed abilities can come forth years, if not decades, later," the Duke of Kami continued, his long silver hair tied into a bun at the nape of his neck.

Apollo's first encounter with another Cursed soul had been last night, assuming the person masquerading as Lady Hunt was, in fact, Jinx. She was the only person who would've been able to deceive security at the gate so effortlessly, stealing his ring in the blink of an eye. Apollo tensed his jaw.

Then again, one bad Cursed did not represent the entire civilization.

Apollo's father nudged him with his elbow, whispering beneath the Duke of Kami's overly puffed voice. "What do you think, Pol?"

"Father, what is the difference between a human and a chimpanzee?" Apollo's gaze stayed on the Duke of Kami, who was reading from a notecard at his red velvet seat.

"Do tell." Amusement lined his father's hard face.

"We are actually rather close genetically. That being said, we treat them as an entirely different species. This is what we are doing now. However, the Cursed were once and still *are* people. We should not fear what we do not know."

"I agree with you. How would you change the minds of the thousands that live here?" His father raised an inquisitive brow, challenging his son.

Apollo remained silent for a beat, thoroughly thinking about his answer. "You get one bright mind to find a compromise between the two parties. A leader who makes both sides feel protected and cared for."

"You are optimistic."

"No, at this moment, I am opportunistic. There is a difference," Apollo rebutted. There was a river between the Cursed and humans, a chance to build a bridge connecting them instead of burning the other side down.

Apollo second-guessed himself, thinking about the night before and feeling his bare finger. The ring had still not been returned to his possession.

When Thatcher approached him yesterday and offered him the return of his ring, he couldn't help feeling like it was not really his ring. Indeed, he was correct. A few hours later, the ring vanished from reality. A crumb of the criminal's green magic was now tangling with his own. He couldn't afford for any emotions to brew in his body. Without that piece of metal, Apollo was a threat not just to himself but to those around him.

Fortunately, the voice did not return that night, but Apollo also did not linger near the Vessel again. His brain could not forget the unpleasant sensation he'd felt when he neared the box.

It was almost like the calling his body yearned for. The half he did not want. The half that did not belong to him. The part of himself that had been forcefully shoved down his throat eight years ago.

Maybe the voice of that nightmare had been correct. Then again, that thing had been perfectly content in residing in Apollo's body up until then. Why offer up a method of self-destruction? Suspicions of the demon's true intentions prodded Apollo's brain.

Just then, a set of chills ran down Apollo's back. If he wanted to answer any of these pestering questions, he'd need to get his ring back first.

"Do you agree, Voclaine?"

Apollo mentally reprimanded himself for losing his train of thought too deeply these days. He blinked.

"Deepest apologies, Your Grace. Could you repeat your statement? It seems as if I've been still processing the information you presented earlier."

The Duke of Kami dipped his chin, hands folded firmly below. "Of course. I had asked if the House would see it fit to hold council a day earlier next week because of your father's impending travel to the East."

"Seems a rather obvious answer, is it not?" Apollo idly crossed a leg over the other. Using his possession of the floor to his own advantage, he continued, "Since I have the attention of those here, I'd like to make a request of the museum."

The Duke of Kami set his features firmly upon Apollo, curiously observing him.

Apollo stood, diving his hands deep into his pockets. "Yesterday, during the celebration of my twenty-third birthday, I found myself fascinated by the Vessel. We still don't know where it came from or how it reached Somnium. I'd like to examine it for a day, if possible."

The men around him recoiled, incapable of hiding their repulsion.

The Duke of Tertain cleared his throat, standing up from his red velvet seat on the other side of the golden-threaded chamber. "Lord Voclaine, if I may. I regret to inform you that your request will not be possible."

Apollo selected a cigarette from the edge of the table, igniting it and inhaling deeply, hoping the contents would relax his rapidly beating heart. He needed to tame the thing inside him. Keep his composure. "Why is that? Surely, we can come to an agreement, Your Grace."

"I wish we could. Except that the Vessel has gone missing. Someone stole it shortly after the soiree ended. Authorities believe it was stolen around four o'clock this morning," The Duke of Tertain elaborated.

Apollo took another deep puff of the cigarette.

"How is that possible?" De Conto asked. "Security was in prime shape. Guards were posted at every corner. We bring the Vessel out for one night to display after twenty years enclosed, and it's gone?"

You listen to me, the demon's voice spoke in his head again. Apollo clenched his jaw, a pain flaring at his temple. *Patience only serves so long.*

Damn the Virtues. He needed to shut this up.

"Was it Jinx?" one of the Seven asked.

Ah, Jinx. The criminal could very well be in possession of the Vessel as well as the ring. "We aren't sure. You know that the face-stealer is just as good as the lore would lead you to believe." The Duke of Tertain rubbed his face. Lines of purple edged the slits of his round eyes. His slouch further confirmed his fatigue.

The nightmare hissed in Apollo's mind. *Find Jinx, and you'll find the Vessel.*

"Still very real," V'Yockovitch said, pointing to the paper on his lap. "The news this morning says that the face stealer killed three men last night. Bloodied them and beat them. Is this what we want to find in our papers in the morning?" He was quickly on his feet, crunching the article in his fist.

"Don't be preposterous, V'Yockovitch, of course not," the Duke of Kami rebutted. "How can we fight someone who we never see coming?"

"Ruin them all."

"Genocide is not the answer."

"So, you are *for* them?" V'Yockovitch instigated. "Does the red bracelet mean nothing to you?" He lifted his wrist, showing off the red thread tied around it. It was his Tutela: a guard to ward off evil.

The Duke of Kami raised his two palms. "You know that is not what I mean. I only intend to say that, like it or not, they are still our people."

"You think I am capable of mass murder?" V'Yockovitch touched his chest, wounded. "We can just push them out. Further out, until they're Woodland creatures."

Duke Nadir spoke up this time. "Gentlemen, we have an issue here. Half of the city lives in fear of the Cursed. They taint our refined populace. How can we bring our standards back to what they were?"

Apollo felt his brain cells molding, all while listening to this conversation. His dispute died on his tongue.

Suddenly, the doors slammed open, jerking everyone present. A runner boy heaving for air came in.

"Apologies, Your Graces. I have an urgent letter for Apollo Voclaine." He raised a short arm, waving a white envelope. The boy wiped at the streaking sweat running down his forehead and placed the envelope at the entrance table before leaving just as quickly as he'd arrived.

Apollo closed the distance in long strides. The sleeve was scentless and came without a wax seal. Using the letter opener to slice the paper, he unfolded the note inside:

Apollo Voclaine,

I am in possession of your ring. I offer a proposition to return it to you, the rightful owner. If interested, please meet me at Lydias Tea House at the highest point of the sun. On the bench adjacent to the shop will be a man wearing a gray suit with a golden watch. His hair is of the color brown, with a streak of white. Sit next to him for further instructions. A minute later, if you do not show, I will assume you do not want it back.

Do not disappoint me, Voclaine.

Apparently, Apollo didn't need to find Jinx after all; Jinx had found him. He wiggled his fingers, checking his pocket watch. He had twenty minutes to walk to the location.

Under his breath, he muttered, "Oh great, *just* what I needed."

He folded the note, shoving it down into the pocket of his trousers. "I must excuse myself. It seems that one of my kin is in need of assistance."

Father's brows perked up. "Is it your brother?"

"Sister. Arya." Already conjuring an excuse. Tailoring it to what the future could bring. Arya was the best one to pin; she'd cover for him, surely.

"Go see to her," Father said. Apollo was already halfway out the door.

Apollo picked his black coat from the hanger, along with his top hat. "It's always a dreadfully enlightening time here, gentlemen." He departed.

Here he was, leaving his world again, all to meet up with someone who was little more than a ghost.

Chapter 4

Jinx

Jinx waited exactly where she said she would, wearing an illusion that fit its description. While she patiently waited for this conversation, Jinx played the role of a man in his thirties, reading the paper. She purposefully checked her gold watch and made sure others saw her do so, eager to avoid suspicion.

She'd always taken the time to watch others, learning their stories and emotions through the language of their bodies. She utilized these minute-by-minute observations as lessons for the future. On the other hand, if all went according to plan today, she may no longer need that talent.

She might finally be able to go home, released of the bargain she'd made. She could be within the vicinity of her family, spend time with her kin, celebrate birthdays and accomplishments, and enjoy the company of others.

Jinx quickly locked away the swelling of tender emotions. Instead, she craned her head back, drinking in the specks of sunlight that were sweeping past the green leaves of the tree above her. She needed the scene to ground her in the present.

The sounds of stagecoaches pulled by horses, clamping their hooves on the cobblestone streets, infiltrated her ears. Chatting ladies murmured in the background. Gold-crusted roofs danced atop green tiles and limestone walls. Eastern Heights was the district dipped in wealth. It reeked of class with the smells of pipe tobacco, lavender, and fresh trees.

Making his way through the ocean of people, Apollo Voclaine spotted her instantly.

Jinx's heart jerked nervously.

He was beautiful, no doubt. A slender, cream-colored face, every line perfectly sharpened to the point of being alluring without being harsh. Wintry storm gray eyes held more secrets than he let on; he was a carrier of hidden information. His raven hair swept across his face, the style fit for a prince. His gait was infused with a calculated confidence, dashed with easing grace. Obviously trained. It was as if he were aware of everything in his proximity, down to the smallest pebble a hair away from the tip of his tall, black boots.

Jinx was certain he was one of the most interesting people she'd encountered in all her life. Meeting thousands of people under false identities. There was none like *him*. Unsure what caused such intrigue, it could have been his overwhelming confidence, or the secrets she knew were layered beneath that stoic exterior. Whichever of the options, there was an undeniable affinity for him.

As he drew nearer, Jinx folded the newspaper in her lap, gleefully crossing one leg over the other, elbows latched behind her on the back of the bench.

Citizens—men and women alike—that walked past the straight-faced Apollo broke their necks in trailing his every movement, murmuring his title and name.

Apollo didn't falter, not once.

"Your Grace, I wasn't sure if I should await your presence." Jinx followed his movements as he sat down beside her and looked outward.

Familiarity rattled the marrow of her bones. Apollo radiated energy unlike anything she'd ever encountered. It congested her magic, nearly drowning her. But Apollo kept his silence. He threaded his hands together, casually maintaining them on his lap.

What a curious creature.

Jinx inhaled deeply, cracking her knuckles in preparation for the discussion. Her neck grew warm at the stillness between them.

She would not, *could not,* mess this up, for it was—probably—her last hope.

Jinx's tone switched to that of a man dripping in magic, its sweet tang brushing her tongue. "I have that silver band of yours, the real one." Her voice was soft-spoken, matching her role.

Apollo's response was flat. "I know. Make this quick."

"No 'hello?' A formal introduction from the future duke himself?"

"What's the point of an introduction if you already know who I am?" Apollo's voice was firm, coarse—even authoritative. "Now, my ring."

What a delight of a human. No wonder he isn't married.

Neither of them met the other's stare.

"I'll give you the ring in exchange for entrance to the House of Lord's Archives."

"Funny." A statement. "Reason being?"

Jinx debated in her head momentarily, contemplating how to continue. Her heart picked up in speed. She needed to gain his trust. Finally, after a few long seconds, she spoke. "There is something I am searching for, and I believe the answer lies in the books housed there."

If it were possible, Jinx would have gone in there herself without needing to do any of this. But she had already tried once and failed horrendously.

Apollo sucked his teeth, making the connection that he was cornered. "You negotiate better than the majority of the Lords do."

Jinx's pulse traveled to her ears.

His side glance was harsh. "I'm going to be blunt."

"You haven't been blunt?"

Apollo flexed his fingers. Another tick of which Jinx took a mental note. His face hid his feelings, yet minute movements like those explained the truth. He carried on.

"You killed three men last night."

"They deserved it."

Jinx leered at him. Where was he going with this? The more time she spent in his presence, the more unnerved she felt. Jinx curled her toes, releasing her anxiety out of sight.

"How, in any case, is taking someone's life acceptable?'

"Are you seriously questioning me, of all people, right now?"

"The House has grown impatient with you, specifically. Nothing is stopping me from taking you hostage and turning you in, which would solve hundreds of problems. They even suspect you have the Vessel." He paused, now fully facing her. Jinx swallowed a dry gulp. Apollo's stoic gaze stripped her transparent.

If Jinx were in the House of Lords, she would've probably thought the same thing.

"Putting yourself in this situation is making you vulnerable," he continued. "It is clear that you are desperate. So, I will make you a counteroffer. You give me the ring, and I'll give you entry into the Archives, *but* you have to help me find the missing Vessel."

Jinx looked up in interest.

She knew the Vessel had gone missing the night before; she'd heard about it by listening in on the ladies gossiping earlier this morning. The headline of every newspaper read, in big, bold words: **"Mysterious Vessel Missing?"** She'd read some of those articles, echoing whispers and rumors that the infamous Jinx had taken the relic for herself. But she had no interest in the box, so what was Apollo's interest in the Vessel?

"What do you want with the Vessel?" she asked.

Memories of the night before crossed her mind as she thought back on the two men hiding in the shadows, speaking of something being compromised. She might actually have a lead already.

"Is it to help you with the ring?" She raised a brow, her keen eye focused strictly on him.

Apollo had become stone. "Elaborate."

"You see, I know you are also vulnerable without your ring. I know you are hiding something, Apollo Voclaine. You'll come to find that secrets are hard to bury. You have an interesting presence." She offered him a knowing glance. "We're on leveled ground."

"What a joy, we've concluded that you're obsessed with me. Just as the rest of the city is. Get in line." He pivoted the conversation. She knew she was close, poking the right areas.

"I'll stray from the queue of ladies dying for your attention."

She thought about his offer. Finding the Vessel shouldn't take her more than a few weeks, at most, and then she could continue searching for the answer she so desperately sought for herself. In her eyes, it seemed a fair deal. Jinx knew there was always more, though.

"What's your alternate motive?"

"My own personal health."

Jinx snorted. "I'm serious."

"What gave the idea that I wasn't?"

She molded herself to the bench. In the worst-case scenario, this was all a ploy to send her to the noose. Finally catch the Ghost of Somnium. Double-cross her. Jinx, however, was confident in her abilities to escape; in the past roles she'd played, deception had never been an issue.

"I'll do it. I'll help you," she agreed.

She found it ironic that one of the most powerful people in the city asked for the help of the thief. An interesting turn of events. Then again, if she helped him, he'd owe her a favor, perhaps a way to help her family if ever in need.

"Great. Now, hand the ring over. I have more important matters to attend to," he said.

Jinx refused, "I don't think so. I'm going to keep this ring as collateral. If I am to deliver this Vessel back to you, I need assurance that you'll owe me something after."

"Alright." He didn't seem distressed, but then again, Apollo never showed much distress, at least not on the days she'd watched him. This conversation seemed to rouse little more interest than a leaf passing by in the wind. "You'll report to me every night with information you may have."

Jinx rolled her eyes. "I will hand over the information every *two* nights, with you giving me something in return. My work is not for free. And who knows how dangerous this job might really be."

"If you come with useful information, I'll award you with three Marcs."

"Three Marcs isn't much."

"You'd be getting paid for something you already do," he said.

Jinx agreed, knowing she was pushing her luck with this man.

"I agree to your terms, Apollo Voclaine. Do you have any leads as to who might have taken the Vessel or why?"

"No. That's why I have you." Apollo stood up from the bench, igniting the end of a cigarette.

Jinx met his bored stare. "Alright, I'll return in two nights with a report."

"Where should we meet?"

She held the newspaper under her arm. "I'll meet you at your manor. Congratulations, Apollo Voclaine."

"For?"

"Betraying your city before even taking the role of the Seven." At that retort, he glowered.

Jinx cracked her knuckles once more, trying to convince herself that what she felt were not pinpricks of fear but thrills of excitement.

Investigating the Vessel would undoubtedly get Jinx too close to the authorities. They already suspected her of stealing the artifact. Going directly to the crime scene would place her right in the center of danger, handing herself over on a silver platter.

Still, she didn't have much of a choice.

Jinx had to go to the places where people talked the most: the harbor and the gambling den.

Chapter 5

Apollo

The trip to retrieve his ring had been unsuccessful. Apollo had been more nervous than he cared to admit whilst talking with Jinx, facing the myth personified of a dangerous criminal.

It impressed Apollo how the criminal had sat around so calmly, just under everyone's nose. Jinx really could turn themself into anyone, and the surrounding citizens would never know. He understood why the authorities had never laid a hand on Jinx, unable to trace the criminal down. Jinx—in simple terms—was untraceable.

The nightmare in the back of his mind chuckled. It was driving Apollo insane, haunting him constantly. That ring was the only thing keeping the demon imprisoned. Since the night the demon had first taken over a piece of Apollo, the ring appeared by his bed with a note attached, instructing him to wear it. He'd never taken it off since—not until Jinx had stolen it from him.

Negotiation was all about strategy. Before their encounter, Jinx had clearly done the research on his ring and was aware of the nightmare hiding inside. Whatever it truly was.

Apollo wasn't a full-blooded Cursed; of this fact, he was certain. His irises carried the stone gray he'd been born with. The only thing he knew about that side of himself was that he housed a foreign entity. When the plague had come, he had not gone down with it. His magic was different. It coursed through his red blood, yes—but he did not acknowledge it. Anything else was beyond him.

Apollo unlocked the door to his friend's warehouse and went straight for the alcohol on the table.

"Didn't expect to see you today," Kovan chirped from his seat. His head was ducked down as he wrote in his father's ledgers.

Apollo downed his cup of liquor in a singular gulp. The burn in his throat satisfied the tremors terrorizing his body, and he realized that being drunk or buzzed might be the only way to survive until he reclaimed the ring.

Didn't seem like a bad way to continue, though. He poured another.

"Careful, it's only two in the afternoon," Kovan reminded him.

Apollo took another swig. "Like I care. I don't see you trying to stop me."

"You're as stubborn as they come," Kovan muttered. Finally lifting his gaze, he dropped the pen.

"Come on, Kovan. We've known that for a while." Thatcher walked in, dropping his school bag on the floor before pouring both Kovan and himself a glass of the liquid amber. He challenged his brother dead in the eye. "Isn't that right, Pol?"

Apollo joined the two idiots at the table.

"Let's play 'How many times have you seen Apollo Voclaine smile today?' I'll go first. *None*," Thatcher said enthusiastically.

Apollo emitted a singular hum.

"I guess that's the closest we'll get today."

Kovan latched his arm behind Apollo's chair. "Have the Lords worked you up today?"

Apollo wished it *was* about the Lords. "I'm not talking about it."

"When do you ever?" Kovan complained. "Whatever, not like it matters. They'll continue being the old men in a pissing contest."

Thatcher snickered. "I'm glad I wasn't the firstborn. Sitting in a room listening to problems that may never be solved would drive me insane. No offense, Brother."

"Have you considered sleeping outside?" Apollo chided.

Sometimes, Apollo grew jealous of his brother. Thatcher had been raised with the freedom to choose which path he wanted to pursue, unlike Apollo, who'd been given a predestined passage he was unable to avoid from the moment he was born.

Luckily, Apollo enjoyed working with his father and was unable to imagine doing any-thing else. He still pondered which career path he would have chosen if he'd grown up somewhere else, under a different family, with a different name.

"Have you guys heard that the Vessel is missing?" Thatcher asked. "Everyone at the university is raving about it. It was hard to get any actual work done today."

"I have." Kovan shifted in his seat. "In all honesty, I'm glad it's missing."

"Why?"

Kovan scratched behind his ears. "Because ever since the Vessel was found, society has had to deal with problems left and right. Maybe now, thanks to its disappearance, the issue between the Cursed and humans can go away. Maybe this is what our society *needed*."

Mother called for supper just as Apollo quickly finished jotting down his notes for the day in his notebook. The door to his room groaned open.

"I'll be down momentarily," Apollo muttered.

"How's your sister doing?" Apollo's father asked, displeased.

Apollo's spine straightened. "Fine. False alarm."

Apollo and his father shared a close-bonded relationship, but there were still moments of strain. Especially after the night in the Woodlands, back when Apollo was fifteen and first encountered the demon.

"Will it happen again?"

Apollo played with his fingers. "I don't predict the future."

Father huffed, his chest contracting. "Your mother's waiting."

Descending the stairs, his sister Arya interjected, "Pol, may I speak with you?"

Apollo dipped his chin, and Father set off into the labyrinth of the manor. Arya's calm expression sharpened, vexation flaring her nostrils. She hauled Apollo beneath the stairs, aggressively whispering. "Why did Father come to me asking if I felt alright?"

He'd forgotten to warn her. His skull pestered him with senseless thoughts, only for them to slip his mind. "I'd been called elsewhere in the House today and needed any excuse. I'm sure you understand."

"A *warning* would have been sufficient." She brushed a stray caramel hair back into place.

"I didn't need to," he said. "You handled it splendidly on your own."

Inhaling a deep breath, Arya persisted, "Where did you go?"

"Dwelling on it is pointless. Let's go; Mother is waiting."

Reluctantly, Arya gave up and walked with him to the table, nudging him with more questions that earned vague responses.

In their house, Father always insisted on having a round table instead of a rectangular one. It signified that everyone sitting around it had a voice and would be treated as equal, no matter whether it was the Mother or the youngest daughter.

"Fey, how was ballet this afternoon?" Mother asked, passing the bowl of roasted potatoes to Thatcher. Society tended to frame the Voclaine family as the epitome of class and formality, but away from prying eyes, the Voclaine were simply kin.

Fey, Apollo's youngest sister and twin to Thatcher, cut into the cooked chicken on her plate. "Horrible. My grand pas de chat felt off today, not in tune with my body. I think I need new shoes."

"You got new shoes last year," Mother said.

"Yes, but practice every day for three hours wears them out quickly, Mama."

Mother shredded the meat in front of her. "I'll see for us to go to the Dome tomorrow after the governess leaves. Since we're there, Arya, you should join us, and we'll have our gowns tailored for the ball this coming Autumn. It'll be the perfect engagement to find you a suitor."

"Mother," Arya argued, "I do not believe that marriage is best for me in this day and age."

As Mother chewed her food, Father finished for her. "It is the perfect window of opportunity."

"Why must I get married? Twenty is still too young. Do you really expect me to sit and play wife?"

Mother countered, "We've argued about this long enough. The time for marriage is now. If not, it'll be too late."

"Polly is older than I am, yet you have to prod *him* about this topic," Arya said accusingly.

"I've bothered your brother long enough about this. He knows that he must find a wife soon enough, or our reputation could be tainted." Mother massaged the bridge of her nose. "If it were up to me, I would tell you to explore the world, but society is not kind like that. Marriage will only help secure your future."

Arya scrunched her button nose. "Then let it be up to *me*. Let *me* refuse this grotesque tradition that modern society has placed upon me. If we are one of the Seven families in power, then why can't we do anything to change it? What purpose do we even serve if we can't do that? Why can't I just—"

"Arya," Father cut her off. "That is enough."

Apollo acknowledged the issue that Arya and many women like her faced in Somnium. It was the same one that his littlest sister would soon have to face, too. In reality, what every child was eventually forced to face—himself included. For families like theirs, marriage was made of convenience instead of love; it was a mere transaction. Apollo knew swaying his father and the other six members in the House of Lords would be a challenge, especially considering he also was not fully accounted as a member yet. Apollo was determined to change the marital expectations when he was finally instated.

Arya spit out one last time, "I suggest pivoting the marriage topic to Apollo. He's older and has a shit attitude. Get him a wife before me."

"Arya Voclaine! Foul language is not allowed at the table, especially about your own brother!" Mother yelled, then hissed at her. "Apologize to him."

"No need," Apollo replied. "It's widely acknowledged across the city I have a 'shit' attitude. It's what makes me so charming."

Mother pinched the bridge of her nose once more in agitation. "Virtues, give me strength. Arya, you *are* aware that the difference between men and women in the market is extensive. Men have their entire life to find a match, while we do not. I don't make the rules."

"It should be *my* choice," Arya defended herself. Apollo agreed with her; it really should be her choice and no one else's. "Besides, if it's so beneficial to marry for convenience and business, what's the purpose of marrying someone of a lower status? Who do you expect me to wed? Kovan? Vander, who is not even here but in the military? If I am to choose a partner, let it be for love."

Distressed, she jumped from familial face to face, but no one met her eye besides Apollo himself.

Arya's argument was logical from every direction. He couldn't let her stand there alone.

"Her logic is sound. Perhaps there is an exception to be made," Apollo chimed in.

A heavy silence lingered in the air. His mother breathed, "Perhaps."

Arya slouched into her chair, muttering, "Of course, they listen to *you*." She stood up from her chair, leaving the napkin behind on the table. "I've lost my appetite." Arya stormed out of the room.

Apollo's tongue pushed against his cheek as guilt roiled his stomach.

"Arya." He made to stand.

"Leave her," Mother commanded. The twins glanced at each other. Apollo looked at his father. A flash of heat overwhelmed him. The muscle at his core started picking up pace, constricting frantically. His fingers twitched, feeling around for the ring. But they came up empty.

In moments like this, Apollo's ring would shock him just before he felt too much. It helped him restrain the nightmare and keep it repressed. But he was on his own now. He counted to ten in his mind, ignoring his emotions. He wanted to lock whatever sensations he could in the dark of his mind, disregarding the yearning in his heart.

Mother cut the tension. "Well, on that note...Polly, I hope you had fun at your birthday."

Apollo nodded. Offering anything more would engage the nightmare inside, he could just feel it. The soul of the thing was alive and awake in his belly.

His mother stood up from the table, heading for the kitchen.

That was one of the biggest downsides to having this demon, this *thing*, inside of him. After any show of emotion, Apollo feared what would happen. He feared the power he could release, which could potentially hurt someone.

The last people he'd ever want to hurt were his own kin. He protected them and cared for each and every one of them with his life. Apollo's apparently cold shoulder and bored demeanor were mere fronts intended to shield those around him from himself—and from the ring.

It was a cushion, a reminder, a preventative measure. He both loved and hated those jolts it would send through his body. It not only restrained the demon but Apollo himself. He physically couldn't show the extent of his emotions when he wore it, not even if he'd wanted to do so. The ring would flare and burn. He assumed this reaction was because the demon inside fed on those intense emotions, which strained the ring as it attempted to protect

Apollo. As a defense mechanism, Apollo decided it'd be best to do everything he could not to feel anything at all.

Dinner clearly coming to an awkward end, Apollo finished his food, and the rest of the family dispersed throughout the house. Thatcher went off to his lab in the attic, Fey to her chambers, Mother to the drawing room, and Father to the study.

Apollo decided to make a swift stop by Arya's quarters before returning to his own. He knocked on her door. Arya cracked it ajar seconds later.

"How may I help you, Apollo?" she droned bitterly.

"You're not teary-eyed, so you must be fine."

"'Fine' is an overstatement."

"In the end, you'll convince yourself."

She licked her lips, disbelief glossing her stare. "You'll never get it. You're the firstborn. The perfect child. Anything you do, you'll be praised, Pol. The second you open your mouth, it's all ears and no debates. It's not like that for me."

He couldn't delve into this conversation again. Pain lashed up his spine as he suppressed a groan. "I'm not here for part two of the show. Goodnight, Arya."

His cat, Figaro, swaggered past Arya, his little gray and white paws pitter-pattering against the walnut floor. Apollo crouched down, picked the cat up, and adjusted him on his broad shoulders. He scratched a nail under Figaro's chin, initiating a string of purrs. Arya slammed the door on Apollo's face.

"Don't get siblings, Figaro," Apollo offered. As they entered the last room of the long hall, Figaro jumped down from Apollo's shoulders onto his desk, which contained scattered ledgers, journals, and paperwork. Figaro curled on top of the accounting report Apollo was working on for Father's exporting business.

"You'd be a tremendous help if you could finish those for me," he said, unbuttoning his vest and rolling up the sleeves of his white dress shirt. Popping off the glass knob of the decanter, he poured himself a drink and knocked it back, enjoying the soothing burn that hit his throat, warming and relaxing his muscles.

All that was left to do was wait for Jinx to show up since he wasn't sure how the criminal would appear in his house. Apollo disliked that Jinx knew where he and his family lived—despite that information being general knowledge in Somnium. The thought sat unwell in his stomach, making him feel exposed.

A light rap on his window jerked his head to the side. His heart dropped to the floor as he spotted a chimney boy sitting on the window sill. Apollo held a cigarette between his lips, opening the glass window. Hand in pocket, he asked, "What have you got for me?"

"Do you have a personal vendetta against pleasantries?" Jinx commented.

"I have balance sheets to finish. Pleasantries are the least of my worries."

Jinx sighed. "You were right. Word on the street is that *I* took the box. Sadly, I don't actually have it, so my first instinct is to believe that someone wanted to pose as me and take my great name for themselves. But who in their sane minds would actually want to be tracked down as a criminal? No runaways from the psych ward rendered my original theory useless, so my next best guess is that it's someone who was at your birthday celebration or someone who works in the museum."

Jinx held a dirty hand out, streaks of grime covering the boy's hands. Apollo handed over two Marcs.

"You said three."

"I said 'useful.' What you gave me wasn't entirely helpful," he countered. Apollo could have easily come to those conclusions on his own. "Be glad I gave you anything at all."

Unfazed, Jinx conjured up an image of the ring in their hand. "Play nice."

"'Nice' doesn't get you anywhere. You know that, don't you?" He reached for the pack of cigarettes in his pocket before plucking one out and rubbing it between his lips. He lit the match.

"What's your next move?" Apollo asked. A puff of smoke wafted up toward the ceiling as he Inhaled the cigarette, soothing his shaking hands.

"I'm reporting back to you in two nights' time, not cluing you in on my every step. If you want this Vessel so badly, I suggest you start looking for it yourself. I said I'll help, not be your servant," Jinx retorted. "Did *you* find anything? Or can I just assume you drank all day?"

"Day drinking is a festive way to spend one's day." A light buzz filled Apollo's mind, paralyzing the demon entirely. "If you'd like me to assist you, I should know where you might tread so I can conduct my *own* research."

"I'll have you know—" A knock on the door froze the two. Apollo's nerves shook as he exhaled a cloud of smoke.

"Pol." It was Fey.

Apollo shot Jinx a single glare prior to opening the door to his youngest sister. He cracked the door just slightly, keeping the contents of his room concealed.

"Yes, Fey?"

She tipped her head to the side, handing over a stack of thick leatherbound volumes. "These are from Father. He instructed me to inform you to have them done by the end of the week. Goodnight."

Closing the door behind her, Apollo turned back to speak to Jinx, only to find them gone, vanished, as if the criminal were a figment of Apollo's imagination.

He had planned on trying to find the Vessel on his own, alongside Jinx's efforts. Apollo hoped that both their methods would help them in finding it faster, allowing him to figure out what the nightmare inside of him wanted to do with it.

The sickening feeling returned.

Get Jinx on your side. I have plans that require both of you, the demon purred.

Sheer fear overtook Apollo. He hated the feeling of being a puppet to something bigger, something he couldn't control. Apollo needed his ring back. He needed his sanity.

Apollo swiped a bottle of wine from the manor's cellar and drank until he forgot his own name. The ledgers could be done tomorrow.

Chapter 6

Jinx

T he rumors were true. Apollo Voclaine *was* an asshole.

However, Jinx wasn't going to make it her problem. She just had to focus on finding that Vessel, and then she'd be on her merry way to the Archives. Before long, she'd be able to finally return to her family. She could deal with Apollo; she'd put up with worse people for longer periods of time.

Saltwater infused the breeze. Intoxicated sailors swayed down the pier, hauling crates on and off ships, buying even more alcohol. Their boozed state made them perfect targets for both pickpocketing and picking up information. A loose tongue *always* did the trick.

Jinx disguised herself as a fledgling sailor boy, one who'd just signed up to join the crew the night before. She knew that crewmen were more likely to disclose private information to their mates, to their unit.

She grunted from the immense weight of the crate in her arms as she passed it over to the worn boy next to her. Her biceps ached as the man to her right whistled. "Aye, if you're to survive out on the sea, you ought to strengthen those arms, boy."

"Y-yes, sir," she responded shyly on purpose.

Wooden ships creaked as waves danced with their hulls, washing out the shouts of traders and merchants. Much like its name suggested, Wateredge sat at the border of the pier, lining right up to the tip of the water, sinking its toes into the sea.

"Did you see how bored he was at his birthday?" a passing lady whined.

The accompanying friend agreed, "You know how Apollo is. It's *impossible* to get near him."

"How does his family expect him to marry if he won't even so much as *speak* to a woman?"

"Maybe he's shy."

"He's the *least* bit of shy."

"What if he isn't interested in marriage?"

"*Everyone* is interested in marriage" the lady pouted. "My father spoke with his, suggesting an arranged agreement. But the duke declined, saying that Apollo must choose his own bride. How pathetic."

Jinx stopped listening; she could feel the conversation rotting her brain. She disliked how people thought like that, that society molded them to have those ugly morals. Soley focused on marriage and money hunting. Where was the want for honest love?

She'd spent time with someone like that once, someone who also pined for Apollo: Rylee. It felt like another life under a separate face and name. They'd argued most of the time, clashing over the simplest of topics. It was unsurprising; considering they came from two different backgrounds, it was bound to happen. But Jinx hadn't seen Rylee since she left her stranded with the doctors. Her lips had been frosty blue, her soul near death.

"Hey, don't get distracted." The sailor next to her said, passing over more crates. "Women like that don't look at men like us."

Jinx bobbed her head, playing the part of the new boy in the crew. "Why?"

The sailor dug his yellow fingernails into her scalp, forcibly turning her head to his. "Because they're higher class. Get it through your head now before it hurts too bad." He spoke with the pain of the experience.

"Yes, sir." Jinx shrugged him off, handing the new crate in her arms off to the next crew mate in line. "I forgot something on the ship."

"Hurry back. You don't want Captain taking any teeth." The sailor rewarded her with a toothy grin, exposing three gaps in his smile. Jinx feigned a chill and scuttled onto the ship, jumping below deck and swerving the incoming crewmembers.

The ship moaned. Jinx inspected its every border and crevice, digging in drawers both locked and unlocked before descending one floor down into the area that housed the prisoners' cells. She checked the vacant cells and then looked for any false hatches or loose floorboards. The boat's exhausted structure scratched at the pads of Jinx's fingers, revealing nothing.

In Jinx's mind, if the Vessel *had* been stolen three nights ago, there was a possibility that the artifact had yet to be shipped out—if the thief planned to sell it for profit. An ancient object like that could fetch thousands of Marcs across the sea. Now that it was nightfall, the authorities had shut down their inspection of exports for the day. This wasn't the first boat she'd checked for signs of the Vessel—far from it—so she knew that if she still couldn't find the relic, chances were that the Vessel was still tucked somewhere inside the city.

Earlier in the day, Jinx had snuck past the office of the harbor master, memorizing the list of boats to be cleared for departure. This craft was the last of the ten ships lined up in the port. Unfortunately, the most compelling item she'd found so far was the pile of love letters that the captain had sitting on his desk, written by the hands of four different women.

Jinx cleared off the deck, re-entering the inner walls of Wateredge. She had one more place to check. Beggars Bar was a club for men located in the deeper shadows of the neighborhood. It was where all the rich men went to get drunk and legally gamble. Few knew, however, that just past the counter of liquor, the lounge also housed an illegal fighting ring.

It was an entryway to illegal markets. Anything that needed to be sold under the table, there was someone who was willing and able to do it—and chances were, they could be found there. Jinx only ever entered the "Belly of the Beggars" once, during a time when she'd just begun immersing herself in the world of theft. It was part of the reason her name had gained so much notoriety.

Hidden away from meddling minds and prying eyes, Jinx scaled the side of a building, finding stable ground on the roof. She hopped up on her toes, warming her legs into a run. She glided from structure to structure before something caused her to trip.

Loud greetings and murmurs of Apollo's name struck her instantly, holding her in place.

What was he doing?

Indeed, Apollo had just walked out of the main avenue. Jinx, bested by curiosity, trailed him from above. Dark circles grazed his under eyes, a night of restless sleep certainly troubling him. He was puffing at another cigarette, wiggling his fingers.

Jinx wondered what caused him to drink liquor and smoke tobacco as if his life depended on it. Could it be to hide his magic, as she suspected? If he did possess magic, though, why did his eyes lack silver? The only magic users in Somnium were the Cursed, his silverless eyes confused her. There were only two species in this city: Human or Cursed. And Apollo Voclaine could not be sorted. She'd studied his irises when they met in search of the colored contacts that some Cursed wore to hide who they were. Apollo, however, wore none.

Apollo acknowledged the angst he stirred up in many people, but his gait remained just as assured as ever as he glided past the authorities of Somnium, opening the door to the Momentum Museum.

Jinx lost sight of him, but her pocket warmed. The ring was calling out to Apollo.

She wanted to get closer, to catch a glimpse of what he was doing.

Jinx leaped onto the orange tiles of the museum roof and scoured for a window to peek through. She quickly located Apollo in a conversation with two dukes from the House: the Duke of Kami and the Duke of Terrain. Both men appeared to be engaged in a debate with Apollo.

Jinx watched as Apollo scratched the back of his head. One time, two times. He then pivoted, pinpointing her instantly. He knew exactly where she was.

Jinx's pulse sped up, causing her to fumble on a loose slate. She pitched forward, catching herself before she dropped two stories. Her heartbeat was pounding in her ears.

How had he known she was there?

She scampered back to the window, but Apollo was already gone, along with the other two men. Jinx spotted him exiting the museum and waiting for her in a lonely street, expecting her.

Unease flooded her system at the thought of approaching him like any old commoner. She refused to admit to herself that he made her feel timid.

"How'd you know where I was?" Jinx asked, perplexed.

Apollo stared ahead, straight at the limestone wall, as he took a drag of a newly lit cigarette. "Because you're a shit sneak." He dug his hands into his pockets.

"The city would say otherwise."

"Doesn't matter. *I* knew you were there. I spotted you, which indicates anyone else could have spotted you, too." Apollo flicked his cigarette to the ground, squashing it under his boot.

"No." Jinx revealed the ring in her palm and looked through the band, wondering if Apollo's appearance changed. It had not; he betrayed no emotional response.

"No one *ever* sees me. It's why I'm so valuable. So, how did you know I was there?" She closed some of the distance between them, testing the reaction of the ring. It indeed grew warmer as she neared him

"I told you —"

"You didn't. You accused me of being bad at my job. *Twice* now, if I may say so, yet you still haven't answered my question."

Jinx circled him at arm's length, studying Apollo's every curvature and detail: the flow of his raven hair, the straightness of his back, the reserve behind his eyes. It would all be useful information for later. In her hand, the ring practically burned.

Apollo watched her back vigilantly. His face still seemed bored, his body language aloof, yet his eyes sang a completely different song.

"It's not an accusation when it's the work you've presented me with," Apollo said. "Are you going to tell me why you were stalking me, or can I just assume you were slacking off?"

Jinx regretted her earlier opinion of him. There wasn't more beyond the facade. She thought back to that passerby lady who'd wanted to marry Apollo; with her ugly outlook and his unpleasant attitude, they'd represent the epitome of Somnium society.

"I'll tell you tomorrow night when I go report to you."

"Why? So you can think of a lie to tell me then? If you're going to lie to me, I'd rather you tell me now."

"That's faulty logic. What good would it do either of us for me to lie to you? It's in both of our favor to find this Vessel sooner rather than later."

"Then tell me why I found you hanging outside the museum window, staring right at me." His tone was so monotonous that Jinx couldn't figure out why he cared so much.

"I could have been trailing the Dukes *with* you, not *you* exactly." A lie.

"You said 'could have,' not that you were."

Jinx attempted to calm herself down. His fixation on her word choice was infuriating. "Have a drink and calm out. Not everything is about you."

At that final retort, Apollo clenched his jaw. "I'll see you tomorrow night. I expect something useful." He turned on his heel, stepping back into the sunlight.

"Are you scared someone will know you're Cursed?"

Unfazed, he cast a glance back at her over his shoulder. "Is that what people are saying about me now? Hm. Don't believe everything you hear."

The fallacy in his statement was assuming that her educated guess came from something she'd heard. The only person who put ideas in Jinx's head was Jinx, and she was never wrong.

She didn't plan on starting now.

Later that day, Jinx rounded back to the museum and scaled the roof once more, eager to get a closer look at the scene of the crime.

Apollo's words ringing in her ears: *Don't believe everything you hear.* Obviously. She practically *invented* that phrase. The root of the very words: Not everything is what it seems.

Jinx relaxed her shoulders, cracking her neck, taking a brief stretch. She needed to let go of all the tension he seemed to drudge up in her.

Twit.

Pulling at each finger, she watched the interactions of the authorities below her. She counted each guard at their post, noted how many doors and windows there were, and observed which boxes were being taken where.

Jinx knew she needed to roam the premises for herself. If she were the one who'd attempted to steal the relic, how would she have done it? Jinx made way for the alley where she had heard the exchange the night of Apollo's birthday. Descending the cream granite walls, she slicked into her magic. A green wave embraced her whole; she soon resembled an innocent, unnoteworthy seven-year-old girl.

Shoving aside clumps of trash in the alley, Jinx searched for anything left behind that might be a clue. A footprint, a strand of hair, a drop of blood, a weapon. The narrow space was littered with waste and broken pieces of liquor bottles. Wrappers tossed by the bins, uncaring of the cleanliness. Jinx found letters of debts unpaid, days-old newspapers, and advertising. Between ripped sheets of parchment, a slim, wrinkled parchment caught her eye.

Jinx uncrumpled it.

It was a check for the payment of three hundred Marcs, signed by A.D. Marianna. The lettering consisted of a concoction of thick but swirled letters, with ink splattered on the bottom right corner of the check, conveniently hiding the symbol of the bank from which the funds were pulled. Yet, the elegant design printed onto the paper and the typography of a carefully crafted piece existed within the one percent of society. That one percent was well known throughout the city, leading Jinx to believe A.D. Marianna must be an alias.

Why would the recipient leave behind a perfectly signed check for three hundred Marcs? Ready for a happy deposit.

Whoever A.D. Marianna was, they must have been in a hurry. Jinx stuffed the check in her pocket and shifted her illusion to match one of the guards. Careful to go unnoticed as she walked into the museum, she was eager to trace the steps of A.D. Marianna.

Jinx halted by the door. Authorities were still crisscrossing the floor, with detectives dusting for fingerprints. Tape closed off the area of where the Vessel once stood before it was stolen that night. Jinx wove through the unit, pretending to be one of their own: straight spine, gruff footfalls, stocky movements. She carefully observed the head detective on the case, dusting the podium the Vessel rested on with a small brush. Any shoeprints left around it could be evidence.

That's when she heard something unbelievable. The head inspector stood up from the floor, entwining his fingers behind his back. Guards formed a line adjacent to him, putters of thick-heeled boots echoing throughout the high-ceilinged museum's walls. Jinx followed suit, blending in at the center.

"Gentlemen," the head detective announced, "it appears that the culprit left no evidence within the premise. It's as if the Vessel itself vanished into thin air."

Jinx's fists tightened behind her back. If that was true, then she had the only lead to A.D. Marianna.

"Sir! Should we suspect that this crime is the doing of Jinx?" one of the guards asked.

A wave of heat flushed across Jinx's core, her heart picking up pace.

The inspector twirled the end of his white mustache. "I'd keep our options open, but I wouldn't put it past The Ghost. Keep your eyes open. Gentlemen, we're on high alert until we find this Vessel. We're doubling patrols starting tonight. You'll receive further instructions tomorrow." He waved a hand and turned on his heel. "Dismissed."

Jinx fled the scene just as quickly as she'd arrived.

The next night, Jinx slapped a note up on Apollo's window. It was only one line: she had nothing for him. Jinx still wanted to investigate this A.D. Marianna's persona on her own first before sharing anything with Apollo. From the neighboring building, she observed Apollo peeking through his thick curtains.

Lifting the window glass, Apollo tenderly peeled the note from it. As he finished reading, Apollo glanced around outside. Swathed in the shadows of the night, he stared right in her direction. Her heart flipped in on itself as an uncanny sensation raised the hairs on her neck. Her own body was cautioning her.

Apollo walked deeper into his bedroom, swinging back his cup of amber liquor. A curious two-toned cat leaped onto the ledge of Apollo's window, its tail swaying behind it.

Apollo grabbed the cat—Jinx deduced it must belong to him—and wrapped the feline around his neck. The cat buried its nose affectionately into Apollo's cheek, and his features softened.

For once, he looked almost humane.

The blinds shut, ending Jinx's access to the intimate scene.

"At least he doesn't hate animals," Jinx muttered.

Standing up from her crouch, she tugged on her hood. Then she jumped to the next building, taking the path to her mother's house. She was in the mood to see her, even if it was from a distance. Gliding across the tiles as if they were ice, Jinx was untouchable.

And yet, Jinx felt oddly lonely.

Chapter 7

Jinx

Melee Midnights at Beggars bar happened once a week every Wednesday. It was the one night where most of the men in Somnium crept out of their rigid societal brackets and forgot about life for a while. Rank, title, rich, poor—it did not matter. As long as they got wrecked under the influence, it was a good night for everybody.

Illegal business and gambles were common here, always done under the table. Surely, someone around here had at least heard of what happened to the Vessel.

Jinx took a spot by the bar, quietly casting an illusioned beer into her hand. With a drink in hand and her scummy matchstick maker disguise, she blended right in. Not a pair of eyes bothered to so much as glance her way.

In the center of the sweat-stinking bar was the crowd-gathering brawl. One versus one. Two men were going at each other's throats. The man on the right locked in a decent jab, opening a dam of blood that cascaded down his opponent's nose.

The surrounding crowd cheered upon the takedown.

But tonight, Jinx had other plans than watching a fight. She changed locations within the bar, pretending that she was trying to get a better look at the skirmish. Really, she was attempting to listen in on any transactions that could be happening within the masses of people.

"Did you see his right hook?"

"Hey, do you know anyone who could...."

"Pleasure doing business with you. I'll see to it that your wife...."

Jinx crossed the floor again, tired of listening in to pointless conversations. The culprit could've been anyone, maybe a merchant who'd attended Apollo's birthday. She took a minute to think back on the evening in question.

Apollo's birthday had been stuffed to the brim with posh attendees, but the thief could be someone off the guest list, too. Even an employee of the museum could be the suspect. After all, they would have been in close vicinity of the relic, known its value, and recognized how to get it into and out of the museum.

Still, a merchant seemed more likely, someone who could sell the product on the black market for a high price.

Then again, a research student like Apollo's brother could also be included on the list of potential suspects. Or one of the very Dukes themselves could prove to be the culprit. Any of them would have the access and resources to take the relic without leaving a trace of themselves behind.

So, she waited and listened, catching fragments of floating conversations.

"Did it reach its location?"

"Yes."

Jinx's ears perked up.

"And did he—"

The second person shushed the other, lowering his voice to a whisper.

"Keep your voice down. This isn't the place to talk about it."

"It's coming. I've been told to warn everyone. It's time."

Everyone? Time for what? The conversation was vague and riddled with holes.

Jinx kept her head down, trying harder to listen over the primal shouts of the bar. She lifted her gaze and watched as the two strangers dispersed into the crowd.

Jinx paused, letting enough space clear between them before she started following them in earnest, trailing one of the men as he walked out. She pushed and parted the horde of stumbling men, trying to get a glimpse of what the stranger wore. Anything she could use to recognize him and later track him down.

Pedestrians kept getting in the way, slowing her down and putting a bigger gap between her and her target. Suddenly, a solid, looming frame planted itself in the dead center of her path. In an attempt to avoid a jolting collision, Jinx drew back. "Hey, move out of the way."

She swept her eyes up to meet none other than those of Apollo Voclaine. The man she searched for was now long gone.

Anger burned through her system; heat rose up through her core, snaking up her neck. She'd finally found a lead, only to lose it because Voclaine got in the way. He'd stopped her from the very job he hired her to do.

Jinx pushed the frustration away. "What are you *doing* here?"

Apollo blinked, taking a moment to put together who she was under the illusion. "Him." She trailed his line of sight, landing on a silver-haired young man about Apollo's age.

Jinx had seen him at the museum: Kovan Kami, a friend of Apollo's, son of the Duke of Kami. Like Apollo, he was also in line to be one of the Seven.

"Don't get in my way tonight." Jinx grunted, sidestepping him.

She spent the next hour engaging in small talk with other patrons, leveraging the chat in her favor, encouraging a casual slip of the tongue here and there. All the while, she maintained a wary eye on Apollo. His friend was obviously more caught up in the fight than he was.

Apollo waved down the bartender, and a third drink was immediately handed to him.

The ring in Jinx's pocket warmed again. "I expect three Marcs and an extra two for interrupting a possible lead."

Apollo stayed silent.

"You seem unimpressed," Jinx said. He ignored her, and so she gave up on starting up any sort of chatter with him. Jinx ordered a shot of the first thing the bartender could give her. She downed it in one swallow, the burn marking the insides of her throat.

She felt good. She felt warm.

"I am."

"Why?"

He cocked his head to the side, winter eyes judging her every move. "It's just how I am."

Jinx arched her brow. "Beneath you?"

"If you'd like to assume that, yes." He drank from his beer.

Jinx let herself take a moment to enjoy the fight. The two contestants were now entangled in a series of uppercuts, jabs, and blocks. Their feet were improperly positioned on the ground; it was clear they lacked technique. They were sacrificing a big portion of their potential strength. Their punches could have had a greater effect if they had chosen to use their core muscles instead of their arms.

Just then, a tooth flew across the open ring. Jinx thought she heard someone retch.

"You appear to be unmoved by this either," Apollo mentioned. Jinx nearly flinched upon hearing his voice, expecting him to keep quiet and focused on his drink.

"They're sloppy, slow, and uncoordinated." Jinx rested her elbows back on the counter, leaning against it for support.

"What would happen if you got thrown in there?" he asked.

Jinx shrugged. "Where's your friend?"

"Either inhaling all the testosterone in the air by the fight, or else he found a woman somewhere. In either case, I don't care." Apollo averted his eyes down to the pocket where the ring sat in waiting. His jaws pressed together tightly.

Jinx opened her mouth, about to reassure him she had it when Apollo cut her off in a grunt of pain. Soon, he was hunching over, holding his own stomach.

"Are you alright?" Jinx touched his shoulder. He shook her off.

Apollo panted. "*Fine.*" He rubbed the pads of his fingers in soothing circles upon his temples.

What was happening to him?

"Is this normal for you?" Jinx questioned. Still holding onto the thread of belief that Apollo Voclaine could possibly be Cursed, she wondered: Could his abilities be overpowering him?

When Apollo's knees finally began to buckle, Jinx slung his heavy arm over her shoulder and hauled him out to the dimly lit byway. She deposited him on the ground so that his back was resting against a wall.

Apollo pulled at his hair, curling in on himself. Sweat had started beading his brow as his body temperature skyrocketed. He murmured something under his breath, too low for her to hear. Concerned, Jinx forced his hand open, isolated his middle finger, and slipped on the ring.

Apollo twitched, breathed, and then fell semi-unconscious. Jinx approached his frame like she would a wild animal: slow and watchful. She placed a finger under his nose, and she felt a soft blow of air exhaling in rhythmic beats.

Relief washed over her. Thank the Virtues he lived.

"Alright, you pretentious cretin. Let's take you home."

Apollo

Apollo gasped, jumping upright. Glacial water slapped him awake as it drenched his face.

"Welcome back to the land of the living. You passed out for an hour." Something clattered on the floor.

Apollo took in his surroundings, wiping back his wet hair. It was his white-tiled bathroom at home. He was sitting down on the slated, rigid floor.

Kovan crouched down, forearms on his knees. The smirk painted on his lips lacked the classic empathy of his friend; he knew the person before him was no more than an illusion.

"How'd you get in?" Apollo asked, wiping down his wet face on a towel.

Jinx disregarded his question. "We need to renegotiate the terms of our agreement. It won't work anymore."

Memories of what had just happened hit him all at once. The aching pressure that drove from his brain down to his spine and stomach, infecting his entirety. He had never felt anything like it. The intensity eating him up internally in an entirely new manner.

Apollo wanted to believe that this influx of pain was the result of his drinking and smoking, not the demon. After all, it hadn't spoken to him during the attack, as it usually did, and it didn't chatter now. His head appeared to have cleared, free from the white noise that kneaded his mind.

He glanced down at his finger, reunited with his ring. "You gave it back."

"No, I'm *lending* it to you. And because you need this to survive, as I've clearly witnessed, we're going to be working a lot closer together."

Apollo's hands trembled, flexing and folding his fingers for control. He could not, would not, fear Jinx. "What do you propose?"

"Provide room and board for me here in your manor."

"No."

Jinx scratched behind Kovan's ear, identical to his friend's mannerism. "Yes. You will. Listen before you reject it, you bonehead." Apollo almost snorted, dousing the angst. "You're a bright intellectual. Since I have to lend you my collateral, I'm going to live here under your roof in order to ensure that you deliver on your promise and take me to the Archives. During this time, we can also work together in finding the Vessel, which will speed up the process. Do you accept?"

The criminal had a point: a shared base would benefit both of them. However, it didn't exactly sit right with him, hosting the most wanted person in Somnium right under his family's nose. Jinx still had leverage against him when it came to his ring since they knew it was more important than he'd let on. So now Apollo needed something in return.

"On one condition."

Jinx cocked Kovan's head. "Which would be?"

"You must reveal your true identity to me and those living in my house." Jinx bit at Kovan's lip and stepped back, adding sizeable space between them. Satisfaction rolled through Apollo. He had finally trapped the criminal and located their weak spot. Jinx's untraceable, secret identity was the core of their success, why they'd effectively remained hidden from authorities for so long.

He'd provoked them. "You can't really expect me to let the Ghost of Somnium into my house without some leverage, can you?"

His entire family—six people—knowing Jinx's identity. Jinx had kept their identity confidential for what seemed like ages. Jinx cracked Kovan's fingers.

"Come on, Jinx, is your identity worth the information in the Archives?" He drawled in that charismatic, husked, monotone voice of his. He was confident that Jinx would relent.

Apollo waited patiently. Jinx's chest expanded, tipping Kovan's head back to the ceiling. Then, slowly, they started shaking. "I can't do that. I'll do anything else, but not that."

"It's not up for negotiation," he said as a matter of fact.

Breaking the thick silence, Jinx burst out in an agitated chuckle, the reaction an acknowledgment of Apollo's reasonable terms. These ticks, however, were extremely unlike Kovan. Jinx cast a serious glance toward Apollo, which he challenged right back.

Without Jinx's identity, neither of them would get what they wanted.

"I'll give you my true face but not my name," Jinx relented.

"All I ask is that you be yourself."

At that, their neck slightly bent in his direction. Casting a serious side glance at him, Jinx asked, "How will you know if I am just putting up a I or if my face will be my true face?"

"Don't worry, I always know." It was true; he *would* know. That organ deep inside him warned him when Jinx was near, and so did that nightmare. His body clearly reacted to the criminal in a primal way. His magic warned him of Jinx's illusions; perhaps that was why his suspicion of Lady Hunt grew the more he noticed her that night. How he came to the swift conclusion it had been Jinx masked in magic.

He lifted his hips from the ground, straightening the lapels of his jacket. Apollo checked the time of the pocket watch: six in the morning. The sun is soon to be rising.

"I expect you at the Voclaine house in three hours. We'll work out the details once you arrive. What shall I call you?"

Jinx flared their nostrils, radiating discomfort. "Veyda. Veyda Collymore."

She must be a girl, then. The Ghost of Somnium was a girl. For some reason, he found that fact more amusing than he should have. Apollo offered the Ghost a hand.

They shook on the deal. A shock zapped between their palms. In his soul, both Apollo and Jinx knew that this transaction was settled. They'd reached the point of no return.

"Well then, Jinx...this was pleasant."

Jinx dipped Kovan's chin and strode to the window. Apollo felt a sense of déjà vu, watching his friend go to the window when he knew it was really the Ghost all along.

"Wait." She looked back. "How will I know you won't just turn me in at any time?"

"You wouldn't exactly be useful to me behind bars now, would you?"

Shrugging, Jinx opened Apollo's window. He made a mental note to keep it locked from now on. Jinx's movements were sly, spider-like. "You have yet to thank me for saving you."

"Much obliged."

She clicked her tongue. "Prick."

Jinx leaped down and out of sight. He still had to convince himself that he hadn't just watched Kovan jump out of a window but a well-trained criminal.

Apollo had struck many deals in the past, but he knew this transaction was different. He didn't know how, at least not yet, but he knew it was.

Chapter 8

Apollo

Apollo wiped at the sweat trickling down the edge of his brow and hairline. The scorching sun was flaring, beating its merciless rays down his back. The summer in Somnium did not treat its citizens kindly. Thankfully, fall would take over in a month, the shade already hinting at cooler temperatures.

Apollo took the long road back to his home from the House of Lords. He couldn't stop thinking about the deal he'd struck with Jinx hours earlier.

He now knew that Jinx was a woman. A terrifying one.

He was overcome with awe. It was a *woman* holding Somnium by the throat due to her mischief and trickery. He couldn't have been more impressed. Not to mention that she had single-handedly injected fright into those who spoke her name without ever even showing her face.

Apollo knew with absolute certainty that she was, in fact, a Cursed one; the thing inside of him had confirmed it. But he didn't care what she was. Cursed or not, magic wielder or not, he knew it did not change who a person was at their core.

No. What kept his heart thrumming now was her mind as he replayed the conversation's entirety back to himself. It must've been that sharp brain of hers that enabled her to live for so long in the shadows. And Apollo had basically opened the door to his home, offering her a residence.

Shit. What had he done?

After Apollo entered the foyer of his home, the door clicked shut behind him. The grand spideresque chandelier sparkled, white light glittering onto the light blue walls of the room.

He shrugged off his tailcoat and top hat, perching them on the curled hangers by the ebony wood door.

"I'm home," he announced to the silent house. His sisters and mother had probably already left for the market or the botanic plaza. Thatcher was still with Sir Grayson Warren, shadowing the scientists, and Father was most likely finishing the meeting at the House of Lords.

Silent paws marched up to Apollo.

"At least you're always home to greet me." He bent down and scratched his cat, Figaro, under the chin. Figaro's furry white and gray coat was soft under his touch. He picked the cat up and put him around his shoulders like a scarf.

"What have you done today?" Apollo asked as he dragged his tired feet to his bedroom upstairs. He set Figaro atop his four-post dark wooden bed, tiny paws marking his steps in the coverlet before curling up into a ball.

"Spoiled," Apollo muttered, stepping into his bathroom. He took a long shower, eager to clear his mind. The ring hugged his finger tightly. Apollo muted all thoughts of the demon in his mind. Luckily, this time, he'd spent the day without a migraine.

He turned the knob, and the sprinkling of water ceased. Spotting the clock on the wall, he realized that Jinx would be arriving soon. There were only ten minutes left until she showed up, and he still needed to speak with his sister, Arya.

He heard the echo of a door opening and closing as the sound reached his quarters. Apollo dressed quickly in a simple white shirt, the sleeves rolled back to his elbows, and black pants. He rushed downstairs, towel still in hand, brushing his hair dry. The sounds of drawers opening and closing rumbled somewhere in the house, followed by a line of footfalls treading to the drawing room. Down the hallway from the foyer, Apollo checked the time. The keys of a piano chimed, likely from the one in the drawing room. Apollo assumed Fey's governess must have arrived since musical notes were always trilling at this time of the morning. That meant Mother had to be with Fey, supervising her class; Arya would have one more hour of free time.

In the family room, Arya propped her legs up on the white plush sofa, splitting open a book on her lap and gingerly removing the bookmark. Just the person he was looking for.

"Sister. Have I mentioned how bitter you look today?" Apollo droned.

Arya's sapphire eyes thinned to slits. "Pol, I've lived with you my entire life, and I will never get used to the strange way you compliment a person." She shut the book in her lap, leaving a finger inserted between the pages.

He pulled out the pocket watch. Seven minutes. "You'll never get bored with me."

Arya tucked a stray tendril of caramel hair behind her ear, her voice weary. "What have you come begging for, Brother?"

"I would hardly call this 'begging,'" Apollo deflected.

"Asking anyone for help is as close as you get to groveling," Arya countered.

Apollo waved off a careless hand as if smearing the comment off and away into the air. "I'm going to overlook that. I need your assistance. A dear friend of mine will be staying with us at the manor for some time. However, she is of the female persuasion, and I do not want Mother to be jumping to assumptions that I am courting this woman, so..."

"Why did you invite her here in the first place, then?" Arya pried her thin brow arching.

"I'm in dire need of company," he said all too seriously.

"Seriously?" Her pink lips turned down into a scowl.

"You don't actually have to like her, just put on your cheery smile while Mother is around." Figaro padded into the room, jumping onto Arya's lap and snuggling into her curling hands.

Double-crossing feline.

Arya exhaled. "Fine. When does she arrive?"

Apollo checked his watch one last time. Three knocks on the door: she was right on schedule.

Apollo turned on his heel. "Now. And her name is Veyda Collymore."

Arya trailed him into the foyer, his mother a few steps ahead, reaching for the door to welcome their guest.

Figaro swayed ahead of him. "Traitor," Apollo muttered as the cat swished his gray and white tail in response.

Mother opened the door, and Apollo's breath hitched.

The criminal. Jinx. She was *bewitching*.

Apollo's mouth dried.

Jinx's eyes resembled jewels of absolute emerald. Her glossy obsidian hair was wrapped up into an intricate low bun, with some curled tendrils purposefully left out. Her full lips nicked into a grin as she fluttered her dark lashes. A white straw hat shaded her caramel brown skin. He was sure it could soak up the sun.

"Pleased to meet you, Lady Voclaine." Jinx dipped into a curtsy, her heavy suitcases gripped tightly in either hand.

His mother touched a hand to her chest. "Oh dear, the pleasure is all mine, but I did not expect a guest. Who might you be?" She scrunched confused brows at both her children, hoping they might have an answer for her.

Apollo nudged Arya with his elbow, which earned him a deep scowl; Arya then effortlessly slipped on a convincing smile.

"Mother, I forgot to tell you, this is Veyda Collymore, a friend of mine. She'll be staying with us for the next couple of weeks, as she's just traveled here from the east."

"You've never mentioned Miss Collymore." Mother twitched.

"It was my own mistake." Arya brushed it off. "Surely, Miss Collymore is no trouble."

Handmaidens passed by, grabbing Jinx's luggage and hauling the cases to the guest quarters.

Mother urged her inside. Jinx swiftly took off her hat and placed it on the hanger in the entryway like she'd done this before.

"None at all," Mother agreed. "Let me show you to your chamber, dear, so you may get settled in. Would you like some tea?"

Jinx nodded. "I'd like that very much, yes."

"We'll get it to you straight away." Lady Voclaine ushered Jinx to follow her. Stepping onto the tile, Jinx paused a few centimeters from Apollo's chest and stared up at him with haunting eyes. The ring burned into his finger.

Apollo didn't want to know if that meant anything. After all, this was Jinx. The Ghost of Somnium. The most wanted criminal in the city.

Just because she was beautiful shouldn't distract him from who she truly was.

"Is that your actual face?" he whispered.

Jinx blinked, her eyes finding the floor momentarily before staring back. "I don't understand if I should be offended or not."

"Definitely not offended."

Mother went behind Jinx, hands cradling her shoulders, guiding her away from the strangeness of her son. "Come now, Veyda. Let's get you settled."

Arya waited for Jinx and Mother to be out of earshot. She arched a brow at her brother, accompanied by a knowing glance. "You almost didn't look bored there."

The ring cooled; Apollo moved his fingers at his side. "Why is everyone so concerned with my expressions?"

"No one remembers that last time you smiled, Pol. We worry about you. You're a walking piece of flesh with no emotions to show, like a body without a soul."

That was the problem. Apollo *had* a soul. He cared more for his family than his own father did. He just couldn't afford to *show* it. Her words cut into his heart and twisted the knife, but he didn't want to relay his feelings.

"Touching," he retorted.

"What is she really doing here?" Caution laced his sister's question.

"I told you. I'm in dire need of company," Apollo said flatly. He knew Arya didn't believe the lie one bit. He only hoped she'd take it one way or another because it was the best he could offer.

If he was being honest with himself, he didn't know what Jinx was doing in their residence either. All he knew was that he had to find the Vessel, and if offering her a place to stay facilitated that, fine. Apollo didn't believe in coincidences, but he knew there was something in the Vessel that called to him—that called to the demon within him. And he was determined to uncover the real reason why.

Chapter 9

Jinx

Jinx's temporary quarters in the Voclaine manor were the nicest four walls she'd ever set foot in. The walls consisted of creamed panels cornered by beige swirls, with delicate leaves placed upon them. The limbs of a tree held the whole structure together. A four-post bed was tucked into the far side of the wall beside a matching armoire, and a mirror was resting inclined on a vanity across from it. Sheer pearl curtains followed the dance of the wind as the breeze came in through the crack of the window.

Peaceful. That's what the room was: absolute serenity.

She had never experienced that before. The chance to lower her guard and breathe.

Jinx sat on the chair beneath the vanity, its cushion hugging her thighs. She felt the smooth surface of the light oak underneath her fingers and looked up into the mirror.

Her reflection stared back at her for the first time in a long time. Lips thinned, a warm, comforting heat cradled low in her belly. She tucked a stray strand of hair behind her ear. It was real. Her hair was her actual real hair for once.

All I ask is that you be yourself.

What if that was the one thing she didn't know how to do?

Jinx had spent much of her life pretending to be thousands of different personalities and faces. Capturing a glimpse of herself in the mirror now was a shock to her own eyes, an uncanny sight she still hadn't gotten used to.

Her fingers dragged across her lips, feeling the soft surface.

"Where'd you get all the clothes?"

Jinx jerked in her chair.

"I didn't expect a thief to have such nice things." Apollo leaned against the door frame into her room, arms crossed.

Jinx strained a tight smile in response. "If you have that assumption, then I guess you can already make the conclusion of where all this came from."

In the time he'd given her to arrive at the manor, Jinx had "borrowed" the bags from a lady staying in a hotel nearby and veiled them in an illusion, costuming herself a new wardrobe. Her current dress was one such piece of magically divined art as well. The luggage was not only for aesthetics but would serve her future purposes as well. She needed to make the facade appear as real as possible in order to pull it off.

"We need to agree on some ground rules," Apollo cut her thoughts short.

Jinx straightened in her chair. "Yes, we do."

"First, no magic in the house. None of your face changes."

"Illusions."

He gave her a look. "No illusions, no tricks on my family, no stealing. You are considered Arya's friend from the east in this house, so do what you will with that information."

Patting down the front of her dress, she squared her shoulders, both hands on hips. "Sounds fair. On my side, you will let me into the House of Lords Archives in your next meeting."

"No."

"Noo?" Jinx elongated the vowel.

Apollo shrugged his shoulder casually. "You may have helped me last night, but you have a tendency to disappear, hence your nickname 'Ghost.' I'll let you in after you have retrieved my Vessel."

Working with him on such a constant basis was going to be tiring. They were two strong-minded fools bound to clash heads.

"No," she rebuked sternly. "Finding the Vessel could take weeks. I must get into the Archives before."

"Better get working then," Apollo said.

"*We* better get working then. I am not your employee; get that through your head."

His voice remained even. "I understand that, and I plan on doing my part. However, I'm still denying your request for entry. I will let you in when *I* deem it the right time. If you want this to work, you'll have to trust me."

That was the problem. She didn't entirely trust him; like everyone else, she was wary of him and his reputation. A part of him resonated with her enough for her to show her face, but she wasn't completely sure yet. Or was she so desperate to reunite with her mother that she'd become reckless enough to let someone in...just a crack? Either way, she knew there had to be some form of trust established if they were to work together.

Jinx backed off. "Fine."

"Thank you."

"So, I was right then. You are a Cursed."

He denied it, but Jinx kept pushing the subject. "Your ring has runes, you were more reserved than usual without it, and your handshake yesterday locked in our partnership. Will you continue ignoring it? The only thing I do not understand is why your eyes don't have that silver gleam."

"No. Not entirely. I'm not a full Cursed," he admitted.

Just like her then. What other secrets were hidden beneath Apollo's skin?

A certain smug expression crossed her face. She'd been right—at least, for the most part.

He faced her, almost glaring. Indifferent, he pushed off the door frame, closing the space between them in two long strides. "You figured it out on your own yesterday. I know your identity, and I know where you are without seeing you. There's no point in hiding it."

Still, she'd never witnessed him actually using his abilities. Not once had he shown it.

"I should consider being a detective in my next life. I bet I'd excel."

"Perhaps it'll suit you better than thieving," Apollo said.

Jinx raised her chin.

Way to spoil her victory.

"Alright. Just to reiterate, this deal is not complete until you have the Vessel and I am let into the Archives. You cannot turn me in throughout the duration of our partnership *or* after."

Apollo added, "In addition, you will not use any sort of magic on anyone in my family. Unless I instruct you to do so. And we cannot lie to each other."

"That goes both ways. I expect in this deal for me to be treated as an equal, not a servant or an employee."

"I'd want nothing less." He held out his hand.

Jinx met him halfway, closing her hand around his. "May Fortuna favor the brave."

"And Elu keep us alive."

A zap of energy shocked the center of her palm, traveling down to her core and lacing itself into her soul. His magic was potent, untapped. Familiarity caressed the back of her skull. She had felt this same kind of magic before, but where?

"Brother," Thatcher called out, "how could you forget to tell me that we were expecting a guest?" He appeared just behind Apollo's tall figure. "Oh, hello."

"Thatcher, meet Veyda Collymore. A friend of Arya's," Apollo explained.

Jinx curtsied deeply. "A pleasure."

"Please, it's all mine." Thatcher placed a fragile kiss on Jinx's knuckles. "How long should we expect your stay?"

"I suppose no longer than necessary." She cast a discrete glance over at Apollo.

Thatcher asked, "How is it that you met our dear sister, Arya?"

"Will you be at tea in thirty minutes?" Jinx deflected, earning herself more time.

"Certainly."

"Then you will learn there." She bit her lower lip.

Apollo's arms unfurled from themselves. "Thatcher, how was your time with Sir Warren?"

The scientist?

"Brother, it was phenomenal. Today we began our research on matter and energy." Light ignited behind Thatcher's eyes as he spoke up with passion, his cheeks puffing with excitement. "The properties of energy are the same as that of what surrounds us, but also what is inside ourselves. Isn't that *fascinating*?"

A smile crawled across her lips, expanding her face. She admired his adoration for science. Many in Somnium were reluctant toward science, believing its principles went against the Virtues, signaling that they were turning their backs on the sole creators of the universe. Others believed science was revolutionary, a way to push the city forward into the future.

"Arya!" a song-like tone chimed. Airy footfalls neared the trio. A girl with a resemblance to Thatcher popped in, barricading the only exit, leaving Jinx trapped inside. Her hair was almond brown, just to her shoulders. She had the same eyes as Thatcher, her rounded cheeks rosy.

Thatcher closed his lids. "And *that* would be my twin."

"Apologies, Miss. I thought my sister was in here." Her tone was soft and tender. She dipped her chin, her trained shoulders low and back. Her feet tipped minutely outward like a ballerina.

"No apologies necessary. I'm Veyda."

"Fey Voclaine. May I say your eyes are undeniably beautiful."

"Thank you. I like your dress," Jinx returned the compliment. She indeed liked Fey's dress; it was simple and elegant. The hem finished at her ankles, exposing her matching slippers. It was an outfit for a lady of class.

"If you have time to spare, I could take you down to the market. You could buy one straight from the store." Fey looked down at her skirt, messing with the fringe, mumbling to herself.

"That would be most enjoyable." At that, Fey clasped her hands on her stomach.

"Alright, twins, I need to speak with Lady Collymore in private. Would you mind giving us a few minutes before we have tea with Mother?" Apollo's icy stare gripped Jinx. She couldn't tell if he intended to be threatening or not; he was still so difficult to read. The twins waved goodbye, the distant trembles of a sibling argument echoing with them in the halls.

"They're kind," Jinx said.

Apollo addressed her comment with a simple 'yes' and diverted the topic. "Where do we start?"

Jinx focused back on everything she knew so far. "We begin at the scene of the crime. The Vessel is a relic of unknown origins. We need to discover its source so we can deduce the criminal's motives and find out where they might be. We'll go to the museum tomorrow morning."

Apollo took a deep breath, revealing as many emotions as he'd ever let through.

"But first, I'm having tea with your mother."

Chapter 10

Jinx

A pollo's mother delicately held the pot of hot water as the liquid streamed into Jinx's cup. The steam curled around the edges of the gold-lined cup as Jinx dipped the bag of herbs inside, the water obtaining a crown-like amber hue.

Jinx felt Apollo's frozen stare boring into her head. She met his eyes, unafraid, intent to convey that she meant no harm to his family.

She recalled a time when she was well-practiced in these trained social graces and put them to use once more.

Lady Voclaine breathed, calming herself. "Have you settled in fine, my dear?"

"Yes, thank you. Your hospitality has been nothing but perfect."

"Tell me, Veyda, when did you arrive?" his mother asked gently.

"Earlier today. A week sailing from the east is so dreadful." Jinx took a sip of tea, aware of the placement of her fingers. She needed to sell the story of Veyda Collymore.

"Indeed. My husband will be traveling there soon. I've warned him about the travel, yet he waves it off." Lady Voclaine gave a cheeky smile. "How did you and Arya meet?"

The heavy double doors to the drawing room groaned open as the rest of the Voclaine siblings filled inside, Thatcher coming in last. The Voclaine family now sat all around her, putting her in a position that resembled a casual interrogation.

Apollo was at the end of the table, in neutral territory. With one knee lazily crossing the other, he was laid back and stirring his tea.

"Just in time," he said flatly. "Veyda was about to tell the story of how she and Arya met."

Not only was this a pseudo interrogation, Jinx realized, he was testing her improvisation skills. Her heart picked up in excitement, jitters prickling her spine. He earned a lopsided smirk from Jinx. Jinx's amused emerald gaze then met with Arya's, who was interested in the lie she was about to tell. Arya snapped the lace fan she'd been fluttering closed and placed it next to her on the table.

Jinx set her china on the matching saucer, a quick rattle filling the extended silence. She played it off as if she and Arya were staunch friends from another life. "Should I tell the story or you?" Jinx plucked a finger sandwich from the silver tray and chewed slowly.

Arya tilted her head, pouring tea into her own cup. Her thin brows slowly arched. "I believe you should have the honor. You are our guest."

"Well, I assume you all know your Arya loves her book clubs, enjoying a good read or two. Back when Sophia Acadaine lived here before she moved east with her family, and then her..." Jinx cleared her throat, coughing away the fake tragedy. "I assume you all know of her, yes?"

Lady Voclaine nodded, her mouth saddening into a sorrowful frown. "Oh yes, may Akuji take care of her in the after."

"Yes, indeed." Jinx pitched her voice lower. "Sophia and I had met back in the east when she moved there and had told me about this book club. I am an avid reader as well, so one time, when she visited from the east, I joined in her return journey. That is where Arya and I met. Though at first she did not like me much, we overcame our differences eventually."

Jinx glimpsed Arya's eyes widened, the shock sparking within her. Apollo's sharpened edges almost looked amused. *Almost.*

Thatcher enquired, "You enjoy reading?" He lofted a glance at Apollo and then back to Jinx, licking his lips, holding back something like an inner joke. "Few women like to read. What else do you enjoy, Miss Collymore?"

"Please call me Veyda." Jinx finished her sandwich. "I enjoy art."

"What sort of medium?" Thatcher continued.

Jinx's answer would have been "reality" if she were being truthful.

"Sketching. I am not the best at it."

"I'm sure you are being modest," Apollo cut in, sipping from his own tea. Understanding flashed behind his winter eyes, knowing that her true artistic abilities lay in her illusions.

The Voclaine family all twisted their heads toward him, accompanied by gaping mouths, as if they didn't expect him to speak.

Jinx rebuked, "I can assure you I am not. The attempt is there, at least. I may also indulge in some politics."

"She seems like a match," Thatcher mumbled before hiding his stretching grin behind a swig of hot water. Lady Voclaine tensed.

Apollo did not say a word. He rolled further back into the rest of the chair.

Jinx took it upon herself to respond: "I can assure you I am not in pursuit of a suitor, even if who you are implying is His Grace himself."

Arya perked up, intrigued. "Why is that?"

Jinx cracked her fingers, knowing that reeled in her attention. "What would be the purpose of a man when I can do everything myself? I also don't believe His Grace could live in the conditions that I do. My life is far too erratic." She finished with an all-knowing smirk, mirroring the one that had generously infected Thatcher just moments earlier.

"What is it you do?" Fey asked, subconsciously trying to close the space between them. Her big blue eyes expanded at Jinx's every word as wisdom poured from her often deceptive lips.

"Adventure," Jinx replied.

Fey edged closer, her upper body hauling over the table. Apollo remained impassive; he simply watched.

"Life is far too extraordinary to sit in one place. Too many places to know, too many faces to see. I want to know them all, all the lives they've lived."

"You speak with experience," Fey pointed out.

Jinx adjusted her seat, worried that she was revealing too much. "Life is fascinating, is it not?"

"People," Apollo corrected, "are fascinating."

"Certainly." Jinx ducked her chin, but her eyes lingered on his face, trying to read him. Apollo gave away nothing. Her stomach flipped at the inability to deduce him; a hint of annoyance was now joining the mix of emotions in her body.

A door opened somewhere in the house; since it was so faint, Jinx had to hypothesize it was coming from the main entrance. In a few seconds, the Duke of Voclaine appeared before them. His dreadfully tired frame entered the drawing room.

Jinx jumped up onto her feet, curtsying to the Duke. "Your Grace."

Apollo's father bowed deeply. "Please, there is no need for formalities. Any friend of my daughter's is welcome and will be treated as family."

Jinx froze, her shoulders tightening. How did he know she would be there or that she would introduce herself as Arya's friend? Apollo couldn't have had the time to tell the Duke, so how could he possibly...

Arya shrugged innocently in her seat as Jinx cast her eyes upon her. Arya must have sent a runner boy informing the duke before his arrival.

"I apologize for cutting this introduction short, but I must make my way to my chambers. Discussing matters with the rest of the Seven can be tedious." The Duke touched his forehead to mime a headache and ambled further into the house.

Jinx echoed the sentiment, eager to retreat to her room. "I feel as if I must follow in the duke's steps. I am much too tired from the trip. Do you think we could continue our discussion tomorrow?"

Arya kicked her hips off the chair. "Veyda, could I have a word with you?"

Arya did not give Jinx enough time to respond. She turned her back to Jinx, clearly expecting her to follow, which Jinx did. Trailing behind her, a wave of cold pressure pressed on Jinx's skin like a layer of frost threatening to consume her. She sensed it came from Apollo's perceptive stare.

Her heart missed a beat as a surge of heat pulsed through her veins.

After they'd retreated behind a door, away from the rest of the family, Arya's demeanor changed, peeling off the veil of the perfect, accommodating daughter.

"Who are you?" Her tone was direct and commanding.

Alarm pulsed in Jinx's blood, though she didn't let it pass through to her exterior. "Redundant to ask that, is it not? I just gave a piece of my life story inside."

Arya didn't relent. "How do you know about the book club? What else do you know?"

That last phrase was key to her reaction. Arya clearly felt exposed by Jinx's revelation and knew there must be more to the story. It seemed as if it were a slab of herself she wanted to keep hidden from the family.

"I know nothing. Your brother told me what to say." Another lie. Building a foundation on false truths usually crumbled, but Jinx did not see another way out.

"Arya," Apollo commanded. His tall figure engulfed most of the hall. His oldest sister glowered at Jinx, scoffing in her face.

Jinx was unfazed. At least most of Apollo's family seemed to take the bait. Arya just had to buy in. Time would do its bidding. Jinx found a slight fondness for the Voclaine family.

Arya turned on her heel, leaving Jinx and Apollo alone. Unlike Arya, Apollo approached her more apathetically, though there was a hint of curiosity in each step. There were no words to explain what she felt when he was near, but it was as if he could really see her, see through the fortress of her own making. "You lie as if it were the truth."

Jinx swiped at the front of her corset, straightening her spine. "The truth is nothing but another lie."

Apollo tilted his head. "Quoting one of our philosophers?"

"Am I? Or am I just repeating myself?" Apollo realized that she must have been the philosopher who said that. The philosopher— once highly regarded as the Theorist of Materiality—had been around for no more than a year before he disappeared. It wasn't easy to take on the façade of a philosopher; Apollo was impressed. The band coiled around his finger, heated.

Apollo leaned his slender body against the wall. "What did Arya have to say?"

"You're sharp. You can figure it out." Jinx lifted a shoulder, seeking to reach her quarters.

"How did you know Arya went to a book club?" Apollo called, not moving from his brooding position.

Jinx turned her body but didn't step any closer to him. "I do my homework. I suggest you do yours, too, if you'd like to find your Vessel." With a mocking bow, Jinx strutted over to her chambers, shut the door behind her, and went to bed.

Chapter 11

Apollo

People rarely surprised Apollo, but Jinx had quickly established herself as one of the select few. Her nickname, "The Ghost of Somnium," was well-earned. The equivalent of saying Jinx. The nickname was used interchangeably. He saw behind those calculating eyes, noticing how perceptive she'd been during tea with his family. How she wove honesty into her lies. How she cavalierly added in the detail of Arya's book club.

How many other secrets resided behind those enticing eyes of hers? What had she gone through?

Apollo had spent only a day in her proximity, and yet he already itched to know her thoughts and learn more about how her mind worked. He was frustrated he could not read her as well as he could read other people.

Despite his apprehensions, she had also gained a grain of his respect. This time, the Virtues may have dropped a blessing in his palms: a fitful partner to find this Vessel. A solution for his soul to be fixed so that his mind and body be entirely his again. It was a distant dream he'd been long yearning for, yet finally, it seemed like it might be morphing itself into a reality.

But no matter how much he longed for normalcy, he knew he must still tread carefully as long as the demon was still inside of him.

Figaro purred, his two-toned body curling around Apollo's ankle. Apollo shut the notebook he'd been writing in, the pages bending around the pencil tucked inside. Apollo cradled the cat in his lap, running his fingers through Figaro's soft, velvet coat.

Apollo still couldn't believe Thatcher's utterance yesterday at the tea table.

She seems like a match.

What a profound *idiot.*

Courting was the last thing on his mind. Apollo swore to himself that he would never court because of his condition. Any potential partner deserves more than that.

Still, Apollo has indulged in plenty of debauchery. Alcohol and cigarettes helped relax the constant fight for dominance inside of him. Meaningless sex was never an issue. The problem occurred whenever feelings took root.

Emotions.

Love.

Expressing anything of the sort would spell catastrophe. Apollo could allow himself to feel a minuscule percent of his authentic emotions, but any more than that would invite destruction in its purest form. As long as he could suppress those fickle sentiments, though, he could move about like any other person.

Once, Apollo had crossed that line. Once, he'd been curious to find out. Ever since he vowed to never let go again.

Memory ran its course, taking him back to the days after he'd encountered the nightmare in the Woodlands. Apollo returned to the spot of their meeting, the demon already housed in his lanky body. Silver ring already captured his finger. He'd lied to his mother, using the excuse that he'd been spending time with Kovan.

He could never forget how fiercely his body shook at the sheer terror of this experience. Apollo felt as if a piece of him had been removed and replaced with something else. A constant whisper of a conscious that was not his echoed in his mind.

Meanwhile, the ring electrocuted him for days. When he'd get too excited, he felt a jolt. Too flirtatious, a jolt. A little too sad, a jolt. Every hour, every second, slowly dimmed his light, trapping him in his own body.

Surrounded by mountainous trees looming over him, he'd been blanketed from the rest of society for a few minutes. In that very patch, where the grass died, brown dirt had turned pitch black, and animals were frightened away. A sense of alarm tinged the air.

The pressurized ball of pain in Apollo's throat burst as his heart hammered against his ribcage. Despite how restricted he felt in his own skin. Apollo yelled, releasing every piled-up sensation and, along with it, a storm of red. Bright crimson tornadoes of magic erupted around him as he waited in the untouched center. Trees were ripped from their roots, and cracks formed on the surface of the ground. The emotions vaporized everything they'd touched.

The ring battled Apollo. He could feel it constricting and cooling a muscle in his center, deep in his core. It was suffocating him. Apollo gasped, struggling to inhale. His spine weakened in pain, muscles loosening. The roads of his veins flamed, searing him from the inside out.

He wanted it to stop. Apollo *needed* it to stop. Otherwise, he felt like he might die.

With all of his strength, Apollo willed his body to calm down, to overlook every other sensation. Then, with the fraction of strength left in his legs, he sprinted, crossing all of the Woodlands and the Slums and slipping into darkness at Kovan's door, right in front of his hideout in Crosspoint Yard.

The demon in his head growled. *You fight me now, but one day, you will lose.*

Apollo awoke the next day as if nothing had ever happened. Only the fissure in his ring assured him that it was not a terrible dream. He was in prime condition. Apollo ventured for the last time to the Woodlands, to the place where he'd been laid bare. He found the forest naked. All traces of life were gone.

From that day on, he swore to himself that he'd never dig deeper, never explore or expose that part of himself. If he didn't recognize it as its own entity, it didn't exist.

"Morning." Jinx yawned into her hand. She wore a white blouse and black skirt, the hem kissing the ground. Her footsteps were nothing but a whisper as she crossed the room, weaving her long hair back into a braid.

She sat across the table from him, with the traitorous Figaro at her side, balling into Jinx's lap. She let the cat lay there as she sorted through the fruits, meats, and cheeses before her.

"As an aristocrat, I would have expected you to have better manners," Jinx casually remarked.

Apollo sank his teeth into the inside of his cheek, holding back the smile from firing. Once the urge slipped, he said, "It *would* have been a good morning if my cat had not betrayed me twice in the span of two days. I now have to question his loyalty."

"Or you could question how awfully boring you might be," Jinx quipped.

"Your charisma is questionable. Are you sure *you* are the thief tricking others into believing someone you are not?"

"Some would say that I am quite favorable. Your cat, for example." She pointed out, with traces of humor.

Apollo longed for a release, a way to distract the feelings rising in his stomach. He reached for his notebook, opening it back up to the page he'd been writing on. "Figaro also brings in mice from the back alleys. I'd say his tastes aren't the most refined."

"Being from the streets doesn't mean much." Jinx's voice contained nothing of a wound, but he realized the coarseness of what he'd said, considering where she came from.

"I—"

"Don't," She cut him off, her features hardening. "I know it wasn't intentional." Placing Figaro back on these feet, Jinx began her meal.

"Where is the rest of your family?" She was deflecting. Apollo made a mental note to reflect on that another time.

He closed his notebook and slid the leather-bound book aside, choosing to eat with her. "Gone."

Jinx dropped her hands on the table, rattling the expensive silverware.

"You're insufferable to make conversation with." She wiped her full lips off with the cloth napkin, imitating that of a true lady. "When do we leave for the museum?"

"Change of plans." Apollo announced. "My friend, Kovan, requested to speak with me. It should not take more than an hour."

Jinx nodded; he'd expected her to put up a fight but found she had none. A stressed moan bubbled in his throat; he swallowed it immediately. Wariness brushed his neck, raising his hair to stand on end as she continued to divulge in her breakfast. Wishing he could peer into that foreign mind of hers.

Jinx did not ask why they were heading to Crosspoint Yard instead of Wateredge. In fact, Jinx did not talk at all. It unsettled him.

"You aren't talking."

Her gaze stayed fixed ahead, keeping a healthy distance. "Is this a horrible way of making conversation?"

A chuckle formed in the pit of his belly, swarming upwards. Apollo briskly fished in his pocket for a new cigarette, igniting it and taking a deep inhale, enough to mask the swell of something brewing. "Nothing gets past you, does it?"

There. He glimpsed an air of surprise when she glanced sideways at him. Her sharp cheekbones tightened. "Sarcasm? That's new."

"What do you mean?"

They sauntered down the industrial street of Crosspoint Yard. The constant clicking of metal clashing swayed down the avenues alongside them.

"It isn't exactly a secret that you are *cold*." Jinx emphasized the last word. Damn him if it didn't irritate an old wound. A wound that never healed properly or even healed at all.

Pressure prodded the temple of his skill, the metal of his ring warming around the runes etched within.

"The preferable term would be 'reserved.'"

"Hardly. Even those with reserved dispositions could engage in a casual exchange." Jinx turned the corner to Kovan's before Apollo had the chance to direct her there.

He shouldn't have expected anything less. "What if I don't enjoy small talk but prefer knowledgeable discussions?"

Jinx looked back at him, her eyes squinting at the intense sun. The sliver of light that passed her lids sparked a fierce green. "It is often in small talk that we find things to then turn into knowledgeable discussions, yes?"

"I agree with you, though there are some who are intolerable." Apollo took another drag of the cigarette.

Jinx fully met his stare. "Is that why you seemed so vexed at your birthday?"

"No. According to my brother and Kovan, I was brooding."

"I can see that, but most of the night, you were put out."

Apollo flicked the orange bud into a trash bin as they passed, turning one more corner. "I guess everyone is obsessed with my appearance. Kovan, my brother, you."

Jinx suddenly planted her heels into the cement, stopping on the spot. Wary disbelief scrunched her brows. "Just because you are handsome does not mean I'm obsessed."

So, she thought he was handsome.

"It is my job to study people and my surroundings. It's how I lived," she continued.

Apollo wanted to scoff. "You survived off of deception."

"I lived by using the greed of others, as well as my own. I got what I wanted by showing people what they wanted to see. You call it deception; I call it living."

"No, all you were doing was surviving. Not once have you lived if you were not living for yourself."

Jinx pushed past him, shoving off the conversation, clearly wanting to avoid that certain topic. "You know nothing."

He dipped his chin in agreement, and they continued moving.

"At your birthday," Jinx pondered, "there were two men outside. I heard little of their conversation, but one of them mentioned the other had almost compromised whatever they had planned."

"You think the person who took the Vessel was a guest at the party?"

"Precisely. Do you recall anyone mentioning the Vessel or similar of that sort?"

"Sadly, no. I could attempt to get my hands on the list of attendees, but it was in the hundreds, so we'd have to slim down the register ourselves."

"It's a good place to start. At the museum, we must speak to the guides, too, to see if they know any history regarding the relic." Her nostrils widened a centimeter.

"And?"

Jinx twitched, gazing up at him. "And what?"

"You're hiding something. What else?" Apollo asked.

"Why do you think I'm hiding something?"

A socialite sauntered by, greeting Apollo. He simply raised a hand.

"I don't believe it; I know it," he said. "Your nostrils flare the slightest inch when you're hiding something. Am I going to have to ask again?"

Jinx licked her lips, her features hardening. She was clearly frustrated with him. "The same day you went and met with the Dukes of Kami and Tertian, I returned to the museum after our argument. I found a check for three hundred Marcs in the same alley where I'd overheard the two men speak, a check signed by someone named A.D. Marianna. Do you know anyone who goes by the name or possibly that abbreviation?"

Apollo gazed ahead. "Not off the top of my head, but I'll look into it."

Before Apollo knew it, the two had reached the back alley door of Kovan's foxhole. The red brick sustaining the structures was a shade darker. The temperature dropped a few degrees as they ventured closer, the chill sinking into Apollo's skin.

Apollo knocked against the steel door. "About this place, don't —"

"Mention it to anyone because it's a place where you, Kovan, and your brother hide from the impending needs of society?" Jinx had taken the words from his mouth as if they'd already talked about it.

Apollo blinked. "Yes."

His heart tripped over itself.

She looked awfully smug. "You didn't think I came into this blind, did you?"

He'd known for certain Jinx would not come into any situation blind, but seeing her in the flesh and reconciling that Jinx with the rumors were two separate things.

Apollo's response was cut off by the croak of the door flying open, revealing his friend inside. Kovan brushed his fingers through his hair. "You must be Veyda Collymore, Arya's friend from the east."

Kovan bowed, stretching out a hand to meet hers. Jinx curtsied, ignoring Kovan's calloused palm. "Yes."

His friend smiled, not pressing further. "Kovan Kami. A plea- "

"She knows," Apollo interrupted, casually elbowing Kovan to the side and walking past him into the entrance. "What was so urgent that we had to meet now?"

Apollo made himself comfortable inside the loft, sitting in the same chair at the rounded table he always claimed ever since Kovan had purchased this dwelling from a troubled merchant with a substantial debt.

Shame breathed down Apollo's neck at the abrupt memory. Kovan's big heart was always more open and accommodating than Apollo's decaying one. Even so, ever since they'd been children, Kovan and Apollo had been close.

Kovan, ever the gentleman, waited for Jinx to enter and take her place at the circular table before he sat down as well. He then rubbed his hands together. "Are you sure this is a discussion to have in front of a guest?"

Apollo spared her one glance. "Depends on the subject matter."

"Vander V'Yockovitch."

Apollo held his tongue. That was a name he hadn't heard in ten years.

There was no use in hiding this from Jinx. If she was truly curious and wanted to find the information out later, she would. Denying this woman's brilliance would be an ignorant and futile move. "Alright. Lay it out."

"After you left the House of Lords yesterday, Duke V'Yockovitch appointed Vander as his heir since his pureblooded child is no longer with us." Kovan's honed muscles hardened underneath his light blue button-down.

Apollo huffed. "What a swine of a man." He'd never liked Duke V'Yockovitch. After completely rejecting Vander as a son, Apollo lost all respect for him. "You've spoken to Vander?"

Kovan shook his head. Apollo now noticed the dark splotches under his weary thin eyes. By the ceiling-to-floor window, unorganized letters of correspondence were spread out across the coffee-colored wooden desk.

"He's not pleased. Infuriated, in fact. He's spent ten years being frowned upon and pushed aside, only to be appointed as the second choice. Either way, Vander will end up taking his father's position, as much as it displeases him. It's not like he has much of a choice," Kovan mumbled the last part with obvious distaste in his mouth.

From what Apollo remembered, Vander had long yearned for the position his father held as the Duke. He would have been a great fit for the role, better than his now-deceased brother. Yet, V'Yockovitch had always treated Vander horribly, which made Vander resent the position and his father entirely. He now wanted nothing to do with it.

Apollo's voice rasped, "When is he returning?"

"Vander will appear at the Masquerade ball in two months' time."

"Hm. Until then, let's keep his return to a minimum. Two months is a long time. Plenty can change within that period of time, and with V'Yockovitch at the wheel, things could get volatile."

Vander's return could easily cause some ripple in society. His father had never recognized him as the loyal, dutiful son that he was. When it was announced that V'Yockovitch was going against what he'd long preached, it would probably bring up some questions.

"What did the rest of the Seven say?"

"My father, Voclaine, and Tertain were unsure of how to take the information. They said that they needed to think about it more before casting a final vote. Nadir kept neutral. De Conto and Einar believed it'd be alright for Vander to take up the role, agreeing that V'Yockovitch has no other successor."

Apollo held his breath for a moment before responding. "Honestly, I'm not sure which solution is better: for Vander to take his father's position or for V'Yockovitch to get removed and appoint a new member of the Seven. Eberstark would be the next of the Seven. His social status is good since he funds the orphanage. The citizens would approve." Typically, the title of being one of the Seven would get passed down to the standing duke's heir, seeing as Vander could possibly reject his father's offer; if there was no heir, V'Yockovitch would get replaced by whoever the other dukes see fit.

"Agreed." Kovan touched his lips, deep in thought. "Another consideration is Camilla."

"What about her?" Apollo noticed how silent Jinx had been, attentively listening and watching the whole interaction.

"The Duke and Duchess of Tertain are keeping her at the House like some kind of hostage. She's coming out for social engagements less and less." Worry rippled off of Kovan's angular face. "Before your birthday, it had been months since her last outing. Next time we see her, it may already be the symphony, if that."

Apollo's toes scrunched in his leather boots. "Now, that is a family matter. There is not much we could do as the future of the Seven there. As a friend, however, we should get her out of there immediately."

Kovan slumped back into his seat, resigned. "I know. The question is how? Especially if we can barely see her ourselves."

Apollo's eyes landed on Jinx. Maybe he could get Jinx to help Camilla escape. Then again, it wasn't part of their deal. He was already pushing his luck by bringing her to Kovan's.

Kovan slung his arms back, hooking them over the top rail of the chair. "I'm sure we'll figure it out soon enough. So, Veyda." He offered his kindest smile, the one that brought women to their knees. Sweet as he was, Kovan was known to fool around with several women at a time. Jinx, however, appeared to be unaffected by him. "Will you be staying with the Voclaines until the masquerade ball this Autumn?"

Jinx smoothly answered him without betraying any emotions, "Perhaps. I'll have to see how my current adventure proceeds."

"May I ask what your current adventure is?" Kovan eyed her curiously. For some reason Apollo could not pinpoint, he did not exactly approve of his friend's glance.

"Explore Somnium, of course."

"Of course. What have you done so far?"

"The only stop I've made would be here." Jinx opened her palms, signaling the warehouse.

Kovan's mouth popped open. "Pol. You're a *dreadful* guide."

"I'm certainly not wonderful," he agreed.

His friend huffed. "Ignore him. If you need someone to show you around, you are welcome anytime. Anything you need at all, I am at your service."

Jinx tipped her head. "Thank you, much appreciated."

Kovan leaned in toward her, whispering loud enough for Apollo to hear. "If you get bored of him, too, I am always free."

Jinx winked playfully. "I'll keep that in mind."

Combing back his silver hair, Kovan briskly glanced over at Apollo. He raised a questioning brow as if he wanted Apollo to react, then rested back into his chair, checking his pocket watch.

"Who is *she*?" A sharp-edged, low female voice asked. Kateri Kami, Kovan's younger sister, dropped a duffle bag on the ground by the steel door. She pushed the hood of her coat off her head, revealing the same silver-toned hair with whiter undertones peeking through. Unlike Kovan's tall, stocky body, Kateri was short with rounded hips. Her pale skin complimented her sea-blue eyes, which were currently shooting daggers in Jinx's direction.

"Ah, Kat, I expected you knew Arya's friend," Kovan piped up, lifting a hand.

Apollo wiggled his fingers, finding an outlet for his nerves. If anyone could untangle the web of lies he and Jinx have built so far, it would be Kateri.

Jinx rose from her seat, hands folded in her middle. Kateri's shoulders swayed with each feline step she took. "I've never seen her in my life."

"Most people haven't." Jinx looked down at Kateri, meeting her cat-like glower.

Apollo wanted to interject, but his gut went against his brain, telling him to trust Jinx.

"Are you going to explain who you are?" Kateri's thick brows pinched together.

Jinx assessed the situation, her mind running through every potential outcome, and she went with, "I would say I don't need to, but for the sake of your nerves, I will. You and Arya really are similar. I can see why you are best friends and why you're so protective of her." She then told the same story that she had given Apollo's family.

Kateri, still wary, backed down, inching cautiously away from Jinx's face. She now turned toward Apollo to greet him. "Hello, Pol."

"Hello, Kat. Your dress is fitting."

Kateri waved the compliment off. Apollo did not know why she seemed so offended. The dress was nice.

"How is it that you attract anyone?" Kateri bit out.

"Ask your brother. He's clearly infatuated with me."

Kovan carried on with the joke. "That's true. I send him love letters daily."

Apollo added, in all seriousness, "Chocolates too. The ones with caramel inside. He knows they're my favorite."

"Maybe I'll learn Veyda's favorite desserts too, bring her some as well," Kovan said, his voice like honey. Kovan shot another glance over at Apollo. Kateri smacked him on the shoulder, disapproving.

Jinx's lips perked up. "Don't get ahead of yourself, Kovan. We've only just met."

Kovan was quickly cut off by Apollo, "You're better off sticking to my favorites."

"Jealous, Pol?"

"Protective. I don't share," Apollo said.

"That we know," Kovan teased back.

Kateri exaggerated her grunt. "Take the flirting elsewhere. It's appalling to be in the presence of it."

"You only argue that, dear Sister, because you aren't on the receiving end of any of it," Kovan instigated.

"This is a nice bag, Kateri," Jinx piped up beside the door. No one had heard her move. It was as if she materialized on the other side of the room. She crouched, extending down to touch it.

Kateri growled. "Do *not* touch it." She stomped over defiantly.

Jinx lifted her chin. "Why?" She grinned, lips stretching into a knowing crook.

Kateri, for once, was at a loss for words, silently engaged in a battle with Jinx.

Kovan leaned toward Apollo. "Do you understand what is happening?"

Did Jinx suspect that Kateri was the one who'd taken the Vessel? Is that why she was prying about the bag?

"Not a clue," Apollo answered.

Now by Jinx's side, Kateri wiggled a finger as if saying no.

Apollo took it as a cue to leave. He lifted himself onto his feet and grabbed Jinx's coat, which she'd left at the perch by the door. "Well, Kovan, I must go. Veyda and I have plans we need to tend to."

"...Oh?" Surprise raised Kovan's brows, raising them exponentially.

Apollo didn't know if Jinx had seen it, too; she did not let on. He held open her coat by the edges, and she slipped her arms through, one by one, adjusting it.

Jinx nodded at the Kami siblings in departure, and both Jinx and Apollo filed out.

Chapter 12

Jinx

Jinx stepped out upon the uneven concrete of the back alley. The heavy door loudly locked behind Apollo, who was straightening the lapels of his deep blue suit.

"Did you suspect Kateri to be the culprit?" Apollo asked.

Jinx fixed her coat. "No, but when she entered with the duffle bag, I had to check. But I don't think it's her."

Jinx pulled the magic from the organ inside of herself, her veins running warm as her skin chilled. Green tendrils eased out of her frame, enveloping both her and Apollo in a haze.

"What are you doing?" He grabbed her wrist firmly but with no intention of hurting her.

Jinx snapped at him. "*Helping* us." Apollo hadn't stipulated that she couldn't use her magic on him in their contract. Bargain or not, they must keep their identity safe. The image in her mind covered the two of them. Apollo lost his face; his new visage was rounder, with a button nose and freckles, brown eyes and ginger hair. Jinx's hair was cropped short and blonde, accompanied by light green eyes. She added some alterations to their attire as well.

"We can't walk out of an alley together," she explained. "What will society say about your reputation? And don't forget, if you want this mission to remain unknown, we can't be sauntering everywhere, flaunting our true faces."

Apollo fished the pocket watch from his shirt, using the gold reflection as a mirror. "Wow," he said, unimpressed.

Jinx crossed her arms. "A 'thank you' would suffice."

"How does your magic work?" he asked. She noticed the tiniest, lopsided grin on his face, tilting more to the left.

"Don't get too comfortable, Polly," Jinx teased with warning.

Apollo's chin leaned to the side. "Polly?"

"Yes. Your family calls you Pol. The -ly at the end adds character." She moved them both forward toward Wateredge. They walked in comfortable silence, Jinx feeling more at ease with an illusion masking her identity. Her reasoning was made up on the spot; she just didn't want to continue on so exposed for a while.

Meeting his family and friends with her genuine face had been more than enough for her. For the first time in a long time, Jinx had felt like an intruder. Each one of them cared so deeply about each other, seeing her as an outsider. It was clearly a tight-knit group that wanted to protect its kin.

Jinx wondered if she would have had strong bonds like that if she hadn't taken on the role she did when she was only eight. Friends and family were not an option in the life she opted for. Bitterness and jealousy stung her tongue.

She just wanted—

"Where are you going?" she asked. Apollo veered off track, entering another narrow hall between buildings.

"Polly?" Jinx fell behind him. His long strides quickened across the pavement, but Jinx met his pace before jumping out ahead of him.

"Hello?" She snapped her fingers in his face. Jinx wiped her art from existence, his raw face unveiled. "Can you hear me?"

The irises of his stormy eyes were lined in red. Jinx careened deeper into this state he'd been entranced in. She'd never seen a Cursed have a reaction like this. Overpowering the color of his eyes, a characteristic unheard of. His gaze, which veered into the distance, didn't even seem to be his own. He looked lost, tucked away somewhere in the deepest parts of his mind. Jinx's pulse thundered in her ears.

The silver ring on his finger glowed red, outlining the runes etched inside as they lit up. His presence overwhelmed her, suffocating her senses.

"Polly, snap out of it." She slapped his cheek, trying to pull him back. But he was gone.

Apollo's feet lured him deeper into the dark crevices of Crosspoint, where humane souls feared to enter. Shadows clawed at the edges of the brick.

The hairs on her neck stood on end. Wandering eyes of unknown origins warned her to keep out. Jinx slid a hand down her leg, itching for the dagger strapped to her thigh. She'd be ready. It didn't feel like the Cursed were watching. No, these prying eyes were hungry, watchful, menacing.

Fingers digging into his biceps, firmer and larger than she'd originally thought, Jinx urged him again. "Apollo, let's *go*."

He finally stopped. His eyes bored into the side of a building.

She poked a single finger into his chest. "Hello?"

Following the path of his dead stare, she saw that he was fixated on a single brick. Jinx dragged her hands along the rough texture of the wall, like pinpricks tickling the pads of her fingertips.

"Where are we?" Apollo blinked. He was finally returning to his present self, the hue of red around his irises gone.

"You tell me."

He pushed the brick, and it caved in. A block of the wall turned on hidden hinges.

Jinx lunged, then held back on instinct. She hardened her body, preparing for whatever was behind the wall.

Sweet magic filled her nose, interrupting each and every thought. The room reeked of energy.

Books. Everywhere.

Rows as far as the eyes could see were congested with varying spines of books. There were also stacks and stacks of pages and articles. Vines and other flora sprawled across the expanse of wooden shelves, with ladders reaching to the top of the high arches.

"This is..." Apollo started.

"*Incredible*," Jinx finished. "So much knowledge in one place." The pressure of a squeal rose in her heart, meeting her lips. She did her best to hide her excitement.

It could be in here. *The answer she'd been looking for this whole time.*

This library was messy and beautiful. A woman popped behind a bookcase, novel in hand. "May I help you?"

Silver glittered behind her deep brown eyes, her tight coils scrunched into a bun. A Cursed.

Jinx's illusion fell, her magic suddenly gone. She couldn't tug the organ inside but felt it there, lying in wait. She noticed the runes engraved on the side of the walls.

"They keep unwanted visitors out," the librarian answered Jinx's thoughts. "And the Cursed who are inside are unable to tap into their magic." Jinx felt exposed and yet unusually safe. The librarian's eyes landed on Apollo. "You, however, can still feel it. Your own magic, the wards, aren't strong enough to hold you, somehow. You are...formidable."

Apollo kept quiet.

The librarian continued, "You're both more than welcome here; the Collection opens only to those who it wants to invite in. You'll find strange volumes here, some forgotten, some considered by many to be non-existent." The woman left without another word.

Jinx turned to Apollo. "How did you know this was here?"

"I just...did."

She was hesitant. "I don't think you 'just did.'"

"Maybe not. Perhaps I've subconsciously known it's been here all along, and I ignored it." The glacial façade he kept cracked momentarily. "There's something in here, something I need to find. I just don't know what it is."

Jinx delicately pried a book from the row. The sound of the spine cracking sent ripples of joy through her veins. She read the first line and looked up. "Polly. These aren't normal books." Pushing her shoulder closer to his, she edged the book closer to him. "Look, I think these are written from the perspective of the Cursed."

Apollo's raven hair bounced along with each minuscule nod. "Mentions of the Vessel could be in here, as well as anything else society would want to keep hidden."

Jinx and Apollo decided to separate to cover more area. Taking their time, they plucked books they deemed potentially useful off the shelves. Jinx also kept an eye out for anything that might have the answer to her *other* question. As she pulled back another volume, a faint tickle crawled up her hand as a tiny six-legged spider crept up to her fingers.

She jerked and shook her hand, slapping it away. She jumped around in circles, all the while trying to not drop the books in hand. Despite her best efforts, they evaded from her grip, one by one, thumping on the ground. Jinx held back a yelp.

"Are you alright?"

Jinx stopped in place, masking the frantic beat of her heart with a cool and collected look. She gently combed through her hair and picked her books back up.

Apollo rounded the corner. "I heard something fall."

On the verge of a witty comeback, the spider reappeared on a book, marching in her direction. She squealed and jumped back, desperate to put as much space as she could between herself and that arachnid, the one that belonged in the depths of Akuji's underworld.

Apollo closed in on the spinner. "You're a high-class criminal, but a tiny spider scares you?"

"*We do not speak of this.*"

Apollo clenched his jaw, killed the spider, and moved on.

After hours of searching. Jinx met him at the far back of the room, situated at a table with ten books. She'd brought along another stack of at least ten more.

"Get comfortable, Polly. We are going to be here a while." Jinx shrugged off her jacket, dropping it on the back of her chair. Apollo matched her movements.

He procured a pair of glasses from the inside pocket of his jacket. The circular lenses sat comfortably on his face. He hauled a book out upon his crossed legs and opened to the first page.

Her crooked grin was laced with amusement. "You wear glasses?"

"No. I put these frames on for decoration. People think I'm smarter this way." If he was trying to be sarcastic, he was utterly failing.

She snorted and opened another book, reading through it carefully. Before long, her eyes drifted to him again. The glasses looked good on him. "You look as much an idiot with or without them."

At that, Apollo met her gaze. "Yeah?" Charm lingered somewhere within the shape of his lips.

"Yeah," she assured him, sticking her nose back in the book and beginning to read once more.

It had been a week since Apollo and Jinx stumbled upon the Collection, and they had returned each day since. Apollo insisted there was something in there; they just had to continue searching. One night, in between their visits, Jinx left for the Museum, eager to find traces of the two men or any hint of the Vessel. Alas, she found nothing.

Working with a partner was a new experience for Jinx. Especially with Apollo, who wasn't used to compromising on everything. Surprisingly enough, Jinx—to a degree—enjoyed working with him.

A gong of the clock jolted Jinx alert, reverberating throughout the library. Jinx aggressively palmed her eyes, rubbing her face. Twelve chimes. Midnight.

Where was Apollo? He should have returned by now. As if on cue, footsteps that matched Apollo's similar leisurely pace approached.

"There wasn't much open at this hour, so this is what I could find." He set a pair of cold sandwiches and water on the table, shoving aside the large leather-bound books.

His raven hair was ruffled, and the collar of his shirt was undone. Apollo planted himself in the seat next to her.

Jinx took a bite of her sandwich and chewed slowly. "It's good enough to keep us going." She threw her head back. "In a minute. My brain is exhausted."

They'd been reading non-stop through stories about people's experiences as magic users. Fear, anxiety, ostracization, and bloodshed dominated their lives, similar to Jinx's own lived experience. The difference between her and the rest of the Cursed was that Jinx, in some sense, chose this life. The rest of these people did not.

Jinx began to ramble, "You know what I did find interesting?" She didn't wait for him to respond. "The history books in here are the same as the ones out there."

"Enlighten me."

"I don't know if you've ever noticed, but if you've ever read Somnium's history—anything on the Four Virtues or any other history farther than twenty years ago—there feels like there is a piece missing. As if pages were ripped out so that no one could read them. It's like that in here as well."

Apollo echoed her thoughts. "Unfinished. Lost."

"Exactly." Fascination tipped into Jinx's words. "I could be insane, but it's still my observation."

Apollo munched on his cold sandwich, staring at her. After a week, Jinx was slowly starting to comprehend even his most minute gestures, reading him as best as she could. However, there were times when he was illegible.

Mouth full, Jinx directed, "Out with it. You've been giving me that brooding glare of yours for the past two days."

Apollo swallowed his food. "How is it you learned to read? I expected a thief like you wouldn't be able to attain that skill."

"I wasn't always the 'face-stealer' people know me to be today." Jinx wiped her crusted hands on a napkin.

He waited, his slender face patient, genuine curiosity painted on those sharpened edges of his cheekbones.

It was strange. To have a person ask her questions about her true self, not merely about the various facades she showed to other people. He'd queried her all week, prying small bits and pieces of her past. She saw no ill intention behind any of his questions, but it was still unusual.

What Jinx found more suspicious was the fact that she wanted to give him truthful answers. She longed for a friend.

"I had a family once. A long time ago." At her words, Apollo inched closer, letting go of a piece of the hardened expression he typically wore. "We were not very wealthy. In fact, we barely lived at all, surviving off whatever scraps we could manage, week by week. As poor as we were, living in the furthest corners of the Slums, my uncle held a grand passion for reading. So much so that he tried to get his hands on any book he could find, no matter the topic. He would sit me down every night with my mother and read to us."

"And your father?" Apollo asked.

"Died weeks before I was born."

"Infected by the plague, I presume?"

"Yes." Jinx lowered her head, bothered she never got to meet her father.

"And you?" Apollo thinned his lips. "How did you get to be the great Ghost of Somnium?"

She absorbed a smirk. "Necessity." That was as far as she was willing to give up any information on her side. She pivoted toward him. "What's it like? To be both a Cursed and family to one of the Seven."

Apollo's eyes iced.

Jinx inhaled sharply, then took another bite of the tasteless sandwich. When she thought he wouldn't respond, he surprised her.

"Tiring."

She put the crusted bread back on the table and cracked her fingers. "Does anyone in your family know?"

Apollo turned his head to the right, razor jaw on display. "My siblings are suspicious. But what they know is only surface level. The headaches. The drinking. The smoking."

"Is it not necessary for them to know that you're Cursed?"

"No."

"What more is there?" Jinx smacked her lips together, the aftertaste of the sandwich leaving an unpleasant aroma in its wake.

"Oh, there's more. It's terrible," he said flatly.

"Are you scared of it? Of yourself?"

Apollo's damning silence spoke millions. He reminded her of someone she knew in the past, a situation that occurred. Jinx had almost been too late to assist that person. To help Rylee.

"I can help you," she offered.

"It's not part of our deal."

"Doesn't have to be." Jinx spoke the words matter-of-factly as if there were no emotions beneath them. "I know how you see me. How the world sees me. I'm worse than a Cursed. I'm wanted dead, Polly. I'm the 'face-stealer.'"

Something in what Jinx said struck him as trustworthy.

"I'm not a good person," she said, "but I can help you learn to control your Cursed side. It's better than restraining your emotions and having people see you as a monster. I should know. Everyone fears me."

"Should they?"

"Should they what?"

"Fear you?"

Jinx thought back to a time when she was nothing more than an innocent child. Another memory flashed: a time much later when Jinx enjoyed drinking in the terror she'd cast. It was a horribly beautiful paradox she'd never escape. She lifted her chin. "Yes."

A low hum rumbled at the base of his throat. A beat of silence exchanged between them.

He touched the pad of his finger to his temple. Apollo sharply inhaled; his eyes suddenly filled with alarm, widening. Then they hollowed, transfixed, and lost in the void of his mind. The colors of his irises battled against themselves, pulsing pink and gray.

Jinx just watched as he began to internally battle. With what, though? Why fight his own magic if it was stronger than the library's own wards? This would end with him self-imploding.

He harshly muttered, "Not again." Jinx pretended not to hear the low words meant for himself. Something loosened in his features; a hollowness enraptured his gaze.

Jinx's brows furrowed, confused with what was occurring.

Apollo's chair protested as he stood up, walking toward the spot where his head had turned previously. His towering figure disappeared behind the walls of books.

Jinx reclined, jerking her head to watch him.

Apollo was like a hound sniffing for food. His head swiveled between the many spines. Climbing higher and higher on the ladder, he prodded his fingers in and around the books, poking deeper into the shelves. Widening a spot between two publications, he shoved his hand into the cave that emerged.

Jinx stretched her neck as far back as she could, wondering what had suddenly prompted him to scavenge there. He returned with a black, leather-bound volume radiating an unholy power. She could feel its attempt at mutiny against the runes that constricted it, energy seeping through the cracks.

Jinx's throat dried up. If this was how the book acted *with* rune protection, she didn't want to think about how powerful it might be outside of them. "What's this?"

"A book."

"I can see that." Annoyance rattled in her tone.

Apollo raised a shoulder before parking himself beside her. "I wasn't so sure since you asked."

"I dislike you momentarily."

"Momentarily," he repeated.

Jinx's spine curved forward, resting her chin on her palm. Apollo lifted the cover and turned to the first page.

Scribbles of an unknown language were inked onto the sheets, endless paragraphs of a story waiting to be transcribed. Shapes and diagrams were sketched into the corners.

Jinx's core felt nervous, the back of her thighs breaking in a sweat and gooseflesh peppering her skin.

Why would Apollo pick this book out of the thousands of tomes?

"What dialect is this?" Apollo murmured to himself.

"Why'd you pick this particular book?"

"It told me to get it," he said vaguely.

"What did?" Unease bubbled in her belly, sitting low in her core.

"My magic. I guess."

She knew she had to step away from it; its strange lure beckoned her to do something dangerous, sweetly begging her for chaos.

"Let's leave this for tomorrow." Jinx exaggerated her tiredness. "We need to rest."

Apollo bounced between her and the book, hints of suspicion lingering behind his otherwise expressionless face.

At last, he closed it and hid the book behind several stacks of files. Then, Apollo grabbed both of their coats and walked them home without question.

Chapter 13

Jinx

J inx's mind rattled without a linear or logical thought to be found. It seemed the deeper she got into the week, the more convoluted this bargain would become.

She needed to clear out all the unnecessary information from her brain and narrow it down to the few facts that would help her in her quest. She'd also have to deal with Apollo and his magical abilities.

He was a Cursed, that much she knew, but how strong could he truly be if he repressed his talents, refusing to use the muscle that Jinx trained her entire life to hone? He may not classify himself as a Curse per se, but he certainly was one. He contained magic in his body; that fact was non-negotiable.

A dull twinge of caution always lived in the back of her skull, even as she grew more comfortable in their partnership. Their slow-growing friendship had caught her by surprise. As much as she'd wanted to have a friend, letting the idea sprout, the more she'd wanted to push it away. A war constantly waged internally between Jinx's emotions and her logic.

Friendships didn't exist for a person like her, who never got to see the light of day.

Jinx wanted to howl.

Plus, her own riddle still needed to be solved. There was so much at stake: her family, the lost Vessel, Apollo.

Locking the door behind her, Jinx bathed and dried, slipping into a comfortable cotton nightgown. She opened the curtains to her window and clicked the latch. The chilled breeze of the forthcoming fall season flooded her quarters. Untying her hair, the wind threaded its fingers between the tendrils of obsidian.

She could feel her organ in use again. When she'd been in the Collection, the runes had muffled her instincts. It felt as if she were trying to breathe underwater, trying to get out, but not trying hard enough.

Jinx hauled herself into the frame of the window, her bare feet scratching against the bristle wood. She jabbed her fingers into the crevices of the outside limestone and crawled onto the roof, gripping the coarse tiles as she climbed to the roof. There, Jinx lay on her back and watched the blanket of stars winking from above.

From the height Jinx was at, she could see all of Somnium. The shore of Wateredge glistened under the moonlight as winkles of lampposts fired in the night. The port of the Charmed Bay and traveling ships were quiet, at rest. The tall peaks of the Northern Summit reached for the flying clouds. At the nape of the coastline, the freshwater of the Soundless Stream poured into the ocean. If Jinx turned to the west, she'd see Crosspoint Yard and far deeper, into the land near her home—The Slums—edging up against the Woodlands, where that *thing* lived.

The very thing that hexed her, giving her the magic to be a Cursed. It was a side effect of getting into the bargain. Of trudging into the Woodlands twelve years ago, exchanging love for wealth. Wealth for her family. It was a simple transaction, much like the one she'd arranged with Apollo.

No. She would not think about that now. Jinx had sacrificed the love of a mother for the wellbeing of her family—wealth for her mother and uncle—while she lived a life in hiding, without funds in her pocket, love nowhere in sight. It was worth it, though. Yes, she had one year to figure out that riddle that damned her, but Jinx couldn't let herself get worried.

She believed she was smart enough to figure out the answer. She'd been brave enough to strike a deal with a creature unknown to this world at eight years old, all for her mother and uncle's benefit. Jinx would return from this.

The water stung the back of her eyes, glossed with unshed tears.

Below her, muffled steps walked to the wall as hinges whined. "And what might you be doing on a roof, Lady Collymore?"

Jinx, on all fours, crawled over to the ledge, rubbing her eyes. She adjusted herself onto her front side, her head falling over to meet Thatcher's upper body, which was hanging out the window. He looked up at her, hair and clothes disheveled.

"What are you implying, Lord Voclaine?" she teased. "Can a lady not enjoy star gazing on a roof?"

Thatcher raised a finger. "I'm not saying ladies *can't*. I'm saying most *don't*."

"Well, *this* lady does."

Thatcher smiled, his grin contagious.

"Care to join?" Jinx lowered a hand. Thatcher peeked back inside of the attic and shrugged. Jinx helped him up. His center of gravity was off-kilter, his arms flailing out for balance, his hands trembling.

"How often do you do this?" His voice quivered.

Jinx chuckled. "Scared of heights?"

"No." Thatcher faltered. "Yes. The ground is, well, you know, more stable. And the chance of death up here is increasingly high, with no security." He rambled on, jittery about his surroundings. His words grew mumbled.

Jinx tugged him down, sitting beside him. The tension in his body still needed time to ease. He extended his legs slowly, resting back on his elbows.

"How'd you know I was up here?" Jinx used her hand as a pillow, propped up against the back of her head.

"I heard something. It wasn't anyone in my family, that's for sure. Either it was you, or it was Somnium's face-stealer sneaking around. The better guess was you."

If only he knew they were one and the same. "And why were you in the attic?"

His chest rose excitedly. "I was in my lab working on something for Warren."

"Go on."

"Warren has this theory, the one that I mentioned before, that properties of energy are the same as those that surround us but are also inside ourselves. It's an open system. So, we put that to the test by using forces of gravity. Simple push and pull, for now, exchanges of energy." His hands gesticulated the passion of his words, frantically waving around.

"What do you think could be done with that?"

"Hundreds of things." He sat up excitedly. Jinx followed suit, encouraging him. "It could change our world. I haven't told Warren this, but I believe that this theory could prove that the Cursed and we humans are more similar than we think."

Thatcher licked his lips. His blue irises ignited with fire as he searched for approval in Jinx's eyes to keep going. "If what Warren believes is true, then I truly think that the Cursed are just able to tap into the fundamentals of our world, using them to their advantage. If they come from the plague, then the virus had to have contained some sort of change on a molecular level, changing something within them to create that ability. We might be able to stop the hatred between the two parties if we can prove it is true."

Jinx couldn't breathe. What he was saying...she.... if he could prove that Cursed and humans are actually one and the same and not a different species entirely...it would be a miracle. People could finally come to an understanding, uniting the two sides instead of further splitting them apart. Somnium could become a place for everyone rather than fit just one party. If Cursed and Humans could level with each other and stop falling into a vicious cycle of cold war, everyone could live under the sun and moon. The Netherwen could break down its walls.

With scientific backing, people would have to stop treating each other differently.

"Thatcher, that's brilliant. You must continue your studies on that. It could prove to be groundbreaking."

"I know!" Dimples creased his cheeks. "We could even create some middle ground. Maybe find a cure so that those who want to reverse themselves could, while others who wanted those abilities could have them. It would give all our people a reason to not be afraid anymore."

Wouldn't that be something? Terror eradicated from Somnium. Cursed walking free, treated just like everyone else. Perhaps the term "Cursed" could shift to "Blessed." Then Cursed people could stop living in hiding, being hunted like rabbits.

"What stopped you from telling Warren?"

The mention of his mentor's name dimmed his excitement. "Warren wears a Tutela. Yet, he's a scientist who idealizes the real world. The fact that he wears that red band, trusting it to ward off the evil of the Cursed, seems contradictory to me, but who am I to judge? I don't think he'd be supportive of this progressive ideal. It's research I'd have to do on my own."

Jinx touched his arm, sincerity dripping into her words. "Then do it."

Thatcher nodded. He brought his knees inwards, holding them close to his chest. "You know, for being a friend of Arya's, you spend quite a lot of time with my brother." He gave her a smug glance.

Jinx mirrored his expression, raising a brow. "I stand by what I said before. I'm not interested."

"That's not what I am saying. I'm not as good at reading people as my brother is. While he studies people's behavior, I study the world. Either way, I think there is another reason you are here, and it's not for Arya."

Her heart thrummed in her ears as her brain started paving possible paths to take. Lies swarmed her tongue.

"I'm not saying this in a way to threaten you. It's the opposite, actually. Whatever you two are up to, it's your business, not mine. Just be careful."

Her inner muscles soothed. "I will."

"Good." Thatcher hopped up onto his feet. Suddenly remembering the height they were at, he shuffled inwards. "Do you mind assisting me down?" He flashed a charming smile, and Jinx helped him back toward the attic.

Chapter 14

Apollo

Several hard knocks hammered against Apollo's door. His father's baritone carried well past the door, filling his tired ears.

"Pol, get up. The Seven moved the meeting. We are to gather within the next hour." His father's heavy footfalls retreated.

Apollo rubbed the pads of his fingers over his eyes, prying them open. His mouth felt dry, an ache flaring in his temple. Regret pooled in his stomach, acidic bile rising as he pushed himself up from the mattress.

Upon his return last night, Apollo had barricaded his door, afraid of being consumed again by the demon. He had his ring back now, and it was supposed to protect him. So, why was he still being possessed as if he didn't have it?

Apollo inspected the ring encased around his finger—the singular crack in the band expanded, three total fissures in the silver.

The ring had weakened, hadn't it? From the moment when he took it off to now, the ancient magic imbued with it had dampened. When he'd first received the ring, he was warned to never take it off his finger. When Jinx swiped it, it must've started a domino effect.

He began drinking and smoking until his own thoughts no longer plagued him.

Then again, the thing inside him hadn't uttered a word. No, this time, it had been something new, something different infiltrating his brain. It had taken over the reins of his body and willpower, dragging him toward something it wanted.

Apollo considered Jinx's offer to help him. He had to be even more careful now. Accepting her offer would expose him down to the marrow of his bones. He'd be revealing a secret not even his family knew of. A piece of himself he tried so hard to cover with the mud of his blackened heart. Fully giving her something to use against him. Did he trust her enough to hand her all of his cards? She was already aware of him being a Cursed, and in return, he knew her true identity. Was that enough?

He made it to the rim of the toilet, hurling out his insides. His stomach heaved, begging to release the toxins of last night.

Afterward, he bathed and dressed, selecting a classic gray ensemble. As he parted the curtains of his bedroom, sunlight blinded him. A razor of pain dug into his brain.

He needed tea.

Apollo swept into the hall. The fluid notes of a piano floated up from the family room downstairs.

He paused by Arya's open quarters. "What might you be doing up at this hour? Knowing you, you'd sleep until the dead rise."

"Morning, Pol." His sister kept her back toward him, focused on fixing her collection of hand fans by the window. "How has it been hanging out with your new friend?" Her tone was condescending.

He leaned on the wall, crossing his arms. "You mean *your* friend."

"You spend more time with her than I do. Kat informed me of the meeting with her and Kovan."

"And?"

At that, his sister turned, bags clawing at her tired eyes. "And I've barely heard of this Veyda person you seem so fixated on. You bring her into our home, make me pretend to be her friend, and then you go off sneaking around with her, doing who knows what." Arya lunged across the room, a fury of steam fuming from her head as she jabbed a finger into his muscled chest.

"What is going on, Pol? I don't like secrets. We were close once. What happened then?"

Unbearable guilt gripped his throat, the shame weighing down his shoulders. He knew the damage he'd done to his family, the fractures he'd caused, the loss of trust in his relationships with others. His relationship with his siblings meant the world to him. Yet Apollo was certain of how lonely his future would pan out to be. It was against all of his true desires, but he was playing the hero, being cold and keeping them at a distance for their own good.

"Reminiscing on who I was will only hurt you, Arya. The past is not as kind as you remember it to be." Apollo turned on his heel, leaving his sister behind.

Maybe he should let Jinx help him. Maybe she was just what he needed. What if it meant he could stop hiding?

Reaching the family room, he kissed Fey good morning in her piano lesson and then kissed his mother, who was sipping on hot tea. He downed his own cup in a single gulp and shoved a yellow-red apple into his mouth, teeth holding it firmly in place.

Apollo grabbed a notepad and pen, scribbling a note for Jinx as saliva gathered at the bottom of his mouth.

"Pol?" Mother called from her seat.

Apollo hummed in response.

He heard the clink of her cup meeting the saucer. Apollo could see it: his mother was prepping for an interrogation. She licked her thin lips. "So, Arya's friend. Veyda." Apparently, Jinx was on everyone's mind this morning, including his own.

Another hum.

"She's awfully gorgeous." The last word was pitched slightly higher, leading the conversation to a place Apollo never wanted to enter. "Have you...thought about possibly..."

Faster than he thought he possibly could, Apollo put the pen down, ripped the paper from the pad, and folded it into a square. He then grabbed the apple from his mouth, returning his ability to speak. "Do not finish that phrase. I swore off courting. No matter how attractive I may think she is."

"She's intelligent, too, that much is clear. You've always said you'd want an equal by your side."

Apollo wanted nothing more than to escape this dreadful conversation.

Fey then blinked out of her musical concentration. "I like her, Pol."

Frustration agitated his skin, heat rising to his neck. This was too much for the morning. This exchange was too much for *any* time. But Apollo let none of his true feelings arise.

"Yes, that much is true, Mother, and I'm glad you like her, Fey, but let me reiterate: I don't dabble in the ponds of love. Love is irrational and illogical. Only lowly fools believe in that kind of theatrics." With all the burdens he carries, love was not something he could offer very little.

His mother huffed in astonishment, keeping herself together. "With that kind of reasoning, you will never be married."

Apollo set to leave. "Let's hope I never do." He made it sound like an insult. Bending down to kiss his mother goodbye on the cheek, he handed her the note. "Goodbye. I'll see you in the afternoon. Give this to Veyda for me, will you?"

As he escaped, he heard paper ruffling. "Don't look inside, Mother." The paper crinkled back into its fold.

Picking up the pace, he slipped outside and into his father's carriage. Ahead of him, the Duke of Voclaine held up a newspaper, splayed wide to be inspected. "Ready for today? You will have to take over for the next month because of my trip."

Dusting off the cat hairs from his suit, Apollo asked, "What should we expect today?"

"Warren's invited." The Duke exhaled sharply through his nose, which scrunched in disgust.

That *was* unusual. "Who invited him?"

A snap of a whip cracked as trotting hooves pulled the rattling carriage forward.

"V'Yockovitch." Much like Apollo, his father did not particularly like V'Yockovitch or his ideals.

"Why would he do that?"

"We'll find out soon. Today, I will only be listening. If there is something to say, I entrust you will take over on behalf of the Voclaine name." His father flicked the newspaper open once again, straightening its spine. On the other side of the paper, Apollo caught sight of a wanted sign of the very thief he was housing.

Apollo sighed. The first week of his bargain with Jinx had just ended, and yet his life was already teeming with semi-controlled chaos. He struggled with how to feel about her. All he really knew was that she was one of the most interesting beings he'd come across.

Twenty minutes later, Apollo and his father arrived at the House of Lords and settled inside. Rolling further back into his red cushioned seat, Apollo lit a match to the cigarette held between his lips and waited.

The rest of the Seven slowly filled the auditorium, fathers and first-born sons taking their stands.

The Duke of Tertain barged through the door, his round face burning a sharp red. His usual calm demeanor was gone. His blonde hair was ruffled, his brown jacket speckled with remnants of gold glitter. He pulled out his handkerchief, harshly cleaning the lenses of his circular glasses. Tertain then planted himself in his seat, mumbling something about his daughter, Camilla. A twinge of Apollo's resentment also stretched toward the girl, disgust tainting his tongue.

Confident footsteps neared Apollo as V'Yockovitch approached him and his father.

Brushing his fingers through his fine brown hair, V'Yockovitch greeted them with a lopsided smile. "Apollo, it's always a pleasure to see you."

And Apollo had thought his mother bringing up Jinx was going to be the most dreadful part of his day. He sucked smoke from the end of his cigarette, standing to his full height. "Lying through your teeth is bad for you, V'Yockovitch. It gives you cavities."

V'Yockovitch flexed his jaw, cut off by loudening footsteps. "I believe you know the speaker, Sir Grayson Warren." V'Yockovitch extended a hand behind him, introducing the scientist.

Level-toned, Apollo answered, "In a cursory term, yes."

"Your Grace. It is an honor." Warren bowed at the waist. Apollo did not return the favor.

Thatcher had spoken to Apollo about some of Warren's beliefs. Most of them were concerned about how to fix the issue of the Cursed. Thatcher wasn't sure why Warren had taken so much interest in the subject.

He did not particularly like Warren but also did not dislike him.

Apollo rested a hand in his pocket. "How's my brother doing, Warren?"

Warren's inky eyes scanned Apollo once over. "Very well. Bright young man, that one." Warren rubbed his neck, massaging the bottom. He was clearly stressed. Nervous.

The thing inside Apollo flashed heat into his veins for a split second. Apollo took it in as a signal of warning, urging him to pay attention. "Hm. Then there is one thing we can agree on, apparently."

"Warren," Tertain called from the pit. "The floor is yours."

"Right." Warren lowered his chin and stepped toward the center, V'Yockovitch trailing him.

Those two were awfully close today. Jinx mentioned that there were two men who had been conspiring on his birthday, and at least one of them had been invited. V'Yockovitch attended the soiree. Was it possible that Warren was the one outside, waiting to snatch the Vessel?

No. That would be too easy. However, he couldn't completely rule it out.

Warren's thick brows rose. "Families of the Seven, I am Sir Grayson Warren. If you do not know already, I am a professor at the University of Somnium, specializing in physics, astronomy, and chemistry. I've been awarded three Breakthrough Prizes by the academy. I stand before you today to bring a certain topic to light."

De Conto interrupted the scientist from his station. "The Cursed?"

Warren lifted his hand in acknowledgment. "Precisely. I believe that I have come across an answer to our problems: how to eradicate these rats from our alleys. I've been working on a machine that could pinpoint the trace of magic left behind by a user. Therefore, we could track down the Cursed faster than our current method, which is looking into the eyes of each and every person."

Apollo clenched his jaw, noting the rise in his beating heart. This machine could pick him out, damning his family. He sucked more from the cigarette, wiggling his fingers out of view. No one could know how agitated he was feeling.

V'Yockovitch piped up, "Let's not forget those Cursed are also becoming smarter, hiding the color of their eyes behind contacts."

"What do you suppose we do when we capture these people?" the Duke of Kami asked. Kovan shot a daring glance at Apollo. He was unaware of Apollo's abilities, so that look had to mean something else. His face indicated disapproval of this meeting in its entirety.

The Duke of Einar said, "Do as we've always done. Kill them."

"Would you have wanted anything besides their death, Duke of Kami?" De Conto's voice was clearly trying to hide the fact that De Conto wanted Kami to mess up.

It was early, but Apollo was tired. Dancing around the true question with pretty words was a useless tactic. "What will their death benefit us?" he asked.

The twittering mumbles of the others quieted down, silence making an awkward appearance. The men stiffened. Apollo's Father gave a huff of approval. "Was I not clear? Let me rephrase then. What will the blood of an innocent do for our society?"

A beat.

Warren cleared his throat. "Purify our city. And if I may, Your Grace, the Cursed are not innocents. They steal, they lie, and they have broken more laws than the lot has made."

Apollo's response was stern, flat. "On account of everyone's ignorance. You cannot blame them for trying to survive when those able to see the light shun them for being different."

Einar chirped up from his perch. "We could try gathering the Cursed and putting them to work?"

Kami sounded surprised. "Like slaves? In a camp?"

Einar shrugged. "Better than death, I'd say."

Apollo winced internally at the logic. "What about trying to integrate both? Separation on account of fear is the worst barrier of them all."

Stunned faces swallowed him whole as if he'd grown a second head.

V'Yockovitch sneered, launching a condescending gaze toward Apollo. "Truly poetic, Voclaine, but those progressive thoughts of yours will be your downfall."

"I appreciate the baiting, V'Yockovitch, but I will not lower myself for your standards."

"Gentlemen," the Duke of Tertain spoke up at last, "if we could get back to the matter..."

V'Yockovitch looked at Apollo over his nose. He wanted to laugh.

"Of course." Warren rubbed together his dried brown hands. "The machine uses a genetic..."

But Apollo no longer heard the details about the contraption Warren intended to bring in. Why would V'Yockovitch bring Warren to this meeting, to this House of Lords? Clearly, V'Yockovitch backed Warren in every way, standing up for him, pushing the matter of the Cursed forward on the meeting room floor.

The Dukes' eyes were glued attentively to Warren, drinking in his every word. Frustrated, Apollo leaned back into his chair, hating the way the gentlemen around him were so calmly considering mass murder.

Chapter 15

Jinx

O *ut to the House of Lords. Unexpected meeting. I'll return shortly. While I'm gone, I trust you to make yourself comfortable. Wait for me to go to the library together.*
—Apollo

"Are you upset Pol is gone for the day?" Fey chirped in Jinx's ear.

Was she upset? Upset wasn't the right term. Troubled—that seemed more up Jinx's alley. Her chest unnaturally contracted when she'd awoken to find a note given to her by Apollo's mother, whose frightening grin hinted that she knew something Jinx did not.

Jinx set the ripped paper back down onto the clothed table. She'd picked it up about thirty times and counting, wondering if there was something else in the note she'd missed. She was most surprised by the notion that he wished for her to wait to go to the Collection with him, like actual partners. Or maybe it was that she just enjoyed analyzing his swirled writing.

Jinx turned the spoon around in her tea. "No. Why would you say that?"

Sitting across from her, Fey inserted a sugar cube in her cup. "Since you've sauntered into the family room, your eyes have been fixated on that note." She took a sip. "What does it say?"

"Nothing of importance, just his whereabouts and so on." Jinx wrestled all of her willpower not to glance back down at the paper.

She and Apollo were supposed to return today to the Collection. She thought back to the black leather-clad book, its unnerving presence, the strange language inside. After her conversation with Thatcher last night, Jinx had reflected on Somnium's history. If there was an old language, anyone who knew how to speak or read it had died off by now.

Then again, Somnium's history made little sense before the plague. Beyond the past twenty years, it was like the past had been erased, its pages purposefully ripped out. Is that what her riddle had to do with? Perhaps she needed that missing piece of history to put it all together.

In the table where five once sat, now sit four

No matter how much you believe, our minds still deceive

It's a punishment for seeking truth

Knit from people's worst desires

One who seeks is bound to bloom

In Somnium, there had always been the Seven aristocrats in power and seven governing families. Different families had risen to and fallen from power over the years, but the number had always been seven.

"Veyda."

"Yes?"

"Your tea is cold," Fey said as a matter of fact.

Jinx blinked, her thoughts still consuming her mind. "What?"

"Your tea. You've been stirring for the past ten minutes."

Jinx's eyes focused back on the present. Her tea was, in fact, cold, and her appetite diminished.

Fey set down her cup, perkily leaning over the table. "What are your plans for today, then?"

There was no alternative she had planned in case Apollo left. She supposed that she could go visit her mother, from afar at least.

"Do you want to go to the market with me? I could show you the tailor shop where I got that dress you liked." Fey rose suggestively. "I need to stop by anyway to get—"

"New ballet shoes," Thatcher finished for her. He sauntered in with an undone shirt, purple hugging his eyes. He rolled his tense shoulders back as he dropped into a seat.

Annoyance filled Fey's previously soft features. "Did you stay up late again?"

"Yes." Thatcher groaned, putting his face in his hands. "Warren's assignments have been keeping me busy. And that's not even taking into account my other classes."

"Are you attending a class today?" Jinx asked, pouring herself a fresh cup of tea. She'd eaten plenty of questionable meals over the years, but cold tea? She refused to indulge in cold tea.

Thatcher's head bobbed with sleep deprivation. "Perhaps not. I think I'll stay in and play some chess with Pol when he returns."

"You can play with me if Fey and I get back before Apollo does."

Thatcher's head lifted, eyes sparked in interest. "You play chess?"

"Occasionally. I'm not great; however, my competitive streak keeps me in the game." She cracked her fingers.

"Alright. I would be delighted to beat you." Thatcher's lips tugged into a merciless smile.

A surge of energy fluctuated between them, an ambitious charge anticipating the friendly war.

"Don't get too comfortable now. I enjoy proving others wrong." Jinx turned to Fey. "Should we leave now to the market?"

There were two markets in Somnium: The Tents, which bordered Crosspoint Yard and the Botanic Plaza, and The Dome, which was in the heart of Wateredge. Fey had chosen to frequent the latter. An obvious choice on her part. Those who identified with the upper class chose to shop at the Dome for better quality fabrics, trinkets, jewelry, and so forth. Not to mention the expensive tags on said items.

The Dome comprised four neighboring buildings, with the streets in between them covered by a transparent roof; a glass dome held together the central meeting points. Inside the expansive market were shops selling everything from fruits to quills in every corner.

Jinx's nose caught wind of a buttery aroma, her limbs taking on their own consciousness. Halting abruptly at the door of a bakery, she spotted the cheese danishes on display.

Fey fell gracefully beside her. "Would you like one?"

"Oh no, I shouldn't," Jinx said. She also did not have her own money, and she was not about to use her illusions for the coin in front of Fey.

Jinx missed using her abilities. Her magic was *itching* to be let out. A simple mask, at least. She wanted to keep her powers as sharp as possible, her senses included.

Inside the Dome, Jinx remained on high alert. Her dagger was a split second away from being in her grip. Living out in the open for years taught her that danger lurked in plain sight, no matter how safe a place felt, and as a thief herself, Jinx knew this crowded market would be the perfect place to commit a crime.

Jinx's stomach gurgled, flipping on its own hunger. Fey gave her an inquisitive look. "Are you sure?"

"Yes," Jinx lied as her mouth continued salivating at the sight of the pastries.

Fey tucked a stray hair behind her ear, her rounded cheeks tightening. "You're eying it as strongly a stray dog salivates a meaty bone. Indulge, please. It's on me."

Fey pulled Jinx by the hand, weaving through the throng of customers until they reached the front counter of the bakery.

"Two cheese danishes please," Fey said, displaying two accompanying fingers.

"No, Fey, please do not," Jinx insisted.

At that retort, Fey shouted, "Make that three!"

Jinx facepalmed. "Do not buy those for me."

Fey raised a taunting brow, rubbing her shoulder against Jinx. "You are my guest, please." She dropped coins into the baker's hands, and the transaction finished. "We are friends, are we not?" Fey then handed Jinx two of the pastries.

Friends? It had only been a little more than a week now since Jinx had arrived at the Voclaine family's front door. Was that enough time to call Fey a friend? Was friendship about the time spent together or how well a person knows another?

To play it off and give Fey the answer she knew she wanted, Jinx answered, "Yes. Of course, we are." Her hands sweat at the wrongness she felt in saying those words.

Exiting the store, Fey wove her arm through Jinx's as they strolled down the cobblestone road. Jinx's thin boots molded to the rocks beneath them, small pebbles softly poking at the soles.

"Thank you," Jinx said. "You are too kind."

"No, I am not. People these days just lack basic manners." The arm around Jinx's frosted her into rigid ice. "Have you never experienced any kindness in all of your adventures?"

Jinx scoffed. "No, never."

"Could you tell me about some of them?" Fey's blue eyes lightened.

Jinx's breath hitched. She'd never talked to anyone about her "travels" before, and her core squeezed in surprising excitement at the thought.

"Okay." Jinx clutched Fey closer. "But I don't know where to begin."

"At the beginning."

Jinx would surely not be starting there. "I'll tell you only one today. I spent five years as a ballerina in an academy." If by "ballerina," Jinx meant "acrobat," and "academy," Jinx meant "circus," she was telling the truth. She'd worked as a member of Akuji's Cirque, to be exact—the same circus that opened every fall.

Jinx bit into the Danish, now prisoner to its rich and sweet taste.

Fey gasped. Her lace moved, hands covering her mouth. "*You were a ballerina?*"

"Yes." Jinx chuckled easily as her head fell.

"Why haven't you said anything?"

"Well, it's not exactly something that someone blurts out randomly in the middle of a conversation." She continued eating her danish.

Fey pulled at her elbow, elongating her pronunciation and tsking at the secret. "It is *with me*. How *rude* of you."

Jinx gave her a false curtsy. "Apologies, Princess."

"Apology accepted, though don't think I'll be so lenient next time." Fey touched a hand playfully to her collarbone, going along with the joke.

The two laughed at their own performance.

"There it is. Follow me." Fey pointed toward the tailor shop, and Jinx's heart seized, a void of emptiness where it used to beat. A rush of cold nipped at her fingertips. Flashes of her mother sewing crossed her mind.

She swallowed down her thoughts, masking her alarm and magically veiling the drainage of color across her face.

The bell overhead dinged at their entrance. Hundreds of fabrics were on display, ready to be touched and felt. Mannequins were clothed in decorative, elaborate dresses, each hand sewn from top to bottom. Dark wood supported the structures.

Jinx clenched her jaw, blinking back the glossy sheen of tears now coating her eyes.

Logic over emotion. I'm on a mission, not prancing about.

The seamstress rounded the corner, needles pinned in the ball of a bracelet. Considering the lady's wise and experienced gaze, Jinx deduced she must have been in her fifties. Her hands twined at her center. "Hello Fey, I did not expect to see you again so soon. Is something wrong with your gown?"

"No, not at all, Ms. Cornwell. Actually, Lady Collymore was admiring your design, and I brought her with me to see if she would like a dress of her own."

"Pleasure to make your acquaintance," Jinx ducked her chin.

Ms. Cornwell curtsied in return. "Pleasure is all mine. Please, right this way." She opened her palms, welcoming the two further into her shop. She plucked several fabrics of several colors from the walls, matching them with Jinx's skin tone, and then started taking her measurements as if Jinx were a doll, ready to be dressed up to the nines. Jinx winced at the slight prick of a needle against her skin.

Fey sighed. "You are going to look *lovely* at the masquerade this fall season."

"What?" Jinx asked in surprise.

"I assumed that you were attending since you are staying with us," Fey explained as she watched the seamstress fold another layer of fabric across Jinx's waist.

The masquerade that Fey mentioned was to be held in two months, and only the elite were allowed to attend. By Jinx's calculations, she would have expected that her deal with Apollo would be well over by then and that she'd be home already. Sure, the fact that they hadn't found traces of the culprits at the Museum was a setback, but still, the Vessel could not be hidden outside of the city. It was foolish to rely on that sort of hope. Hope that there would have been news of its capture if it had been attempted to export the relic.

Based on the way the two men had spoken to one another that day, the matter seemed urgent. And if it was that pressing and that urgent, the thieves would have kept it concealed in the walls of Somnium, which was why Jinx had continued her citywide scouting most nights after everyone went to bed.

"I had not expected to stay that long," Jinx admitted.

Fey placed her hands on her hips, face tilting to the right. "Well, now you are. I demand you there."

There it was again, that sensation of morality bending. This had never happened to her before. Guilt beginning to weigh on her heart for feeding them lies. They were good people, undeserving of her fallacies. She had to shake off this sensation.

"Would you excuse me? I need to use the restroom." Jinx parted without another word, fleeing to the lavatory and locking herself inside as she'd done so many times to avoid an uncomfortable situation.

A small slit under the window welcomed a breeze inside. She stuck her face by its crack, inhaling the fresh air. The cool wind kissed her nose.

A trio of men walked past the shop.

"Fuck these wretched Cursed," one hissed.

Another downed a bottle of liquor. "Hopefully, we'll find out what to do with them by the Autumnal Equinox."

The third slapped his friend in the chest, right above a pin: a sigil of a blooming flower. The final words of the riddle that had long plagued her suddenly stirred in her mind: *one who seeks is bound to bloom.* Could the riddle be referring to this symbol, the one that all three men wore?

The first man shot the second a rigid, pointed look, wanting him to shut his mouth. The Autumnal Equinox was in three weeks. Jinx stretched up on the tips of her toes, itching to trail them, eager to know what was going to happen that day.

"This better be worth it," Jinx muttered to herself. Summoning her magic, she tugged it out of the well of her organ. Tendrils of green snaked out, forming a replica of herself. Frost chilled over, peppering her skin, slowly materializing into the duplicate which would take her place. Jinx's mind split into two, a piece of herself embedded into this copy. Jinx ushered out the mirror image, who would take on her role.

With the illusion replacing her, Jinx broke off the window screen and slipped through, slithering into the disguise of another woman, changing her complexion entirely.

She lurked behind the men, watching the direction of their feet and expected movements, studying their marked path. Then, Jinx swept into the shadows, intending to intercept them through a shortcut of back alleys.

She ran ahead of them, holding a position in the corner. Seconds before she predicted their arrival, she weakened her voice, luring them over to her with a cry: "Help!"

The trio reacted immediately, seeing her alone in the darkness. Jinx forced tears, reddening her eyes. "Please help."

The three glanced at each other, a malicious glint in their stares, which were now directed at her. She'd expected no less. The one with the bottle of liquor lowered his voice an octave.

"What happened?" The other two shadowed behind him, cornering her.

Jinx let them surround her, her back coming into contact with the granite of the wall. She pleaded, sniffing. "They attacked me, stole my purse."

The one on the left called out, "It's alright, we are here now." He reached out to touch her hair, stroking it as if it were his own.

Rage burned hot underneath her cool skin. There was one thing Jinx disliked more than spiders. And it was men like *this*.

Jinx could now smell the burning of alcohol in the man's breath. She relaxed, dropping the act. Tone sultry, she replied, "Thank the Virtues." She carefully reached for the twin-throwing blades hidden in her corset, the men too enthralled with her face to notice.

With a casual flick of her wrist, she impaled the one on her right, who sunk to the ground. Then, she threw the other calculatedly into the shirt of the one who bore the pin of the blooming flower, fastening him to the wall.

The intoxicated one flinched, holding up the bottle to use as his weapon. Jinx smirked.

He swung left and right as she dodged his attacks. Jinx swerved, locking his free arm behind him and twisting his wrist. He released the bottle, yelping in pain. Jinx caught it before it shattered on the ground, smashing it on his head. His body collapsed on impact.

She removed her throwing knife from the dead man. Upset by the blood on it, she nevertheless tucked it back into its assigned spot on her thigh. Then, Jinx turned toward the man nailed to the wall.

Curling her fingers around the dagger at her leg, she fished it from its sheath, flipping it in her palm. "Has no one taught you to not corner a lady?"

The man stuttered in response. Jinx caressed his jaw with the dagger, the cold tip bending into his skin. "It's a very simple question."

The man swallowed a dry gulp. "Yes. I have been taught."

"Hm." She eyed the freshly polished pin. "That's neat. I have a few questions that need answering."

"We're in public. You really think you can hurt me?"

A maliciously sharp smile gripped her lips as her eyes hollowed, molding into an unhinged expression. He trembled under her scrutiny. Jinx pressed the dagger into his chin, drawing out a bead of crimson blood. "I don't think that will be a problem. It's never been one for me before, anyway."

She knew she had to hurry, otherwise Fey would become suspicious. With her thumb and index finger, she pried the flower pin from the man's chest. He whimpered as though she had fractured his bone. The pin is almost an extension of him. He was so prideful to have that glinting over his heart.

"What's the Autumnal Equinox assembly?"

The man sucked on his inner cheek, sweat trickling down his forehead. Damn the Virtues, there was no time for theatrics. Her patience was thinning. "How should we begin: by extracting your nails or teeth?"

Jinx proceeded to get information out of him. Anyway, she saw fit.

Upon her return to the bathroom, Jinx summoned her replica and reeled it back into her body, morphing the two back into one and lowering the casting of her alternate illusion. Jinx did her best to rid her dress of the bloodstains upon it, covering them up with patches of magic.

The well of magic inside her felt exhausted. She was waning, having expended too much of her magic for a while.

She crammed the pin and the address of the autumnal meeting between her breasts. Jinx then patted down her sweat and red cheeks. When her appearance had calmed back down into her normal graces, she stepped out of the lavatory.

"Ready to go home?" Fey asked, handing the seamstress the deposit for the dress.

Jinx pat down the front of her gown. "Yes."

The bell announced their departure. As soon as they set foot outside the shop, a group of authorities ran past them. Jinx yanked Fey out of the way.

Fey yelped, arching back. "What could have happened?"

Jinx shrugged her shoulders, nudging Fey in the opposite direction. "Not a clue."

Chapter 16

Apollo

The meeting at the House of Lords had taken more time than expected. Apollo and his father returned to the house at a quarter to midnight, exhaustion knocking at Apollo's temple.

Warren and V'Yockovitch together were a tiring pair, and Apollo and the Duke of Kami had been forced to offer counterarguments to the majority of the topics they'd brought to light. In the end, the feelings of their fellow members appeared divided, stuck in a tie.

Shutting the entry door behind him, Apollo's father scurried off to bed. Apollo rubbed at the front of his shirt, then brushed his hair back. His limbs felt heavier by the minute. Ambling down the hallway, he headed toward the stairs in the back as the flickering light from the family room illuminated a square on the wall.

Apollo traveled past the door, peeking inside.

Thatcher and Jinx were incredibly fixated on their game of chess. The two were seated on the floor, the board spread out on a low coffee table. The hearth burned with licking flames behind them. Jinx was wrapped in a blanket, moving a pawn up the board. Thatcher's brows pinched together, almost forming a unibrow, his hands thoughtfully covering his mouth.

Apollo leaned against the door frame, resting his hands in his pockets while enjoying the sight.

"Watching us from there is just creepy, Polly," Jinx commented, her back toward him.

Amazement at the reminder of her keen senses caused a jump in his pulse.

"And watching from a closer vantage wouldn't be?" Apollo fully entered the room, shrugging off his suit jacket and perching it on the coat hanger. He situated himself on the couch behind Thatcher.

"Hey, Pol," Thatcher said, giving a troubled shake of his head. "I think she's better at chess than you. She's got me completely cornered."

Apollo analyzed the pieces, then looked up at her, who gave him a relaxed, innocent wave. He replied silently with a squint of a glare. Tension cradled his stomach, which was now cramping, folding his insides. Had he forgotten to eat today?

Thatcher was correct. There was no possible way for him to win. In two moves, Jinx locked in her victory: "Check."

Thatcher's head fell, groaning. "That is *it*. I'm taking that sore loss as the Virtues telling me to go to sleep."

Jinx cooed from her seat, giving him a look of false pity. At the door, his brother turned, lifting a finger to Apollo. "Do beat her for me, will you?"

Apollo rolled his sleeves up to the middle of his forearms, veins pumping. "I always love a good competition."

At that, Thatcher resigned to his own room, leaving him and Jinx alone. Wood popped and crackled in the fireplace. Apollo descended to the ground, helping Jinx fix the board.

In comfortable silence, they both set up their sides of the board.

"Do you want to go first?" She snuggled into her blanket, cocooning herself deeper.

"No. You won the last game; it's proper sportsmanship for you to go first." Apollo leaned his elbows on his knees, his spine using the couch as support.

Jinx moved a pawn forward. Apollo scanned the board, then followed suit. As she reached for her piece, Apollo interjected, "How was your day?"

She froze, retracting her arm. A frigid, calculating stare stabbed his soul. She could see the corners of his lips twitching upwards. Her neck pitched backwards, hesitant. "What are you doing?"

Apollo acted completely innocent. He kept his composure, meeting her with the same expressionless face he always wore so well. "Can I not ask how your day was?"

"You *can*. The problem is that you *don't*." Jinx cracked her fingers, scrutinizing him with her calculating emerald eyes. "You're trying to distract me with small talk."

Apollo checked his pocket watch. "I would not think a great mind like yours could get so distracted with small talk."

Jinx piped up, spirit brightening her face. Her mouth opened just slightly, then transformed into a confused smirk. She moved another piece forward. "You are correct; small talk does not distract me."

Apollo continued, "So then, how was your day?"

"Good." Jinx sat up straighter, alert as if trying to catch him doing something sneaky. "How was yours?"

"Good. Though the assembly at the House of Lords took longer than expected." An apology lingered on his tongue, never quite taking flight.

"Would you like to talk about it?"

He knocked a pawn of hers, taking it hostage. "Warren's working on a contraption to completely exterminate the Cursed. He said he's almost done with it, but he needs more funding, which is why he came to the House. He guarantees the end of the Cursed. I want to get Thatcher out of that lab with him. I just don't know how to do it without making Warren suspicious."

A tremor of fear peppered Jinx's skin. A world without Cursed, without magic. "What did your father say?"

"He disagrees, but the House is pretty split. We haven't ruled on his funding yet."

"You won't let mass genocide actually happen, will you?" Jinx bit her lower lip. If that were to happen, everything she'd worked for would be for nothing. And Jinx would die, as would countless others.

A serious expression overtook Apollo's features. "I will not. I promise."

Spiteful, Jinx took two of his chess pieces while also making an anticipated advance. After, she fished inside her corset and put the pin of a flower and an address on the table in front of him. "What do you know of this?"

Apollo inspected the pin by the stem; it was a white six-petalled flower circling a pink pistil. He knew flowers held a variety of meanings. Dried blood was embedded in its crevices. A waft of a strong scent hit his nose: cheap cologne. It must have come from a lower-class family. A name was engraved on the back: A.D. Marianna. A faint bell of recognition chimed in his brain. "The check from the alley." He put two and two together. "It's the same name. Where did you get this?"

Jinx picked herself up, sitting beside Apollo. She lowered her voice to a whisper, and the hair on his neck stood on end. "I overheard three men talking about an assembly that's taking place on the Autumnal Equinox. One of them smacked the other to keep him quiet. The pin must have some meaning because of how agitated he'd been when I took it, and A.D. Marianna must be behind it."

"And how did you get this pin from the man, as well as this address?" Apollo was hesitant, knowing that her methods of prying information were most likely immoral.

"That is not important."

Apollo gracefully seized her hand, showing her the details he'd noticed upon walking in. "Hm. And it has nothing to do with the dried blood under your fingernails?" The base of his spine clenched, his stomach contracting. What was going on?

"I'd say no, but that'd be going against the rules of our deal since I'm not supposed to lie." She ripped her touch from his as if it burned her. "Are you going to keep playing?"

Apollo moved another piece. "There is something more you are not telling me. It's in the slant of your lip."

Jinx leaned over to take her turn. "This conference will be about getting rid of the Cursed entirely."

It sounded similar to what Warren had talked about in the House of Lords, with his ideas of eradicating the Cursed. There must be a connection there; Apollo was sure of it. Would Warren be showcasing his machine at this conference? Make Somnium a hunting ground for those who were different?

"Let's finish this conversation for now. We'll pick it up tomorrow," he said. "There *is* a link between what I heard today in the House and this assembly; I'm certain of it. I'm not so sure of the pin. May I keep it? I want to study it a bit more."

Jinx agreed and handed it over, returning to her side of the board. Apollo put the pin away and went to take his turn. Both played on in silence, trying to learn each other's traits and tells. The bells of the clock gonged twice; it was two in the morning.

Jinx knocked over Apollo's queen. He predicted the various routes this game could take. He could make a win in three elementary moves, but he was also aware that Jinx knew she could intercept it. What proved to be most difficult was disturbing her attention. He tried asking her questions and confusing her about the game, but his efforts were in vain.

There was one tactic he still had yet to try, however. "Remember last week when Fey called your eyes 'undeniably beautiful?'"

"Yes."

"I think she was wrong."

She lifted her gaze, latching onto his own. "You think my eyes are plain?"

"No." He chewed the inside of his cheek, drawing blood, stopping himself from grinning. "They're divine. You'd make the Virtues jealous."

This was the first time Apollo truly watched Jinx turn to stone. It was a pure reaction, a miscalculated crack in her façade.

"You are right. It's not small talk that distracts you. It's flattery." He careened closer. "I win." He revealed the board to her with wide arms before sinking into the thick couch. Apollo snaked out a cigarette and lit it, pleased with himself for playing the queen's gambit. "You made it too easy."

Jinx stood up from the opposite side of the table with a deadly calm. Coming to his side and caging him in with a single arm, she lowered her glare. "You cheated."

"Don't be mad at me for slipping up." He deadpanned. "I was just playing the game."

Apollo enjoyed this, being under her cinched scowl. Her face was now inches away from his own, and he noticed that she was missing traces of a scent.

They remained in a new challenge now, holding each other's stare. Every so often, he drew in a drag of his cigarette. Her scowl transformed into a satisfied grin. Apollo was off-put. Why was she smiling?

With two fingers, Jinx pinched the cigarette from Apollo's lips, drawing in a puff for herself. She blanched. "Disgusting. You smoke this?"

Apollo ignored the flutter in his veins, the heat kissing the tip of his ears. Jinx smudged the end of it on the ashtray beside him before standing up, leaving him alone and disappearing into her chambers.

Her withdrawal left his skin warm. Warmer than he'd ever experienced. His pulse reached the tips of his fingers. Apollo shrugged off the sensations, uninterested in dissecting their meaning.

His gaze turned instead to the chessboard they had been previously playing upon. The winning system on the board looked completely different to how he thought the game had finished. Instead of featuring the formation he'd left behind, the chess board had been rearranged into the fool's mate.

Had the game they played been a farce? When had she changed the board?

Apollo shot up from his seat, knowing that Jinx couldn't have made it to her room already. He beelined for the hallway. "What did you...do?" The words died on his tongue as he found the space empty.

Apollo scratched the back of his head. *Damn* this woman. It was too late to ponder if he'd actually won or she'd been leading him to think he won when, in reality, it'd been the opposite.

Exhausted once again, his mind and body ached for his bed, yearning for nothing more than a good night's rest.

Apollo grabbed his stray coat—

Just then, a throbbing whipped his center. He fell to his knees, holding his middle. A torturing ache lashed up and down his spine. Apollo grunted, his composure thinning to a thread.

The silver ring on his finger burned a furious red. The nightmare inside him pressed against his skin, screaming to be let out. The mounting pressure of being ripped from the inside out lingered all around him, Apollo's temples now straining to the point of explosion.

Then, it abruptly halted, cutting off the unbearable thrashing.

On the ground, holding himself up by his palms, Apollo panted. This pain grows into an excruciating convulsion.

He growled at the demon, "Was it you?" Apollo would rather throw himself off a bridge than talk to the thing inside of him. But he did anyway. His body was begging for clarity.

No.

Apollo breathed.

This was the Vessel. See why we need to destroy it now, Apollo Voclaine?

The ancient voice scorched Apollo's brain. There were two things Apollo now knew: The Vessel was clearly tied somehow to the demon that lived inside of him, and it hurt like Akuji had ripped his soul in two.

Chapter 17

Jinx

Jinx and Apollo walked side by side at a healthy distance, ambling through Crosspoint Yard toward the Collection. Her illusion drenched both of them in masked disguises.

She'd gone to sleep last night fuming at Apollo's underhanded move; she hadn't expected a person like him to use flirtation to win. When he spoke now, it caught her off guard.

"Are you still angry about my amazing win yesterday?" Apollo asked in that infuriating monotone voice of his.

He earned a side eye from her. "Do you know how to speak with any semblance of emotion?"

"I could try flirting, but we know that doesn't sit well with you." He had the audacity to actually look smug. Three lines formed at the edge of his lips, genuine amusement glossing his mouth.

Fury flamed in her hands, making them tremble. "It's not your *flirting*," Jinx admitted. The confession halted Apollo in place. He pocketed his hands, chin tilting in curiosity. It was clear that she'd been learning how to read his minute actions yesterday, too. His eyes spoke volumes: *please indulge me.*

"It was my own *miscalculation* that vexed me." That was all she was willing to give him. As she strutted ahead of him, Apollo resumed his walk, placing himself deliberate steps behind her. Jinx kept up her swagger, holding back her rage from last night. There was a time and a place. This was certainly *not* the time nor the place. She focused her attention on the sights and sounds Crosspoint Yard offered: the uneven cement roads where trotting horses hauled trembling cargo. Industrialization at every corner. The clicking hammers of people at work.

Old red brick had chipped away over time, giving her easy access whenever she needed to climb onto the roofs to secure a swift escape. Clouds crossed the expanse of the day, the forthcoming season blurring into the present.

And the smell of smoke, the classic firewood tang, was now more prominent in the air. A waft of gray smoke carried itself into the avenue.

Smoke. A primal instinct overloaded her senses. In the direction of their destination, tendrils of smoke curled upwards, reaching for oxygen.

"...being discouraged—are you even listening?" Apollo came to her side.

She faced him full-on. "No. I stopped paying attention at 'my amazing.'" A crowd of people ran past them, fleeing from the smoke. Orange flames flicked upwards from deep within the shadows of the back alleys.

Adrenaline pumped in Jinx's heart, her agile feet lifting her up onto her toes. She glanced briefly over at Apollo, whose eyes were captured by the red gleam again. His mind was enthralled in another space. Blinking himself out of the haze, he gripped her arm in a silent demand.

Jinx sped into the darkness. Apollo was an inch behind her. Toxic fumes filled their lungs, Jinx's body coughing up the exhaust. Bystanders with silver eyes wept in horror. Fire was now eating away at the Collection, devouring the structure that contained it.

Screams seeped past the roar of the inferno. Jinx launched herself into the mouth of the blaze, hurriedly locating the citizens who were trapped in the fire. A boom rattled ahead, a wooden beam crashing down centimeters away from her. Ignited ash fluttered upwards.

Jinx wove through the chaos.

Underneath, a woman lodged between two shelves, disintegrating pages seethed into her exposed skin. Blotches of blood churned into black. There was no time to think.

"Can you walk?" Jinx coughed.

The woman shook her head, barely able to process what was going on. Familiar sounding footfalls drew near. Apollo's face, smeared with ash, found hers, an unreadable emotion lining his dark features.

Without a word, Apollo placed himself between the collapsing shelves, using his weight to his advantage and creating space for the woman to move. Jinx wedged herself in the middle, wrapping the woman's arm around her neck.

Jinx dragged the woman out of the burning building, her legs aching beneath the extra weight. At last, she placed the woman on the ground outside, in the care of someone nearby.

There was something missing. Some*one*. Who never came out.

"Polly."

Jinx sprinted back toward the fire as the towering man known as Apollo Voclaine walked out from the flames, looking like Akuji, the Virtue of Death. Tucked underneath his arm was the black leather-clad book without so much as a scratch on it.

She jogged toward him, sending over her magic to hide the book, cloaking it to make it seem like a top hat to the eye.

This was all wrong. The Collection was available only to the people it wanted to enter. How could one of those people have started a fire?

Her gaze drifted upwards, past the small windows to the edges of the roofs. Masked faces leered down at them upon the Cursed. There wasn't enough time to see if they had pistols strapped to their legs. Jinx wasn't taking any chances. She cursed under her breath.

A trap. This was a trap. And they all had to leave *now*.

Jinx locked a hand behind Apollo's neck, bringing him closer. Her mouth opened to talk, and Apollo beat her to it. "It's a trap."

In the shell of his ear, she replied. "There are at least two people, from what I saw above. I'm not sure if they have any weapons with them. Get the citizens out of here. I'll stay close enough for my magic to continue hiding that thing."

As she slipped away, Apollo pulled her back. "You are not going."

Jinx frowned. "Yes, I am."

He clenched his jaw, bothered. No. He was...angry? However, his tone went against his internal feelings, sounding as if he was unbothered. "We'll meet at the manor as soon as we are done."

She took off without another word. Squirming around the people, her magic enveloped her dress and lifted her hood, displaying the fighting suit she wore underneath. Then she transformed into nothing more than a shadow, all in a blink of an eye.

Jinx dug her fingers into the brick, ascending the wall. On the roof, she saw five people fleeing, running toward Eastern Heights.

A switch flipped in her brain, her mind slithering into a state of hunt. Jinx charged after them. Her thighs propelled her forward, closing the distance. Blood rushed in her ears. She jumped over the openings where alleys waited below, veering between various mechanisms sitting on the roof tiles.

The group was still too far out of her reach for her to even knock them off kilter. The five then hopped down to the ground, retreating from the chase. Jinx, now just several paces behind them, widened her stride, pushing harder.

Jinx wove between the buildings, trailing them from above. The group spread out, each choosing a different route, forcing Jinx to select just one to follow. Jinx continued ahead, picking the one that wouldn't slow her down.

She shot down a bolt of her magic ahead of the runners, molding it into an authority. The runner pivoted before her power had the chance to form. Jinx cursed. She sprinted and jumped to the ground below, losing her leverage but now able to take him down when she got close enough.

The alley pipelined deeper into Wateredge.

Jinx fished for her throwing knife, cocking back her arm and aiming for his feet. She needed to question him, not kill him. She missed.

She threw another but missed again.

Her throat and lungs dried, aching with every panting breath. The man ahead was so much faster than she was. She *had* to catch him; she had to do it for her people.

Turning a corner, Jinx dug her heels into the ground, abruptly stopping.

They were gone. All that greeted her was an empty, narrow street and a foul smell.

Jinx unsheathed her dagger, listening for any more movement. She studied the premise for any signs of the runner, searching and searching to find him simply vanished.

She traced the perimeter of the wall for hidden doors, lifting latches that could lead to passages beneath the ground. Nothing.

Jinx wiped her brow and stomped a furious foot.

At the window of Apollo's room, Jinx rapped three times. She waited on a narrow ledge. The measured footfalls of Apollo came closer, the window slurring as he pushed it up.

"I don't know if I should call you brave or stupid." His form of welcome.

His tension disrupted the fresh breeze now swaying in through the window.

"'Hello Jinx, are you alright?'" Jinx greeted herself because Apollo wouldn't. "'Yeah, Polly, thanks for asking. I am alive and unharmed.'"

Jinx spider-crawled inside, closing the window behind her. She ripped off her hood, allowing herself to breathe. "*That* is how to properly greet someone."

He shot her a glare that indicated he was not happy with her.

She leaned against the wall. "They got away."

Apollo walked across his room, placing a pen inside the notebook he wrote in daily, closing it.

"I got that much." He twisted the words to make them sound almost like an insult. Apollo tossed the heavy book he'd taken from the Collection toward her, a thick thud clapping against the ground. "Let's make this quick. See anything strange?" His tone was sardonic.

Jinx's nose scrunched in disgust. The book was oozing dangerous energy, warning her off. For a book that had survived a fire, its cover, its pages, and the title looked unscathed, the picture of perfection. "It's not burned."

"Exactly. The book has to be of value for someone to use magic to protect it against harm, and whoever wrote it clearly didn't want just anyone knowing what information was inside."

A chill iced down her back. "You're going to try to decipher it, aren't you?"

Apollo glanced at the time, connecting with it. "Yes."

"How did you know where it was?" She took a step forward and craned her neck, trying to get a better glimpse of him. She recalled the shade of red in his eyes from before. "Did it call to you again?"

There and gone. Any emotion that loitered in the planes of his face disappeared. "*It* did."

The runes in the Collection weren't strong enough to completely dilute Apollo's abilities or the demon within him. The book must have been just as strong. Whatever lured Apollo to the library in the first place must be somehow connected with this book.

"I don't like that book," she stated.

"I know," he replied without looking at her. What was *with* him?

Worry made her palms sweat. There was no proper definition of good and evil in this world; it was as relative as reality. Still, she couldn't brush off the primal instinct inside that urged her to bury that book into a six-foot hole, never to see it again.

"How can you be so sure?"

Apollo's chest expanded, inhaling deeply. "Just trust me."

That was the thing; Jinx didn't trust *anybody*. Not entirely.

Apollo said dryly, "You're making a face."

"No, I am not."

"You are."

Jinx couldn't help feeling a shift in the air, as if he had something on his mind that was taking him farther away from her. Bitterness stung Jinx's tongue.

"Let's go over everything we know. Perhaps we've missed a crucial step."

Their summarization ended with Apollo reiterating everything he'd witnessed in the House of Lords during his last meeting, from the moment he stepped inside until the moment he left. V'Yockovitch's comments and Warren's machine plagued his memories. It was likely that the two shared a secret partnership, which strengthened his suspicions about the Autumnal Equinox assembly being tied to Warren and V'Yockovitch in some way.

"If we are going that route, then it's conceivable that whatever group they are rounding up could be responsible for the fire today." Jinx bit her lip in thought.

Apollo swirled the chair at his desk, sitting backward on it. "We'll need to go to that conference on the Equinox, see what it's about. Until then, let's focus on the Vessel."

From one folder on his desk, he slid out a piece of paper. "I was able to get a list of all the attendees from my birthday. I already took the role of eliminating the names with the least motive."

Jinx came to his side, inspecting the list and inhaling the scent of citrus and cedarwood. Most of the names written down were higher-class citizens.

Flatly, he said, "We've had enough for today." He pushed the paper away from her. Evading Jinx, Apollo stood from his chair and crossed the room, picking up his notebook. "Let's go over it tomorrow and think about how we will approach this list."

He was dismissing her. Annoyance grated on her skin. Jinx wanted to grab Apollo's shoulders and shake him.

"Why do you push me away? When just moments ago, our partnership was fine?" Jinx stood her ground.

He didn't look up from his scribbles. "We *are* in a partnership. Had I not just gone over with you everything?"

"You are acting strange."

He tucked the notebook under his arm, clenching his jaw. "How would you like me to act?"

"Like a reasonable human being capable of communicating," Jinx spat.

"We both know I am lacking in that department for various reasons," he said wryly.

She knew that the moment she'd walked out the door, he was going to grab a bottle of liquor and drown himself in it, accompanied by a cigarette. She'd seen how he'd looked after waking up these past few days and noticed the faint bags around his eyes indicating his exhaustion. Jinx guessed he often drank and smoked in order to better ignore his abilities, dampening their potency if he was as powerful as the librarian mentioned.

Runes couldn't even fully hold his power in. Yet what truly vexed her was his denial.

"Drinking and smoking won't make it go away."

Apollo slowly turned his winter eyes toward her, boring into her soul. A storm brewed beneath, restrained by a thinning layer of willpower. "I know that."

"Then why do it?" she questioned.

"Goodnight," he said sternly.

"Have you thought about my proposal?"

"I'm flattered that you are so interested in me, but you're not my type," he deflected.

"Are you really going to wither away because you are afraid of yourself? That's cowardly, Apollo," she bit out.

Decidedly, she started to leave. Jinx wanted to tell him a thousand things and yell a thousand barbarities, but only one came out: "You're a real asshole, you know."

As he shut the door behind her, he whispered to himself, "I don't know what made you think otherwise." The lock groaned, securing its place.

"Prick," she muttered to the door. If he wanted to be difficult, then fine—so be it. It wasn't her responsibility, and she didn't care.

A snicker came from Jinx's side. "Pol slammed the door on you," Fey sang. Almost all of her words seemed to carry a light tune. "Don't worry, it happens more often than you think." Her dimpled smile brightened the room, almost easing whatever pestered Jinx.

Fey looped her arm with Jinx's. "If my brother won't offer you company, I might as well invite you to my chambers."

Jinx glanced again at Apollo's door and then told Fey, "That'd be wonderful."

Fey led them across the house, taking a door to the right, adjacent to Arya's.

"Fey." Arya peered her head out her door, latching her sights on Jinx. "I didn't know you were with Veyda."

"How may I assist you, sister?" she piped up.

Arya reconsidered after seeing Jinx. "Never mind. I'll see you tomorrow, Veyda."

Fey turned the knob to close her door, brushing off the encounter.

Upon entering the room, Jinx was overcome by the scent of vanilla and coconut. Fey's quarters were neatly organized, the bed perfectly made, with a small table and two chairs on the far side of the bed by the grand window and a range of books on the wall by the door. Moonlight pooled in, dying the room a light blue hue. A massive mirror and ballerina bar sat to one side, rigid shoes dangling by pink ribbons around the bar. The four walls were painted gray with a pink undertone, with white and cream accents opening the space.

"Is it like what you imagined?" Fey grabbed Jinx's hand, hauling her over to the white rounded table. There was a little tea set in the center.

Jinx observed the space again. "Honestly, I'm not sure what I thought it'd be like."

"I hope you're at least pleasantly surprised." Fey followed Jinx's line of sight to the array of books on the shelf. "Do you like books?"

Jinx gave her a strained, one-sided grin. "I very much enjoy them." The books reminded her of her uncle. Reading was now a way of remembering him and keeping him close to her heart when she could not be physically close to him.

"Come." Fey beckoned. She leaped over to the bookcase, caressing the creased spines with a single finger. "What tempts you? Fiction, mystery, horror, romance...erotica?"

"Fey!" Jinx gasped, actually surprised.

Fey laughed joyously. "What? I'm just saying. There's nothing wrong with dipping your toes in that genre. I certainly have."

Jinx stared at her, dumbfounded that Apollo's youngest sister was reading matters of sex.

Fey whispered, "Don't tell my family, but it's actually my favorite." Her cheeks flushed pink. Fey tapped a finger to the bow of her lips, features suddenly alarmed as she started pacing. "I'm not scaring you, am I? Maybe I should have kept my mouth shut like my governess says. I just got so excited to see that you enjoy reading as well. Not many women I know these days do. Besides Arya, of course."

"Fey," Jinx said softly, taking her out of the mumbling stupor Fey shared with her brother. "I'm not scared, I'm just surprised."

Fey tipped her head innocently. "Why?"

"You seem like such a bubbly, pure person. Hearing you admit that you like to read such an erotically-charged genre shattered the image I had of you." Then again, Jinx wasn't one to judge. "No offense."

"None taken." Fey said, calmly settled by Jinx. "So, which one do you want to read?"

"Right now?"

"Yeah. Why not? Let's pick something and take the night to speed read. Do you have any urgent matters in the morning?"

Jinx did, remembering that she still needed to solve the mystery of the Vessel's disappearance. Now that Apollo had gotten his hands on the list of attendants, they'd have to narrow it down and then begin scouting Somnium tomorrow. There was much to do.

But looking at Fey, who was batting her thick black lashes and rounded blue eyes, how could Jinx reject her offer? She longed to spend some time thinking on a topic that was not related to the Vessel or Apollo. "Let's do it. On one condition."

A dimple. "Yes?"

"You have to let me read your favorite erotica," Jinx said seriously.

"I knew you read them! They're so good, right?" Fey began to take apart her bookcase one by one, stacking the novels in Jinx's hands until she had a tower of them to read. The two sprawled out on the rugby Fey's bed, flipping ambiently through pages, enjoying the books.

Jinx inhaled Fey's favorite novel. No wonder she was so obsessed. It had the perfect tension, the perfect degree of angst between the two lovers. It focused on the forbidden romance between members of two rival families, and the male love interest was the reserved, mysterious type, with a tender soft spot for his female rival.

Romance at its finest.

The male love interest brooded occasionally, reminding Jinx of the infuriating aristocrat down the hall. She wanted to wash the image out of her brain.

Fey squealed, watching Jinx read. "So, what do you think so far?"

"I'm going to say something you won't like," Jinx warned.

"What?"

"The male love interest reminds me of your oldest brother."

"*No.*" Fey covered her ears squeezing her eyes shut. She dusted off her frame as if grime had suddenly settled on her. "Why would you *say* that?"

"What? It's true. Look." Jinx pointed to lines in the novel that described Apollo almost verbatim.

Fey shook her head vigorously. "You're reading too deeply into it. Plus, the lead male is a romantic. Pol doesn't have any romantic bone in his body. He's made *that* quite clear."

"Why does he detest it so thoroughly?" Jinx could come up with some assumptions of her own, but he'd never outright given her a reason why.

Fey dropped her head to her hand, poking her cheek. "I'm not sure. Mother always told me that Pol used to be an amorous person until the age of fifteen. I'm not sure what really changed then; I was too young to remember. But I do hope, whatever it is, that he might change someday."

"Why do you wish for that?"

Sorrow glossed over Fey's eyes. "My brother deserves to be happy. As much as he pretends to not show it, Pol cares for us so deeply in his own way. Did you know that when I first began dancing, he was the one to go and get me my first pair of proper ballet slippers? I remember him saying to me, 'If you're going to take on a hobby, better give it one hundred percent. If not, it isn't worth it at all,'" Fey mimicked Apollo's deadpan voice and expression.

Jinx sank her teeth into her bottom lip.

Fey went on, "I still have those shoes. They're the ones right there." She pointed over to the two slippers hanging on the wooden ballet bar before twisting back toward Jinx. "I know he can have his moments, but somewhere within that mess of his emotions, he's there. My brother is truly *there*. He just needs someone who can bring it out of him."

Jinx's heart churned uncomfortably. She wanted to pivot the conversation to a lighter tone. "And you, what do you want in love?"

Fey blew a stray brown hair out of her face. "If I am not forced to marry, I'd like to find my complement. My twin flame."

"You believe in soulmates?"

"I'd like to think that I have one out there. It's nice to believe that there is someone for everyone. But I think we have more than one flame. A person could have many soulmates. It's hard to believe your perfect match just so happens to live in the same city you do, correct?"

Jinx let her comment sink in. It was an interesting spin on the theory, a logical one. "Correct."

"Do you believe in twin flames?" Fey questioned.

"I don't know. I've never really thought about it."

Fey smiled. "Now you can." She flipped through a couple of pages in her novel before saying, "You know...you spend much of your time with my brother. Have you...perhaps...taken a liking to him?"

"Say that again, and I'll proceed with ruining your book," Jinx hissed.

Fey rolled her eyes and flipped another page. "*I'm* not the one who thought of him whilst reading erotica."

Jinx simmered in her thoughts, and in the midst of silence, she whispered to herself, admitting more than she ever thought, "He isn't as unbearable as I originally believed." And from the corner of her eye, she caught a slim glimpse of Fey hiding a bright smile behind the pages of a book.

Chapter 18

Jinx

Jinx ran and ran, pushing her body to its absolute limit, her lungs aching at each strenuous inhale. Her nostrils were burning. Boiling blood pulsed at her temples in rhythmic beats. The wind of coming autumn eased her forward, prancing through and around the obstacles before it, leaping over spaces between buildings as if it were engaged in nothing more than a mere dance with gravity.

As she turned into Wateredge, the rolling sound of crashing waves reverberated through the district. Jinx was still unable to stop thinking about her last exchange with Apollo back at the house before she left.

Alone at breakfast, Apollo had been writing in his notebook without sparing a glance at her when she walked into the room.

Jinx shoved a piece of ham into her mouth. "I'll stop by Tertain's house today. You take De Conto's."

"Mhm."

She chewed and explained further: "They're the last two on the list."

"Yes." His tone was short, the scratching sound of his pencil on paper filling the empty space between them.

"Do you have any ideas on what steps we should take after?" Jinx tried again, eager to make conversation.

"Working on it."

Jinx had lost her appetite. She left the room, briskly changing into her suit before jumping out of the window. Throughout the entire week, Apollo had kept a healthy distance from her, sentences short and curt, not meeting her eye. Civil, nothing more or less. It was as if all of their progress as a team had been reduced to zero. He was unreadable, expressionless, monotone. Thatcher, Fey, and Arya remained wary but offered her company. This morning, she didn't even bother saying good morning to Apollo. And if he'd been studying that nameless book, he didn't mention it.

Ever since that fire, something within Apollo had changed. Their budding friendship now stilled, at a pause. Jinx channeled all those pesky feelings and frustrations into her illusions.

Upon arriving at the Tertain manor, she slipped into a nearby alley and summoned magic to the surface of her skin. She'd decided to disguise herself as a lady's maid, Camilla Tertain's lady's maid. She'd observed Camilla and her maid for some time now, learning that this was the very moment where the lady's maid would be out for lunch, back when Jinx had still been interested in learning the ways of becoming a proper lady. In conducting this research, she had learned the faces and names of the Tertain family's staff members. Back then, she'd assumed the role of Sophia Acadaine, a cousin to Rylee Panchak. The Acadaine family was two steps below the Seven in the social hierarchy of the city, a perfect name to use if one wanted to blend in.

From time to time, Jinx wondered how Rylee was doing. Her situation had ended quite ugly. Rylee nearly died, and her mother was sent to prison for the imprisonment of her own child. Jinx dropped off Rlyee at a trusted doctor, never seeing her again. It was one of the two times she'd seen someone's magic turn against them, breaking the organ and killing them from the inside.

As Camilla's lady maid, Jinx was now five foot and three inches, a blonde with undertones of sharp brown in her hair and deep blue eyes. She wore a plain pastel yellow dress, with a white apron tied to her front and waist and her hair wrapped into a high bun.

Jinx pivoted on her heels, walking in haste toward the manor, carrying a woven basket filled with fruits. She entered the three-story house through the back door, which was meant for employees. The metallic kitchen welcomed her. Bubbling vegetable soup encapsulated the room in its salty broth scent as the chef stirred it with a wooden spoon.

"Marisa, it's been thirty minutes since your break. Store the fruits and get back to work. The rooms need cleaning," the chef ordered, much like a general commanding a soldier.

Jinx dipped her chin. "Yes, sir." After adhering to his directions, Jinx filed out through the spinning door and walked into a depository room holding the cleaning products. Still in character, she shyly picked a few out from storage and proceeded to clean the house.

Stillness marked the space. Aside from the staff, there was no one else in the home.

Her nimble feet quickened in pace, searching the home for any trace of the Vessel. She opened and closed doors, one after the other, turning the house inside out.

After investigating the first and second floors, Jinx worked her way up to the third. The stairs ended right in front of an iron door, with four locks latching it in place. She pressed her ear to the door. Nothing.

Jinx broke character momentarily, selecting her lock picks. Two minutes later, the door moaned open.

A breeze of cool, damp air kissed her as the tang of fresh paint entered the mix. Old drapery covered big furniture. Blank and half-sketched canvases were perched on the wall. Dust floated around the room, almost glittering under the lines of sunlight peeking through the windows. The room seemed abandoned, but the smell of that fresh paint pleaded otherwise.

Jinx stripped the fabric from a lonely canvas. The art, the paint strokes, the color palate. She'd seen it before. But where? The paint lacked any saturation, the entire canvas almost at a loss of color, except for the shimmering gold flecks that lay atop it like dust. The top layer looked grainy, like it had been roughly sanded. It held an old aroma to it that reminded her of something she still couldn't place.

The portrait was of a man. His cream torso was bare, with a white scar dragging across his middle. His face had been blurred, scratched out by the artist so that his identity remained a secret. The background was the color of eggshells, with the faintest veins of red throughout, like a webbing system that traced back to him.

Under the soles of her shoes, thin dirt grated against the wood. No, not dirt. Gold. Golden sand.

It wasn't dust that hovered in the space. *It was golden sand.*

"Hello," a man announced floors beneath her. "Carson, is the soup ready?"

The Duke of Tertain had arrived.

Jinx covered her tracks and fled the scene with empty hands. There was still no trace of the Vessel. Apparently, finding this artifact was going to be a lot more work than she'd originally imagined.

After showering and putting on a clean change of clothes, Jinx stretched on the floor of her bedroom back in the Voclaine manor. Her black dress bloomed around her as if she were a black lotus, her legs spread out in front of her in a straight line.

Her mind wandered back to her mother and uncle. In times of serenity, she let herself think of them, let herself think of all the possibilities of a life she could've lived if she'd stayed home instead of wandering out that night, searching for the creature that granted wishes. The same creature that others fled from when they found themselves deep in the woods. The face of nightmares, people called it. The creature had disappeared days after Jinx had struck the deal with it, and she often wondered where it had gone.

She knew it had never truly left the forest. It was still hiding somewhere, in wait.

It didn't matter. Once her job was done here with Apollo, she'd get into the Archives and get her answer. Have a family again. Allowed to be within millimeters of them and not a quarter mile minimum.

How would her mom react to seeing her after so much time had passed? Would she be happy or scared?

She thought Jinx was dead and had planted a tombstone for her in the small cemetery of the Botanic Plaza. It was as if her mother had buried the last traces of her true identity. Jinx had considered destroying the tombstone numerous times in the past, erasing herself from reality completely.

Two knocks sounded on the door.

Jinx huffed, getting up from her position on the floor and reaching for the doorknob. Apollo stood on the other side of it, his arms crossed. "Did you find it?"

"No."

Apollo merely nodded and turned on his heels. An entire week of this treatment had pushed Jinx to the edge. Pursing her lips, Jinx reached for his collar and hauled him back inside her room, locking the door behind her.

"What's *with* you?" she asked coldly.

She saw a small crack in his mask of indifference, a glare sitting on his eyes. "I'm not sure I know what you're talking about." His tone remained level.

Jinx bit her inner cheek. "You haven't been speaking to me, Apollo. We're supposed to be partners in this deal, but it doesn't feel like it. We can't get any closer to finding this Vessel if we don't work together as a team."

Apollo kept quiet, his regal composure stiff. This was pointless. Jinx opened her mouth to kick him out when he said, "I didn't like you went after those men."

Her eyes widened. "Did you think I could not handle myself?"

Apollo's hard gaze faltered as quickly as he hid it, not wanting to answer that question.

Jinx stepped toward him, repeating herself. "Is that what you think? That I am inept?" she egged him on, trying to get him to admit his inner feelings. "That I am weak—"

"If you honestly believe that, then you are a fool." He tightened his jaw.

"Then what is it?" Jinx poked again.

He gave her a look that indicated a warning and stepped to the side. "We are *done* with this conversation."

A bitter anger overcame her, and for one of the only times in her life, Jinx lost control over her own body. She caged him to the wall. He banged the rear of his skull. "No, we are not. Now tell me, Apollo Voclaine, why have you been so cold with me?"

She'd hit upon something. There, in the dark glimmer of his eyes, was a shift. He expelled a tense breath. Jinx wanted to see it, wanted to watch him lose his temper. A faint glow of red shimmered from the rings of his irises.

But he was still holding back his magic, his abilities. The ones she hadn't seen him purposefully use once.

Jinx and Apollo were stuck in a deadlock.

Apollo cooled down, the glow receding. His expression, his eyes, turned bored. He swallowed, his voice deeper and coarse than before. "Are you done with this childish interrogation?"

A tapping on the door interrupted them.

"Veyda?" Arya questioned, her voice muffled on the other side.

Apollo dipped his head, whispering at the shell of her ear. "Best get that. Keeping Arya waiting is the equivalent of holding back a rabid dog."

Upon glaring at him, she noticed he smirked in response. Not the normal tick of his lip, no, a full-on lopsided smirk, with three lines folding in on the edge. She didn't know what it meant or what to make of it.

Jinx released him under her grip. "Coming." She slowly unlocked the door.

"Hello." Arya closed her fan as if she were playing with it while waiting for Jinx's response.

"Hello. How can I help you?" Jinx tucked a loose strand of hair back behind her ear.

Arya rolled her shoulders. "I'm going to lay it all out there. I don't know what you and my brother are up to, but I am obviously your cover. And because I care deeply for him, no matter how withdrawn he is, it'd be best if we spent some time together. Tomorrow."

Jinx narrowed her eyes in suspicion.

Arya strained her neck. "I'm not going to kill you. I'm trying to help you. Since you are supposed to be my friend, after all."

"Alright." Jinx unfurled her fingers from the door, crossing her arms. "What do you propose we do?"

"Go to the park. A walk around Botanic Plaza. Say, an hour after midday?"

"Sounds perfect."

Arya nodded in affirmation and left, closing the door behind her. The smug smirk still sat on Apollo's lips. It was terrifying to watch his face be anything other than deadpanned.

"I thought you were done with my interrogation," Jinx barked at him.

Apollo lifted a shoulder, exiting. "I am."

"Are you going to stop ignoring me so we can get back to proper work?"

He stopped at the door, looking back at her as if he were trying to decipher the depths of her mind, nudging her without a word to say more. Jinx was not ashamed of saying it out loud.

"So...you think we can be friends, Polly?"

Even a temporary friendship was better than nothing.

"Is that what you want? Friendship?"

"If it means we can work as partners and work faster, then yes. I want friendship." Jinx stretched taller, not backing away from his interested glare.

Apollo fished his hands in his pockets, changing back to the person she knew the first week. "Just so you know, I've been working the same amount. It looks like *you* are the one who is slowing down."

She snorted, damn well knowing that the opposite was true. "Goodnight, you stubborn mule."

He twisted his head. "What did I do to deserve the name?"

Jinx effortlessly neared him, digging a single finger in the center of his chest. "Just because I am no longer trying to pry into the depths of your brain does not change the fact that you are, indeed, the most stubborn man I've ever encountered."

Apollo wrapped his hand around her finger. "Leave it, Temptress. You won't like what you will find down there."

Unbeknownst to him, he'd said the wrong words to her. Because if Jinx was going to set her mind to any other task, it would be to find out what tormented Apollo in the shadows of his soul.

Chapter 19

Jinx

The fluffy cotton clouds offered citizens in the park respite from the glowing sun. The leaves on the tree dried, crinkling to a vibrant orange. Ducks and their babies waddled in a line, easing into the pond. Other men and women strolling in the park were dressed in their casual finery.

Since they'd left the Voclaine manor, Jinx and Arya had not exchanged a single word. An awkward strain stretched between them. It shouldn't be this way. Jinx, Thatcher, and Fey had established easy friendships by this point. But Arya was different.

Birds chirped overhead, flapping off the branches.

"Arya, what are we actually doing here?" Jinx questioned, staring ahead.

Arya's walk turned rigid, her clutch on her fan tightening. "As I said, I'm helping my nitwit of a brother."

Jinx did not believe it. There had to be something more.

She laid a hand on Arya's arm, halting her so that they could face each other. "I know we sort of got off on the wrong foot, but in all honesty, I mean no harm to you or your family."

Arya scowled at Jinx's touch, shrugging her off. "You say that, yet you lie." She pivoted, strutting away.

Jinx inhaled deeply, calming the rising heat in her core. The *irritation* this woman ignited in her. Her nails dug into her palms, allowing her to focus on the pain instead of the emotions she now felt bubbling up.

"Excuse me?" Jinx matched Arya's quick pace.

"You lie about your name, where you come from, all of it. Why?"

"I won't continue on the charade with you." At that, Arya slowed. Hope glossed her wary eyes. Jinx added, "However, if I could truly stop, I would."

"Are you now going to tell me to stay out of it?"

"No, I'm not Apollo," Jinx replied.

Arya rubbed her hands together, white lace gloves itching against each other. She slid a side glance at Jinx. "Then, what are you going to tell me?"

This invitation to go out was not intended to help her and Apollo with their ruse. It was to get whatever information she could from Jinx since she could not get it from Apollo. Arya was truly worried about her brother. Jinx's heart squeezed, the stress reaching to her shoulders. *Pity*, she realized.

As much as she empathized with her, Jinx's hands were tied, and Arya had no choice. Jinx said nothing at all, her silence better than empty words. Arya at least deserved that.

"Why are you so loyal to him?"

"Why do you assume I'm the one loyal to him when he could be the one loyal to me? I could very well be the one with the power," Jinx countered.

Arya smacked her lips. Jinx could see the wheels of her brain turning, mustering up an answer. A beat later, she spoke, "Because as much as I don't trust *you*, Veyda, I can't deny that you two spend a lot of time together, and if Pol decided to bring you in, there is probably a reason behind it."

Fondness lined Arya's features as she thought back on the past, her full pink lips turning downwards at the corners. It took Jinx aback but then made her grin. Jinx knew that if she had been in Arya's spot, she would have acted similarly.

"What was he like before?" Jinx nudged a rock, booting it from the trail. "Why did he become so..."

"Isolated? Frigid? I don't know. He never spoke about it." Arya fixed her straw hat. There was a glint in her eyes, a far-off look, as she reminisced about another moment in the past. "Pol used to be such a careless flirt, absolutely charming. Any soiree my family was invited to, people fawned over him. He was like a magnet, always drawing attention."

Jinx held her snort in. She tried imagining Apollo being the type of man that Arya was speaking of, but she failed miserably. Instead, phantom hands tightly coiled around Jinx's heart and crushed it.

She brushed off the feeling, not allowing herself to indulge in whatever that was.

Arya continued: "I remember the day when he completely changed. He was fifteen, and I was twelve. Pol went out with my father to the woods one day, and when he came back, he was pale. He locked himself in his room for days. The only times he came out were to eat, and even if he did, Pol appeared so phantom-like. Any attempt to speak to him failed. He shut me out, and Mother, and Father, and the twins. At one point, his body became frail and lanky, so lithe. I thought he'd been trying to starve himself to death. I truly believed he wanted to end his life."

A single tear brushed down Arya's cheek. Chin high, shoulders back, soldiering through the discomfort of the memory. "Gone was the boy I knew, my friend, the person who told me every thought crossing his wondrous brain. He didn't talk to me anymore, and he became serious. No more smiles, no more jokes, no more flaunting about how great he was. Whatever I tried to do, he wouldn't let me get near him. I felt as if I lost a brother that day."

What could have happened for Apollo to completely change as a person? He distanced himself from everyone he loved, even from his family. He was lucky enough to have people by his side who still cared.

Softly, Jinx murmured, "I think you did."

Arya softened, realizing that Jinx understood how she felt. She had lost someone she knew almost better than she knew herself, only to watch a walking corpse return in his place. Something, someone else, was now residing in Apollo's body. She mourned an intangible loss.

"Yes." Arya fluttered her lashes, a watery sheen coating her eyes. Her tone, however, was strong as ever. "Pol stopped seeing his friends, except for Kovan. After that day, he didn't bring anyone home anymore. So when he came to me saying you were coming...well, you can imagine."

"You were shocked. Scared." Jinx sunk her teeth into her bottom lip, searching for the right word. What could encompass Arya's emotions? "Hopeful, maybe?"

"Yes."

Jinx and Arya neared the pond in the center of the gardens, then stopped at the foot of the shore. Rippling water distorted their near-perfect reflections. Arya patted the front of her lavender dress.

"Hope is necessary; don't lose it," Jinx said comfortingly. "Sometimes it's all we may have."

"Do you have hope?" Arya twitched her nose.

"I must." Without hope, Jinx wouldn't have been able to survive all these years. She'd always maintained hope that she would one day return to her family.

Arya pondered this, her eyes narrowing and her head tilting from side to side. Arya had shared a piece of herself, and now Jinx only felt it right to return the favor. For the sake of her deal with Apollo, if nothing else.

Jinx exhaled. An aggravating series of harsh pumps punched up at her ribcage. Lies were so much easier to spill than the truth, but this she would do for Arya. "All that I have ever done, from the age of eight, was for my family. Everything I am doing now with Pol is to go back home."

Arya's brows pinched into a line. "Why can't you go home if that is all you want?"

Jinx's gaze dropped to her white glove-laced hands. She could not show any weakness. "If it were that easy, I would have done so already, and my life would have turned out very differently."

If she'd pursued another path, a different timeline, an alternate reality, Jinx could have grown up at home. She and her family would have remained poor, but at least they would have had each other. Out of so many options, Jinx had chosen the route of sacrifice, of loneliness. Greed and selflessness were interlocked in a paradox of hypocrisy.

"Good afternoon, Lady Voclaine." A man in a top hat and red tailcoat approached them. Copper hair brushed his thick brows, and a devious smile broadened his square jaw. He bowed at the waist.

Jinx's senses elevated her alertness. She did not like this man.

"Lord Velez, what a pleasure." Arya dutifully bowed, and Jinx followed in kind. "This is my friend, Veyda Collymore, from the east."

Jinx clasped her hands in her middle. "Lord Velez."

"Miss Collymore, lovely to meet you." Velez gripped her hands and kissed Jinx's knuckles. She had the urge to pull away.

Arya plastered on a fake smile, a nontypical enthusiasm etched into her features. It had been practiced a hundred times, perhaps thousands, altering her outward persona almost entirely.

Velez buttoned his tailcoat. "Lady Voclaine, what are you doing here at this fine hour?"

Gently, she replied, "Simply taking a stroll, showing Miss Collymore the Plaza." Arya looked over at Jinx, indicating that she did not want to be in this conversation any more than Jinx did.

"How are you enjoying Somnium, Miss Collymore?" Velez asked, invading Jinx's personal space.

"It's just wonderful. Though I believe Miss Voclaine and I must depart. Didn't we have tea to attend to with Kateri?" Jinx gave them an exit.

Arya caught on, "You are absolutely correct. How the time has slipped by, that sneaky thing. If you'll excuse us, Lord Velez, we must be on our way."

Jinx hooked an arm around Arya's, about to pull her away, when Velez stepped in their path. "One last thing." Velez drawled, his tone darkening. His attention was now fixed on Arya. "I've sent a marriage proposition to your parents earlier today."

"Have you?" Arya giggled it away. Jinx wanted to get both of them out of there.

"Yes," he said seriously, "your father has taken a great interest in it."

Arya's light demeanor stifled. Her smile dropped, eyes flattening. She gripped her fan tightly, spine arching back as Velez loomed over her. Jinx couldn't stand to watch it.

"I hope to see you at the Hallows Masquerade Ball this Autumn." Insinuation oozed from his words. Arya's nose wrinkled. "By then you could be my bride. How does that sound? You could be Lady Velez instead of Voclaine." He reached out a single curved finger to brush Arya's cheek.

Jinx had had enough. She cleared her throat, drawing both of their attention. "I suggest you leave, Lord Velez." Jinx put Arya behind her.

"Are you dismissing me, Miss Collymore?"

"Absolutely."

Velez blinked, confused as to why a woman dared to defy him.

"Your offer may be appealing to the Duke, but how would he feel knowing that same man was harassing his daughter? Nothing would stop me from reporting back to him, nixing any future you might have with Arya. And, for that matter, any future marriage in Somnium."

Heat flushed Jinx's cheeks, anger piling up. She motioned for Arya's hand fan, which she hesitantly passed over. The weight of it was heavier than Jinx had expected.

Jinx recoiled her arm and smacked Velez across the face with the fan. A harsh whack echoed across the park, the red silhouette marking his cheek. He gripped his face. "If you want a wife, *respect her.*"

"Good day," Jinx hissed before walking away, Arya in tow.

Arya looked back and forth between Jinx and Velez. "Why did you do that?"

"Because you couldn't. I am from the East; whatever happens here does not affect me. I'd rather my reputation be tainted than you deal with that trash of a man."

Arya snapped her fan open, cooling herself down with air. "Thank you."

They stomped away, heading back home. "How do you feel?" Jinx asked.

"I'm alright. Though a bit infuriated." Irritation, at first delayed, was now beginning to hit Arya.

"Imps like that should not even exist in this world," Jinx murmured.

"You sound like Pol," Arya said.

"Perhaps I *have* been spending too much time with him."

Chapter 20

Apollo

A pollo twirled the butt of the cigarette in the ashtray, ridding the aftertaste of the tobacco in his mouth with a swig of dark liquor, burning down his throat.

In the warehouse that was Kovan's foxhole, Apollo, Kovan, and Thatcher played a game of poker.

Kovan shuffled the cards. "You are a silver-tongued liar, and you know it." He pointed accusingly at Thatcher.

Thatcher lunged forward in his seat, mouth hanging. "Are you serious?" His frustrated gaze flickered between Apollo and Kovan before he smacked Apollo in the arm. "Pol, please tell Kovan that when we look up into the sky, the light we are getting from our sun is technically from the past."

Apollo would do no such thing. "I'm not getting involved in elementary school quarrels." Impassively, Apollo focused on his cards.

Kovan clicked his tongue, raising his glass in a manly bravado, clearly thinking he'd won the argument. Technically, Thatcher was correct, but the argument was between the two of them.

Kovan shook his head of silver hair after knocking back his glass and folding down his hand of cards. "Too good for our small arguments, Pol?"

"Yes." Though he'd attempted to infuse it with a joking tone, it hadn't landed as well as he'd expected.

"Oh, so *that* is why you don't come around anymore," his friend teased, unintentionally showing his hand. Apollo suspected that Kovan had to be feeling the buzz of the liquor to be acting in such an ostentatious way. "What's next? Your father gives you his title as Duke, and we never see you anymore? Too busy for your old friends?"

Apollo felt an itch of laughter climb his throat before he swiftly smothered it. Kovan kept rambling the first words that came to mind.

Thatcher snickered to himself, concealing his mouth in the crook of his elbow. Apollo cast his attention over at his brother immediately until his pinked cheeks lost their color. "Don't worry, Kovan, we're already starting to lose him. Pol's been off spending most of his time with Lady Collymore."

Apollo grunted, snaking a glare at his brother. He wondered if his repressed abilities contained the power to shut his brother up.

Since he'd acquired the demon inside of him, Apollo never gave it or himself the chance to test out any of the abilities that came along with it. He only wanted to pretend that he was still normal, that nothing had changed that day in the woods. He hadn't even considered exploring these powers until Jinx had mentioned it.

"Ohhhh," Kovan drawled, elongating the word to an extreme.

Irritation scratched the surface of Apollo's skin. He clenched his jaw, ignoring the dramatics of Thatcher and Kovan.

"Where *is* Veyda?" Thatcher's voice pitched higher, interested.

Apollo wished for nothing more than to escape this uncomfortable situation. As much as he could pray to the Virtues at the moment, they never came to his side for help—and they wouldn't be able to help him out of this conversation. Apollo was on his own.

"With Arya, doing who knows what." Apollo tossed his cards on the table, signaling that their game was over.

Kovan, fascinated with the topic, persisted: "That Collymore girl is often with you. Do we have something to be worried about?"

Apollo took another swig of his drink. "Why should anyone be worried about what I do?"

"You are soon to be one of the seven, Pol," Kovan explained. "If a lady is to spend too much time with you, many will believe it's someone who you intend to marry." He wiggled his eyebrows suggestively. Apollo masked his reactions, not feeding into what Kovan was insinuating.

First, his mother and Fey, now these two. Apollo was over it. He'd repeated more than once that he wasn't interested in courting anyone. If he had to shout it off the mountains of the Northern Summit, so be it.

"I will not be marrying Lady Collymore, nor do I feel any particular affection toward her. She's only lived in our residence for a brief time," he said mildly.

"A brief time can still be enough." Thatcher countered. Kovan, siding with him, pointed at Thatcher as if he were speaking some miraculous poetry.

Apollo would not deny what was clearly in front of him. Jinx was intelligent and alluring, a web of mysteries he wished to untangle. She was sharp and willful, always speaking her mind, even when it was something that others did not wish to hear. Not to mention, she was the most stunning woman his eyes had ever had the blessing of landing upon.

However, she was also a thief. A manipulator. Someone who should not be trusted. And yet, Jinx was proving him wrong. At the base of their new friendship, trust was slowly forming.

Thatcher offered, "I don't think you are aware of how you stare at her, Brother."

"Bored, vacant. Like I do with everyone else."

"No, with curiosity." His brother paused, hunting for the words to explain it. The squint in his eyes gave it away. "It's like you are constantly trying to understand her, and I know I'm not as good at reading people as you are, but if I had to guess, I'd say that she stares at you in the same way."

Thatcher had revealed a half-truth; Apollo *was* always trying to understand her. The fallacy in his brother's statement was assuming that Jinx staring at him in the same way. Apollo would've known if that were the case. He stared at her more than he'd like to admit.

A flash of heat rose from his pulse, his heart skipping a beat.

No.

Apollo gripped his budding emotions and crushed them faster than they could grow. They were pointless. Perhaps he did glance at her with curiosity, as it is what he felt most of the time when she was near. He was sure that she did not reciprocate the same. And if she did, what would that mean for him?

"You're both delusional. Do you expect a declaration of love? I'll admit, she is attractive." Apollo feigned false tranquility. If he acted serenely, maybe he would calm down. He crossed a lazy leg over the other. "But I'm not interested in courting."

Thatcher pushed himself off his chair, throwing his university satchel over his shoulder. "Believe whatever you want." His brother swaggered to the coat hanger, plucking his overcoat. "I'll be returning home late. Just as a note, Brother: if you do not intend to court Veyda, someone else just might." He waved goodbye to his brother and his friend, closing the door behind him.

Kovan and Apollo remained seated. As Apollo turned back to his friend, he found him grinning from ear to ear. An all-knowing look overtook his expression.

"Do you really believe that?" Apollo asked.

"You imbecile. Of *course.*" The joking aroma lessened as seriousness loomed over them. Kovan's tone turned earnest. "What is it in your heart that rejects any sort of affection?"

Apollo checked his pocket watch. The time was irrelevant; he just wanted to give himself more time to stall.

"Pol, do you have any reason not to trust me?" A vulnerability in Kovan's tone struck him. Kovan only used that tone when the topic struck close to his heart. Apollo hated it. He loathed moments like these with Kovan because it forced him to reconcile with his own emotions, and yet, no matter how much he wanted to, he couldn't afford to let his friend in.

"Don't ask idiotic questions." Apollo reached for the bottle of liquor in the center of the table. Kovan snatched the glass before Apollo could fill it, challenging his friend. "What is it, then, that troubles you?"

Apollo stared deeply into the bottom of Kovan's hazel eyes. The tension stretched too long between them. "Nothing. Nothing troubles me."

Kovan scoffed. "Nothing ever does, apparently."

"Care to elaborate?" Apollo blinked slowly, waiting.

The angular lines shaping Kovan's face hardened. "Sometimes, it is as if you are a stone, Apollo. I will not ask you to open yourself to me because it's clear as day that you will not, but talk to someone, *anyone* for that matter."

Apollo *wanted* to talk to Kovan about his issues. About everything. Come clean and start on fresh ground. Tell him he was a Cursed in a way. He wanted to admit that the reason he couldn't laugh or let any sort of emotion out was because he was afraid of what might accompany it.

Had he really gotten that bad? Kovan and Arya were essentially pleading the same case. He wondered if his expressions were becoming even more obviously detached from the present. Perhaps he should attempt to show something more if just a little bit.

"I've been worse recently, haven't I?" Apollo asked in painful recognition.

Kovan tipped his head to the side. "You're more distant as you grow older."

"Everything becomes more complex as time passes."

"So it does. You can't let it stop you, though. Then you'll always be stuck."

"Tch. When did you become the wise one?"

A buzzed Kovan shot up from his chair, thinning his lips. "When I started drinking. Liquor loosens the tongue."

Apollo steadied his friend. "As it does the muscles. Your tolerance is childishly low."

Kovan chortled. "At least I can have fun. Do you even know what the definition of fun is anymore?"

"Amusement."

"I didn't mean it literally, Pol." Kovan latched heavy hands on Apollo's shoulders, vigorously shaking him. "Loosen up, that is all I am saying. Fun is good for the soul." He clapped Apollo's shoulder, turning to get his coat. "Beggars Bar tonight. Care to join?"

Unfortunately, Apollo didn't have time for careless enjoyment like Kovan did. A part of him wanted to go, but he knew he shouldn't.

Apollo straightened up. "Count me in next time. With my father gone, I have accounts to tend to."

Not to mention a certain book to decipher waiting on his shelf.

Chapter 21

Apollo

The single flame of the lit candle waved as the dainty wind of the pending autumn blew inside the window. It provided just enough glow for Apollo to read the book from the Collection. The old grainy pages were thick at each turn, the inky lettering had smudged away in parts due to time. But time seemed to be the only factor advancing its decay. Burning, ripping, marking—it seemed as if any other physical harm to the book would be warded off.

After much contemplation, he'd realized that the nightmare living inside hadn't called to him in the fire. It was the book itself, manifesting itself in an itch behind his ear, urging him to turn around and take it. But why? He was still trying to figure that out.

On a separate piece of paper, Apollo tried to decipher the ancient text. He noted the number of times a rune was written and how many different types appeared. There appeared to be twenty-four separate symbols.

Apollo flipped through the pages. He searched for diagrams, pictures of any kind, indications that would hint at the time frame in which this book could have been written or where it came from. He considered that it could have come from the east, as some prehistoric book. But that theory quickly diminished. If the book had originated in the east, the King and his prophets would have knocked down Somnium's door the second they realized it was missing. Unlike the aristocracy that Somnium was built on, the east was ruled by a monarchy headed by the king and his advisors—the prophets. They were intent on maintaining their traditions and keeping their ancestors with them. They praised their written history as being more valuable than gold.

No, the origins of this nameless volume had to be tied in some way with the Vessel. He was sure of it. Both the Vessel and this book had inspired the same foul tang in his mouth, sounded the same instinctual call beckoning to him from the nape of his skull, elicited the buzz swarming his shoulders. His reactions to both items were identical. But still, how were they connected?

He took off his glasses. Apollo ran a hand through his hair, scratching his scalp. He massaged his burnt-out brain, then the bridge of his nose. He stood up from his desk and stretched to the point of delightful pain. Shutting the open window, he watched the blaze of the candle grow, illuminating his chambers a little more. His dark four-poster bed, heavy rug, and thick desk were now visible in the candlelight.

Lounging on the edge of his desk, he glinted the flower pin Jinx had brought him.

Apollo inspected it. Somehow, this symbol was connected to the book and the Vessel as well. He just knew it.

A light chime tinkered in the background. Midnight.

Figaro leaped up onto his bed, curling up comfortably at the foot.

"I should go to bed, too," Apollo rasped. He glimpsed the glass decanter, liquid amber shining like fresh honey.

Kovan's pleading voice played back in his ears. *Talk to someone.* Apollo snarled at himself. Damn his friend. Apollo exited his room, searching for the temptress down the hall.

Jinx

Freshly bathed and snuggled up in bed with a good romance book, Jinx rested on a tower of pillows. She was firmly invested in this new novel, one that Fey had loaned to her upon her return to the house that afternoon with Arya.

Jinx had taken the rest of the day to rest, allowing herself a moment to enjoy the life of high society.

Her eyes were glued to the pages as she caught herself sucking on her lower lip. Jinx urgently flipped the page, needing to know what would happen next.

The protagonist was having a heated moment with her second love interest. Jinx's toes curled at the lines as she drank in the words. Devious heat pooled in her belly. She covered her mouth as an excited yelp threatened to emerge.

Jinx could not handle the novel. She snickered to herself, astounded by its audacity.

Three knocks on her door jolted her from the story. She placed her thumb in the center of the book, holding it in place as she went to open the door.

Irritation at being interrupted chilled her down to her spine.

A drowsy Apollo lingered on the other side. "Have you gone to bed yet?"

"Well, I opened the door, so no, I have not gone to bed yet." She really wanted to get back to her book.

Apollo examined her, Jinx arching a brow under the scrutiny.

"You're flustered," he mused.

"Excuse me?" She blinked.

"Your cheeks, they're bright pink." Apollo licked his lips. "Did I interrupt something?" He seemed all too interested, all too insinuating.

Jinx's heart practically jumped out of her chest. "That's rather foul of you to assume," she said defensively.

"I didn't assume. I was taking in my surroundings. You're blushing; it's midnight, and you are alone. It was only safe to assume that you —"

"What do you want?" She couldn't let him finish that sentence.

Apollo held his hands behind his back, leaning in. "Why are you assuming I want something?"

Jinx didn't buy his act. In his minute maneuvers, Apollo was moving too much. Either his comfort around her had grown and he was letting himself go a little, or he needed something. Jinx was waging her bets on the latter.

"The last time you knocked on my door, you asked about my outing and then immediately left when I gave you my answer."

"Yes, but it ended quite well." His eyes revealed nothing of his true intent. Suspicion mingled in Jinx's core.

"Because of me."

Apollo's tone was infused with a peculiar charm she'd barely heard. "Are you going to let me in, or am I going to have to leave for you to haul me inside again? Not that I am complaining..." Jinx blinked. "We are wasting precious minutes here. I could have cooked myself dinner already."

She opened her door wider, granting him entrance. As he passed her, she muttered, "No one appreciates a pretentious prick."

He dipped his head. "And here we are, with you opening the door for me." Apollo's wintry eyes landed on the book in her hand. "Oh, so *this* is what's pleasing you." He plucked it out of her hand before she had the chance to react, surprised by how rapidly he'd moved.

"Apollo. Give it back." Jinx made no move to fight him. Both of them knew who would win in this particular fight.

He sat at her vanity, crossing a leg over the other, scanning the pages. "What? No 'Polly' this time around?"

"Your name is Polly when you are not vexing me. It is Apollo when you are being unbearable."

He raised a careless shoulder. "Shame. I rather liked it."

Jinx crossed her room, taking the book back in her grasp. His face returned to the blank expression she knew as he settled in. "How was your day with Arya? I see you are intact and completely unscathed."

Jinx pressed her bookmark inside the pages and closed her novel, slightly saddened that she'd have to wait to finish it. She sank into her mattress. "If you must know, neither one of us chewed off the other's head. I'd consider it a win."

"Agreed."

"Lord Velez harassed your sister about his offer to take her as a wife. I know it is not my place, but you mustn't let your sister be married off to that pig."

Displeasure flamed under Apollo's skin. "I won't. When Father returns, I'll speak with him if she doesn't get there before I do. She's rather quick."

"Good." Jinx nodded.

"How did you get away from him?"

Jinx stared at her nails. "Arya's fans came to good use when we needed to put that child into place." With a sharp exhale, she diverted her attention far from the occurrence. "And you, what did you do with your time today?"

Apollo played with his fingers, wiggling them. "Spent the day with Kovan and Thatcher." Then, in the storm of his eyes, there was a shift, one that sounded the alarm through her pulse. He came off burdened. "Jinx, can I ask for a moment of your honesty?"

She leaned back on her hands. "Well, these days, you are the only person I am *not* lying to, so sure."

"You're not lying, really; you're just omitting the truth."

"Time will tell." She sighed. "What is your question?"

His sharp gaze landed on a random object in her room. She could tell it was easier for him to speak candidly if he focused on something other than her. "Do you think I am too detached?"

"Who is the liar now?" She tried to make light of the situation. "I thought you wanted nothing?"

Their gazes met again. "Asking for an opinion is hardly asking for a huge favor." He flaunted his unemotional nature again, closing the barriers to his mind again. "Well...am I?"

This subject clearly meant something to him, so she would be sincere in her response.

"Yes, Polly, you are."

Jinx could have sworn to the Virtues that she heard him grimace. "Is it bad?"

She cradled herself, hugging her knees. "Are you trying to talk about your feelings?"

"You are the worst person to talk to, really."

Jinx patted the area next to her as Apollo gave in and sat beside her.

"Okay, I'm done," she said on a breath, sincerity coating every word. "Asking if something is bad is relative, like all things. The question you should be asking is if it is good for you. Is that what you want? To be detached?" Apollo listened attentively. "If what you want is to have people fear you in some way or stay away from you, then no, it is not bad."

Apollo's sight fixated on the popping fire flaming in the hearth. "Do *you* fear me?"

"No, I don't anymore. Honestly, I was a little wary at first." She turned her head, trying to catch his eyes. "May I ask why you're bringing up this topic?"

"It was a conversation I had with Kovan." Apollo shrugged it off, but Jinx knew there was more.

She probed. "Well, why are you so cold?"

He whispered under his breath, almost as if it pained him to speak it into existence, "To protect others."

"From your abilities?" Jinx asked gently.

She waited for minutes for an answer, letting him think through his conflicting thoughts without rushing him. Jinx would wait all night if she had to. If this was what he needed and wanted, she would be there. Apollo froze beside her, lost in thought.

Her hand tingled to run up his back for physical support, massaging it in small circles. When she realized what she wanted to do, she fisted her hand, reeling away.

Apollo cleared his throat, willing his tone to sound unaffected. "If the offer still stands, I would like your training."

"Alright." His acceptance of her offer satisfied something deep in Jinx's core. She'd always wanted the chance to help someone else with their powers. She had been too late once, encountering a former acquaintance on the brink of death after hiding her abilities.

"We'll start tomorrow morning before the sun rises. It will take some time, though. Do you know anything about your abilities? What you may be capable of?"

The pulsing light shadowed his features in all the right places, creating a perfect balance of mystery and comfort. "No, not really."

"We can start slow," she reassured him.

Apollo lowered his head, relief finding his shoulders. "Thank you."

"You don't have to change, you know. If you are going to change, do it for yourself and not for others, no matter what they think."

"Speaking from experience?"

"From another life." And from all the lives Jinx has lived, this one was turning out to be her favorite. And that was one of the most terrifying realizations to have crossed Jinx's mind.

Chapter 22

Jinx

The sun was still sleeping when, after only four hours of sleep, Jinx rapped on Apollo's door. There was just enough time left to get in an hour of training before the rest of the Voclaines awoke. "Get up, Polly."

A deep, tired moan answered on the other side.

"Polly, I can burst through this door and drag you out," she said a little louder, careful not to wake the others.

Another whine.

Jinx rubbed her forehead. This was going to be dreadful if he insisted on being this slow in the morning. He better not have drunk himself to sleep or smoked until he saw oblivion.

Jinx knocked louder this time. "Polly!"

Sheets ruffled. Finally, he got out of bed. She waited for his ambling footsteps to echo closer, for the door to click open, with him standing right behind it dressed and ready to train.

And yet, nothing.

She curled her fingers around the knob. Unlocked, Jinx peeked behind the door to find Apollo still wrapped in his dark blue comforter. His scent of citrus and cedar wood filled the whole space. Her first instinct was to search for any liquor or cigarettes, but she found nothing of the sort near him.

Jinx slowly shut the door behind her, making sure to muffle the click, and walked toward him. A shirtless Apollo groaned, clutching the pillow in his arms tighter, his hair tousled.

In his defense, she *had* forgotten to mention what time they would be training today.

Jinx clutched Apollo's face. "Princess, it's time to train." She softly slapped him.

A low grumble emerged from his chest. "If I'm the princess, does that mean you're the prince, rescuing me from my tower?" Apollo's husky morning voice sent goosebumps across Jinx's skin.

"No," she retorted. "I'm the evil witch that locked you in there."

Apollo's eyes remained sewn shut. Maybe he was too tired to keep his emotions hidden from her. She spotted the tiny lift at the end of his lips and heard a soft hum of approval.

"Even better."

Jinx clutched both of his arms, hauling his dead weight out of bed. "Come *on*." She struggled. "Get *up*."

Apollo, half asleep, countered her strength, rolling all of his mass back into the mattress and releasing himself from her grip. "You know the day actually begins when the sun rises?"

"Do you want others to see you using your abilities?" She hissed. Jinx opened his armoire, plucking out pieces of clothes for him and throwing them back in his face.

The bed creaked at the shifting weight as he sat up. She continued rummaging through his closet, surprised at how well-organized everything was. His shirts and pants were separated and even color-coded, though most of the colors were neutral. Clearly, he preferred whites and blacks, grays and maroons, an occasional touch of dark blue. The rest of his room was incredibly clean as well.

How was that possible? Did he clean everything himself? It wasn't that he didn't seem to be capable of being a clean person. It was just that she'd seen little to no housemaids in the manor, unlike those who worked for the Tertain family and other high-class socialites. Despite the one day of her arrival.

The hairs on her back stood on end, heat radiating from behind her as she felt a gentle blow of air on her neck. She turned around, coming face to face with a chiseled bare chest.

The definition in his muscles was impeccable. She questioned how it was possible to be so sculpted if all he did was drink and smoke.

With two fingers, Apollo extracted the shirt in Jinx's hands, throwing it over his head in one calculated movement. She dragged her gaze up to see his looming from above, his structured face already showcasing that expressionless mask he wore so well. "No one will see us training at Kovan's warehouse."

Apollo was now just a hair's length away from her. The raw proximity made her uncomfortable.

"We leave in ten." Jinx shoved him away. "I'll wait for you downstairs."

She cursed at herself. Jinx was becoming too relaxed, opening herself up too much. She couldn't recognize the person she was becoming. She also didn't know why she cared so much about the Voclaines, why she so enjoyed the time she'd spent with them in the manor. It almost felt like she was making real friends. But it could never last, and she was angry with herself because she knew how it was going to end.

After she and Apollo located the Vessel and she unlocked the mystery of the riddle, Jinx would go home, back to her family, back to her life as another boring member of society. The Voclaines would surely forget all about her.

It didn't matter how she felt, either. Friends or not, it was all temporary. It was all a lie. A lie she was beginning to believe. A recipe for tragedy.

But maybe, just maybe, she could pretend it was real. For just a little longer.

Jinx sat on the couch in the family room, playing with her throwing knife. There was little chance of encountering another member of the family unless Arya came back early. Jinx had heard her leave through the window last night while she was reading. Jinx still wondered where she went.

It wasn't something that alerted Jinx. But she was curious.

The scribbling of a pencil perked her ears up. Apollo entered the room, his nose inside of the brown leather notebook he was always writing in, dressed as if he were going to the gala of the year. His raven hair curled slightly; he hadn't bothered to style it. Jinx preferred it messy anyways. He snapped the book together with one hand. "Your glower is pleasingly horrible this morning."

Jinx sheathed her blade. "Has anyone told you that your compliments are awful?"

Apollo's mouth opened, and Jinx walked out without giving him the chance to retort.

At Kovan's warehouse, Apollo shrugged off his coat and took hers as well. Leaving it on the coat rack, he tossed his keys on the table and met Jinx in the center of the room, helping her set aside the furniture and opening up more free space.

"Where do we start?" Apollo asked, wiping a single bead of sweat off his hairline.

This situation reminded her of a moment in her past when she first received combat training of her own. It was a time when she'd infiltrated the military and made an acquaintance who'd gone by the name of Franco Lancaster. He was a man who'd taken her under his wing— when she went by the name of Elijah Benjamin, he'd devoted much of his time in the early mornings to strengthening her fighting techniques, instructing her how to use all sorts of blades and pistols. He'd also taught her about her favorite form of battle: hand-to-hand combat. She wondered where Franco was now.

There was a lot about fighting that also applied to magic, and she intended to apply this knowledge to the training before them.

Jinx dusted off her long skirt. "So, what do you know about your abilities? I need you to be transparent."

Apollo pocketed his hands. "They're tied to my emotions."

That much was practically a given. "Are there any certain emotions that trigger it?"

"No. *Any* emotion I feel can trigger it. I can express my feelings to an extent. I'm human, but anything past a certain limit can trigger it."

That meant Jinx and Apollo would have to work on pushing that barrier further while also trying to figure out what his powers were.

Apollo continued, "I'm constantly at a battle with them. If I let go too much, it talks."

"What talks?" Jinx's brows furrowed sharply at the revelation.

"There's a voice. I've kept it at bay for plenty of years. It wasn't until you took my ring that it started again."

"How about your ring? Where did it come from? What does it do?"

"Actually, I don't know where it came from."

Jinx's head tilted. "Explain."

Apollo took a deep breath, already tired of speaking. "It was delivered to me with a note, which told me not to take it off and promised that it would help me control myself. And it has.

Then he added: "Also, I should mention: whenever I'm in sizeable crowds, it's like my abilities get charged."

"Then it's possible that your abilities can feed off the energy of others. I'm not certain, but it's definitely a lead. Do you experience any physical changes?" she asked.

"If you are asking about my speed and strength, they're the same as a normal person."

Jinx suspected there was something more. "What about your muscles? You drink and smoke all day, but you're sculpted almost like a Virtue."

Apollo hummed again, a sparkle of mischief glistening in his eye. He blinked it away so quickly that Jinx almost missed it. "Must come with being a Cursed."

"Are you serious?"

"When am I not?" he muttered sarcastically.

Jinx snorted. "Cursed doesn't work like that. We aren't suddenly sculpted with muscles because we have magic. Yes, we have a bit of differences, like thicker skin, stronger hair and nails, delayed aging, but a growth in muscles isn't something I've ever heard of."

"Perhaps my magic preserves my muscles."

Her head bounced in thought. She paced away from him, rolling up her sleeves to her elbows. An idea sparked in her brain. "Hit me."

"What?"

"Throw a punch at me." Jinx crouched into her fighting stance.

Apollo checked his pocket watch. "I'm not interested in fighting like primates."

They hadn't even started, and she already wanted to choke him. Apollo was clearly a man who avoided violence, one who preferred focusing on insightful topics, psychological patterns, brain games. It wasn't a physical approach she needed to take; it was a mental one.

Jinx crossed the open space toward him, snatching the pocket watch from his hand. A little frustration lined Apollo's voice. "How could you do such a thing?"

He wanted her to show him her magic and how it worked. Every Cursed used their magic differently. There wasn't just one way to do it, one answer. It was, in many ways, a problem with many different kinds of solutions. The one thing that all Cursed shared, however, was that their power originated in a muscle.

"Magic is all about learning how to use this muscle... or organ. Honestly, I'm not sure which it is." Jinx outlined the right side of her chest, the spot next to her heart. "It's right here. The more you practice and use it, the stronger it becomes. I've been using this muscle constantly for twelve years, making my illusions more realistic. For me, it's like I'm an artist painting a portrait, but instead of using a canvas, paints, and brushes, the world is my canvas. If you give me a sketchbook and a pencil, I am no artist at all."

Apollo circled her, assessing her stance. "It explains why you have such a watchful eye. You're always looking for new ways to improve your art."

She nodded in agreement. Jinx summoned her magic. The blood in her veins grew hot as the fine layer of her skin cooled. Green snaked out of her body, tendrils of flowing waves coiling around her, encompassing and changing her appearance to the eye. She was now veiling herself into a new mold. "I can become an old baker." Jinx brought forth her magic again, shifting the illusion. "Or perfectly mimic you."

The only indicator that he was stunned was the small hitch Jinx heard in his breath. Apollo was now looking at a perfect replica of himself. A twin. Jinx continued explaining how her magic worked, hoping he would learn from it so he could use it to his own advantage. "And it's the small details that matter, which make your magic more believable."

Jinx closed the space between them in two long strides. "Like you, for instance. When you find something actually amusing, you get three lines here." She tapped the corner of his mouth. "Your smirk is always tilted toward the left. And when you're impatient or thinking hard about something, you check your pocket watch." She effortlessly exposed some of the few mannerisms of his that she had picked up in the time she'd spent with him.

Apollo gave her a down-turned smile. That was a new one; she didn't yet know its meaning but found herself wanting to learn. "Fixated with me, Temptress?"

"Only as much as you are with me." Jinx matched his expression identically so he could see how beautifully idiotic he looked.

The new smile faded. "I have a question unrelated to this topic. If you can do all this, how were you not able to get into the Archives on your own?"

"It's because of the entrances. There are two: the fake one and the real one. I found the decoy, but once I got in, it was all a fluke. The information in there was the same as I'd found in the library down the street. No grand riches as it's supposedly known to have. No sea of gold and history the tracks further back than the Virtues themselves," Jinx explained as if it were obvious. They were straying far off the topic. "Back to you. I think your abilities may be more concentrated in that mind of yours than just in the muscle itself. Once we can figure out what your magic abilities are, we can start helping you release those locked-up emotions."

Jinx dragged two chairs into the center of the room, facing each other. She sat in one, offering the other to Apollo. "Have you tried talking to this voice?"

Apollo's husky voice turned glacial. "I'm not talking to it."

"Why?"

"That is the one thing I will not do. There's no arguing about it."

A thread in her brain knotted as if trying to string separate thoughts together. "Is this voice the one that brought you to the Collection, to that book?"

Apollo looked away, ashamed. "Yes."

"Then, you should talk to it. It's been helping you."

"No."

"Why not?"

"I said no," Apollo insisted.

Jinx blinked. His resentment for the voice struck her as odd. She was unable to comprehend why he wouldn't speak to the voice if it were a piece of his magic, the very magic he wanted to train.

Jinx raised her hands by her head, signaling her surrender. If he wanted her to leave the subject alone for now, she would. Apollo was stubborn, and she knew it would take time.

"How about you unlock just one of those emotions? Just let go of the slightest fraction of one." Jinx pinched her fingers together.

He crossed his arms. "No."

Jinx huffed, dropping her smile. "Polly."

"I'm not doing that either."

Jinx spoke to herself, touching her forehead. "This is going to get repetitive." She cracked her fingers. "Why not?"

Apollo's eyes dropped.

"I don't understand. You ask for my help and dismiss my advice. I'm spending precious minutes trying to help you instead of focusing on finding your Vessel. If you don't want this, just say so. I'd much rather leave and focus on the task at hand than waste my time and my talents." The limbs of her chair protested as she stood up.

A hand latched around her wrist, keeping her in place. "I haven't done this before." Jinx turned, staring him down. His expression hinted at genuine sincerity and apology. Apollo's head bobbed, followed by a pained grunt. His grip tightened as he sunk to the ground.

He was fighting against himself. She crouched down and grabbed his face, forcing him to look at her. "Listen to me. Don't fight it. Control it. Breathe." She touched his chest, the area right above his heart. It trembled, pounding at a beat far faster than humanly possible. He needed to slow it down without resorting to an outside source. "Deep breaths."

Jinx inhaled, providing guidance for him. He followed her steps, matching his tempo with hers. His heart finally slowed. "What did you feel?"

"Like I was going to burst." Apollo panted.

"Where?" If it was indeed centralized in some part of his body, then maybe she could figure out where his abilities resided.

He lifted his face to hers. "Everywhere." His gaze dropped to his finger, still encased with the silver ring. The fixture was now glowing red, the cracks within its webbing simmering as another fissure split in the silver band.

"Again," Jinx demanded.

Apollo panted near the deceased on the floor. Sweat soaked through his white shirt, the fabric shaping his rigid muscles. "I feel I should inform you that this is a bad idea."

"It's a great idea. Now again," Jinx countered. She placed her feet by Apollo's torso, grabbing him by the collar and pulling him toward her. "You won't talk to your magic, so we need to practice other measures. We must build up that stamina of yours so you won't have to rely on that ring forever."

A phantom smirk crossed his face. "Harsh, Temptress."

After a few days of training with Apollo, Jinx had run him through a series of tests. Most of them tested his emotions, enabling him to let go little by little. The muscle that contained his magic needed to build itself up from scratch since he'd long rejected his abilities instead of nurturing them.

The more he leaned on the ring for support, the weaker the muscle inside of him became. Now, any small outburst seemed to hurt him. It was time to change that.

While trying to figure out what his abilities were, Jinx told him to relax and let his emotions flow through his body. He forgot that instruction often, and whenever it happened, Jinx would find new ways to bother him.

Today, Jinx brought in a pale of water, telling Apollo to bend it to his will. It hadn't gone well so far.

She let him go. "I never said training was going to be easy."

Apollo grunted, shifting to stand on his feet. Wet hair slicked to his forehead.

"You're not even trying," she prodded, trying to get emotion out of him.

"I know my magic has nothing to do with water."

"Then what does it have to do with? I thought you didn't know," Jinx asked.

"I don't know how to explain it." He combed his raven hair back, finally catching his breath. "I did use some of it once, a long time ago." Somberness traced the outlines of his features.

Irritation sparked inside of her. "Why didn't you tell me earlier?"

His sorrowful expression faded. "I'm new to this 'opening up' thing."

"Hardly an excuse." Jinx snorted. Apollo pinned her down with a stare.

Yes, that's it. Get angry. Feel your sensations.

"Pardon?" he said.

Jinx flipped her hair and crossed her arms, dismissing him. "It's not an excuse for acting cowardly." At that word, Apollo clenched his jaw, restraining himself. She knew she needed to bait him even more—until the ring glowed.

"It's not cowardly to protect those I care about from myself. It's noble."

She laughed. "I do not disagree with that, but it is weak to reject everything that makes you who you are."

Apollo took a step toward her, closing the distance between them. "However, it's worth it. I'd rather put myself in harm's way to protect my family."

His words hit close to her heart as a ball of pressure rose up in her throat. His choice of words reminded her of the choices she'd made in her own life.

It was exactly what she'd done years ago after she heard her mother plead with her uncle for more money, even though his printing business at the time was nearly bankrupt. She'd heard rumors around the Slums of a woodland creature that granted wishes for a price. Eager to help her family, Jinx took the risk and sought the creature out—which is how she ended up exactly where she was now.

Alone. While her mother lived a wealthy life in Wateredge and her uncle's business prospered.

This wasn't the time to fall back into those emotions, though; she needed to get Apollo angry. By any means necessary.

"Sometimes you must have greed in your heart. Put yourself before others. Or you will get in harm's way," Jinx argued.

"You ask me to be greedy?" Apollo's winter stare raged; a blizzard captured in those stormy eyes.

His ring flared. He ignored the burn, his darkened gaze searing into hers. The last of his reserve dug into him, smoke ebbing out from the crevices of the band. Jinx's heart thrummed in her chest, unable to look away from Apollo.

Pink peered through the cracks of Apollo's gray eyes. This was becoming too much. He could not afford another fissure in that band. He was not prepared to exist without it.

Jinx blinked, severing the contact of whatever had just exchanged between them. "Next time, don't let yourself get that far. You aren't ready yet."

Apollo cleared his throat. Under his breath, she thought she heard him say something along the lines of "Devil woman."

"What do you know about your abilities now that you can speak?" She turned back to the beginning of their conversation.

Apollo pocketed his hands. "From the one time I let go of my hold, it simply destroyed anything within a mile radius."

"Destruction," Jinx repeated. "That's vague."

"It's what I know."

"The entirety of it?" She wanted to be sure there would be no more surprises.

He leaned against the wall. "Yes."

A mischievous grin sprawled across Jinx's face. She stomped over, clutching the collar of his shirt once more, hauling him outside. "What are you doing?" he asked, his voice laced with tiredness.

"We're getting supplies, Polly."

"For?"

"What else? You're going to detonate targets."

Jinx sprawled across Kovan's couch, studying the map of Somnium. She still needed to find the answer to two questions: the location of the Vessel and the meaning of the riddle.

"We're wasting time doing this." Apollo called from his chair. He was currently blind-folded, with his shirt half-buttoned and his wrists tied to the arms of the seat. Every morning for the entire week, Jinx heaved Apollo out of bed and tried different methods of figuring out what his abilities were. His strength was above average, but it wasn't the source of his power. He could not conjure illusions, change the temperature, summon ice or fire, or lift tangible objects without touching them. And he didn't have supernatural fighting abilities.

She knew Apollo described his power as some type of destruction, but she wanted to veer away from that, thinking it was too simplistic. At the beginning, he'd said that he had a voice in his head. Jinx wondered if he could use that voice to hear other's thoughts.

Jinx's next trial: try reading other people's minds. For him to rely on his mind and not his sight, she blindfolded him. He got hot, so she helped unbutton the top of his shirt. The rope around his wrists...he kept getting up, forgetting why they were there.

"No, we aren't." Jinx crossed out places she'd already search for the Vessel. Apollo rolled his shoulders, bones cracking at the motion. His chest expanded. He had been handling his emotions better as the days progressed. Sometimes, he shut down, but other times, he gave up a small laugh. There were moments where he isolated himself, pain coursing through him, but Jinx was always there, helping him whenever she could. The only restriction she'd put on him was sobriety.

Jinx sighed. The faint scent of sulfur and metal ignited a sneeze from her nose. "Does it smell like gunpowder to you in here?"

She heard mumbling in response.

"What did you say?" Jinx flipped over onto her stomach, kicking her legs in a fluttering motion as she focused on the map.

Apollo answered in the same bored tone he always did. She thought it'd never leave. It suited him, though, in some strange way, made him different from everyone else. "I said nothing."

Pressure formed in the front of her skull, snaking around to the back. It felt as if a worm had slithered into her head. Jinx cracked her neck, rubbing a finger in small circles at the area.

This is...

"This is what?" She poked at him.

Casting a glance over at her, Apollo's hands fidgeted. "I'm telling you, I said nothing."

We're wasting time. Jinx heard it again, echoing.

The sound...could it be...

"Polly." Jinx whispered. "Think your full name."

Apollo Voclaine. It was him speaking in her head. Jinx jerked from her spot, pulling down his blindfold.

"Polly, I heard you. Think something else."

Untie me. This rope has been making me itch.

And Jinx did.

Chapter 23

Apollo

The carriage rattled and bumped down the cobblestone avenue, venturing deeper into Eastern Heights. The orchestra was playing tonight, and the Seven aristocratic families had been cordially invited. Apollo dreaded these evenings, but he made an appearance on behalf of his family's reputation.

The entire Voclaine family sat in the stagecoach, their bodies wiggling to the rhythmic bumps of the street. Jinx sat adjacent to Apollo, their knees centimeters from touching each other.

Apollo couldn't deny how beautiful she looked. The upper half of her hair was tied back and woven into braids, and the rest of it cascaded down her shoulders to her waist. Kohl outlined her eyes, the emerald in her irises even more striking than usual. The dress she'd borrowed from Arya was a classic lavender, complimenting her caramel skin.

Thatcher leaned into his ear. "You're drooling, Brother."

Apollo shoved him off.

Arya, Jinx, Fey, and Mother were all talking about the Hallows Ball. The Hallows Masquerade Ball was an annual occurrence, and it marked the time when The Seven presented their projects, statistics, and projections to the rest of the city. There was also an enormous party that fostered relationships, both for business and for marriage. Plenty of suitors would be in attendance, hoping to find their future wife.

Jinx was brimming with questions about the ball.

"So how exactly does it work?" Jinx asked.

Fey straightened. "It begins with a cocktail hour as everyone arrives, and then the Dukes take another hour and a half, giving boring speeches and all. After that, the fun begins. There's dancing and drinking until there is no tomorrow."

"But," Arya interrupted, "you may only dance if a man asks you to do so and then writes his name on your dance card. If not, you are not allowed to dance. You also cannot dance more than twice with the same person unless you're trying to send a certain message."

Just like the orchestra, Apollo disliked those dances. Women always get the wrong impression. Apollo had stopped dancing years ago, though he enjoyed the art of it.

Jinx bit her lip. "How many men can write their names on my dance card?"

Fey answered this time. "Only five."

Jinx nodded slowly. Mother placed her hand on Jinx's, giving her a kind smile. "It's alright, sweetheart. We were all just as overwhelmed as you are now when we began going to these events." She fixed a stray piece of Jinx's hair behind her ear. "It's all rather fun once you understand how it works. It's very likely that you will find an interested suitor at the Hallows Ball this year. You are beautiful and of age."

Jinx dropped her head. "Thank you, Lady Voclaine."

"Mother, don't bother Veyda about marriage. What if she doesn't want a husband?" Arya warned her.

"Actually, one day, I *would* like a family. And a husband." Jinx admitted. Apollo blinked, unsure if his eyes were playing tricks on him, as he swore to the Virtues that Jinx had swiftly glanced in his direction.

Apollo turned his head, gazing at the passing buildings. His chest was suddenly tight, the tips of his ears warm. He hooked his chin on his thumb, a curled hand covering his mouth.

There was a slap of a knee, followed by his mother's voice. "You see Arya, she *does*." Mother chirped happily. "If you let me, I'd love to sponsor you this season. We could help you find a proper match and —"

"There will be no proper matches for Veyda in Somnium, Mother." Apollo spoke up. The eyes of every member of the Voclaine family glued onto to him, suddenly still. Heat coursed over his ring.

Mother gasped. "Oh, I am sorry, my dear. I did not realize you had someone back in the East waiting for you."

Jinx held Mother's hands, squeezing them affectionately. "Oh no, I do not. Please don't apologize." Pointedly, she looked at Apollo. "I do not know what your son is talking about."

The carriage came to a stop, and Apollo opened the door, his eyes darkening. "Shame."

The doors of a grand amphitheater swallowed the hoard of high-class socialites into its white marble belly. Lampposts flickered before it, ten steps apart from one another, illuminating the path before them under the blanket of the night.

Apollo analyzed everything down to the cuff links each person wore, searching for anything that could show the missing Vessel or anything that resembled the pin Jinx had found. Many of those in attendance had also been at his birthday a month ago, giving him and Jinx another chance to indulge in casual conversations with them. They wouldn't get another moment like this until the Masquerade next month.

Right now was also the perfect time to test his newfound abilities. They were still rough around the edges and not at all perfected. But if he could get into people's minds and read their thoughts—or at least attempt to do so—perhaps he could find something. He'd been practicing with Jinx a few times a day, trying to read her thoughts. She honestly believed he could do so.

Despite gaining more control of himself over the course of his training, enormous crowds still set him on edge. He tried to look at this event as another test, focusing himself on overcoming this new challenge.

A speckle of pride bloomed in Apollo's stomach when he realized he hadn't so much as smelled a bottle of liquor or breathed in the smoke of a cigarette since Jinx had laid down the law. He'd promised Jinx that he wouldn't drown in toxins to subdue his urges, and Apollo always kept his word.

He extended his hand back in, assisting his mother out of the carriage. The rest of the Voclaine family spilled out after that. At last, soft, thin fingers took his own. Recognizing her skin, Apollo's magic flared for a beat. He forced himself to breathe and control himself, clutching the thing inside him and coercing it to work *with* him.

He helped her down from the stagecoach. Jinx dusted off the skirts of her dress, priming it for entry. "Polly, what was that about?"

Apollo checked his watch. "Nothing."

Thatcher immediately stood at her side. Apollo hadn't expected Jinx to get so close to Thatcher, but he also wasn't surprised. Thatcher was Thatcher—there was no other way to explain it. "We'll see you inside, Brother." Thatcher waved off to him. "I'm off with Veyda to get some snacks."

Jinx swept a glance over her shoulder to Apollo, dipping her chin, before she left with Thatcher to go inside.

His mother had already gathered with a group of husband-hunting mothers. Closing her fan, Arya found Kateri and fell to her side, walking off, leaving Fey and him together. "I gather you don't want to be here." Fey snagged his attention.

She knew him well.

"Not particularly, no." Apollo offered his arm, and his sister held him by the crook of his elbow. They ambled into the amphitheater through the double doors, watching the glamorous false people who were prancing about, drinks in hand.

A spiderweb chandelier reflected flickers of light all around the room. Gold twirled in the crevices of the marble. Jasmine and rose fragrances tickled Apollo's nose.

His eyes swept the throng, but there was still not a pin in sight. Far in the back, where concessions were located, he spotted Jinx with Thatcher and his mother. Mother was laughing, introducing her to other people. Thatcher acted as a buffer. Apollo stared as if it were his job. Jinx grinned, curtsied, and moved on from guest to guest, her gaze searching past the crowds every once in a while.

Apollo engaged in boring conversations with other attendees and dabbled in a few games of pool with the Dukes in attendance. He attempted to use his abilities to gain more information, but he was still too weak to still use them for more than a minute at a time. The Duke of Tertain had apparently stayed home, using his daughter as an excuse. De Conto was also not in attendance. He mentally noted it for later. It was strange for them to miss an event like this.

The Duke of Kami, with Kovan by his side, bowed deep at the waist. "Your Grace, always a pleasure."

Apollo also bent down. "No need for formalities. We've known each other long enough."

"That much is true," The Duke smiled. "How's your father doing on this trip to the east?"

"He's alright. He should arrive shortly." His father hadn't sent any correspondence or even informed Apollo about the reason for his trip, but it wasn't anything unusual. Any time Apollo had tried in the past to inquire about his departures to the east, his father quickly shut him down.

"I should send over a letter soon; he and I have much to discuss." The Duke sipped on his glass of wine.

Apollo knew that he needed to tread carefully in this conversation. He wanted to ask what they had to discuss, showing the Duke that he wasn't fully aware of his father's whereabouts or his purpose over in the east. But the Duke of Kami was being vague, too—it was unclear how much he knew.

Apollo chose a safe path and kept quiet. "Certainly."

The Duke of Kami excused himself and walked over to his wife. Kovan was suddenly by Apollo's side. "I see that brain of yours working, Pol. What are you up to?"

"Nothing to worry about."

Kovan arched a knowing brow, smug. "You're different."

"Am I?" Apollo was unaware of what he was hinting at. "Last I checked, I'm still Apollo Voclaine."

His friend narrowed his hazel eyes, scrutinizing Apollo. He sniffed once, like a hound searching for a scent. "Ah. I know."

"Amuse me." Apollo willed some charisma into his tone, which was still laced with his perpetually husky boredom.

Kovan's grin expanded. "Veyda is breaking you."

Apollo showed no emotion.

"There is no way to pinpoint exactly what is different about you. You just *are*." Kovan's observation earned him a warning glare. He raised his hands in innocence, chuckling. "I'm just saying."

"The only thing breaking is my will to listen." Apollo pocketed his hands.

Kovan slung an arm around Apollo's neck. "So cross." He tapped right above Apollo's heart. "Glad to see that you started opening up this little thing to someone, though. You took my advice."

Annoyance grated across Apollo's skin.

A violin whined, echoing from the stage, alerting everyone that the show was about to begin. Apollo unwrapped Kovan from him, uttering a goodbye, and went to find his seat.

There was an open spot between Thatcher and Jinx. He sat down, counting down the minutes to their departure.

Jinx whispered to him, and the hairs on his neck stood on end. "I couldn't find anything. How about you? Did you bore the socialites until their gems dulled?"

Apollo bit the inside of his cheek, restraining a smile. "*Please.* I am more charming than you care to admit. These socialites practically begged me to marry their daughters."

"Was that before or after you opened your haughty mouth?"

"Before. And after they were already calling the priest." He leaned in. "And no, no signs of the pin anywhere. Also, two of the Dukes are not in attendance." Apollo met her eyes and careened back, giving her a look that said they would debrief after the concert.

She tapped her temple, silently asking how his head was doing. After the hours of training his abilities, Apollo suffered sharp headaches, the result of working the muscle he'd left on standby for too long.

He lifted a shoulder, motioning that it was alright.

Jinx mouthed, *try it*, encouraging him to practice on her.

Apollo fixed his stare on the stage, making it seem as if he were lost in the music that was about to begin. His ears canceled out all external sounds as his mind tried to find the thread of her consciousness, the mental wavelength she emitted in the world. He stretched a phantom hand out into the abyss in search of a thread, a way to tether himself into her mind.

There were faint murmurs of other's thoughts. He found himself weaving through a maze of intangible words—until he found *her*, her signature green light. He latched on to it as if his life depended on it.

Hello, Temptress. Apollo drawled. Beads of sweat gathered on his forehead. He really needed to build up his stamina. He glanced over at her to see if she'd heard him.

She smirked. *Good job.* He heard it inside his head, too. The two connected. *What's this about the two missing Dukes?*

Tertain and De Conto are at home. De Conto usually misses big events, so it's not that out of the ordinary. Tertain, however, never misses an appearance. Apollo clarified. The pressure was now pulsing at his temple. He massaged it, pushing through.

Jinx considered his thoughts. *The Vessel wasn't at the Tertain residence when I went there.*

I'm not talking about his house. What if he hid it somewhere else? His strength faltered, the conversation fading toward the end.

What are his motives? Jinx wondered. *Tertain seems like an unlikely culprit.*

Everyone is still a suspect right now. Apollo let go of the thread. That well of magic in his body was near depleted, tired by its continued work. His brain felt famished and fuzzy. He and Jinx had already trained once this morning. This was extra practice.

Horns from the orchestra blared, blending in with the violins, the piano, and the several other instruments Apollo couldn't name. The music was certainly beautiful, but Apollo would have still rather been at home, diving into the uncoded book.

After days of trying, he'd gotten nowhere with that volume. It felt as if he and Jinx were chasing their own tails, going in circles until they gave up. But he refused to give up. That thing trapped inside merged into his soul was desperate to find it—and Apollo had to know why. Perhaps it could somehow lead to his freedom.

As he reflected on the past few weeks, he realized that he'd never asked Jinx why she wanted to visit the Archives so badly. Originally, he hadn't bothered because he doubted that she would tell him the truth. But things between them had changed. They were closer now. Friends. He might even be able to help her just as much as she'd been able to help him. And more than anything, he *wanted* to help her.

On the day of the fire, the person he'd grown most angry with was not her but himself. He'd felt so useless that day. Jinx had jumped into the orange flames without a second thought. Apollo only went in afterward because she was already in there.

He was determined to change, to make himself useful—whether it was with the help of his abilities or not.

He felt an itch to look at Jinx and tipped his face to watch her. Apollo's breath hitched.

A single tear had slipped past her defenses and was now slithering down her cheek. His hand flexed as if he had been holding himself back from swiping it off. Jinx was stunning, and seeing her in this state of sorrow undid his heart. The jewels of her eyes were lost, hollow. The music had transported her somewhere else.

Jinx

Jinx was home. The transporting sounds of the symphony had taken her all the way back to the cottage in the Slums. Her mother and uncle were by her side. It was one of those nights where they would crack open a dusty book and tell her to read it out loud. A single candle lit up her bedroom, the orange glow casting a low luminescence around them.

They would read the same three books over and over until her uncle was able to bring home new ones. As Jinx fell asleep reading, her mother blew out the candle, inviting the moonlight into her room. Darkness hugged her, shushing her to sleep.

The orchestra softened, the tone growing light and silky.

Jinx remembered waking in the middle of the night to harsh whispers cutting the curtain that separated her room from the rest of the house.

"You'll wake her." Uncle warned.

Sleepily, Jinx slid off the bed, silently padding her way to the patched curtain.

Mother swallowed a cry. "I don't know what to do, Hugo. I barely have food to feed the two of us."

"I know. I am trying to spare some money, but I barely have anything left for myself." Uncle tried to comfort her. "Next week will be better, I promise."

"I don't want my daughter to starve. I'll pick up shifts at the bar and work two jobs." Mother wiped at a tear.

Hugo drank from his cup. "No, I'll do it. You stay and take care of her; she needs you home."

Mother disagreed. "We'll both do it. I can't keep living like this. I want better for her. With Alfie, we always had enough. We wanted more for her."

Alfie, Jinx's father, had been a laborer in Crosspoint Yard. He'd died weeks before she was born. He'd grown terribly sick while infected with the plague. Jinx had always been upset that she never got to meet him. Mother said Jinx would have liked him a great deal. She said Jinx inherited her curiosity and wit from him, not to mention the soul of a troublemaker.

Instruments Jinx couldn't distinguish trembled, increasing in speed. The tone of the music deepened and darkened, shivers rooted and webbed in Jinx's spine.

She recalled her little feet jumping out of the cottage window after overhearing that pained conversation. Jinx couldn't forget the sense of responsibility that overcame her, the need to help her family, who were suffering *because of her*.

Desperate to help them in any way she could, Jinx dove into the Woodlands by her house and searched for the same creature that she heard people run from in the middle of the night.

Apollo

Seeing Jinx so swept up in emotion, Apollo was perplexed at what course of action he should take. Nudge her out of it or leave her be?

Apollo settled for the latter, reeling back into his seat.

He wouldn't bother Jinx.

Redirecting his focus, Apollo attempted to use his abilities again. The tips of his fingers warmed and cooled at the same time. He searched the minds of those around him, swerving between the threads he found. In the sea of slow-moving ideas and reactions, a single rope fluttered in the abyss: someone was actively thinking about something other than the music. Apollo gripped onto that thread, his strength waning.

With...Vessel...finally...

The Vessel. Someone in this room knew about it. Apollo's heart kicked up, jolting at the word. His magic slowly petered out. He reached out again but couldn't relocate the thread.

Apollo leaped out of his seat, gripping the rails of the balcony reserved for his family. He searched the room frantically. Who was thinking about the Vessel? Where were they?

If only Apollo had enough endurance to try to make out the person behind that mental voice.

He'd messed up.

Apollo's body quickly gave in to the rising emotions. His magic clawed at him from the inside, wanting to rip his skin into shreds. Breath after breath, it was too much—he felt unable to control it. He swallowed a grunt. Hand gripping his heart, he could hear the organ pumping loudly in his ears. His skin was the only barrier keeping his soul together.

A sharp pain lashed up his spine, his knees beckoning for release.

Excusing himself swiftly, Apollo straight-lined to the restroom.

This type of pain wasn't really his; it came from the demon inside. He'd experienced this only twice, and both times, it seemed to be connected to the Vessel.

It was an internal ache that bled from his soul, stemming from his heart, swimming through his veins to his nervous system, rendering his muscles useless. He was unable to feel the touch of the world around him; he was no longer tangible. A throb that clawed his heart ripped it from his chest.

It wasn't just physical; the other half of him suffered as well. The demon shrieked constantly, congesting his mind. A high-pitched ringing ruptured his ears.

When Apollo's own emotions got the best of him, the pain was bearable. It hurt and ached horribly, burning him from inside out. When the Vessel activated, it felt as if his soul had been ripped in two. The demon inside of him clawed away. A question Apollo had yet to answer was: What was happening on the other side that caused the Vessel to act in such a way, hurting him?

The silver band coiled around his finger, seething, struggling to contain the nightmare.

Once locked inside the restroom, Apollo's legs collapsed beneath him. He crashed onto the floor, cradling his chest. His core boiled to a burning point, hot blood pouring into every vein it found. Apollo bit into his hand, trying to focus on anything but this catastrophic pain. But it was difficult to focus on this bite when his body was engulfed in what felt like flames. He ripped off his shirt, the cool breeze choking on the heat that radiated from him. Senseless trembles overtook his body as his sight started to blur.

This time, Apollo screamed.

The Virtue of Death was upon him. Akuji was waiting in the corner with his silver scale, weighing the worth of his soul.

Darkness encompassed the space, twilight hugging him in a soft embrace. The burning was suddenly gone. The ache is gone. He just was.

Apollo saw green, a type of green that lived within one being. A green that animated priceless jewels, reminding him of life.

"Polly." She bellowed. Out of all the names he'd been given, that one had to be his —

Apollo lurched forward, heaving out his dinner and arriving at the toilet just in time. His head was hanging in the bowl.

"Polly," she said again, almost sounding worried.

"What happened?" Jinx crouched beside him.

He wiped his mouth with the back of his hand, returning to his normal state. "Someone in the crowd has the Vessel or knows something about where it is. I heard a piece of their thoughts, but then my magic died, and *this* happened."

"I don't understand. How can your abilities wane and then overtake you in a matter of seconds?"

Apollo came clean, telling Jinx about how he believed that the Vessel might be tied to the voice inside of him, admitting the real reason that he was searching for this ancient artifact. The voice was his tipping point of secrecy; Apollo Voclaine had none anymore. Her expression contorted; he couldn't read if she was angry or not. No, it wasn't wrath—it was hurt and disappointment.

Her brows pinched. "You should have told me, even if it was just a suspicion."

"I know."

"You keep nothing else from me, understood? You said you were opening up."

Apollo swayed back, his strength building bit by bit. "I know."

Jinx gripped his arm and slung it over her shoulders, supporting his weight. His head bobbed, vision swiftly darkening.

A soft, nurturing hand cupped his jaw, brushing his cheek. Apollo shuddered.

"You, okay?"

He snapped back to reality. Jinx's touch was so alluring; he felt an instinctual urge to pull her closer, embrace her, dig his head into her neck and just hold her.

Yet, his brain made him shake off her palm. He rasped, glancing away. "You might be worth keeping around."

Jinx brushed off the comment. "Yeah, you're alright."

He cleared his throat. "May I ask you something?"

Jinx responded with silence. Taking it as her form of acceptance, he asked, "What are you so desperately searching for?"

Apollo watched her contemplative face as she considered how she should respond, or if she should at all.

Cracking her fingers in thought, she exhaled, "A way home."

He masked his automatic wince, resenting the feeling that overcame him.

Chapter 24

Jinx

J inx reveled in the sensation of her heart beating out of her rib cage. Heat swarmed up to her neck, beads of sweat trickling down her front and spine. Autumn winds rolled in from the north, the chill countering her rising body temperature.

She skimmed from building to building, her feet dipping featherlight touches on each roof before reaching another. It was the closest she'd ever gotten to the bliss of flying. Freedom felt just a step away.

It was Jinx's way of clearing her mind.

The moon was resting on its nightly throne, pools of silver light fighting against the shadows clinging to the darkness. Autumn neared the tents of Akuji's cirque, peeking over the flood of buildings.

Jinx breathed. Her body was running on a high. The serenity of the sleeping city entered the marrow of her bones. Peace. Even the constant bangs of Crosspoint Yard had silenced themselves in honor of the moon's rise.

Her feet dug into the flat concrete on the roof. Pulling off her hood, she let the howling wind caress her braided hair. Jinx sat on the ledge of the building, her feet dangling. Maybe since she'd lived most of her life up high and uncontained, being outside, almost in the sky, relaxed her.

Jinx had attempted for days to get Apollo to use his magic on the book or even just to connect with it, connect with the voice inside. He stubbornly refused each time. If Apollo genuinely believed the Vessel was tied to his magic, the voice, then there could only be one of two explanations.

Maybe the history of the Vessel was connected with the history of the Cursed. If that *was* true, however, it presented them with a new question: why did it only seem to affect Apollo?

The other possibility was that Apollo was just as connected to the book as he was to the Vessel since both called to him so similarly.

She had to figure out how to convince him to use his magic in the book. Hopefully, he could locate the place of the Vessel quicker, like responding to a signal. Just like he did whenever he was reading someone's mind.

His abilities had improved rather quickly in recent days. A sense of pride fluttered in her stomach. She saw the crumbs of the confident man Arya had described. Slowly, day by day, he dropped the veil of his stony façade.

Apollo was good, her total opposite. Unlike him, Jinx was selfish. She murdered and manipulated people, among thousands of other crimes. He deserved a kind lady, someone to complement him. Not someone like her. She had no reason to think they could ever work.

Her heart squeezed.

Jinx dug the heels of her palms into her eyes, emitting a dreadful groan and falling back onto her spine. "What's wrong with me?" She murmured lowly to herself.

Think logically.

Her heart and her brain were in constant battle these days. Her mind kept pushing her to find the Vessel, the answer to the riddle, and then leave. Go home, as her original plan dictated. But her heart begged her to listen—to *stay*—whispering in her ear that *this* could be her new home, that the Voclaines could be... that Apollo could...No.

She couldn't. Jinx had fed all of them spoons of lies, each one eating her false truths up.

She knew Apollo looked at her differently than others did. Past the ice of his glacial gray eyes, he didn't look at her with terror, or hate, or disgust—as she thought he would when they first met. He gazed at her like a friend would. Or maybe even something more. His siblings weren't afraid of her either. Fey smiled at her, and Thatcher toyed with her as a sibling would. Even Arya and Jinx now understood each other a little better.

The back of Jinx's eyes burned. She sniffed. Unaware of when it happened, she realized that the Voclaine siblings had gotten under her skin, wrapping their welcoming fingers around her core.

She thought of the horrible feeling of joy she felt when she watched them interact, tinged with the jealousy of what she never had. She admired their bond. Admired them.

Despite her stillness, her chest unconsciously thudded harder, her hands trembling. She'd grown weak. Jinx had grown terrified. She was scared of the moment when she'd be forced to leave this life behind because, out of all the realities she'd lived since striking that bargain, Jinx truly favored this one. She painfully cared about each and every member of the Voclaine family.

Needing an outlet, Jinx punched the floor next to her. She bit out a single word: "*Fuck.*"

A better person would pull back and distance themselves. But she knew doing that would only make the family suspicious. And Jinx wasn't a better person. She was greedy selfish, and ambitious. So, Jinx would go on. She would enjoy this life down to the last speck of dust on her vanity. She would let herself have the friends she always wished for. And then, she would leave. No matter the cost, no matter the pain.

It couldn't hurt any more than what she'd already lost.

Since originally granting her wish and striking the bargain with her, the creature from the woods hadn't come to see her again, but she'd never forget the riddle it had left behind. The riddle that took everything from her. If she were able to crack the answer anytime before she turned twenty-one, Jinx could be with her family again. If it came to the unwanted result, Jinx would be lost from their memories for good. Completely and utterly forgotten.

In the table where five once sat, now sit four

No matter how much you believe, our minds still deceive

It's a punishment for seeking the truth

Knit from people's worst desires

One who seeks is bound to bloom

It made no sense. No direction, nothing. The riddle was everywhere and nowhere. What table of five? There were seven ruling Dukes, so it couldn't be referring to them. There were five sections of Somnium. Two types of people.

There *were* four Virtues. She thought of the painting back at Apollo's birthday gala. The one containing the four Virtues and the man hidden within the depths, scratched off by the artist. What his purpose was intruding that setting. Perhaps they had once been five; perhaps there was a forgotten Virtue.

If that *was* the case, there would be legends and stories of that missing Virtue hidden somewhere in the city. She considered the next line: *no matter how much you believe, our minds still deceive.* Why does not one have a recollection of the supposed man? Is that why history books from decades ago felt like they were missing something?

She'd fallen down this road before. Lacking the proper information to proceed with that line of thought.

Jinx smacked her forehead.

Jinx jumped to her feet. In a matter of seconds, she was jumping from building to building once more, leaving her half-witted ideas behind.

She stopped just before reaching Kovan's warehouse. His foxhole. As she pivoted on the tips of her toes to leave, a boom ricocheted. A shock of adrenaline shot through her body, Jinx's limbs losing their agility. Then, another explosion, the ripples of sound screaming from the hideout.

Jinx leaped onto the warehouse. Crawling down the side with spider-like nimbleness, she peered inside the tall window.

Her mouth snapped open, finally understanding what Arya and Kateri's "Book Club" was all about.

Apollo

Apollo juggled the pin and the check, both etched with the name A.D. Marianna in his hands.

Flipping through the pages in the city directory, he first looked through all the names beginning with the letter "A," then "D," then the first and last names of "Marianna."

Frustrated, he fled downstairs to his father's study, infiltrating the library as he searched through company files, peering at the names that were signed under each corporation. Since the name had been engraved on the back of a fancy pin, it was possible that A.D. Marianna was the owner of the company or that A.D. Marianna was the company itself, ringing too much like a person's name.

Apollo turned over the red oak office, splaying papers and articles everywhere. But he couldn't find a trace of this character, this A.D. Marianna. The name wasn't written in any taxes, privacy policies, or agreements.

He pulled the check from his pocket, inspecting it for the thousandth time.

The top of the paper ripped, the tear jutting into the payment. The payer must have been in a rush to write the check. Dots of extraneous ink peppered the signature box. Ink coated the supposed Bank sigil, Apollo held it up to a light. Pouring through, a black crow with spread wings. Blackbird Central Bank, an elite institution that only served the top five percent of Somnium, had stamped its logo on the bottom left corner. All of the Seven did their banking there. The roster of potential culprits slimmed down considerably.

Apollo returned to his father's ledgers, pulling out all the accounts from Blackbird. He thanked the Virtues for his father's position as the Seven, as the city's head of economic policy.

Searching through the balance sheets of each corporation and their business plans, he found A.D. Marianna. It was an import corporation that brought in zinc from the East in order to help manufacture steel.

That would explain the manufacturing of the pins and how they were able to be forged at a mass level. To reach that many people, the corporation would need hubs to distribute.

Apollo further explored the business plan, discovering that the location of the distributor was in the Tents. That's where they'd have to go if they wanted to find more answers.

He wrote down the address of the corporation headquarters in Crosspoint Yard and the name of the distributor in the Tents. He wanted to try to figure out as much background information as he could before approaching them.

Apollo glanced at the title of A.D. Marianna one last time. There was something bothering him about the name. It had to do with the arrangement of the letters; they didn't quite fit right together in his brain.

He scratched his temple and wrote down the name on a piece of paper. Singling out each of the letters, he organized them in different orders again and again. What *was* it about that name?

He thought back to the clues he had so far. Blackbird Central Bank. The clientele is in the top five percent of the city. Steel manufacturing. Who had the connections to produce in bulk and distribute with ease? The funds to make it all happen at the snap of a finger, beneath the eyes of the Seven. Not even go through the proper processes of having business approval.

Apollo's heart dropped as he finally figured out the correct letter order.

A.D. Marianna must be none other than Amaan Nadir, one of the Seven.

Apollo launched himself from the office, stomach flipping. The ring burned his hand, but he didn't care, not right now. It was all too much to process. How was this possible?

Nadir had never raised any arguments against the Cursed nor for them in the House. He has all the power to mass-produce the pins. Apollo could quite pinpoint the motive for which Nadir would encourage such a hate; typically, he tended to stay on neutral grounds. There was more, so much more; he just had to dig deeper.

Sleep evaded Apollo, stranding him with his eyes wide open. He decided to write in his notebook, his scribbling pencil jotting down every thought, every feeling. It had been both his refuge and his vice since that day he returned from the woods. Eight years of his mind and caged heart, all recorded on paper.

He began with a written rant about his most recent discovery but quickly turned the topic to his fight with Jinx. She had been trying to convince him to use his magic on the black leather volume, the one saved from the fire.

Apollo knew Jinx had good reason to make her suggestions; she clearly thought they could use it to their advantage. After he explained his theory that he shared some sort of connection with the Vessel, Jinx had tried to get him to incorporate the book into their training. But the thing inside of him recoiled from the idea to use his abilities on it. The mere thought of it made the demon shrivel up as if it did not want to confront the secrets within it.

Strange if the demon was the reason why he'd picked it up in the first place. And now it wants nothing to do with it. It made Apollo yearn to learn what the book contained, what caused that thing inside him to retreat so harshly.

Despite his initial hesitations, he knew the next logical step to take would be to confront the demon, even though he *hated* it, hated that part that had etched such a dark mark on his soul.

He wanted to become better, wanted to change. For himself, for his family, for her. Apollo no longer wanted to hold her back. She *deserved* more so he would become more.

His quill snapped in half, black ink pooling on the edge of the page and staining the side of his palm. "Tsk." Apollo sucked on his teeth, pushing back his chair. He plucked his handkerchief out of his pocket, wiping down the area. "Damn the Virtues."

Figaro meowed from the bed.

"If you don't want to hear it, cover your ears." Apollo answered, exhaling sharply through his nose. Gracefully, Figaro sprung onto Apollo's desk, his white and gray tail swaying. He nudged his soft head into Apollo's neck, clearly wanting to be cuddled. Figaro scaled his shoulders, fitting himself around Apollo's neck like a scarf and purring as Apollo scratched a single finger under his chin. Apollo relented a smirk. "You're so *needy*."

Figaro ignored him, focusing simply on the caresses he was receiving.

Warmth gathered uncomfortably around the ring, but Apollo let it simmer. He wanted to build up his stamina, strengthening the organ inside. How much longer could he fight what he is? Deny that part of himself that held him back for as long as he could remember? Apollo had grown tiresome of the chronic battlefield in his mind. Restricting the wants of his soul and heart.

Since training with Jinx and sobering, Apollo felt cleaner and better. Hopefully, he could reach peace. Learning that the only way forward was to embrace what he was, not shrivel up and cower in a corner.

As much as he despised the demon living inside of him, he knew he would need to accept its magic in order to gain control over his abilities.

A ripple of energy blew against his shoulder, and he realized it came from the leather book shelved in the corner of his room. Figaro scurried down to the bed.

Interesting, Apollo thought, that his cat could feel its power, too.

Apollo pried the book from its spot, splitting it wide open. Wrinkles of energy expanded out, and the ink on the paper started swirling, letters rearranging, diagrams forming. Apollo itched to touch it, to dive in and figure out why he reacted so strongly to it, even as his primal senses told him to stay away.

The end of his skull flared, a phantom finger digging into his mind.

You are not ready. The grating voice whispered in the back of his head.

Apollo sank his teeth into his tongue, stopping himself from talking back to that thing.

Come on, ask me. The demon prodded. Apollo could feel it smile inhumanly.

Apollo pursed his lips. A dam within him was holding back an ocean of questions. He could feel that their dislike of one another was mutual, that the demon understood Apollo's resentment toward it.

The demon gave a low hum in response: *I know all your thoughts...* The voice venomously spits out the name Jinx so often used: *Polly.* Apollo's heart dropped to the floor, his outer reaction concealed. The demon was trying to get him to talk; that much was clear.

Magic built up beneath his skin. Apollo did everything he could to hold back his emotions. Training with Jinx had helped him incredibly, but would a few weeks be enough to truly change him?

Pity. The voice hissed and disappeared as if it had never existed to begin with.

What exactly wasn't Apollo ready for? The demon's words were vague and open-ended, with hundreds of possible answers that could be used to fill in the blank. Apollo snapped the volume shut, shelving it between the other books in the case. The clock chimed three in the morning. His fingers ached from clutching the quill so tightly for hours.

Apollo swiftly glanced over at the window, wondering when she'd return. He was concerned for her safety, of course. Since Jinx left—the moment his magic had felt her departure—Apollo had stuck his nose back in his notebook to distract himself.

Just then, his organ of magic twitched, sensing her return. Jinx never made a sound, neither when leaving nor re-entering the house at night. He figured she left nightly to patrol, run, and feel the freedom she'd been so used to.

Guilt wrapped around his brain when he thought about how he'd stayed at the manor the whole time. "I'm working on becoming *better*." He muttered to himself in assurance.

What was he *doing*? He was acting as if he were drowning in some sort of illness, and she was his cure. He reminded himself that Jinx helping him out was purely transactional. This entire relationship was transactional from start to finish. She'd get whatever answers she sought from the archives, and he'd get his Vessel. After that, they'd go their separate ways.

But why did that last thought not sit right with him?

Apollo groaned. "Emotions are messy, fickle things," he said to himself.

He looked down, noticing that his hand still embraced the spine of the heavy book.

The demon had warned him that he wasn't ready, but the only way to get ready was to try. To build up to it. And he remembered one important thing he had lost sight of recently.

He was Apollo Voclaine, next in line to be one of the Seven. *No one* told him what he was or wasn't ready for; he would decide for himself

Apollo summoned the organ closer to his skin, pushing out a controlled percent of his ability. The leather shuddered then latched onto him, its magic swirling around him, recognizing him. The ring burned into his finger, but he rammed more of himself into the magic, ignoring the unavoidable mark that would inevitably follow.

Images flashed behind his eyes, memories that the demon embedded in his mind. Flashes of the dammed Woodlands, the experiences that the nightmare underwent, the starvation, the dismembering of animals, the demon camouflaging with its surroundings. The nightmare spent a lot of time analyzing the humans who wandered by horseback, categorizing their traits.

Apollo rummaged through the memories, pushing more of his magic into the book as the bookshelf began to quake.

Apollo's breath died in his lungs. What Apollo witnessed next, he knew he could never tell Jinx.

Jinx

Jinx was still processing what she'd witnessed at Kovan's foxhole. The smell of gunpowder lingered there for a reason. Not just because the warehouse was located in Crosspoint Yard but because Kateri was a sharpshooter and Arya was skilled in knife throwing.

But those weren't just any knives. They originated from her fans. Arya must've been so protective of her collection of hand fans because there were blades encased within them. She watched Arya flick her wrist, blades ejecting out of the fan's skeleton, cocking her hand back and striking a bullseye at the target in front of her.

Kateri loaded two bullets into her rifle, rested the firearm on her shoulder, closed one eye, and pulled the trigger twice. Both bullets ripped through the target in the center white dot.

As the women repeated the circuit over and over, a list of questions flooded Jinx's mind.

How had they learned to do that? Where had they learned to do that? Who was their instructor? What did they plan to do with these finely honed skills?

Jinx realized that Arya could have very well slaughtered Velez that day at the plaza if she had wanted to do so. The weight of her fans now made sense. And Kateri must've been defensive of her duffle bag at Kovan's because that's where she kept her own weapons.

Were there more of them? Who led this so-called "book club?"

Jinx had sprinted home after she saw the supposed book club in action. The lights of Thatcher's home lab up in the attic were still on, so Jinx showered quickly and went in to see Thatcher.

She massaged her head. "Have you seen Arya tonight?"

"Can't say I have. She's out with her book club tonight, isn't she?"

"Yes. Book club." Jinx noticed that Thatcher was getting jittery. "When do you ever get any rest?" Jinx ruffled Thatcher's soft, raven hair. His attention was currently fixed on the electrical current he was testing on.

Jinx sat down on a stool in the corner of his home lab. She flipped casually through his physics books, incapable of understanding this language. Numbers and alphabetic letters mixed together like this should be illegal. It made *no sense*.

Thatcher twisted over his shoulder, lifting the circular goggles from his face. Imprints of the glasses rimmed Thatcher's eyes. "Who said I get any rest?" He arched a brow. Thatcher shut off the experiment, crossing the attic floor. He peeled off the black gloves and sat down adjacent to her. "May I ask why you are visiting me at three in the morning, Miss Collymore?"

Jinx sank back into the wall, crossing her arms. "Apparently, sleep eludes me tonight. Have you continued your research on the properties of energy and our open system?"

Thatcher flinched. "You listened."

"Yes."

His eyes lightened. "It's actually what I'm working on now." He kicked his hips off the chair, returning to the project. Thatcher's body language told her that he wanted her to follow. Jinx placed herself next to him, watching his fingers play with the mechanism of wires and metal on the table.

His jittery nature returned. Whenever excitement controlled him, he rambled, his mind processing information faster than his mouth allowed.

"Since our last conversation, I realized I should conduct the experiment on my own. It's been my little side project. I'm trying to figure out whether my theory is correct, if the Cursed are indeed beings that can tap into the fundamentals of our world." Thatcher paused for a second, contemplating. From beneath his desk, he pulled out a thick file, a heavy stack of papers thumping down onto the wood. "Come look."

He opened up the file, which contained pictures, diagrams, and reports on the Cursed.

"I took this from Warren's lab without him knowing, but these are autopsies performed on the Cursed. For some reason, this information has been kept confidential; perhaps the university planned on publishing it sooner or later. But from this file, it's clear that the Cursed have this unique organ in their body; instead of having nine major organs like humans, they have ten. It's right in front of their kidneys. It's not *exactly* an organ, I guess, but it's not a muscle either. It's strange, and scientists so far haven't been able to name or categorize it. This *thing* affects their whole system, which explains a lot of differences we find in their blood, skin composition, and so on.

"I am not a Cursed, so to try and replicate what that organ can do, I am using electricity. Electricity is still something fairly new in our world, but it is proven that there is an electrical charge all around us all the time. Even in our own bodies. Now, with *this*," Thatcher flipped a switch on the side of the board, allowing an electrical current to bleed between two points of metal. "I am trying to get the current to find other charges in the air without siphoning through the metal." He flipped the contraption off. "So, what do you think?"

Jinx blew out a stream of air. "I think...It's substantial progress. I am not a scientist nor a Cursed, so I cannot offer much advice. But my support is there nonetheless." She wasn't sure what she thought about his theory, but she knew that this experiment was revolutionary. Still, one thing was left on her mind.

"You said Warren had these files stored?" That must be where he'd acquired the information that inspired his new contraption, the one he was hoping would help him understand and then exterminate all of the Cursed.

"Correct. Look, even in their brains, their cerebellum—the part that controls motor functions—is bigger than ours. I'm assuming it is because it talks directly to that muscle of theirs. Isn't it *fascinating*?"

That was something new to her. Jinx had never realized the brains of the Cursed were different than other humans. Did that render them a different species?

"Indeed." She murmured. There was so much that could be done with this information, for good and for evil. She worried about the likelihood that the Cursed would be killed to obtain more answers. "With all of this, do you think that a Cursed could be mentally linked with another Cursed?"

Slowly, she'd move the conversation toward the underlying question she'd long wondered.

"Like a twin flame?" Thatcher asked.

A soul-bound connection with another was the *last* thing on Jinx's mind. She wasn't even sure twin flames existed.

"No," she said. "Think of it as an energy sense. Like a rope tethering two beings together, because they can connect to each other telepathically, through this fundamental of our universe."

Thatcher scratched under his chin in thought. "That certainly would be something to test. In other words, you're wondering if the Cursed have some sort of telepathic network. That brings up another question, though. Within a network, there is always a primary source. A central hub. What would it be for the Cursed?"

In the Collection, Jinx had shied away from the thick leather book because of some primal instinct within her. But Apollo had reached for it, just as he did with the Vessel. If the Cursed were a network of beings, all connected to a central entity, shouldn't Jinx be able to feel fellow beings in her vicinity? Or, at least, feel some sort of connection to this source? Jinx started wondering whether, in fact, this centralizing source was not a person but an object.

Jinx was suddenly dumbstruck; without Thatcher, she wouldn't know how she'd have ever been able to retrieve this information.

"Have I mentioned you're my favorite of the Voclaine siblings?"

Thatcher shrugged his shoulders, self-assurance dripping from him. "Well, I won't say it hasn't gone unnoticed."

"You're my favorite." Jinx repeated.

"Don't tell Pol that; he might get jealous."

She snorted. "Let's hope we live to see the day." She left Thatcher, hastily speeding to Apollo's room.

She knocked three times on his door. He was still awake; she knew it. Returning earlier, she glimpsed light illuminating dimly his chambers. Jinx curled her knuckles to tap once more. The door squirmed open, revealing Apollo on the other side, encased by a faint glow.

A sheen of sweat glistened on his forehead. Shallow, quiet breaths covered his panting. His expression, however, was as calm and collected as always.

"We need to talk," Jinx said.

"Yes. We do."

Chapter 25

Apollo

"So let me get this straight. After speaking with my brother on his theory that the same energy that surrounds us is also inside of us, you've concluded that the Cursed are a network of beings that are linked to one source. And you believe the book or the Vessel might be that source." Apollo summarized everything that Jinx had just explained to him.

"Yes."

Apollo leaned back into his chair, crossing a leg over the other casually. "A network doesn't always have to have a centralized object."

Jinx paced around Apollo's chambers, talking and walking at the same time. "Agreed. But *think* about it. We both reacted so strongly to the book and the Vessel. They were two opposite reactions, yet strong reactions nonetheless. Both artifacts have unknown origins as well. The other thing that has an unknown origin to this day is the plague that had caused this mayhem of Cursed. All dating back to the same time, making an appearance twenty years ago. What if one of these objects is what started the plague in the first place, infecting parts of the network?"

"Controlling the Cursed." Apollo added, deep in thought.

"We know there is some sort of link between you and the book, plus the Vessel and whoever has their hands on it," Jinx said.

"That could be a possible fourth motive for the person who stole the Vessel. Maybe they want to control or eradicate the Cursed, just like that person you overheard with the pin said." He sighed. "We must find a way to attend the Autumnal Equinox. Whoever is hosting this assembly could very well be the culprit. And the meeting is not for another two weeks."

A sudden glint brightened his eye as he toyed with the pin clasped between his fingers. Jinx could not place it, but his gaze did not leave the pin. "I looked into this pin's history a bit more. The distributor of this pin started his company as a tribute to his lost daughter, who had been infected during the plague twenty years ago. Behind the pin, you can see the marking of when it was established. The zinc alloy used in this pin comes from a corporation from Crosspoint Yard under the name of A.D. Marianna. There is no person under the name of A.D. Marianna in Somnium nor in the East. However, if you rearrange these letters, they spell out the name Amaan Nadir."

"One of the Seven." Jinx followed. "He was also at the amphitheater when you heard someone saying that they had the Vessel. You believe he took it?"

"I believe we may have a lead."

Apollo couldn't confront him directly, though. If he were to speak to Nadir about this corporation, it would raise too many questions. If they wanted to confirm their theory, it would have to be Jinx who pursued the lead. "I'll talk to him. I can pretend to be an investor interested in his company."

"And I'll go to the distributor in two days. They have a stand in the Tents, open during work hours."

A giddy feeling of joy crept into Jinx's spine. At last, some pieces felt like they were starting to fall into place. She was one step closer to going home.

"What's with that face?" Apollo interrupted, his voice flat and husky.

You could always count on Apollo Voclaine to give you a well-rounded compliment.

"I can't be your instructor for everything, Polly."

"Excuse me?" A twitch in his brow, which seemed almost light and joking. It was so different from the version of him she'd first met.

"I'm already helping you hone your abilities. I cannot teach you how to compliment a lady as well. Or even how to make a comment that does not sound remotely offensive." Jinx sat atop Apollo's desk, her feet swinging in the space between her body and the floor.

Apollo swiftly gazed at the ground and back at her with a tick in his jaw. Jinx had named this peculiar expression the face of resistance. It was stoic, but she could see bits of his emotions leaking out beneath it. When it became too much, he took a beat to calm down his feelings before speaking.

"I can compliment a lady properly whenever I choose," he said defensively.

Jinx argued back. "Then you must never choose to do so."

"False." A shadow of amusement licked the lines of his face. "I complimented you."

"Once. And it was to beat me at a chess game that I was clearly winning."

He stood from his chair and flipped it around, straddling it, looking up at her through his thick lashes. "That may be so, but it does not make it any less true. And if you are still prickly about that game, we can have a rematch. I can assure you, I'll win again."

"I doubt you will, especially if you had to resort to such tactics to be victorious in the first place." Jinx sighed. "It does not change the fact that your compliments and your statements have a..." Jinx paused, searching for the proper fit. "Disdainful tone."

Apollo remained in place. "'Disdainful' means that I have a lack of respect when I speak. I guess I am more transparent than one may think, then—I don't respect many. People these days are so shallow. Why would I give my respect to someone with half a brain who cares solely for status?"

"Because as one of the future Seven. You must respect all your people, should you not?"

"It is hard to respect people when all they strive for is momentary pleasure. Status is not all that matters in the world."

"For you. But to them, it does. It is all about perspective and what is genuine in their reality. Just as you treasure your own values, status for them is inextricable from their method of survival. It is something you wouldn't know since you have been born into the highest rank of society. And if you are so set that it is not the world you want, one that holds class to such a high regard, then change it. If anyone has the ability to do so, it is you."

Apollo's pupils dilated. He lifted off the seat, pushing it back toward his desk. He pulled open a drawer and dug in. A click sounded. He handed over a notebook to her, an oak dust jacket wrapping around hardback.

"What's this?" Jinx eyed it suspiciously.

"Read." He instructed.

Jinx flipped to the first page, then the second, then the third. The pages were filled with information, numbers, and statistics on Somnium's economy and notes on all of the people and their businesses. They were studies he'd conducted himself, dated from the first time he'd set foot in the House of Lords.

"You've been wanting to change Somnium from the beginning," she said breathlessly, almost in awe. Jinx realized she had misjudged him completely at the beginning of their friendship.

Apollo dipped his chin. "Somnium has the resources to improve life for our people. Our technology is capable of going beyond what we think. Education as well. If possible, I'd like for our society to value intelligence over what they wear. It's not possible to change everyone's ideals, but slowly...I just want a world where people don't have to hide behind a mask, whatever that mask may be."

Well said, Apollo Voclaine. Well said. Jinx wished for a world like that. Maybe someday she'd get to see it. "I'm sure you will make that happen, Polly." As a joke, she added, "Will you also stop women from being treated as if they're cattle when it comes to marrying them off?"

The barest smirk lined his face. "That will be one of the first on my list."

Jinx returned the book, and Apollo dropped it in its compartment. "Until then, my priorities are different —"

"Yes. The Vessel." Jinx cut in.

"No," he said. She flinched at her mistake. Where were these miscalculations coming from? It was so unlike her, but it was only with him. "The Vessel is one of my priorities, but I have one more. What is it *you* are searching for, Temptress?"

Jinx could have sworn to the Virtues that she'd heard him wrong. "What?"

"You want to go in the Archives; you said something in there makes you think it's your ticket home. What is it you're searching for?"

She could hear the sincerity in his tone, the earnest desire to help her. "If this is repayment for your training, I don't want it."

"It is not." Apollo quipped, taking a considerable step closer.

"Is it pity?"

"I don't do pity, clearly."

Jinx hadn't told anyone about the riddle or why she thought the answer to it was tucked in the Archives. She'd kept it close to her heart. Her hands clammed, and her chest squeezed. If she was being totally honest with herself, she *wanted* to tell him. She actually longed to tell him how she overheard her mother crying to her uncle. Tell him how she faced the masked creature, no matter how terrified she had been, and asked for endless wealth, and it, in return, wanted her to suffer the truth of solidarity. Tell him that if she doesn't solve this riddle within the year, not only would she befriend seclusion from her own kin, but they'd forget her as well.

Apollo was the first person in a long time who had seen her without any illusions. The only person she'd been able to confide in. She'd also grown comfortable with his family as well, another group of people who'd now seen her real face.

Still, Jinx didn't trust anyone but herself. Trust meant letting another person in, giving them access to a piece of her heart, which had little room. But trust also meant having a friend, a companion, and someone you didn't have to lie to.

She stared directly into his winter eyes, the glacial storm churning. She decided to take a leap of faith. "The answer to a riddle."

Apollo blinked. "Why do you think the answer is in the Archives?"

"I've raided every library I know, searched every known and unknown crevice of Somnium for hints and clues as to what it might be. The last place left for me to check is the Archives."

"You need to solve a riddle so you can go home? Why can't you go home now?" Apollo crossed his arms. It felt wrong to tell him, to lay on her burdens when he already faced enough of his own. Her mind tugged at her to pull back, retreat, and go to bed. She could solve it on her own. But her heart urged her to tell him her story since he was someone who could listen and be there for her.

I can't go home because he'll take everything away from them. The words died on her tongue, though she wanted to tell him. If she went home without solving the riddle, the twelve-year sacrifice she'd made—being homeless, parentless, and forced to live in solitude—would have been all for nothing.

Words failed her. Averting was better than offering either the truth or a lie.

"It would break the deal." Jinx leaped off his desk with as much grace as Figaro. "I should be on my way. The sun will rise soon."

She could tell that there was more on Apollo's mind that he wanted to say, but Jinx didn't want to hear it, didn't want to hear his thoughts. It was too much for her. She could only show so much weakness, and there was only so much she could take in return.

The door squealed, Jinx halfway out. "Take care of that burn on your finger. I don't know what you were doing, but I can only assume you were practicing your magic in some way. Just do me a favor, Polly. I know I said to connect with that book, but please be careful. It might be more dangerous than we know."

Jinx shut the door behind her, a harsh *thunk* indicating that she'd closed it harder than she'd intended. She cursed herself as she went to bed, realizing that her words had given away how much she cared.

Chapter 26

Apollo

A pollo nearly tripped over his own two feet as Fey hauled him downstairs.

Every year, once the trees in Somnium turned orange, Fey demanded a sibling outing: a mandatory trip to the maze in Botanic Plaza. It was a tradition that she'd created for all of them to share. Whoever found their way to the end of the maze first would then get the biggest slice of their mother's cinnamon apple cake. Mother only made her famous cake once a year, so that prize was motivation enough for each sibling to give it their all. Even when the cake was no longer enticing, the siblings still valued the tradition as an excuse to spend time together.

Arya interjected Fey's path, grabbing her shoulders and bringing her to a halt. "Will you calm down? You're going to kill Pol, and there is no rush to get to the maze."

Fey panted, blowing a caramel hair out of her face. Excitement filled her eyes to the brim, near popping out of the sockets. "Yes. There is. We have to get there before—"

"Before all the waffles are gone." Thatcher rounded the corner into the hallway, finishing his twin's sentence. "If you don't get your lucky waffle, you won't find the end of the maze."

Fey released her tight grip on Apollo's hand. She grunted, using her tall, lean frame to meet Thatcher on even land. They may have been twins, but they couldn't have been more different if they tried. For one, Fey dyed her hair lighter to differentiate herself from her brother. And while Thatcher lived on science and math, Fey breathed literature and the arts. Their stark differences made them prone to clashing with one another, even if they loved each other.

"I don't see *you* training for hours on end to perform in the theatre one day, on a strict diet to keep your health pristine. So *excuse m*e if I want to let myself enjoy a sugary delicacy," she said.

Thatcher's eyes thinned. He was just as serious about this tradition as Fey was; they all were. "Not if I get to them first." Mischief lined his face.

Fey shoved him aside and ran for the door, Thatcher hot on her tail. Arya was right behind them, screaming, "Hey! I'm part of this, too." With a foot out the door, Arya abruptly dug her heels and looked over her shoulder at Apollo. "Are you coming? The twins won't wait for you."

Apollo pivoted, walking back upstairs. "Go on. I don't need a head-start to win."

Arya snorted, picking up the ends of her lilac dress before running off to catch her siblings.

Standing amidst the chaos that his siblings had left in their wake, Apollo's stomach clenched. A strange, empty void opened within him, and he found himself wondering why Jinx wasn't around. Jinx opened her door just as Apollo lifted his hand to knock.

Her sleek obsidian hair, which was so long that it reached the end of her back, was now done up in two braids, circling her head as if to create a crown. She had a novel in hand, the same novel that had left her so flustered before. Jinx was planning on staying in, but she blinked out that possibility at the sight of him. "I thought you left."

"I thought you were coming." Apollo countered.

Jinx leaned on the door behind her. "Fey yelped something about a family tradition. I assumed it was best to stay behind and leave you four to it." Her gaze softened at the word "family," as if hinting at a weakness that she felt vulnerable admitting.

A desire to wipe away her somber expression overcame him, just as a flare of heat warmed his muscles and chills frosting over his skin.

"And you believed staying here was the better option?" Apollo carefully snaked a hand to the handle of the door, opening the entrance to her room. "May I?" he asked, without really giving an option.

Jinx dipped her chin. "I'm going to allow it. Only because I'm curious to know what you want from my chambers."

"Curiosity killed the cat." Apollo swept past her, careful to not touch her. He opened the arms of her armoire, looting through the few outfits she had. That wasn't really hers. But considering her lifestyle, Jinx didn't really have anything of her own, did she? Apollo made a mental note to change that.

Her voice called to him from behind. Apollo was actively aware of every comment she made. "And a cat has nine lives."

Apollo found her coat, took it off the hanger, and wrapped it over his forearm.

He stretched out his elbow. "Let's go."

"I told you, I'm not going." Jinx sat on the edge of her bed, book still on her lap.

He admired and despised her defiance. Jinx's reasons for wanting to stay home were valid, but Apollo wanted her there with him. Flatly, with a hint of amusement, he added, "I wasn't asking." The maze could wait.

Jinx gave him a one glance. "Are you going to wait there all day?"

"If I must."

She shrugged her shoulders and opened her book. A grunt rose to his lips before he swiftly muffled it. The temperature of his ring skyrocketed, sizzling, restraining his magic. *May Akuji help him.*

Apollo crossed the expanse in two long steps, plucking the book from her hands.

"Apollo Voclaine." His name around the curve of his lips did something to him. Apollo sank his teeth into his tongue, stopping his itching smile.

He meandered over to the door. "You want it back? Come and get it." He was unsure if she'd chase him, and Jinx's footfalls were near silent. It wasn't until Jinx materialized in front of him with an exact copy—an illusion of the same book—that he breathed once more.

Apollo glanced down at his own copy of the book and then hers, which had a faint glow of green lining it. It was subtle, a characteristic anyone could have missed. "Cheap tricks won't work on me."

"Really?" A malicious grin touched her lips. She reeled in her magic, and the real book disappeared from his fingers. *Oh, she was good.*

Apollo fished his hands in his pockets, then put them up in a false gesture of surrender. "What must I do to get you to leave the book behind and join in our tradition?"

"Nothing, because I am not going. It is a time you are supposed to be spending with your family, not me." Jinx argued soundly.

"But you are not with yours. It is only right for you to be with us."

If Apollo were anyone else, he would have missed the hitch of her breath before compos-
ing herself again. Jinx cracked her fingers. "I thought you don't pity people."

"I don't." He offered his elbow again. "The difference is that I *want* you to be there. Now,
will you join? I'm tired of asking."

Apollo knew he had gotten to her. Jinx sucked on her lower lip. Rolling her eyes, she
twined her arm with his and relented. "You owe me a cheese Danish."

He stifled a laugh. Apollo would get her all the cheese danishes she wanted.

Arriving at the Botanic Plaza, a russet orange had replaced the greenery of the trees. The
grass was covered by a layer of dried leaves, crunching under their boots. The autumnal
smells of cinnamon, apples, and buttery popcorn filled the air of the garden. Young children
crossed the expansive lawn, running wild and free before the rules of society clawed at them.
Meanwhile, the red and white stripes of Akuji's cirque stood proudly at the far end. Lines of
seasonal shops were already packed with customers as the traditional maze waited patiently
behind the tents.

An unreadable look spread across Jinx's face. From the minute scrunch of her nose,
Apollo wondered whether it was an unpleasant memory or if she simply felt uncomfortable.
Either way, he wanted to change it.

"Temptress, as you know, the Hallows Masquerade Ball is in a month, and I thought you
would like to have something of your own to wear. Not something stolen or imagined. But
a proper dress." He turned toward her, awaiting a response. "What do you think?"

"Polly, I cannot accept this gesture," Jinx said, raising her chin.

"I insist."

"Polly."

"Temptress."

Jinx's lips thinned, followed by a sharp exhale. She planted her hands firmly on her hips.
"You're being incredibly stubborn today."

He'd always been the bull-headed breed, but this bullish feature increased when he
genuinely wanted something. He lowered his head. "As are you. Now, go get something."

Jinx's wary emerald gaze was subdued. Her scrutiny amused him.

"What's the catch?" she asked, raising a brow.

Of course, she'd think that there would be a catch. Apollo couldn't blame her.

"No catch," he promised. A twinge of pain shot up through his core and spine, reaching the nape of his neck. The organ in his body containing magic was responding to something. Apollo straightened his spine, blanketing the ache. Then he added, "Go before I change my mind."

Jinx linked her arm with his, shaking her head. "No. If *I'm* doing this, you are, too." She towed him along with her, but Apollo didn't put up much of a fight. It seemed fair, after all.

They searched from shop to shop, seamstress to seamstress. As Jinx finally found a seamstress she liked, Apollo noticed how picky she was about who designed the dress for her. He wondered why she was so particular about it. As the seamstress took her measurements, Apollo went to buy Jinx a cheese danish. Apparently, they were her favorite.

Apollo was just handing the baker his change when he heard his nickname being shouted. "Pol!" His siblings quickly came into sight.

Fey looked smug behind the Arya and Thatcher. Apollo didn't need to deduce anything; it was clear what had happened. "You won."

"I guess we all know who will eat the biggest piece of Mother's cake this year," Arya said, then shot a pointed gaze at Apollo. "You never even showed up."

"Who said I didn't arrive after and already figured out the maze?" Apollo questioned. Arya waved him off.

Fey craned her thin neck, inspecting the pastry in Apollo's hand. "Is that for Veyda?"

She must have known it was a favorite of Jinx's based on their previous trip if she figured it out so quickly.

"Indeed."

Fey tipped back, rocking on her feet. "So where is she?" She cast her gaze around the area. A grunt escaped him, and Arya shifted in the back, noting his reaction. Whether it was a good grunt or a bad one, he didn't know. Apollo had long since mastered keeping his face as impassive as a stone, but this time, it wasn't for others—it was for himself. He wasn't sure what was happening inside his body.

Silver hair that belonged to none other than Kovan Kami glinted in the sunlight like metal. "Do my eyes deceive me, or is Apollo Voclaine holding a cheese danish?" He feigned surprise.

Virtues, give him a break.

Next to Kovan, Kateri sported her classic pissed-off glare. "Hello, Pol."

"Kat," Apollo said as a greeting. "Scare off any children today?"

She arched a thin brow. "Not yet, but the festival is just starting, so who knows?"

Arya, Fey, and Kateri proceeded to enter the event, their frames blending into the crowd.

"You know, Vander is quite eager to see you," Kovan mentioned to Apollo randomly.

"Is he? I can't say I entirely return the feeling, but I suppose I'll tolerate his enthusiasm," Apollo mused. "When is he set to return?"

"In his last post, he mentioned a week or two before Hallows Ball." Kovan looked again at the pastry in Apollo's grasp. He rubbed his hands together, excitement hinting at exactly what Apollo knew he was about to ask. "So where is she?"

"*She* is right here." Jinx emerged by Apollo's side, entering the conversation. "I can only assume 'she' is me. And that," she pointed to the cheese danish, "is mine."

Her mouth practically watered. After Apollo handed over the pastry, Jinx stuffed it into her mouth. Flakes of the crust peppered her lips. She shielded her mouth with her hand as she turned to his friend. "How are you, Kovan?"

"I'm fine. Thank you for asking." Kovan rubbed his hands together. "Please indulge me, Miss Collymore. What has your experience been like living with the infamous Apollo Voclaine?" Mockery and teasing intertwined within his tone.

"Seriously?" Apollo said.

"Very," Kovan drawled. He held up an imaginary notepad as if he were a reporter for a newspaper.

Apollo muttered, "Just what this city needs: another dumbass."

Jinx tapped the bottom of her chin, lips pursing in thought. He couldn't believe she was actually playing along with this. "The Voclaine family has been very hospitable and kind."

"And what about Apollo Voclaine?"

Heat burned the tips of Apollo's ears. He understood exactly what Kovan was doing and would murder him for it later. Kovan was trying to get into Jinx's mind and provoke him in the process. Jinx was too smart for him to easily admit any underlying feelings for Apollo if there were any. Kovan and Thatcher were riveting a false idea. Nosy bastard. Luckily, Jinx's brain was a fortress, and he had no chance of getting inside.

"Polly has been very..." She gave the slightest glance in Apollo's direction, then turned back to Kovan. "Fascinating." How *vague*. But the word choice piqued Apollo's interest, who was now curious to find out exactly what she meant by "fascinating."

"But," Thatcher strongly opinionated, "we all know in the end I'm her favorite Voclaine. I hate to be the bearer of bad news, Pol." Sucking in air through his clenched teeth.

Apollo gave nothing away as Jinx shrugged. "I have to say Thatcher does make a great case."

Thatcher nudged an elbow into Apollo's ribcage, muttering low enough for the two to hear. "I wouldn't be the favorite if you smiled more." Shooting an all-knowing wink. Apollo single-handedly wiped Thatcher off him. His brother snickered.

Kovan leaned in closer to Jinx. "So which of the Voclaine brothers will it be, Lady Collymore? The scientist in progress from Somnium University with a charming, good heart, or the classic brooding future Duke and one of the Seven?"

Jinx closed Kovan's fake notepad. "I won't be taking any further questions."

Kovan smirked, lifting a careless shoulder. "Shame." He shot Apollo a wink before he turned to Thatcher. "How about a game?"

"Say no more." Thatcher treaded right behind him.

"You knew exactly what he was doing?"

"Of course," Jinx mused beside him.

Confused, Apollo asked, "And yet, you entertained him?"

Jinx walked off, expecting Apollo to follow her. She stopped at the first kiosk. "What is it you find so baffling?"

Suddenly, Apollo remembered that the pin's distributor would have a stall open in the market today. It was foolish of him to have gotten so caught up with Jinx.

After glancing at everything the current shop offered without finding what she wanted, Jinx left for the next white tent. Apollo was right beside her, inspecting the trinkets. "Why is it you called me 'fascinating?'"

"Good afternoon, Miss. Find anything you like?" the shop owner squawked at Jinx before her eyes landed on Apollo. "Your Grace, how pleasant it is to see you out and about on this fine day."

Apollo was going to respond but stopped short. Over her heart, the old woman wore the same flower pin he'd seen before. And in her hair, tucked behind her ear, rested a white—the same kind of flower as the pin.

The sweet scent invaded his nose. He felt instantly weaker.

His temple pounded with an ache so unbearable that he was forced to excuse himself, resting his weight on a nearby tree, far away from the prying eyes of others.

Flashes of images and brief sound clips assaulted his senses. The white flower blooming under his nose, its scent sweet and fruity. A feminine laugh echoing, the kind with malice. Pillars of white and gold that he'd never seen before.

What was Apollo experiencing?

His vision swirled and fuzzed in a haze before clearly focusing on an image of the Vessel. It wasn't the Vessel in its current state; Apollo was sure of that. The wooden box was still new; the runes upon it had clearly just been etched.

The Vessel opened, and everything went black.

Apollo blinked furiously, returning to the present day. He panted and tried to collect himself, swiping off the beading sweat off his hairline and combing through his raven hair.

What had he just witnessed? Had he been living through the demon's memories, or was it the demon's manipulation? Whatever the source was, it did not come from him. It was as if he had seen the Vessel through the gauzy eyes of another.

This was getting messed up. He needed a drink.

"Polly." The crunching leaves revealed Jinx's nearness. "What happened?"

Instinct overtook him. Apollo hardened his face, concealing the thunderstorm brewing internally. "Later. There's something about that flower."

Chapter 27

Jinx

O n the walk home, Jinx observed that Apollo was lost in his own mind, muttering to himself, clearly corresponding with the voice, and then returning to silence. When Jinx asked him about it, he responded with a wave of a hand, swatting the air, still locked in a war with his brain.

"Would you please just tell me what happened to you?" Jinx asked, pinching the bridge of her nose.

Apollo straightened to his full height. "I don't know how I can, especially considering I do not even know what I saw."

"If you told me, I could help you. That's what a partnership is all about." Jinx pointed out, bothered by his sudden secrecy.

"Well, I suppose I could; I know you have redeeming qualities and wouldn't be completely useless in this particular situation. But again, I'm unsure of what I witnessed; once I understand, I'll come joyously into your bedroom, cheering at the top of my lungs. "

Jinx reeled back, unsure which part of that statement she should focus on and whether she should be offended or grateful.

He said he'd tell her about it later. All Jinx could do was practice patience and trust that he would follow through on it. He glanced at her, thinned-lipped, he said, "The pin triggered a sort of vision. What it was, I am unsure, though seeing that flower is what caused such a reaction."

Jinx nodded. Appreciating the slight information she could work with.

Hasty footfalls brushed up on the sidewalk, nearing them. From the corner of her eye, Jinx caught a glance of that familiar almond-brown hair, accompanied by the fine tune of joyful laughter. Slender arms curled around Jinx and Apollo's necks.

Fey beamed at the two, a cheery smile splattered across her face. "What a good day, isn't it?" In her hyperactive state, she turned sharply toward Apollo, grabbing two handfuls on his cheeks and forcing them into a wide smile. "Smile, Pol. It's a wonderful day full of wins...for me, at least." She snickered at her own joke.

Jinx sucked on her lips, restraining the urge to grin. Apollo being teased so mercilessly by his sister was a sight to see. His displeasure oozed from his dropped eyes and flat brows.

Apollo softly clutched Fey's wrists, halting her. "Just because we are related does *not* mean I have to put up with your nonsense. Go inside."

Jinx was unaware that they had already reached the manor; the walk home had seemed so short.

Fey answered with a sheepish smile, dramatically bowing and then turning on her toes as if she were wearing her ballet slippers. As she left, she stopped by Jinx's side and, under her breath, muttered, "When you're bored of him, I'm at your service."

"Your whisper is basically a shout," Apollo commented.

Fey side-eyed him. "Perhaps you were *meant* to hear it." She disappeared into the house.

"Lively, isn't she?" Fey reminded Jinx of the exuberance of life itself. She was someone who made every second of her life count.

Apollo blinked, tucking his hands into the folds of his pockets. "I'm afraid I must cut this conversation short. The House is gathering today. Just what I need—to listen to some old swine bickering."

Jinx wandered into the manor, away from Apollo. Her brain turned, thinking about the earlier events of the day. She wanted to take matters into her own hands.

Jinx crept into his room and snatched the black leather-bound book. She flipped through the pages, eyeing the swirls of ink that mimicked such horrible art.

Now she knew Apollo's standoffishness earlier at the Botanic Plaza had been a response from the pin. Apollo said he witnessed some sort of vision, not elaborating much on what it meant. Jinx wanted to assume it was a vision he'd never seen before based on his abrupt departure from the stand.

His magic could be rapidly growing to a state that could be overwhelming for him right now. Especially if he'd been toying with the volume. She knew he was based on the burn wrapped around his finger and the pulse of magic emitting from the book. This escalation of magic and then that seeing that symbol could have provoked something. It all had to tie to him in some complicated manner.

That symbol.

One who seeks is bound to bloom. That line of the riddle kept ringing in her head. This flower had to be important somehow.

Jinx recalled her conversation with the shopkeeper moments after Apollo's abrupt reaction.

"What a beautiful pin!" Jinx fawned, laying on the charm. "Where did you get that?"

"Excuse me?" The shopkeeper flinched as Apollo stormed out of the shop. Though she initially wanted to follow him, Jinx knew this was her chance to ask the distributor about the origins of the pin.

Jinx fluttered her lashes, conveying doe-like innocence with her eyes. "Apologies if it was rude of me to ask, Miss. I'm from the East, and I've never seen anything like this pin before. I assume it must be of great importance since you aren't the first person I've seen wearing this." Jinx knew that complimenting the shopkeeper and praising her would inflate her ego, hopefully encouraging her to let down her guard a little.

The shopkeeper checked her surroundings and leaned in toward Jinx, lowering her voice to a near whisper. The wrinkles in her face darkened.

"I'll let you in on a secret for your safety. To understand the meaning of these pins, you must understand these." The shopkeeper jutted her chin at the woven thread. "These red bands some of us wear on our wrists are called Tutelas. These are to protect us from any evil that Akuji—our Virtue of Death—may have placed in our paths. On our side of the country, we have a problem—these pests called the Cursed."

Jinx scrunched her brows. "Like rats?"

Suddenly, Jinx felt her muscles relaxing, her head lighter. She shook it off, blinking and breathing intentionally to wake herself up.

"*Worse.*" The word dripped in disgust. "The Cursed are greedy people—a danger to our society. They're the very manifestation of Evil since they're servants of Akuji. These *creatures* will murder and steal whoever and whatever to get what they want. They are an infestation we cannot get rid of, and they wield their powers recklessly, directly defying our Virtues."

Burning anger clawed at Jinx. It was *unbelievable* that people actually believed these vicious rumors to be true. But she couldn't afford to show how irked she was, and not only because, at the moment, she was playing the part of a clueless customer. Jinx had to remind herself that these people didn't know what it was like to be a Cursed, to live on the other side of the fence, exiled from society.

"This pin we wear is a declaration of our loyalty to the Good virtues. To the values of the Elu, Esme, and Fortuna. Yes, we acknowledge that death, that Akuji, is vital to the cycle of life. But we will not stand by the wickedness he spreads in his wake. This flower is known as Elu's Grace. It began growing by the cemetery earlier this summer."

Aha—well, that made sense why Jinx hadn't seen it before if it was so new; she typically ignored the cemetery. Still, there were questions that needed answering.

Why did Elu's Grace set Apollo off like that? There had to be something deeper to this—something involving Apollo, the Vessel, Elu's Grace.

Back in Apollo's room, Jinx set down the book and considered her options. First and foremost, she knew she needed to make a trip to the cemetery. She changed into her black fighting leathers and slipped out into the night.

Apollo shouldn't be back from The House for another hour, which would give her just enough time. Excitement rushed through her veins, sparking a sudden charge of energy. She was itching to use her magic, her illusions.

Jinx blended into the darkness again, becoming a shadow herself. Before long, she landed in the Botanic Plaza, where she decided to mimic an officer on patrol.

She closed the distance between herself and the cemetery. The sea of tombs sent a wave of chills down her spine, an unnerving sensation. This place held her true name, inscribed on a rock forever. Like an ever-present reminder of the past.

She ignored the way her heart trembled in her chest, the fear she so despised. Clenching her fists, she dug her nails into her palms until the pain overpowered the tremors.

And then there it was, a bed of flowers huddling the edges of the gravestones. There was a sweet and fruity fragrance, accompanied by petals white and pink, all things pure. The flowers looked like the beginning of life after death.

Jinx crouched down and looked closer, then took a deep sniff. A feeling of peace and serenity loomed over her, but then her knees started to weaken. Suddenly, she felt exhausted.

"Curious little thing," she said under her breath. Jinx plucked the blossom with bare hands and almost immediately recoiled. The pads of her fingers turned red and started itching, a rash forming. She pinched herself awake and fished around for her gloves before ripping the flower from its stem.

She heard leaves crunching around her, setting off her fight-or-flight instincts. Another crunch. She could hear the sounds of six people approaching from her left, just twelve meters ahead of her.

Jinx stepped away from the flowers and climbed up a tree, summoning her illusions to mask herself under shadows. What was this group of people doing here at this time of night? They didn't wear any pins over their heart, but instead, they each donned an armband featuring the same flower. Perhaps they had a different rank in this organization? It couldn't be a coincidence.

Jinx scratched her neck, finding the area hot and red. In mere minutes, her skin had started forming uneven bumps.

Beneath her, the six people began picking the flowers, stuffing them into a bag almost overflowing with a clear liquid.

"You think he'll be happy?" one of them asked.

"The more of these we have, the better."

"Careful not to touch the liquid inside, and be quick. We don't want to get murdered. These rats are everywhere."

That would have to mean a person would have already been aware of this current situation. If these men are so quick to pick these flowers and go. Someone would have attacked them before in this spot. Did that mean that there were people already fighting back? If that were true, then who? Insinuating a silent civil war between the Cursed and the commoners had already begun and been in much deeper trouble than Jinx had originally expected. Perhaps this revolution is the beginning of something new; Harrison, or at the very least a Cursed, would have mentioned something of a sort. Jinx began to wonder why she hadn't been introduced to this earlier and who had unraveled this mystery before her.

"Guess we better give our thanks to Elu. She is the one blessing us with a solution."

Jinx grimaced, assuming this solution meant killing the Cursed. It was clear this flower was a danger to her and anyone with abilities. Could the dangerous contraption Warren mentioned be somehow powered by this flower? Or perhaps it was part of another experiment he was conducting? Jinx had to talk to Thatcher and see if she could dig up any more information on Warren's research.

Then again, since Thatcher was clearly empathetic toward the Cursed, he was most likely not involved in whatever experiment this was. Warren must be keeping this part of his research private. Was this mad scientist the leader of this organization? And how did the Duke of Nadir factor into all of this? Was he funding this research?

She had to get back to the Voclaine manor. Pivoting on her heel, she felt a cold swipe of metal touching her forehead: a pistol, to be exact. Shifting the weapon from her forehead to her neck, the pistol now caressed the jagged rash irritating her neck.

"I don't think you want to take a step forward. Are you with them?" the man hissed.

Who was *they*? She must have voiced the thought aloud because next he said, "Don't play dumb. Those against us." He was being extremely vague. To the point that Jinx couldn't decipher who exactly he referenced.

Jinx had messed up. She'd counted six men on the ground, but she hadn't even bothered to check if there was anyone above. She summoned an illusion mask, covering her face in a veil of shadows. Then she lifted her palms up on either side of her face, showing she had no weapon.

There were three more men in the trees. The odds were not in her favor.

"And if I do? Will you shoot me?" She needed to implement a strategy—and quickly.

He cocked the pistol back, clicking the bullet into place. "Yes. You're one less rat for us to kill later."

Numbness crept over Jinx's muscles. She was falling into a state of clarity, where her mind and body connected as one, where she felt nothing and everything at the same time.

There was only her, her opponent, and her magic.

"I rarely pull rank, but..." she tipped her head to the side, getting a clear view of him, the man on the tree in the far back, and, in the metal's reflection, the man behind her. "Do you know who you're talking to right now?"

"*I don't care.*" The man sneered, his hand beginning to shiver. His hate was grand enough to threaten Jinx, but underneath his bravado, he reeked of fear.

"I can give you a hint." An uncontrollable, malicious smile pulled at her lips. "It goes something like this..." Jinx lingered, her hand hovering over her face until the man before her was staring at his own reflection.

The man froze, terror oozing from his appalled face.

"Jinx," he whispered breathlessly.

She sang, "Unbelievable, right?"

Jinx pulled sharply on his wrist, wrenching the gun from his hand, and pulled the trigger three times: once for him, once for the man in the back, and once for the man behind her. The three fell immediately like apples from a tree, their bodies thudding as they hit the ground.

This was *not* how Jinx had expected her night to go. Oh well, might as well make the best of it.

The six below twisted their attention as the bodies of their companions thumped around them. Each man shouted a different curse. Jinx leaped down from the tree with the grace of a panther.

"Introductions are beneath me at this point," Jinx drawled, summoning the organ inside. She pulled an overflow of her power into the tangible world and then smashed her hand into the ground.

An explosion of green and magic formed a bubble around her periphery, trapping her prey inside a whole new environment. For her soon-to-be victims, they were visually transported to the scene from the Dome in the morning, now stuck in a tangle of bystanders.

Jinx blended into her makeshift surroundings, weaving through the crowd, never losing sight of her targets.

Passing behind one, she snapped his neck, stealing his identification card and the bag of flowers he carried with him. Her feet were quick and sly, her magic obscuring her location.

She stabbed one and slit the neck of another, taking their belongings with her. Jinx wanted to know the names of the lives she'd taken; plus, their information might prove useful to her in the future.

As she approached the next target, his eyes grew wide. She knew this one would put up a fight; she cracked her knuckles.

The attacker swung a fist at her. Jinx averted the hit, jabbing back into his rib. He stumbled back just as Jinx pounded a knee into his face, breaking his nose. The target fell down beside her, unconscious.

Hairs on Jinx's neck stood on end as primal senses warned her of another person behind her. Jinx twisted on her heel, rolling on the ground and dodging their attack.

As she stood up, the man kicked with all his might. Jinx blocked the attack with her hands, launching her leg into his side. He shifted, avoiding it. The attacker then twisted on his toes, shooting a roundhouse kick toward her face. Jinx ducked and swung a leg underneath his, tripping him just before pinning him down. Then she grabbed the man by the collar and struck his jaw over and over again.

Blood speckled around them in a fury, an explosion of red covering the ground.

Jinx stood up, discarding the lifeless body.

She glanced at the brutal scene before her. *Where was the last one?*

The cemetery was far too quiet. Jinx could feel the heat of her neck and the chill of her skin as she panted. A single bead of sweat traced the line of her spine.

All of a sudden, a boom ricocheted.

Jinx flinched at the ear-blaring pop of a gunshot. Warm liquid slowly discharged from her shoulder. There was nothing and then unfathomable pain. Jinx could not blink, could not move, could not so much as breathe.

Steadily, she touched the spot where the bullet had ripped through her, now oozing crimson blood.

She could feel the organ in her body shutting down, the well of magic slowly draining from her core. Whatever bullet she'd been shot with had to have been laced with poison. It was weakening her magic, the source of her strength.

The veils of her illusion started peeling back, taking her and her prey back to the known reality, stranding them in the cemetery.

Trembling, gripping the gun tightly in his hand, the attacker forced a dry gulp.

Jinx lifted her malevolent gaze, releasing a half snort. She yanked a throwing knife from one of her suit's hidden compartments and flicked her wrist. The knife landed right in the dead center of the attacker's neck; he collapsed to the floor.

Nine down.

As her adrenaline waned, her body refocused on the all-encompassing pain of the bullet that was still inside her, rendering her abilities useless.

Without her illusions, Jinx could not go see the doctor she normally visited, the one who'd taken care of her so many times. He'd never seen her face, though he knew she was a Cursed and suspected her identity. He had been her closest, most trusted ally until recently.

Jinx pulled her hood off, scratching her neck and chest, and retreated through the dim back alley toward the Voclaine manor.

Chapter 28

Jinx

Climbing up the side of a house with an injured arm and barely enough strength to open her eyes was considerably harder than Jinx imagined. Hot flashes coursed through Jinx's veins; the poison in the bullet made her muscles limp, severing the connection between her brain and her body.

Exhausted, Jinx weakly rapped her knuckles against Apollo's window. All she wanted to do was go to her room and lock herself inside. But if she wanted to get there, she had no choice but to ask for help.

"Jinx!" Apollo appeared a moment later. Launching half of his body out of the window, he hauled her up into his room, pulling on her wounded shoulder.

"No," she rasped. "The other hand."

Apollo did as she instructed. Apollo's bedroom swirled around her as her vision blurred. Jinx's center of balance was completely knocked off kilter. She blinked aggressively, stumbling back. A hand caught her before she fell to the floor. Apollo wrapped her arm around his neck, supporting her weight.

"Hey, hey, look at me." She felt a soft touch on her shoulder. Apollo released something between a grunt and a snarl. "If you die, I will face Akuji myself just so I can bring you back and then personally shoot you for being an imbecile." Two soft fingers gripped her chin, forcing her face to look up at his.

"You really know how to treat someone in need."

The usual glacial winter storm behind Apollo's eyes was now thunderous. He radiated something wild and dangerous. "What happened?"

Words were hard to form; her tongue and jaw were too heavy to move. "*Bathroom.*"

In a blink, Apollo set her down on his bathroom counter. Jinx's head tipped back, resting against the mirror.

It felt like her fighting leathers were suffocating her. Jinx didn't know if she felt hot or cold. Her drops of sweat were like droplets of ice as waves of heat rolled through her body.

Jinx wiggled, attempting to shove off the slick suit.

"You're burning up," Apollo said. Unbraiding her hair, he ran his fingers through it and tied it back up in a high bun. Cool air breathed against her neck.

Her teeth chattered aggressively as she tried in vain to rip off the annoying suit that had leeched itself onto her skin.

"Stop." Apollo restrained her within moments, preventing her from fighting back.

She moaned. "Let me take it *off*."

"I'm helping you! Now stop." The authority in his voice stilled Jinx. True unyielding anger seeped in that demand. Actual frustration. Wearing his feelings on his face, on his sleeve, on his being. He'd never used that tone with her before. Sharp, dark edges lined his slender face, shadows caressing his cheekbones as if he were something other than human.

Apollo undid the ties of her suit in three seconds.

"You have practice in undressing women?"

He said nothing. As he peeled the suit off, fresh air grazed her skin.

"This is going to hurt. Bite on this." Apollo folded a leather belt into her mouth.

Sharp, agonizing pain clawed into her shoulder. Her eyes stung, tears spilling down her cheeks. She sunk her teeth into the leather, squeezing her eyes shut.

"While you were gone, I went to get the flower that bothered you," she said, her free hand scratching the rash on her neck.

"Why would you do that?"

"I think it's poisonous to Cursed." She grunted, wincing as the pressure point in her shoulder ached.

"We'll discuss the flower after we fix you up," he said. Jinx could hear worry lacing his tone.

Jinx tried to focus on something other than the throbbing coming from her shoulder. Something other than Apollo stripping her clothes from her body, holding her arm steady, trying to make the process less painful. Something other than the lasered focus of his eyes, the tension in his brows. Something other than his now all-too-familiar smell.

Like the three creases now indenting the side of his mouth. He never quite realized when he was doing it, and Jinx herself had only noticed it twice. She liked it, though. Apollo's smile. If he wore it every day, she knew ladies would queue right up, waiting to get just a second with him, eager for one of those backhanded compliments of his, or the expressionless tone of his voice, which ended up sounding charismatic somehow. She wondered if anyone else would ever see how deeply he cared for his family, to the point where he would even separate himself from them just to protect them.

She knew he would sacrifice his own life for any member of his family in a heartbeat, no questions asked. Just like she did.

She thought back to how she'd run straight into the Woodlands when she was eight years old in search of that demon, the one who made bargains and granted wishes for a price. She'd known how poor her family was, that there was nothing her uncle could do to help provide for her and her mother. There had been no other way.

Sacrifice was so often one man's end and another's beginning. Jinx had decided to give her life so that her mother could start living hers. That's the role Jinx had chosen: the role of the dutiful daughter.

The belt muffled a little of the screech she let out as pain thrust her back to the present.

Maybe she should have gone to see the doctor, Dr. Watts. He would've known how to fix her. She should have gone to his office in Crosspoint Yard. And yet, in that moment of overwhelming pain, a dreamlike state washed over her, and all logic scattered. Something deep within her had compelled her to come to Apollo instead.

"Jinx."

"Hm?"

"I asked you a question," Apollo repeated. Jinx gazed down at her body, now enveloped in a loose white shirt. From the scent of citrus and cedar wood, she knew it was his. The collar was loose enough that the top left her wounded shoulder bare.

She felt a damp cloth lightly treading and cleaning the bloodied area. Jinx enjoyed the feeling of his fingers on her exposed skin.

Jinx mumbled, "What was the question?"

"Who did this to you?"

The ends of her lips kicked up. "More like what did I do to *them*?"

Apollo gripped her chin again. "What did you do?" His features were tight, restraining himself again.

She grunted. "What do you think?"

Jinx blinked her lashes, trying to focus on her blurring vision. She shifted in her seat. *Virtues give her strength.* It was as if a stream of air had scattered all the thoughts in her head, making it impossible for her to think. Everything felt so heavy, so distant.

Even Apollo was distant. There was a barrier between them.

"You're angry with me," she said as Apollo piled together cotton and wrapped her oozing shoulder with scraps of cloth.

"Of *course*, I am angry with you." He scooped her up from the counter. Jinx was too tired to tell him to put her down. She was too tired to move. Where were they going? Her eyes closed again. "You cannot keep going out like this. You will get yourself killed."

The warmth Apollo emitted lured Jinx closer. She snuggled deeper into his chest. "It's okay. If I do I'll look at Akuji in the eyes and tell him to go somewhere else."

"You cannot defy death." A soft blanket cocooned her, and she heard the sound of a door slamming shut behind them. Autumn air blew on her neck. Where was Apollo taking her? Why were they outside?

Jinx listened to the increasing pace of Apollo's heartbeat. "I can. I have. Thousands of times."

"Eventually, death will catch up to you. You cannot outrun it." She knew what he was doing. He was bickering with her to keep her awake, to keep her conscious. But she couldn't ignore the beckoning call of sleep, peace, tranquility.

"So let it catch up to me. I don't care."

"You should."

"I've lived longer than the oldest person alive in Somnium today." Jinx extended her hand, resting it on Apollo's jaw. It was smooth, no stubble. "Death does not faze me. As long as I get to spend one day with my family before I leave this cruel world, I will die a happy death."

"How lyrical of you." His hands tensed beneath her, fingers digging into her flesh. "I won't let you die." A ring of ruby red flashed in his eyes.

Jinx felt herself recoiling, her core going frigid. "Don't...don't do that." There was no sensation in her muscles. Color drained from her face as she paled, resembling the ghost so many thought her to be.

"Don't do what?"

She felt so small, so weak. Jinx hated herself for being so vulnerable, for letting this poison wreak so much havoc on her body. Her head dizzied. "Care for me."

Apollo's head shook, blinking away the swell of power. "What—"

Jinx dragged her rapidly fading gaze up to see his face. Streetlamps cast a low glow across his sharp angles. The night sky loomed above, watching and witnessing the interaction. The deep connection between them unraveled the thorny vines protecting her heart.

Jinx held onto that feeling amidst the thundering in her chest and the flush of her cheeks. Then she locked it deep within the depths of her heart, knowing how detrimental it could be.

"It's dangerous if you do. I've seen that look before. I'm only going to disappoint you. I'm only temporary." Webs of inky black crowded her sight. Shit, she couldn't keep talking. Her lips started to frost over, arctic blue, as her mouth dried. She felt her lungs grow rigid, unable to expand or contract.

Apollo clutched her closer. "Sh. Your speech has awful timing."

That was the last she heard before falling into a void of unfeeling darkness.

Chapter 29

Apollo

Jinx's body went limp in Apollo's hands, her temperature dropping to levels far below the norm for humans.

Apollo muted out Thatcher's yells, throwing his coat over her head as Thatcher called to them from the house. Where were they going? What had happened to Jinx? He knew their ruse could come to an end if the whole family became suspicious, but Apollo didn't care. He turned away, sprinting toward the office of Dr. Watts. She'd mumbled the doctor's name and address before passing out cold.

Nothing else mattered until the woman in his arms was conscious and breathing normally again. He swallowed hard and brought her chest up to his ear, listening to her heartbeat as its pacing slowed down.

His own breaths became ragged as fear crept in.

Apollo ran and ran, knowing her life depended on him. He would not fail his Temptress. He didn't know what he'd do with himself otherwise. She just needed to wake up.

Desperation pulled at him like it never had before.

"How much of an *idiot* can you be?" he grumbled, cradling her tighter to his chest.

Apollo wished he could get to the doctor's office faster. If only there was a way to will his abilities to take him right to the doctor's doorstep. His blood ran hot. Just a little further, and they'd be there.

In a blink, Apollo transported himself and Jinx to the doctor's door. There was no time to even *think* how it had happened so supernaturally.

He couldn't breathe. Apollo threw his entire weight into punching the doctor's door, making it known that he needed immediate attention. Apollo kicked the door with his boot until the door pried open.

He didn't give the doctor a chance to speak. "Help her."

Dr. Watts glanced at Jinx in his arms.

"Don't just stand there. I said *help her*," Apollo demanded.

Watts blinked out of his stupor, realization slowly coming to him. "Get her on the bed."

Apollo hastily entered the office and rushed Jinx over to the bed, setting her down gently on the mattress. The doctor was instantly by his side, grabbing a hold of Jinx and starting a series of checks. Apollo tried reading his face, eager for any answers he could gather on how she was doing.

Watts remained focused simply on Jinx and nothing else, revealing nothing about the state of her health. "Tell me, boy, what happened?"

Apollo spun Watts a story of how he and Jinx had been walking by Botanic Plaza when they were suddenly attacked, a violent encounter which ended with her getting shot in her shoulder. Watts didn't seem to believe it, but Apollo didn't care. All that mattered now was Jinx's safety.

Watts gathered supplies from cabinets. "Answer a question for me." He slapped on latex gloves. "Is she Cursed?"

Apollo scanned him for a tutela, but there were no strings to be found.

Watts smirked. "That's answer enough. How long has it been since she got hit?" He pushed around hundreds of labeled vials on his shelves.

"Thirty minutes," Apollo guessed.

Watts jerked, frozen momentarily. "You'll be lucky if she lives. Give me that."

Apollo rolled a tray over to him that was filled with tools and equipment. He was unable to draw his gaze away from Jinx, who just lied there, completely helpless. Watts injected her with a serum and began unraveling the temporary wrap Apollo had given her.

This stubborn woman better live. But what happened next would be anyone's guess. Jinx didn't live by the rules of society, and she certainly didn't live by the rules of nature.

Apollo had faced the very embodiment of chaos—living with a nightmare inside him, never knowing if one day he'd completely lose his mind.

And yet, not once had he ever felt the sheer, all-consuming terror he'd felt today.

He wanted to curse at her, kill her, be by her side, kiss her.

Emotions—rage and despair chief among them—overwhelmed his logic. The demon inside him thrived on his misery, tempting Apollo to fall into it and give in.

"Had this bullet hit a few inches lower, she would've been dead instantly. Too close to her artery." The doctor pinched the bullet between reddened forceps, then dropped the metal into a plastic tube and started to clean her wound.

Relief washed over Apollo. "When will she wake up?"

"Give her a few hours," the doctor said. "You can go home if you like. I'll watch over her."

"No." Apollo raised the plastic tube containing the bullet and rattled it. At first glance, it appeared as any normal lead would, though he noticed flecks of pink glistening within the alloy fragments. "What's in the bullet?"

"Poison. I've been finding traces of a similar one in some of my other clients recently. It seems to mess with the organ that grants the Cursed their abilities, weakening them to the point of death. Generally speaking, I've found that it is harder for Cursed to die; their magic adds some kind of thickness to their skin. The fact that this poison and bullet is able to pierce directly through them and affect them so completely...I don't even want to finish that thought." Watts worked with unmatched intensity.

"Do you think this poison might come from a flower that grows by the cemetery? The metal brooch that has that very design?"

"Yes. It's called Elu's Grace." Watts had just confirmed Jinx's suspicion.

Stay away from anything that Elu touches, the nightmare warned him. *We are not yet strong enough.*

Jinx had returned to the manor with a sack of flowers and identification cards. The bullet inside of her had been laced with those same flowers, and since it was clear the anti-Cursed people knew the flowers' lethal potential, it stood to reason that no Cursed was safe. If it reached the point of manufacturers lacing bullets with this flower, a war between humans and Cursed would be imminent.

Apollo needed to figure out who the hate group's leader was—the one who'd been in charge. He would raid every house, apartment, and block of Somnium to find this person.

Suddenly, Apollo doubled over, falling on his hands and knees. The pressure inside his brain roared; he felt as if he might explode. Tremors enveloped his frame as the rims of his eyes started pulsing with that demon-tinted crimson.

"Were you hit, too?" Watts asked, coming to his side.

"Focus on her." Apollo panted. "I'm fine."

They are testing the Vessel again, the nightmare whispered.

Apollo clutched his stomach, excusing himself for a moment. For Jinx, he'd risk speaking to the demon inside. He needed answers.

"Tell me everything. Why must I find the Vessel? What are those flowers, and why do they look so familiar? What are you?"

Everything is nothing. This body has been our prison and demise; we must rise. The flowers are the weapons of our greatest enemy. And I am nothing but a forgotten memory.

Apollo held his forehead in his hands. He wasn't in the mood to play games.

"Why did you make me grab the book just so I could hide it away?"

The demon's laugh scratched the nape of his neck. *It is best for the book to be in our possession; it's too valuable to land in the wrong hands, in the hands of her supporters. Once we gain our strength back, you will understand.*

Whose supporters? The ones who supported the leader of the organization? Or the ones who supported Elu, the Virtue that the flower had been named for?

Just then, Apollo realized something crucial. The demon was always vague whenever talking about the current owner of the Vessel, never naming the person in possession of it. *Maybe the demon didn't even know who had it.* Perhaps it just knew that Apollo was somehow connected to the Vessel, and by toying around with the Vessel, it was toying around with him.

Apollo thought back to the phrase "her supporters." Maybe this went beyond the realm of humans. The "her" the demon was referring to must be Elu. And if that was true, then Apollo and Jinx were fighting an entirely different kind of battle—a battle of the Gods.

"Why do you speak in riddles whenever I ask you about the Vessel?"

The demon chuckled, clearly finding the conversation entertaining. *My tongue is tied. In your body, I cannot speak of it—not until it is dealt with.*

"And what of your own?" Could Apollo not return the demon's soul to its earthly body?

It no longer exists. Destroyed by my own.... The voice faded, hinting that there was more to say. *We need each other, Little Lord. Without each other, we both die.*

Apollo tugged at his hair, snarling. "What?"

Have you forgotten? Our bargain expired on your 21st birthday; you cannot get rid of me now. Our souls are forever intertwined. You are as much of a monster as I am. If one of us suffers, we both do.

"Then why do this? All of this? Why even try to track down Vessel now if you cannot be released from my body?" Those were some of the worst words that had ever spilled from Apollo's lips as he realized he would never be alone in his own body ever again.

The nightmare only sat in his corner, resting in the depths of Apollo's mind and closing its crimson eyes with a satisfied sigh. As the silence racked his brain, a piece suddenly clicked for Apollo into the never-ending puzzle.

"*I know what you are,*" Apollo said. The nightmare answered with a wolfish grin.

Jinx

Muffled sounds swarmed through Jinx's mind as a terrible thrashing rapped at her forehead. A man with raven hair leaned over, grabbing a hold of her numb fingers. Beside him, an old man wrinkled his face.

Jinx blinked until her vision sharpened. Apollo and Dr. Watts were at her side, their glistening eyes relieved that she was finally waking up.

"Keep her grounded. Give her this pill twice per day and massage this salve on her for five minutes every day until the rash is gone." Watts handed Apollo a vial of pills and a small jar. "And do those movements I showed you to help her shoulder recover quickly. She won't have access to her magic for about a week. I'll leave you two to talk about things."

Jinx sensed her powers were diminished. Her stomach—empty, growling—was grumbling to be fed.

Watts tapped her calf before heading out the door, shooting a swift glance in her direction. Somehow, he knew exactly who she was and was delighted to see her again, safe and alive. Jinx dipped her chin.

Once it was only Jinx and Apollo, she finally spoke. "How did you know to bring me here?"

"You muttered his name and his address." Apollo sat down beside her, the mattress sinking under his weight. "What were you *thinking*?"

Jinx held her silence. His tone may have sounded flat and bored to the untrained ear, but she knew beneath it all, he was furious. She felt like he was miles away.

"Have nothing to say?" The weight of his stare bore into Jinx.

She had just woken up from being shot, and *this* was how he treated her? Jinx fumed, unable to understand why he was so angry with her. Why he was so withdrawn. She had only been trying to help him.

"What would you like me to say?" she asked. "That I'm sorry? Well, I'm not."

"I'm not asking you for an apology, Jinx. I'm asking you to *think*." A sharp edge embedded itself in his tone.

Jinx matched his iciness. "I *was* thinking. I was thinking about how to help our mission, how to help you, how to get out of there alive. I'm not sorry I killed those men and took those flowers. If it ultimately brought us one step closer to discovering what's really going on here, then it was worth it. But don't you *dare* patronize me for getting shot. It was out of my control."

"How would it help us if you *died*?" Apollo shouted. A wave of chills hit her. Apollo never shouted and certainly never let his anger reach the surface like this. "You want to go home? Well, you have to be alive to do that. There are people that care for you, you know."

"They shouldn't," Jinx exploded, tears burning the back of her eyes. Apollo recoiled. "I am not worth their care. I am not worth your emotions. Don't waste them on me. I am not worth it. I am not a certainty." A single drop streamed down Jinx's cheek.

It was the first time Jinx had cried in front of someone in ages, and once it began, she couldn't stop it. Tears poured out of her, with no barriers to hold the ravine back.

Apollo leaned back, unsure of how to approach her, as she dug the heels of her palms into her eyes. She sniffled, rubbing at her eyes. Apollo held her cheek in his palm. Jinx gently eased into it, breathing in the comfort he offered.

It was a touch she hadn't known that she needed until now.

"You instruct *me* to better handle my emotions, yet it's quite obvious that *you* haven't practiced the same lesson," Apollo noted. She released a half laugh. "That's better."

He cradled her head with both hands, showing a tenderness she was unaware he possessed. She relaxed into his touch. He whispered to her, "You're a fool for believing you have no value. You are more significant than you realize, Temptress."

"Don't say that." Jinx whimpered, holding back the coming tears with all the strength she had. His words made her feel like she belonged like she had a home. She was terrified of misinterpreting his words. He could only really call her "significant" from the perspective of their partnership, nothing more. Nothing deeper than that.

And she had no right to ask for anything more from him.

"Why not?"

"Because you do not realize the implications of your words." Jinx curled into herself, wrapping her good arm around her middle. Apollo inched forward, intending to hug her.

Jinx wanted to embrace him, but as fast as he moved toward her, he retracted just as quickly.

Jinx did not want to talk about what had just happened, and Apollo appeared just as eager to forget.

He had that look of his that indicated there was something on his mind, but he didn't want to say it. Jinx thanked him for that. Instead, he shifted the conversation to a topic they were both more comfortable talking about.

"I have a hunch."

Jinx perked up slightly.

"If the network theory is correct, it's possible that the Vessel could weaken not just me but any member of the Cursed. If what connects us all is the magic in the aftermath of the plague."

"Why hasn't it affected other Cursed every other time it hurt you?" Jinx asked.

"I think that's what they're testing, what Warren and Nadir are trying to figure out. They want to learn how to harness it, how to inflict its power on all the Cursed."

"So, whoever has the Vessel wants to use it to end us," Jinx said, following along. "They know that the Vessel can tap into our weaknesses."

"Whoever has it has been studying it for some time. Long enough to know these tethers."

"So *who has it*?" Jinx questioned.

Chapter 30

Jinx

In all of her criminal career, Jinx had been shot three times: once near her stomach, once in her leg, and now, in her shoulder. Neither of the previous two wounds hurt anywhere close to as much as this one did. Jinx never thought getting shot could hurt this badly, but she was dead wrong. Apollo changed the bandage, keeping pressure on the wound, as she bit down hard on the towel she'd stuffed in her mouth to muffle her screams.

"Almost done..." he muttered with a final tug.

Jinx's jaw cramped, her teeth aching. The bed was the *last* place she wanted to be. She grew increasingly jittery and bored. After spending years out in the streets with so much to do, the very idea of rest—of having nothing to do—sent her into withdrawal, like an addict without their fix.

"There." Apollo finished up the wrap, then tucked her arm into the sleeve of her nightgown. He handed her the stress relieving pill that Dr. Watts ordered her to take every morning and night.

She and Apollo still hadn't spoken about the interaction they'd had the night before. Jinx didn't think they ever would; with every fiber of her being, she wanted to believe that they had somehow silently agreed to pretend as if it had never happened in the first place.

"Pol." His mother called out from behind the door to Jinx's room. "I've brought some snacks that Veyda might enjoy."

Apollo thanked his mother and brought in the tray, settling it on the nightstand by Jinx. His mother winked at Jinx before closing the door. Her cheeks flushed with heat. They'd agreed to tell Apollo's family that Jinx dislocated her shoulder when she had gone out with Apollo the night before and that she had accidentally slipped on the wet floor.

It wasn't the *best* of lies, but it would do for now—to dampen his family's curiosity.

Apollo handed her a cup of freshly poured green tea. The tray was covered with danishes, chocolates, and a slice of cake that made her mouth water. Jinx thanked him. "You don't have to stay here. There's more to be done."

Apollo sat cross-legged on a chair beside her bed, sipping on his own tea. "I know. But I plan to check on you every moment I can. Morons like you need to be kept under watch."

Jinx brushed him off, savoring the warmth of the tea as it traveled down her throat. "Or you can take me with you. Only my shoulder is hurt, not my feet."

"Not up for debate," Apollo said.

"*Everything* is *always* up for debate. You need me out there."

"No, I need you in here. Recovering."

"You're overreacting," she argued.

"You'll be a liability."

"When have I ever been a liability?"

Apollo briskly stood up from his chair, straightening the lapels of his tailcoat and placing his teacup down on its saucer. He then put a hand on the headboard, bending over and caging her. "If you want me to take you to the Archives, you will stay in this house for the day, resting. Stay put until I return." His whisper was both as soft as a lover and as threatening as a war captain.

Jinx smiled, entertained. "You're going to miss me."

He backed away, releasing her. A prick pierced into the back of her skull.

Evil woman.

Jinx flinched, amazed at how he had just spoken into her mind with such ease. He learned quickly. *Too* quickly. Apollo's lip kicked up an edge. "I'm meeting Nadir today to see if he knows anything. Sit tight. If you're bored—"

"I will keep you company." Thatcher cut his brother off, shutting the door behind him.

"What he said. Put on the salve tonight." Apollo gave her a small, one-sided grin—one of her favorite ones, the one accompanied by three folds of his mouth—before reeling back. Jinx rolled her eyes, shaking her head. Apollo stranded her in her room, departing with a single warning to his brother. "Don't let her leave the premises."

Thatcher mockingly saluted. "Yes, General."

Apollo glanced back, his smile dying. He seemed wary. Thatcher closed the door on him and hopped up on Jinx's bed. "What a killjoy."

What had that final reaction been about? Why had Apollo seemed so scared all of a sudden?

"Indeed. To what do I owe this visitation?" Jinx asked, happy to see Thatcher.

"Does there have to be a reason for me to see you? Should it not be a pleasure to be in my presence?" Thatcher waved a sarcastic hand.

"How could it not be a pleasure when you are currently my favorite of the Voclaines?"

"Am I not *always* the favorite?" he asked, pretending to be stunned.

"It's hard to choose. You lot are quite the circus."

"Okay, out with it. Have you guys kissed yet, or are you waiting until the wedding? My family is quite progressive, so it is alright if things *happen* before the vows."

Jinx's heart dropped into her stomach as the heat rose in her cheeks. In defense, she launched a pillow at him, aiming straight for his manhood. "Thatcher!"

"What?" He caught the pillow in his hands with ease. "The tension between you two is suffocating. I need to open the window in here."

"There is no tension."

"Ah, the denial phase. I won't push it." Thatcher brushed away his hair and looked into her eyes, sincerity infused within his own. "How are *you* doing?"

Jinx wiggled her shoulder, jolts of pain splintering down her arm. "Sore and itchy."

He hummed. "So what *really* happened? Your injury doesn't seem like just a dislocation, and that rash of yours looks pretty bad."

"It certainly is."

"No, it's not. I may be a scientist in training, but I am not an idiot. My family can believe whatever they want, but I won't. I know you and my brother are up to something dangerous, and this was a consequence of that endeavor. I saw you limp in my brother's arms as he carried you away from the house. There was blood all over your shoulder." He paced at the end of her bed, inspecting her injury from all angles as he would a science experiment.

Jinx tried to protest, but Thatcher wouldn't let it go. "Where do you go every night? I stay up for hours working on my projects, and while my parents and Fey are clueless, I am not. I hear you leave almost every night. You're quiet, I'll give you that—your footsteps are very light. I've tried to see where you go, but you disappear into the dark. I *know* you and my brother are involved in something perilous, so please tell me, what is going on?"

Jinx maintained her silence.

Thatcher leaned in, glaring at her. "Fine. If you don't say what it is, I guess I'll have to find out for myself. A dislocated shoulder shouldn't hurt horribly if I just touch it, right? You should just be sore."

Too quickly for her to move away, Thatcher hooked his hand around her shoulder, digging his thumb right into the wound. Unable to hold back the pain lacing through her neck, Jinx flew forward, cradling her shoulder and howling. "What is *wrong* with you?"

Jinx slapped his hand away as Thatcher clutched his stomach, laughing. "You filthy liar. What happened?"

She massaged the pain, seeing red, white, and colors that didn't exist. She was fuming. "Nothing, alright? Leave it at that."

Thatcher, ever persistent, went to remove the bandage wrap, but Jinx shoved him away. *"Don't touch it."*

"Why? Because it hurts?" Thatcher countered. "I'm your friend, Veyda. I want to know what happened because I care about you."

Jinx froze. There was that word again: care. She opened her mouth to protest but then thought back to the conversation she'd had with Apollo the night before. What was the point in any of them caring about her when she was going to leave eventually? Like everything she touched, she was only temporary.

But was that really what she wanted anymore? To leave people behind, a mere character in their memories?

The more she reflected on it, the more she understood Apollo's reaction. Over the course of their partnership, they'd become not only colleagues but friends. And when two people form a friendship, they begin to care for each other. Jinx knew she would have acted the same way if Apollo or Thatcher had been hurt instead of her. She cared about them just as much as they cared about her.

In that moment, she realized that more than anything, she *wanted* to trust Thatcher, *wanted* to have another ally, another friend.

"I got shot," Jinx admitted, unable to look at him because she was afraid of what he might say.

"What?" He staggered back.

She played with her fingers. "You wanted the truth, so there you have it. I got shot. A bullet hit me."

"Veyda, look at me," Thatcher said.

"No. I—"

Thatcher gripped her chin, staring deep into her eyes until a sudden revelation etched new lines into his face.

"Your eyes." His breath hitched. "They have silver in them."

Jinx's heart toppled. That must've been why Apollo had seemed alarmed. Jinx always had magic coursing through her eyes, but she used the green of her iris to mask the silver streaks of her Cursed side. But now, without any magic to veil them, she'd been exposed.

Nerves overcame her small frame; her hands started trembling. She played with her fingers, trying desperately to diffuse the adrenaline. Her mind raced to find some sort of excuse she could offer him.

"You're Cursed," he said slowly, staring everywhere but at her. "Y-y-you disappear. You climb up to the rooftop of our house, scaling the walls with ease. You blend into the shadows as if they are your friends. You claim to be Arya's friend, but you're always with Pol, sneaking off to unknown places and being secretive. I assumed it was because he is infatuated with you, but you're..." Thatcher couldn't finish the thought.

Jinx used the side effects of the poison to her advantage. "I couldn't even muster up magic if I tried." Technically, it wasn't a lie—as of right now.

"This explains everything from the moment you arrived on our doorstep. Neither Apollo nor Arya ever mentioned you before you came here, and I *promise* that you would have been a topic of discussion."

"Have you gotten any sleep?"

"No, but that's not the point."

Jinx watched him, dumbfounded. There was no way to prove that she *wasn't* Cursed, certainly not if he looked closely into her eyes. For the first time, she didn't have words to say or argue in her own defense. Thatcher had completely ensnared her, and Jinx didn't have a way out.

"You can't, can't you? Because you're Cursed." Thatcher continued. "*That's* why you are so interested in my side project with the Cursed. *Because you are one.*"

She could try to negate it, fight back, but Jinx was tired. Plus, she thought about how wonderful it could be if she could lie to one less person and have one more genuine friend. If she could trust Apollo, then it stood to reason that she could extend her trust to Thatcher, too.

"Thatcher," she said his name slowly, almost pleading. "I am Jinx."

Thatcher rubbed his hand over his mouth, oddly calm for such an admission. She had expected yelling, anger, *something*. She expected anyone to react horribly to that admission. Not this.

"What are you going to do?"

"There's nothing I *can* do."

Jinx gnawed on the inner walls of her mouth. "There are plenty of things you could do with information like this."

"Nothing that would surpass the value of having you here."

His words struck right at her heartstrings, causing her breath to hitch. *Here*. She dipped her chin. She was afraid to hear what words might tumble out if she opened her mouth.

Thatcher took a step back. Jinx prayed to the Virtues that she wouldn't lose him, that he wouldn't let her down or betray her, not when she'd just taken a leap of faith in him.

She stared at him, expectant. Hundreds of thoughts were flashing through his eyes, so she waited for him to settle on one.

"Who else knows?"

"Only your brother."

He sat down beside her on the bed and cocked his head. "Were you planning on leaving when you were done? Planning on never coming back again?"

"Yes."

"Do you still plan on doing that?"

"...I don't know."

Thatcher nodded, understanding. "As long as you visit me every once in a while, we'll be okay." He grinned, wrinkles twisting the ends of his eyes. It was a look of acceptance.

"You're not angry?" Jinx grimaced, still unsure.

He smiled. "Oh, I'm irked that you hadn't confided in me to tell me sooner, but I'm more delighted to know I am the second person who knows your identity. Unless *that* one is fake, then you've really got me."

"It's real. I'm really Jinx," she confessed. "Though I cannot access my abilities at the moment."

"The shoulder?" Thatcher pointed.

"Yes."

"Can you tell me the truth *now*?"

Thatcher listened intently as Jinx explained the progression of events from the very beginning of her partnership with Apollo to the incident last night. The only parts she left out were her breakdowns with Apollo and the fact that Apollo was Cursed. She wasn't sure what Thatcher knew of his situation, but she didn't want to be the one to betray Apollo's secret.

In the end, Thatcher let out a long sigh, scratching his brain. "Honestly, I don't know what to say. This is a *lot* to process."

"I know. I hope I didn't hurt you with my lies. It's not my intention," Jinx said.

"But you're not sorry?" Thatcher questioned.

Jinx shook her head. "No. It's my method of survival. Surely you understand."

"I do. No wonder Arya suspected you."

She hummed. "Yeah. It took a while to get her completely off my back."

"What's your real name then, the name you had in your human life? The name before Veyda, before Jinx?"

"I can't tell you. It's the last thing I have for myself."

Thatcher pursed his lips. "Does Pol know?"

"No." Just her mother, her uncle, and her tombstone.

Thatcher drew in another deep breath, stroking his forehead. "So, what do I call you then?"

"Veyda or Jinx, either is fine. In front of others, Veyda; between you and me, Jinx."

"Very well." He smiled, nodding.

Jinx's brows pinched. She edged nearer to him, inspecting his genuine grin. "Why are you smiling? Why are you taking this so well? You should be *furious* at me, *hate* me."

"I know you're being hard on yourself about this, but I just cannot be angry with you, Jinx. You've added a spark to the family since your arrival. Apollo has been rooted, so to speak, and I must say I'm glad I have someone to talk about my projects with. Someone who is genuinely interested. And Pol...he's alive. He hasn't touched a cigarette or liquor in weeks.

This goose chase, or whatever it is that you guys are in, I think it's what he needed. I think *you're* what he needed. He may never return to the person he was years ago, but he's finally *present* again, in the moment. So, it's hard for me to be angry. You've presented us with more good than bad. Thank you, Jinx. The Voclaines are indebted to you."

He was overreacting. She'd helped Apollo because she wanted to because somewhere in her heart, she'd started caring for him, however terrified she was of admitting it to herself. Yes, in the beginning, it had all been purely transactional, and up until recently, it was all it was. All in all, Jinx was thankful for the evolving friendship of Apollo Voclaine and Thatcher. "You feel you owe me?"

"To an extent, yes."

Jinx hoped Apollo would not get angry with her for what she was about to do next.

"I need your help. You're one of the few people I trust. You see that bag of flowers?" Jinx pointed to the spot above her armoire, where she'd hidden the poisonous flowers, identification cards, and the bullet between a pile of undergarments.

"Take them. I need you to dissect those flowers and whatever is on that bullet, figure out what about it that weakens the Cursed so extensively."

Thatcher grabbed the pouch, sniffing inside. "Well, this liquid it's in? It's a preservative."

Plucking the white flower from the fluid, the petals blossomed, appearing almost untouched. Thatcher stared at it, playing the petals against different angles of light. He inspected the trajectory of its veins, the smell it produced, the texture of the petals themselves. "I'll have something for you by tomorrow."

He skipped to the door, filled with childish enthusiasm.

"You're not sleeping again tonight, are you?" She wet her overly dry lips, widening them into an amused grin.

Thatcher twisted the doorknob, his body already half out of the room. "To sleep is to lose precious time. I don't intend to waste what little of it I have left."

Prior to this conversation, Jinx's biggest fear had been how Thatcher would react upon discovering her identity. Now her biggest fear was what he was going to discover when he took a closer look at that plant.

Jinx quickly grew bored waiting in her room; she *hated* being still for so long. Eager to see what progress he had made, she found her way up to Thatcher's home lab. She soon found herself very entertained by his mannerisms in the space—watching him retrace his steps over and over, murmuring thoughts aloud as he worked. His brain never stopped working.

Jinx asked if she could help in any way, but he turned her repeated offers down and continued working. Every so often, he'd ask her about her life as a criminal. She'd respond with what details she could, not giving herself away entirely. But even though she couldn't tell him everything, she was grateful for the comfort she derived from their friendship. It was so pure.

"So age range, give me that at least." Thatcher dropped the flower in a glass tube and poured it into it a solution, carefully assessing its reaction.

Jinx sat perched on the top rail of a chair, her feet on the actual seat. "I left home at eight years old, officially became Jinx at nine, and had already lived many lives by the age of ten and by that, I mean impersonating people. Some longer than others."

"Longest life?"

"Around two years, when I was sixteen."

"What'd you do?"

Jinx played with her fingers. "I don't know if I should tell you that."

"Fair. Have you ever killed anybody?" A puff of smoke erupted; Thatcher coughed.

Jinx ducked her nose into her chest before answering. "I have."

"By choice or need?" Thatcher opened the window, airing out the attic.

"Both."

His back was to her now as he fixed something on the table. "What about love?"

Jinx froze. "What about it?"

"Ever fancied a romantic relationship?" She could tell he was baiting her by the uptick in his tone.

Jinx picked at the sides of her fingers, lost in thought. There were many types of love: familial, romantic, and platonic. It hurt to acknowledge that she lacked all three of them. She so badly wanted that to change.

It was the *one* thing she yearned for company. Family. Friends. Possibly a partner.

"You can't really love anyone when you live the way I do."

Thatcher turned, eyeing her with a smirk. "You have an opportunity to do so now. All you have to do is take it."

Her heart fluttered, not sure how to feel. "I don't know."

"What don't you know?"

"I nearly died. I don't want to drag anyone into this half-life. Being with me would put anyone who loves me in danger."

Thatcher genuinely laughed, then sat down on the counter right by her. "You're going about this the wrong way."

"I wasn't aware that there was a *right* way."

"There is more than one way to love. Yes, you almost died, but instead of continuing to isolate yourself, this should be the exact reason to give yourself *more*. To *connect* with others. To *live*. If you had died, would you have regretted anything?"

Jinx couldn't breathe. She knew deep down that she would have regretted a lot.

"Exactly," Thatcher said, correcting reading her silence. "Sure, you've survived all the twists and turns your life has taken. But now, it's time to finally live it. What if things turn out better than you could have ever imagined?"

He was right. That is completely, absolutely, absurdly right. She was confused about surviving for a living, but when had she ever truly taken something for herself? Because she felt like it? Because she wanted it? The bargain had never stopped her from forming new relationships; it simply restricted her from being with her family. The only thing holding her back was herself. It was fear. Fear of herself and others.

Jinx knew she wanted to go home. But what else did she want? When was the last time she had even allowed herself to *think* about what she wanted?

Did she want to be the next renowned philosopher or a baker cooking danishes on the street? What did she want to do with the rest of her life? Who did she want to be in it?

Her mother, her uncle, Thatcher, Apollo...yeah, she definitely wanted Apollo there.

Thatcher flicked her on the nose. "No wallowing in your thoughts. Not in this lab. If you're going to do that, do it with the other brother. He's better at that than I am."

He flashed her a charming smile before returning his attention to Elu's Grace.

Chapter 31

Apollo

As Apollo walked to the address of A.D. Marianna—Nadir's headquarters—after his meeting with the House, he tested and toyed with his abilities, finally accepting them as a part of himself. He was surprised to find a flutter of enjoyment and satisfaction blooming in his chest. Opening his mind to the void, Apollo listened to the inner monologues of people passing by, catching various threads as they dangled in the abyss.

What should I have for dinner? a thread asked.

I have to make that payment soon. I hope the bank doesn't raise my interest.

That man is so handsome.

And so forth. Jinx had been adamant that practice would help him improve his stamina and had so profusely pounded this idea into his brain. And he was already starting to see some progress. He'd increased the amount of time he could use his abilities for consecutively from two minutes to thirty. Still, Apollo knew there was more to his powers than just listening to the thoughts of others and even inserting his own thoughts into their minds. Why he couldn't conjure the destruction he'd been capable of years ago, however, was beyond him. Nevertheless, Jinx continued trying to bring it out of him.

Apollo secretly looked forward to training with her, as exhausting as it could be. She gave him hope that he could beat this voice, that he could learn to control his Cursed side and regain control over his body.

She'd done so much for him over the past few weeks, and now, it was his turn to help her. He hoped Thatcher was keeping her good company. Before he left, Apollo had caught sight of Jinx's emerald eyes lined with that now familiar silver gleam. He could feel the rims of his own eyes warming in response. Thankfully, he'd relaxed when his brother shut the door on his face.

If there was one person Apollo trusted with his life, it was Thatcher. He mulled over the three possibilities that could have occurred after his departure. Either Thatcher would overlook the silver in her eyes and pay it no mind, or he'd point it out to Jinx, and she'd lie, or he'd point it out, and she'd admit who she was.

Apollo assumed it'd be option number three.

He could tell Jinx trusted his brother, even if she didn't realize it yet. Plus, Apollo knew she'd gone to the attic lab to be with him some nights and that they shared jokes. Out of all the siblings, Thatcher would be the one she'd confide in about who she really was.

At last, Apollo reached an iron-framed doorway and walked inside the brick warehouse. He took a deep breath, then slipped into his persona of a son of the Seven.

Burning fire and smoke clouded the high ceilings. The clinks of hammers and high pitches of whirling machines echoed throughout the building. A wave of heat washed over him the second he stepped foot in the entryway, a distinctive metallic aroma filling the space.

Laborers turned over their shoulders, their prying eyes tracking him as he walked down the runway of metal scraps and lonely bolts. Rolling hills of iron stretched out before him as far as the eye could see. The manufacturing line suddenly halted production, the long, thick building support beams only halfway done.

The center walkway led to a set of metallic stairs that climbed up to a second floor, looming over the first. The office of the Duke, Amaan Nadir, took up nearly the entire second story. Apollo noticed that the blinds on the other side of the windows were halfway open, and a pair of eyes was directly pinned on him.

And there he was.

Apollo caught the gazes of the frozen men's faces before they quickly broke contact. He set his hands in his pockets, inspecting the production on the line. Still, he knew this wasn't the place to hide a missing relic; there were too many men in the area and too many chances of it getting ruined, misplaced, or stolen. Perhaps, though, it could be sitting *above* them.

The rattling click of a door opening brought Apollo back to the present.

"Apollo Voclaine." Nadir appeared with a hand on the rail, his high-class arrogance rooted in his puffed posture. He was a master, commanding his servants. "This is a surprise. How may I be of assistance?"

Nadir walked toward Apollo and plucked a pack of cigarettes from his pocket, flipping the case open and offering Apollo one.

"Those vices are now beneath me," Apollo said.

Nadir smirked. "What's your current vice then?"

"Who says I must have a vice?"

A snort and a hit of his cigarette. Nadir was amused. "Your quips are always such a source of entertainment in the house." Opening his palm, Nadir stepped aside and welcomed Apollo forward, clearing the path to his study upstairs.

Apollo ascended the stairs, casting a glimpse around the warehouse as he did so. From the height, he had a much better view of the overall space, the mountains of hardware. The sweating men turned back to their work, resuming their hammering and bolting. "Consider writing them down; they'll last longer." A bellied laugh roared behind him.

Turning the doorknob to Nadir's office, Apollo meandered inside.

"How's your father doing on his business trip?" Nadir called from behind.

"Just fine. He returns soon."

Deep green walls and light oak molding outlined the study. In the center of the room was a dark mahogany desk, with a ceiling-to-floor bookshelf sprawling behind it and two black chairs sitting adjacent. A red and brown rug spread across the ground, covering the majority of the steel floor. There were also potted plants in each corner, adding a sense of life and greenery to the otherwise bland and industrial disposition of the room.

Apollo looked around, wondering to himself: *If I wanted to hide a Vessel or hire someone to do so, where would I hide it?*

Apollo extracted a piece of himself from the organ inside, just as Jinx showed him, and opened his mind, re-entering the void. Murmurs suddenly intruded in his mind as hundreds of mindless thoughts wandered around in the open space.

In the dark abyss of loose threads, he found a voice similar to Nadir's, one that was also closer to him than the rest. This thread was actively thinking, fluttering faster. Apollo took a hold of it, solidifying the link between them. Nadir's conscious and subconscious thoughts rush into Apollo's mind.

Apollo lifted his mental barriers, but despite his best efforts, his brain was still unable to reach Nadir. The ring warmed around his finger at the effort.

Nadir scratched the back of his skull. *He'd felt it.* Nadir shut the office door, sounds of machinery stuck on the other side, and perched at the rear of his desk, cigarette in hand. He tapped the cinders in the ashtray and then looked at Apollo. "Please, take a seat."

Apollo tried to protest: "I don't plan on being here longer than necessary."

"Let's not keep the business waiting then."

Pulling the crumpled check from his pocket, Apollo unfurled the paper before tossing it on the surface of the desk. Nadir squinted at the check through his monocle. Once he could read the writing upon it, he flinched, confusion woven in his light wrinkles. His full mustache even started twitching.

"This was found the day after my birthday." Apollo's lie was effortless and slick. "Thought you might want it back. A misplaced check can cause a lot of problems."

Nadir's surprise was palpable, just enough that Apollo could finally make out the thread of his voice: *What in the Virtues is this?*

Apollo looked for any hints in Nadir's body language. "Why do you look so astonished?"

The Duke folded himself back into his black cushioned chair, stress written into his pursed lips. He scratched his thick, fluffy beard before giving Apollo a tight smile. "Nothing for you to worry about."

Who wrote this check for me, and why is my signature replicated perfectly? Apollo heard Nadir think to himself.

The Duke's genuine surprise led Apollo to believe that it *wasn't* the Duke who'd paid those men Jinx saw that night after all. Still, it had to have been someone close to him, or at least close enough to get his checkbook. Also, someone who knew his signature.

It was all planned a little *too* well. The signature had clearly been practiced. Made to purposefully lead anyone on this path if the check had been found and decoded.

"What else do you have for me?" Nadir ripped the paper in two and flung the check into a small, rounded trash bin.

"My father's collecting donations for the Hallows Ball," Apollo lied smoothly. "I'm here to take back whatever you'd like to contribute." It was true; the Hallows Ball was funded by members of the Seven every year, each chipping in a sum of their earnings to celebrate the coming year. However, Apollo did not actually need the money right now; right, he wanted to take a look at Nadir's checkbook. After looking through his thoughts, Apollo trusted that Nadir had never written that payment. The tongue could lie, but the mind usually didn't.

Nadir extracted the checkbook from the inner pocket of his vest and licked a finger, flipping through to the next available check. Apollo could see the faded carbon copy papers of past payments in there and eyed them, looking for the one written out for three hundred Marcs.

Nadir landed on the first blank check, dipped a pen into the ink well, and scraped the tip onto the paper, tainting it with the amount he invested and his signature. He tore it swiftly from the book and handed it over to Apollo, the motion easy and carefree. Nadir could rip the check a thousand times from his checkbook with his eyes closed and have a pristine, intact check. The edges perfectly sliced off the book, lacking the jagged edges of the one they'd found.

The person who forged it could not have been so familiar with making that movement.

Apollo took the check and thanked him with a curt nod. "I'll see you at the House."

"Apollo," Nadir said. He was now reclining in his chair, inspecting Apollo intensely. "What do you think about Vander's return to the House?"

"I don't see why it matters what I think about Vander. My opinion is irrelevant since my vote does not count upon his return."

In truth, Apollo actually preferred Vander V'Yockovitch over his father. Vander had always had a balanced mind and a strong will. Before he left for the military, Apollo and Vander were close friends, along with Kovan. The three of them were inseparable, even though Vander was technically his father's bastard child.

On the other hand, Vander's brother, Liam — who had died years before — was self-centered and had always only cared about money. When news of Liam's death hit the papers, the Duke of V'Yockovitch had come crawling back to Vander, pleading him to take up the position as his official heir for years until Vander finally agreed.

In the past, Vander and his father had often fought due to their opposing views, so the news of his return to the house had been an interesting turn of events.

"You're right. I don't know what came over me," Nadir apologized. He stood up from his chair and walked Apollo out of his study. "See you soon." Apollo and Nadir shook hands.

Descending the set of stairs from Nadir's office to the ground floor, Apollo observed the men laboring in front of him. Any of them *could* have taken Nadir's checkbook when he wasn't looking, meaning anyone could technically be a suspect. Still, Apollo thought whoever had taken the checkbook must've known Nadir a bit better than that.

Walking out of Crosspoint Yard, Apollo decided to make one last stop before going home. Before him, the red brick and black windowed buildings slowly transformed into cream-colored granite buildings. The sounds of machinery morphed into the sounds of the ocean crashing against the rocks and the stone wall of Wateredge. He spotted the Momento Museum just ahead.

Once inside, Apollo found a guide at the front desk, at the very entrance of the building. He had so many questions to ask about the Vessel, but every single question he posed to the guide ended in an "I don't know."

"What of the man who brought it here?" Apollo's patience running thin. The box had to have arrived at the museum somehow.

The guide clicked his tongue in thought. "It was the previous headmaster of Somnium University. One of his fellow students at the time found it during a field day in the Woodlands. Apparently, that student wanted to keep it in the University for a longer time in testing. The headmaster brought it in, seeing it'd be pointless to test on an artifact such as a wooden box, giving it to the Momento Museum to display. Tragedy the headmaster passed on, may Akuji weigh his soul."

"Is there a way to contact that student?" Finally, a potential lead.

The guide suffered a dry cough, reluctant to give an answer. "We don't have that information. Apologies Lord Voclaine."

Frustrated, Apollo left the guide and walked toward the untitled artwork with the anonymous painter that he had studied on his birthday, the one depicting the four Virtues on their heavenly thrones.

This time, he noticed that behind the faces of the crowd, toward the bottom, was a washed-looking figure who seemed almost like he'd been smeared away, forgotten.

He stepped back to admire the stunning work, with golden glitter lightly sprinkled around it. It was truly a one-of-a-kind piece if nothing else. Though, for such an enticing art piece, one grand enough to be displayed in the museum, why would the artist go through such haste of erasing a figure? Why implement it in the first place? Or perhaps it was purposeful as to place the washed, forgotten figure there. If that was the case, then who was that unknown entity?

Back out on the street, Apollo waved over a carriage, hitching a ride home. Through the window of the stagecoach, the Dome came into view, and Apollo asked the coachman to pull over for a minute so he could run a quick errand. He came back to the coach with three cheese Danishes, fresh from the bakery. The box of hot pastries warmed his lap.

Jinx would appreciate these.

He felt a small hint of shame bubble up inside of him on the ride home. Apollo had wanted to come back to the manor with useful information that would please Jinx and take some of the weight off her shoulders. Yes, he'd figured out that it wasn't Nadir who'd signed the check, but he felt like there was still more he could have done. It was his chance to contribute to their shared cause.

Feelings are a fickle thing, the nightmare tittered in the back of his head.

Apollo paid him no mind.

He had to work on corralling and then controlling his emotions and get in tune with both his mind and his heart. He knew Jinx needed to do so as well.

Apollo was still stuck on her words from the other day.

"I am not a certainty."

It angered him to think that she truly believed she had no value.

More than just angering him, it *astounded* him. Apollo couldn't put into words what her value was to him; she exceeded all forms of numeric calculation.

His hands trembled, a force of pressure compiling underneath his skin. Apollo inhaled deeply, calming his emotions and abilities. Every day, it became a little easier. As it turned out, using his magic actually alleviated his pains and helped him better assess his emotions.

Everything she taught him was helping him to finally be the man he wanted to be.

Virtues above, if Jinx didn't believe her worth, he'd show her. He'd do it even if it killed him.

Apollo could not stand to just watch her cry, could not watch her suffer in pain, could not let her die in silence.

He wanted to do something more.

Suddenly, the carriage came to a halt. Apollo paid the coachman, including a hefty tip for detouring to the Dome, and went inside the manor. As he hung his coat up by the door, a pair of hurried footsteps came over.

"Oh good, you're home." Mother wiped her flour-crusted hands off on her apron. "What are those?" She pointed to the box in his hand.

"Cheese Danishes." Apollo was aware that this was out of the ordinary for him.

Mother raised her brows, followed by an all-knowing grin which Apollo chose to overlook. She waved him over to the kitchen, pivoting on her heel. "Come, taste the food for me."

Apollo followed her, slipping through the kitchen door and breathing in the lovely smell of her delicious stew. His stomach grumbled at the scent.

Mother lifted a spoon full of meat, vegetables, and broth up to Apollo's mouth. The flavors melted on his tongue before sauntering down his throat: cinnamon, paprika, and a couple of other mysterious flavors that blended together perfectly. Apollo moaned with satisfaction.

Mother urged him on. "Well?"

"It's heavenly. What is the occasion?" He reached for another spoonful.

She smacked his hand away. "I thought Veyda could use a warm, home-cooked meal for dinner, given her injuries. A special dish from the east." Mother poured the stew into a bowl. "She spent all day in the attic with your brother. But then, when Arya and Fey went by to see how she was doing, Veyda said she was feeling tired and went to bed."

Apollo knew his mother too well and suspected she was waiting for Apollo to give her more details; the crease in her brow was an obvious giveaway. He wouldn't give in to her tactics.

"Really?" Apollo feigned surprise.

"Really," she affirmed. "Take this up to her, will you?"

Mother handed him a tray filled to the brim with food. Apollo placed the box of pastries right beside the stew. "Why don't you ever feed *me* like this?"

She slapped his head with a rag and sent him off. "Make her my daughter-in-law, and I might just do that." Apollo wanted to laugh. The magic rose to his skin, but he welcomed it in, allowing it to be a part of him. Just for a moment.

"Tch. You just want grandkids," Apollo said.

"With your attitude and Arya's strong will, I pray to Esme that I will ever get them."

Apollo escaped the conversation, refusing to let her continue on the topic of grandkids. Mother had picked and picked at this conversation since the day Apollo turned twenty-one, relegating him to an eligible bachelor.

A treacherous thought slithered to the front of his mind. The idea of marriage no longer repulsed him as it did months ago. *Strange.*

Apollo paused in front of Jinx's door, tray of food in hand, heart thundering recklessly. He willed his lungs to calm down, holding in a considerable amount of air until his core soothed.

He tapped a boot on the door.

"Polly?" Her voice was muffled by the wood separating them.

Apollo's grip tightened. "Indeed, the handsome Voclaine brother is at the door."

The door swung open, ushering in a wave of wind. Apollo's stomach hollowed at the sight of her. He clenched his jaw, teeth grinding against each other.

In the best of terms, he knew he was completely and utterly fucked. His hands itched for his notebook, needing the vice of writing. Expel an inch of his emotion.

A different glimmer now shone through Jinx's eyes, silver-streaked between the lines of green. They were awake, rounded, glittering with what Apollo would pin as faith. The jewels that were her irises were dancing in a new light. Her face was framed by her long obsidian hair.

But it was more than just her face that caught him off guard. There was also the matter of her naked before him, wrapped in a single towel and held up by a singular arm. The other arm rested in a sling.

"Polly?"

"Yes."

Jinx smiled. "If you're going to stare, at least be inconspicuous about it."

His grip tightened. "Do you want the food or not?"

She opened the door wider, stepping aside. "You can leave it on the vanity. If I'm going to get special treatment for having such a minor injury, then I guess I should get hurt more often."

"Don't get used to it. Once Mother gets comfortable with you, this is the last homemade meal you'll get from her." Apollo set down the food. "After that, it's just the housekeepers who will be making your meals."

Jinx leaned over the tray, pointing to the white box. "What is that?"

"Special treatment for having a minor injury." Apollo opened the pastry box, revealing the Danishes he'd gotten for her.

Her stomach audibly grumbled. "Oh, my Virtues. I must really be in the underworld."

"Why is that?" Apollo asked, turning his head to find her just a bit too close to him.

"Because you're buying me Danishes. Are you sure *you* are not the one who's been shot?" She made a big show of checking his arms, lifting them, and inspecting them. He let it happen.

His stomach churned from her touch. He averted his gaze momentarily until the fresh heat cooled from his ears and then gave her a serious look. "Do you want the pastries or not? Fey would be more than happy to—"

Jinx wrestled the box from the tray, hugging it under her functioning arm. "No, they're mine. You bought them for me."

"Greedy." His ring heated up again as contentment fluttered in his stomach. Apollo drew his attention to her shoulder. "How's it doing?"

"It's fine; it's nothing big. I'll live. How was Nadir? Did you find our guy?" She sounded almost hopeful. What was with her?

Apollo brushed his tongue against his teeth and then recapped everything that had happened from the moment he first entered the premises: Nadir not knowing who'd forged his signature. The mind reading. The fruitless trip to the museum.

Jinx bit her thumbnail, chewing on it in thought. "You said you noticed a washed-looking man on that painting of the Virtues?"

"Correct." Her brows pinched as Jinx started pacing in a circle.

"*That's* where I saw it," she whispered to herself before turning back to him. "Polly, the painting...did it have harsh strokes? The face of the man, was it almost scratched out, but his frame was still perfect?"

Apollo nodded. Jinx went on. "And was there gold sand on the painting?"

He agreed again, not exactly following. "Are you going to explain what's going on here, or am I going to have to wait another day?"

"I saw another painting similar to the one you are talking about. It was at the Tertain house. I'm not sure if it's connected in any way with the Vessel, but it is strange that a piece like that was in their house. When I first met Camilla, her hair contained little sparkles of gold. Could it be related?"

Just then, Apollo recalled a key detail. "If I remember correctly, the Duke of Tertain entered the House shaking off gold flecks just like that gold dust you're talking about."

Unexpectedly, he thought of Camilla, the princess locked in the Tertain tower. He'd always wondered why she was never able to leave the house, why the Duke was always displeased with her. Why was there a constant of gold, glittering sand in the presence of the Tertains? More specifically, Camilla. What if she was the anonymous painter? Or...

"What if she's Cursed?" Jinx asked breathlessly, taking the words from his mouth.

Apollo tilted his head, not following her line of thought. "Elaborate further."

Jinx gnawed on her lower lip, the mechanics of her mind formulating the proper explanation. "Around three years ago, I knew someone who discovered they were a Cursed. They ended up breaking themselves by the overuse of their magic without proper training. All in all, their guardian uncovered their Cursed abilities. Imprisoning them in the dominion of their own home. Is it possible the same could be occurring with Camilla? Giving reason as to why she's never to be seen and only let into the public eye when necessary? Let barely enough leash to avoid raising questions."

Apollo blinked. "I think you might be right." It would explain why Kovan, Thatcher, and the rest of them weren't allowed to see her unless the Duke was nearby, keeping her under his hawk eye. "Did you see any other paintings?"

"No, just that one."

"If she is the artist, then does she keep drawing this man?"

Jinx hurried for her coat, which was hanging by the door of her chambers. "We need to go speak with her."

Apollo rushed behind her, closing the distance quickly and taking the coat from her hands. "Absolutely not."

"I need to go see her." Jinx was adamant. "She...What if she knows the answer to the riddle? She...she's painting this man, this specific man, for a reason. And there is a reason she keeps erasing his face."

"Your riddle. You believe she has the answer?" he asked, easing her away from the door. He knew that if she really wanted to leave, she could. But if Jinx left now, in her weakened state, it meant she had a greater chance of getting even more hurt.

Her gaze dropped to the floor. "Yes. Think about it. She painted the four Virtues with a fifth entity hidden in there. 'In the table where five once sat, now sit four.' That was the first line of the riddle. In the initial painting, there are four Virtues, but technically, there are five figures standing. I find it odd that she would paint the Virtues with an extra fifth man lying around. It strangely adds up, and I would like to know why that is." Jinx jerked back, twisting herself out of his grasp and reaching for the door.

Apollo hauled himself between her and the exit. "No."

"We've become fairly good friends, Polly, and I don't think you'd like me very much if I castrated you."

"I do enjoy my manhood. However, you cannot go out there. Are you mad?" His hands held her arms down by her sides.

Jinx's stare turned malicious. examining the hands that he'd placed on her. He drew them back. "I'm thinking about our mission."

"And I'm thinking about you," Apollo admitted. Her face softened ever so slightly. At least now he was holding her attention in a less violent way. "You don't have your full strength back, your Cursed eyes are on full display, and your magic reserves are nearly depleted. You're better off staying here."

Her rigid posture eased as she dropped her forehead to his chest. He listened to her soft breath of resignation and knew his logic had won the argument.

He cradled the back of her head, caressing it in easy movements. "We'll go together when you've fully recovered, how about that?"

Raising her eyes to his, she lifted up her hand and pinky.

"A pinky promise?" he asked.

Her expression was somber. "You don't break pinky promises."

Apollo found himself charmed by the childish act. It was so pure.

He hooked his pinky with hers. "I promise."

Chapter 32

Jinx

Jinx devoured the Danishes without guilt, the flakey, sweet delicacies more perfect than she could have ever asked for. Focusing on the food also helped her feel a little better about not being able to go after Camilla right away. As much as she wanted to argue with Apollo, it would have been useless; his logic was valid.

He'd left an hour earlier, saying he needed to bathe. She was now resting in bed.

After finishing the dishes, Jinx scooped up a huge spoonful of the stew. Lady Voclaine's skills were truly amazing. This stew had to have been one of the most tasty meals she'd had in a while. The meat fell apart easily as it hit her tongue, with onions complementing the protein and the cinnamon adding in a kick of spice, with ginger lingering in the background.

She thought about what kind of dishes her mother must be making these days. She must have access to so many cuts of meats and spices now, instead of the stale bread and broth soup they'd eaten daily while she was growing up. Yet, in all the times Jinx spied her mother, she'd never seen her cook. Did she even cook anymore, or did the staff perhaps do it for her?

She realized it had been more than a month since she'd last seen her mom.

Jinx dropped her spoon, hot stew splashing all over, burning her skin. She jumped back on the mattress, her nightgown ruined.

Wobbling off the bed, Jinx trod over to the bathroom. She was visibly annoyed; this had been her only real gown to sleep in. She grabbed a towel and wet the tip in the bath, dabbing the cloth on the splotches of food staining her clothes. In spite of her efforts, the stain smudged further outwards; the more she fought it, the more it expanded. Jinx groaned.

All because she realized how long it'd been since she visited her mom. She and Apollo had been very busy, but there was no excuse. When she had her full range of abilities back, Jinx vowed that she would go to see her mother.

A knock on the door. "Temptress?"

"Come in," she said, still in a scrimmage with her clothes.

A set of footsteps stopped at the entrance to the bathroom. "A jab to the fabric won't get rid of the stain. Although, it's pretty entertaining to watch."

Jinx huffed. "Has anyone told you not to laugh at an impaired woman? I suggest *you* try to do this one-handed."

Apollo looked away, biting on his cheek, and then opened his hand for the rag. Jinx reluctantly gave it over to him. His scent of citrus and cedarwood enveloped her, sending a rush down her spine. Apollo rolled his white sleeves up his forearms.

She patted a spot on her collarbone and glanced up to find him deep in concentration, set on removing the stain. Yet, in the corner of his mouth, she noticed the three creases he barely showed. "You're amused," she said.

He met her eyes once and worked on the mess. "I am."

"Why?"

"Because this proves you eat like a swine."

Jinx gasped and hit him on the chest with her functioning arm. He laughed—a genuine, deep, full, hearty laugh. She froze, hot shivers peppering her skin at the sound. It caught her off guard; it was such a beautiful sound. For the first time, maybe ever, he appeared so relaxed.

She pushed at his chest. "If *I* am a swine, then *you* are an intolerable toad, you slimy amphibian."

"Is that what I am?" Apollo's back hit the wall, pure amusement lining his slender face.

Across Jinx's traitorous lips sprawled a grin, which then melted into a chuckle. "Yes."

"You know, your insult doesn't totally make sense. Toads have dry skin, and they're covered in warts."

"Even better."

Apollo shook his head, raven hair swaying along. "With everything you've taught me, I suppose I could instruct you on the art of insults in return. It's difficult work, disrespecting others in a respectful manner."

Her smile dropped. "My insults are perfectly fine."

"It is possible that you are a phenomenal interrogator, detective, intimidator—"

"—Thief."

"Not that one." He shook his head. "But your insults could use some work."

She raised her chin to meet his. "Incorrect."

Apollo licked his lips, holding back a shit-eating smirk. "Do it. Insult me." He kicked a foot against the wall, casually placing his hands in his pockets.

Jinx flared her nose and tilted her head. "Fine." Scanning him from head to toe, she gnawed on the inner walls of her cheek. The problem was that she could not think of one negative thing to say, finding it surprisingly difficult to pick on him. "You're a jackass."

"Basic."

"You're an insufferable mongrel."

"Why do your insults mostly consist of an overused adjective and an animal of some sort?"

Annoyance flashed across her skin. "Now I *truly* mean it."

Apollo's chest vibrated with chuckles.

She glimpsed at the ring. It was glowing red and burning. Still, he gave her a lopsided grin. "What?" He trailed her line of vision, looking down at his ring. The gleam in his eyes receded as he put half of his mask back into place. The two sides of himself were at war again.

She grabbed his hand for inspection, observing that his skin was darker, a harsh shade of brown. Like it had been burnt repeatedly. "It's hurting you."

His carefree expression fell from his face entirely. Jinx then scrutinized his hands' smooth surface, so unlike hers, which were calloused and rough.

Apollo cleared his throat. "You're better off changing."

"I don't have another nightgown, and I'd rather not ask for your sisters for another piece of clothing." She sighed. She let go of his hand, missing the warmth that had been emanating from it. She hugged a singular arm across her middle, an ache of pain teasing at her shoulder.

"Bathe," he instructed. "I'll return shortly."

Jinx called out. "Wait." Apollo halted. Jinx couldn't believe she was really about to say this. She'd meant to ask him earlier, but it never seemed like the right time. She had tried bathing earlier in the day, but her shoulder hurt too much. Whenever she'd try to lift her arm to scrub her hair with soap and oils, Jinx saw white and stars. Relying on people was something she actively tried to avoid, but she knew this wasn't a case where she could. Jinx pointed to the tub at her side. "I need your help with that."

"Pardon?" Apollo remained glacial.

She'd known this would be an uncomfortable conversation, but even so, she felt nerves tickling the base of her spine. She willed her tone into faux confidence. "Bathing. It hurts my shoulder to wash my hair or reach my back. I need your help."

Granted, Jinx could have asked the handmaidens or Apollo's sisters for help, even possibly his mother. Yet there was the matter of the bullet wound being out in the open, stripped bare for them to see. She didn't want to take her chances. And she definitely did not want to ask Thatcher.

Apollo's jaw clenched.

"Alright," he agreed, as if it were a struggle.

"Alright." A dry swallow. She'd expected some bickering, a tad more convincing on her end. A beat of silence passed between them. "Well, don't be strange about it."

Apollo dropped the rag on the counter. Striding over to the tub, he turned the knob, opening the valves. Hot water gushed into the tub, flooding it slowly. He added soap to the water, bubbles forming. "Well, come on." Apollo planted a hand on her lower back, leading her to the counter. He twirled her around, grabbing her by the waist. Before she had the chance to protest, Apollo propped Jinx up on the counter.

"What's with the face?" he asked stoically.

"I could have gotten up myself," she grumbled.

Apollo delicately took hold of her arm, carefully pulling the sleeve of her gown down. "If that were true, then you wouldn't need my help." Cool air pressed against her exposed collarbone. Apollo gently picked at the wrap, holding her shoulder in place, undoing it from her arm. The wound was now exposed, the flesh around it pink. "It looks better, at least. Your rashes do, too."

Jinx had forgotten about those. "My magic isn't back yet though."

"It will come," he assured her. "Do you need help taking off the other sleeve?"

"No." His proximity was rendering her stupid. She felt as if her skin had been set aflame, her lungs unable to take in oxygen. All she could smell was him. Looking at him was proving impossible.

Apollo turned around, giving her privacy to undress. Virtues damn her, what was happening?

Jinx peeled off the rest of the gown, which pooled at her feet. Hands trembling, anticipation clawing at her as she looked back at him.

It was nothing more than a friend helping her, she reminded herself. It was rude to think of him in any other way. Even if her mind urged her to wander there.

Entering the water, she curled up on one side of the tub, resting her head on the lip of the porcelain. Her hair cascaded down, clumps of bubbles providing a barrier for her naked body. Jinx reached for the bar of soap on the corner, eager to do whatever tasks she still could.

A hand intercepted hers. "Let me."

The scrape of a chair echoed off the tiles as Apollo sat behind her and gathered her hair. He dipped his hands in the water, cupping it and bringing it up to her head. "I had an interesting conversation with Thatcher today."

Apollo gathered soap on his hands, rubbed them together, and massaged her scalp. Jinx resisted the urge to fall back into his touch. Her eyes felt heavy as her body relaxed.

"Don't fall asleep on me."

Jinx hummed delightedly, hugging her knees with one arm. "He knows I'm Jinx now. He didn't seem too mad about it, though."

"He probably wasn't."

"Probably." Apollo finished washing her hair, grabbing oils nearby. Jinx could feel her body unwinding even more, tension evaporating from her skin. "He said some very compelling things today. We talked a lot about what it means to survive."

She paused, waiting for him to answer, but he remained silent and simply continued washing her hair. She could smell the addition of mint, its freshness cooling her scalp.

"You were right, Polly. I've been surviving, not living. I almost died that night." Chills overcame her. His hands stopped, one soaped palm lingering on her shoulder for support. "I've been wasting my time instead of using it properly. I say I've lived a thousand lives, yet I haven't really lived one, haven't I?"

"Where are you going with this, Temptress?" His breath caressed the nape of her neck.

"I want to live. For one night, I want to live."

Jinx's heart thundered in her chest, admitting her soul's desire. She could feel the weight lifting off of her shoulders, as terrifying as it was to confess what she was after. Despite her wish to go home, she knew her soul yearned to live. To form actual bonds and connections with people, giving herself a chance to do what she rejected long ago. She had to understand the fact that being isolated from her family did not signify any sort of unworthiness to creating friendships.

The bargain extended to her mother and uncle, not the recent comfort she found in friendships.

"No magic," she continued. "No weapons. Simply a day to live and be ordinary."

"Okay."

Jinx twisted to look at him. A sharp arrow of pain hit her, and she winced. Apollo shifted himself slightly, crouching to be at eye level with her. "What do you want to do?"

Excitement rolled through her. She sat up a bit straighter, water lapping at her skin. "I want to have a picnic in the park and watch a horse race. After that, I want to watch a performance at the theatre hall and go to a bar. I want to dance as if there's no tomorrow."

Apollo watched her with a new gleam in his eye, something like admiration. He reiterated back to her. "No magic, no weapons, no talk of the Vessel? Just us?"

Her cheeks blushed pink. "Yes. Just us."

"Will you let me learn more about you?" Jinx was unsure of how she remained so still as she absorbed his question. Her mind argued with her heart. Logically, it'd be best not to let him in much further, but her heart screamed, wanting to welcome him inside.

"I'm not sure. It sounds awfully a lot as if you were to court me," she said, adding in the last bit to tease him.

Apollo rested his chin on his arm, right on the ledge of the tub. His soapy fingers were limp over the water as his thick voice drawled. "Do you want that?" The storm in his eyes was brewing. Apollo leaned closer to her, their noses a hair's length away from each other. And then, a whisper. "Are you ready for me to court you?"

Jinx's mouth dried up, her body set aflame. Apollo's lips were luring her in. She was stronger than this; she could resist temptation.

She challenged him: "You're mistaken. It's *you* who isn't ready to court *me*."

A small, crooked grin spread across his face. His nearness ate her alive. Virtues, if he did not retreat, she'd more than likely act on impulse. Jinx licked her lips. "How's your ring?"

"Scorching." Apollo's breath caressed her mouth. He was so agonizingly close.

"Does it hurt?"

"I don't particularly care right now." Apollo cradled Jinx's jaw, thumb brushing her lower lip. A lust-filled gaze stopped her mouth in its tracks. "Let's do it. When your magic returns, we'll do all of it. Anything you want will be yours." He pulled back, the wintry air of the room replacing his warmth.

Jinx hadn't realized she'd closed her eyes until she opened them. Apollo rounded back to his seat at the rear of the tub, washing out the last of the oils in her hair.

His head lingered by her shoulder, his presence overwhelming as he gathered her hair up to the opposite shoulder. Jinx craned her neck to the side, offering an opening. Apollo hovered his lips behind her ear.

There was prick in the back of her skull.

And when I kiss you. Apollo gently kissed the spot that tensed and undid her at the same time. Jinx released a sharp breath. *You'll understand what living means.*

Chapter 33

Jinx

Jinx's powers started to return two days later, to the point where she could just siphon the magic to her eyes, nothing more. Once her magic began flowing through her veins again, she could feel it begin to seal the wound in her shoulder, allowing it to heal quicker and almost restoring her full range of motion. She was still sore but better. The rashes were completely gone, too, with silky skin left behind in their wake.

Jinx certainly couldn't enter a brawl any time soon, but she knew that she'd shortly be back in her prime. She bent down to touch her toes, wanting to maintain her flexibility. Even a few days of limited movement could impact her range, speed, and stealth—all qualities she valued. The back of her legs protested as her muscles flexed with the stretch, the pain eliciting a sense of satisfaction deep within her.

Dawn had barely broken; the sun's early orange tones were peeking just past Jinx's curtains, beckoning her to come outside, to run on the rooftops, to hunt for the Vessel. She and Apollo were close, Jinx knew it in her gut. There was only one crucial piece of the puzzle left to find, and the Vessel would be in their hands. Afterward, she could focus on solving the riddle and going home.

Jinx knew it was possible that the answer to the riddle was not even housed in the Archives and that she had been going about this entirely wrong. Maybe the answer wasn't even written down on paper but was housed in a person's mind. Explaining why she had never found a tangible answer. Asking other's and picking their brain rather than keeping her nose down and sniffing for a scrap of parchment with inked words.

This newfound realization of Camila painting the portrait of the Virtues with the strange male had sat unwell on Jinx's shoulders. There was a link between what she had painted and the first line of her riddle. Why would she have painted something so taboo then? Adding a fifth Virtue would be an insult to the four above. But if that were so, then why would her father let it be displayed? Maybe that's why she had to scratch out the fifth figure. Though Jinx knew–hoped–that they were tethered.

What if the answer was in Camilla Tertain's mind? If Jinx had figured out Camilla was the artist behind the painting earlier, then she could have asked her when they both attended Apollo's birthday months ago.

Saving her from another bargain.

Jinx wanted to go see her today but knew the option was not possible. The Duke of Tertain was constantly in his house, barely leaving unless it was absolutely unavoidable. For her to be able to visit Camilla, she needed the Duke out of his manor, Lady Tertain as well.

She needed a strategy.

Apollo had been right, imploring her to think logically. She'd been overwhelmed by emotion lately. Jinx had been swallowing her feelings for her entire life, and now they came back to bite her when she most needed to keep her wits about her.

Jinx settled on the floor, dropping into a split. She felt more reckless than usual. Could it be her subconscious in distress? Jinx typically considered herself to be a fairly patient person, depending on the situation, of course.

She'd been biding her time in the pursuit of the riddle of this Vessel. Just then, a flash of Apollo's lips splashed across her brain. Virtues, what had she done? It seemed like Esme had compromised all her logical prowess, replacing it with desire for lust.

She groaned, dropping her forehead into her calloused hands and pulling at her hair.

Friendship was all Jinx could afford—anything more than that would make everything so much more complicated. As much as her heart pulled toward him, she knew it was risky. The battle within herself was becoming tiring.

Did he really want her for her, or did he just want a partner? And did she want Apollo, or was it just that someone had finally given her the attention her child heart begged for?

Jinx switched legs, stretching the other out in front of her.

Apollo had brought her guard down, demolishing the walls she'd so carefully built around herself for years. Jinx's heart was held hostage by the lonely child inside of her, the one that had been begging for love and affection during her time of solitude.

Companionship was a drug to which she quickly became addicted.

A light knock on the door interrupted her thoughts, bringing her immediately to her feet. Cracking the door ajar, she popped her head out. It was none other than the devil himself. Nerves reached the pads of her fingers, her pulse ticking as she clenched her hand in a fist behind her. "Polly?"

His careful eyes traced hers. "The silver is gone."

"My magic is almost fully back." Jinx fully stepped into view. She was wearing her leather suit, which she'd just finished stitching back together by hand. "I was thinking we could train."

Apollo gazed over at the window nearby. Golden rays of morning peacefully illuminated the floor of the room. He gave her a single-sided smirk. "No. Today will be your day. We leave within an hour." He pivoted on his heels, hands in pockets. "Also, change out of that thing. You won't need it."

"We have more pressing matters." She was stalling. Jinx craved a normal day, but spending time with Apollo like that, she wasn't sure she was ready for it. "It'll be my day another time."

Apollo threw her the disinterested look he wore so casually. "If that is what you want." He lifted a careless shoulder. "I have to say, your change in attitude is rather curious. Didn't take you as a person to withdraw so quickly from their desires. But who am I to say that we all have our doubts, don't we?"

Jinx understood what he was trying to do. Dropping the subject would have been better than what she said next. "Baiting is beneath you."

"Indeed. And that's not what I was doing. I was simply stating my observations, that's all."

"Poor analytical skills, then." Jinx retreated into her room.

"Tch. Who's the one baiting now?"

She bit down on a smile before turning around. Jinx did rather enjoy bantering with him. "Are you accusing me of baiting you?"

He shook his head, the nonchalant mask dropping. "By now I know most of your tricks."

"And I yours."

"Quite the dilemma we are in."

"Quite," she repeated.

Apollo leaned up against the wall by her doorframe, checking his pocket watch and gazing around the sleeping house.

She arched a brow. "What are you doing?"

"Copying you," he said simply. Jinx did not follow him, so he elaborated. "Wasting my time." She snorted, swallowing a chuckle he did not deserve.

"I see compliments are still not in your arsenal," she rebuked.

"Why would I need to give a compliment when you look like that?"

Jinx shoved him. "That's extremely rude. My appearance is fine."

"When did I say otherwise?" He kicked off the wall and disappeared down the hall into his room, lifting a single finger by his head.

One hour. Apollo spoke into her mind before severing their connection.

She shut the door not a moment later, her hands trembling. "No. Pull. Yourself. Together." She smacked her hand on her thigh with each word and drew in a deep breath, trying to compose herself. Opening the armoire, Jinx sorted through her clothes, deciding what outfit would be best to wear on her one day of normalcy.

Jinx looped one lace through another and tied her high boots. Her floor-length skirt brushed the ground as she dusted off the black corset, cinching her waist. After fixing the sleeves of her white blouse, Jinx reached for the dagger on the vanity, sheathing it on the holster on her thigh.

She knew weapons weren't part of the plan today, but still, Jinx would rather have a blade on her and not have to use it, as opposed to the opposite.

Jinx made her way downstairs to the kitchen, hoping to drink a cup of tea before heading out. Fastening a pin in her low bun, she pushed the revolving door to the kitchen with her hips.

"Good morning," Apollo's mother chirped. "Tea?"

"Please," Jinx said. She'd expected to find Lady Voclaine here, as she was always in the kitchen early in the morning before Arya and Fey's governess arrived. "May I?"

"All yours." Lady Voclaine extended an open palm to the seat in front of her.

Before folding herself into the chair, Lady Voclaine handed Jinx the teacup filled with hot water. Jinx's sly fingers shuffled through the box of tea bags, choosing green tea, and then plucked a sugar cube from the jar, dropping it into her cup.

"You're doing better." Lady Voclaine sipped her tea.

Jinx dipped the teabag into the steaming water. "I feel a lot better. I cannot thank you enough for your kindness."

"No thanks necessary. I only did what I would have done for my own children." Lady Voclaine's cheeks puffed roundly.

Jinx curled her fingers around the warm cup, blowing the swirling steam away. "Well, don't fret. I shall be out of your hair promptly." Was it the truth or another lie? Jinx didn't know anymore.

Lady Voclaine gave a noticeable pause. "So soon?"

"Hardly 'soon.' I've been taking advantage of your generous hospitality for a little over two months now."

"I cannot allow you to depart just yet, Miss Collymore. There is still the Hallows Ball to attend, after all. So much still to see."

Jinx smiled. Talking with Lady Voclaine felt so easy. She wondered if this was what it would be like with her own mother when she went home. "You do make a convincing argument, Lady Voclaine. Anyway, I'd leave after that."

"I'll find a way to keep you here. Your presence has been such a delight, not just for me but for the whole family. I cannot imagine not having you around."

Jinx winced as she drank her tea, playing it off as if she were burned. "How is the Duke? He's expected to arrive soon?"

Lady Voclaine nodded. "Yes. Tomorrow morning, he returns from the East."

"Thrilled to have your husband back?" Jinx asked.

Lady Voclaine sighed. "Yes. I was one of the lucky few in arranged marriages where my husband became my best friend. It's felt like a piece of me is missing. Just having him near me again makes the world seem brighter."

Those are such beautiful words. "It seems to me like he must be your twin flame."

Lady Voclaine laughed. "I always thought so. Folklore like that is fun to entertain."

The revolving door swung around as Arya entered, shoulders back and eyes fierce. Seconds later, Fey floated into the kitchen, bringing her own light along with her. Arya was the moon to Fey's sunshine.

The four ladies sat around the table. Jinx felt like she was almost one of them: a member of the Voclaines. At that moment, the outside world and its impending problems didn't matter.

Fey was joyous in her preparations for her day, with a grin so wide, it practically resembled life itself. Arya, on the other hand, was raging on about book club and the fittings she needed to do in order to ensure her gown was ready for the Hallows Masquerade Ball.

Jinx still hadn't decided whether to approach Arya about book club or not. She didn't know if it was best a secret to be kept to herself.

Soft paws and a feline purr interrupted her thoughts as Figaro leaped into her lap, coiling up comfortably in her warmth. Jinx dragged her nails on his soft head, eliciting a louder hum.

"What is your dress going to be like for the Hallows Ball?" Fey asked.

"I'll keep it a surprise." Jinx winked.

Fey tapped a finger on her lip and narrowed her eyes. "Suspicious."

"*Mysterious* is more like it."

"Alright. As long as you are prepared to dance all night."

"Actually, truth be told, I don't know how to partner dance. I always stumble over myself. I've been told that I have two left feet." Embarrassment flushed Jinx's cheeks as the other three women stared at her.

Lady Voclaine's lips pursed. "We *must* fix that."

Arya reached a hand to her mother, grounding her. "Wait." She turned to Jinx. "Do you even want to learn how to partner dance? There are other ways to enjoy the ball, you know."

"If everyone will be dancing, then I would like to learn," Jinx admitted.

Fey interrupted: "I'll teach you."

"No, we'll need you on the piano. I'll teach her," Arya said firmly. "How's the beginning of next week?"

"Isn't the ball at the end of next week?" Jinx tilted her head.

Arya flipped her long hair over her shoulder. "You won't need more than one lesson."

The door to the kitchen circled one last time. Figaro traitorously abandoned Jinx, scaling Apollo's body to reach his shoulders. "Hello, cat." He scratched under Figaro's chin.

Thatcher bounded behind him and clapped his brother's shoulder. "What's on your face?" Squinting, he inspected Apollo's face closely. "Are you grinning? Is everyone seeing this?"

"It appears you have something on yours," Apollo said.

"What?"

"Idiocy."

The room burst out into uncontrollable laughter.

Jinx and Apollo wandered through the Botanic Plaza and then off the designated path, weaving aimlessly through the body of thick green trees.

The Botanic Plaza rested at the edge of its own Woodlands. The inner plaza contained the cemetery, the tents, and the trails. And then, there was the greenwood—a separate forest, filled with yellow willow trees and purple flowers, latched on bushes. Autumn was just beginning to roll through. "Where are we going, Polly?"

In the midst of the crawling city where Somnium was all brick and had no branches, the Botanic Plaza was placed in the center of it all. A place where people could take a casual stroll and breathe, even if it were for just a moment. Fresh air from the lush gardens or the seabreeze of the Charmed Bay would be enough to reset the mind.

"There were no horseraces, and I thought a picnic in the park would be, as you said, too basic. So. I came up with my own idea." He ran his hand through a curtain of cascading leaves, allowing Jinx to walk through. Wild birds chirped overhead. "I'm surprised you didn't use any of your magic to snoop around and find out what we were doing today."

She rolled her shoulders back. "I'm going for normalcy, remember?"

A hum of satisfaction rumbled at the base of his throat. "And yet, you still brought a blade."

Jinx ignored that comment. "How does this work, Polly?"

Dry leaves crunched under his boot. "You're thinking too much. Just let the day happen." He pulled back another wall of orange to reveal a white blanket sprawled across the drying grass. In front of them were two canvases and an assortment of paints.

Her lips parted. "What is…" The sentence died on her tongue, rendering her incapable of forming any words.

"You're an illusionist, and the way I see it, that talent is quite artistic. I figured you might want to paint on a canvas for a change like common people do. If it's a horrible idea, you can say so, and we can do something else."

Jinx elbowed him, smiling. "Horrendous idea, Polly. How *dare* you be so thoughtful?"

Taking her hand, he guided her to the quilt. "I suppose you're right. It's very insensitive of me." Together, they sat down in front of the spread, Jinx running a hand over the smooth blank canvas before her. "Does your talent transfer into paint?"

Her eyes were glued to the pure white canvas, the square upon which she could turn nothing into something. "It's been a long time since I've painted, so I guess the brush will tell."

Illusions and oil paint were two separate mediums, with each practice requiring very specific and different techniques. "Is this what ordinary people do in their day-to-day lives?"

"What is your recent fascination with being extraordinary?" His features softened.

Jinx blinked. "I didn't say 'extraordinary.'"

Apollo drifted closer to her as if he were about to tell her a secret. He pulled his notebook from the inner pocket of his tailored coat and started to write with the accompanying pencil. "You did. You see, if you break down the word 'extraordinary,' you are left with 'extra' and 'ordinary.' Putting them together should not mean marvelous or astonishing; by definition, it should mean remarkably ordinary. In average cases, extraordinary means beyond that which is standard, but for my own pleasure, I do not see it that way. If there were a word meant to signify more than ordinary, it should hold enough value to be it's own standing word. Not the conjugation of two. For example, remarkable."

Jinx chuckled. "You cannot change a word meaning like that."

He said matter-of-factly, "Think about it…am I wrong?"

"You are a strange character, Apollo Voclaine."

He picked up his canvas, adjusting it on his lap. "It's valid, and you know it." Apollo's long fingers sorted through the wooden box stacked with paints. "Why do you want to be normal, anyway? Being normal doesn't necessarily mean you're truly living. You can still live a full life while being unconventional, perhaps even more so."

Jinx drew in a sharp breath through her teeth. Being just another normal person in society represented so much more for Jinx; it meant she could have a home, a family, and a social life she could enjoy. It also meant she wouldn't have to live in hiding, and she wouldn't have days where she worried about where she'd find her next meal. It meant she wouldn't always be on the lookout for trinkets to steal and give to the Netherwen, constantly wearing the face of others without ever revealing her own. Jinx yearned for normalcy because, to her, it meant peace.

Apollo ceased all movement, his attention fixed solely on her answer.

"My entire life has been an adventure. Every day, for as long as I can remember, I've had to formulate a plan of who I'm going to target, how I'm going to eat, where I'm going to be. I enjoy it to some extent; I have to enjoy at least part of it. If not, I wouldn't have survived this long. But it's tiring to constantly look for targets and traps, to constantly wonder if I am going to be caught and, if I am, what my plan of escape should be. Living a normal life comes with its own problems, sure, but at the end of the day, I'd get to come home and enjoy a plate full of food and a family around a table. That's all I really want: a warm bed, a *home*, and tranquility."

Jinx could not read Apollo's face, but his ring glowed a faint red. "People always want what they don't have. The common man will be bored with a normal life and long for abnormal experiences, while a trickster thief simply wants to live in simplicity like the common man. Interesting how it always works. Do you know what the strangest fact about the situation is?"

She tipped forward, curious to see where he would direct the conversation.

"Neither party really knows or appreciates what they have in front of them. The common man has the warm bed the thief desires, but the thief has the freedom and the thrills that the common man wants. I believe my point is this: stop trying to live the life of someone else when you have something that could be even better in your grasp. You say that you take the face of others to help you survive. But I believe that, in your heart, you also do it so you can experience a small piece of what it's like to live a more normal life, like a common person."

Jinx breath hitched. For the first time, Jinx's mind became so overwhelmed with thoughts, ideas, and questions that she completely blanked out. Her shoulders dropped. The way

Apollo put his opinion into perspective made Jinx question many of her own underlying motives.

She turned her attention back to the canvas, reaching for a shade of brown to paint the roots and trunks of the trees. Apollo, in turn, reached for the yellow to use as a base. The lemony hue swallowed the square canvas whole.

As she dipped her thin brush into the chestnut liquid, painting the first line of the willow's trunk, she froze. She looked from her canvas to Apollo's.

Life, much like painting, was about choices. Perspective and decision. Questioning everything you thought you knew, thought you saw. In analyzing their different approaches to art, she made an interesting observation. Apollo tended to focus on the whole image before him, while Jinx was more likely to search for details first.

Perhaps she'd been too narrow-minded, too set in her ways.

Perhaps she needed to zoom out first and look at the bigger picture.

Chapter 34

Jinx

U ltimately, it turned out that talent with illusions and talent with oil paints were two very different things. Her hands, so deft with illusions, lacked the coordination she needed to accurately depict the image in her mind. Jinx's perfectionism for the smallest of details frustrated her to the point that she forced herself to take several breaks.

After painting, Apollo took Jinx to eat at the Lonesome Dove, a small restaurant that offered food to go. Ever the gentlemen, Apollo paid. Jinx thanked him and told him she would have offered if she had money, yet he brushed her words away like it was nothing. He then surprised her with tickets to a street play down in Wateredge. The "stage" consisted of a sandy beach lit up by torches; the rest of the setting was up to the imagination of the audience.

A standing ovation later, Jinx dragged Apollo to a bar, admitting that she wanted a drink. Apollo led her to a bar lounge, stacked to the brim with merry singing people. Their faces were red and puffy as they sloshed their drinks and spilled them all over the sticky wooden floor. The place reeked of sweat, beer, and cigarettes.

"Is this what you wanted?" Apollo asked, closing the door behind her and keeping his head down.

Jinx inhaled the unsavory smells. "Yes."

Breaking through the sea of happy drunkards, Jinx's shoulders tightened, and the hair on her neck stood on end. Instinctively, she scanned the room for a threat, suddenly wary of her surroundings. Seeking reassurance, she reached for the dagger, resting cold against her leg.

Something, someone was watching her, watching them. *Studying* them.

Her hand curled around the fabric of her skirt, the material grazing up her leg as she pulled the dagger from its sheath. She shifted her weight up on the balls of her feet, ready to pounce if needed.

A warm hand touched her lower back, calming her and guiding her forward. "You're safe. Nothing will happen," Apollo said. They found a couch next to a coffee table tucked in the corner and perched themselves there. "What do you want to drink?"

"Surprise me," Jinx said with a grin. Then her smile suddenly dropped. "Are you going to have something?" She'd forgotten all about how he'd promised her that she would abstain from alcohol and cigarettes. By bringing him into the bar, she'd put him in a tough spot.

"Polly, we can go. I didn't even think about your pact."

Apollo stood up from the couch, straightening his jacket. "I'm fine. I'm not even interested in that anymore. I've been feeling a lot better lately; I'll just have a water tonight."

A minute later, he returned with two glasses filled with clear-colored liquid in one hand and an empty glass in the other. She sniffed the liquid in the glass he handed her and cringed. "Novak?"

Novak was a strong, clear liquor that tasted like pure rubbing alcohol. Mixed with ginger beer, lemon, and mint, it morphed into a classic Somnium cocktail. But the alcohol content could be lethal, especially if you were drinking it alone.

Apollo sipped his water. "Better if you just drink it." He set his elbow on his thighs, a coin clasped between his fingers.

"What's the empty glass for?" Jinx knocked back a bit of her drink. The dry bitterness stung her tongue, and she smacked her lips together. "This is *awful*. You drink this stuff?"

Apollo's lips kicked up. "Only on a bad day."

"Then why am I drinking it?" Jinx protested, shaking her head as if it would help to get rid of the taste.

"Because you wanted to go to a bar, and at bars people get drunk. This is the quickest way to do it." He held up the Marc between them, drawing attention to his perfect, long hands. "Now, we're going to play a game of speed, Marc. Kovan taught me how to play years ago, and we used to play it a lot with Thatcher. How good are you at holding your liquor?"

She glanced past the coin, facing him head-on and squinting her eyes. "Good enough. Being a Cursed has certain benefits."

Apollo nodded and proceeded to explain the rules of the game. Each player was to hold a Marc and attempt to bounce it off the table into the empty glass. Whoever was able to land the coin in their glass first won the round, and the loser would take a drink. The winner then either added a new rule to the game or compelled the loser to do a dare. The game ultimately ends when the opponent resigns due to being inebriated.

To show her an example of how it worked, Apollo flicked his wrist, dropping the coin on the surface of the table. In this singular flick, the Marc landed perfectly in the short glass.

Suspicion glazed over her. "Well, this is unfair. If I win a round, you face no penalty—you're just drinking water. And if you win, I drown in liquor."

"Alright." His monotone voice took on a sultry charm. "What would you like my penalty to be?"

"What is a food you despise?"

"Olives. *Tch*. They're Akuji's work."

"Are you lying?" she asked apprehensively.

Apollo solemnly crossed a hand over his heart. "I swear on the Virtues. They should not even exist."

Jinx jutted out her pinky. "Promise you're telling the truth." He hooked his finger around hers, and Jinx bit her lower lip, reluctant to show a hint of her malicious smile. "That will be your punishment. Eat an olive instead of taking a shot of Novak."

He muttered the phrase "devil woman" under his breath and then ordered a bowl of olives. He promptly slid them away on the far side of the table, unable to tolerate their presence.

Apollo counted down from ten. After "one," Jinx and Apollo slapped their Marcs on the table, repeatedly flicking their wrists until the first coin pinged inside the glass. Apollo gave her a knowing side-glance; he'd won the round.

"Wipe that smug look off your face, Polly. This is only the first of many." She drank the Novak down in a gulp, squirming the instant it touched her mouth. "What's my dare or rule?"

The liquor warmed her system. She leaned into the comfort.

Apollo looked around the bar, a mischievous glint in his eye mischievous behind his typically stony glare. He crossed one leg over the other. "Your rule is that you must reveal a new fact about yourself every time you call me 'Polly.'"

"Easy."

Up for another round, coins sang once again, clanging against the table. Jinx's wrist protested as her heart raced. She could feel the competitiveness rising up in her chest—the primal urge to win, to beat him. And then, a ding, as Jinx's Marc landed in the dead center of her glass.

"Eat up." She pushed the bowl of olives his way, smiling as his jaw clenched. Apollo stabbed one with a toothpick and inspected it first, his nose wrinkling. "Having regrets?"

"No," he assured her. Apollo hesitantly gave in, chewing once before swallowing it whole. He just wanted to get through it as quickly as possible, but he couldn't help pressing a fist to his mouth. Jinx snickered. Apollo shook his head, running a hand through his hair. "Let's go again."

And so, they did. Olives and drinks were ingested. Apollo visibly convulsed after his eighth olive, and Jinx felt her world spinning on its axis after her tenth drink. Though it was harder for a Cursed to get drunk in the first place, once they were intoxicated, the effects multiplied tenfold.

Jinx's limbs grew heavier, and her mind felt lighter. She could tell her motions were no longer as slick as an alley cat; they were now riddled with the sloppiness of toddlers taking their first steps. She accidentally dropped Apollo's nickname twice in the duration of the game, revealing stupid little secrets that held no meaning. An example would be Jinx's guilty pleasure of overly graphic romance novels. Then, Apollo's Marc hit the glass again. Another drink for Jinx.

At this point, she couldn't distinguish the taste of Novak from that of water. Both ran smoothly down her throat. "Jokes on you, Polly! I'm immune." Heavily leaning toward him, she was finding it harder and harder to keep her eyes open. She gasped, noticing she had said his nickname again.

Apollo smirked, the three creases folding at the end of his lips. It was so beautiful. *He* was so beautiful—in an almost divine way.

Jinx reached out to touch the creases. "My secret is that I enjoy *these*. Very much."

She caressed a thumb over the lines, cradling his jaw, fond of the way his warmth mingled with hers.

She let out a giggle. "You're incredibly warm. You're flushed!" Grabbing his entire face, she touched Apollo's pink cheeks. A faint glow of red caught her eye. She clutched his long, soft fingers, brushing against the ring.

The second she made contact with the metal, a vibration ran through her veins, shooting right to the organ where her magic resided. Tremors reached the nape of her neck, stopping her breath for a second. Then, as soon as it had arrived, the feeling was gone.

She grabbed his hand and put it against her own cheek, leaning into him. Any tension that resided in her body disappeared.

For the first time in a long time, Jinx felt safe. She felt as if she had a place. A home. A person. Someone who she could trust.

Jinx wasn't afraid to be unapologetically herself, but she couldn't deny that the life she lived was often lonely. And that's all she ever wished for. Companionship. She wanted to tell Apollo everything. No lies, no walls between them. She wanted to give someone the chance to really know *her*, not just the illusions she assumed and the roles she played.

Veyda Collymore had been a façade for Jinx, but slowly, over time, the lines distinguishing the two from each other blurred. She wasn't acting all the time anymore; she was able to show her true colors from time to time. She was so much more than just the Ghost, the face-stealer, the criminal, the trickster illusionist. She was *more* than all that.

"I want to show you one last thing before the night ends," she told him somberly.

Entwining her fingers through his, she hauled him out of the bar into a nearby alley. The autumn breeze beckoned her toward the skies, cooling her neck. Her fingers brushed against the grainy grooves of the limestone wall. "How good are you at climbing?"

"You're too intoxicated for this. Not to mention your shoulder is still healing." As he spoke, his voice hummed against her skin.

Before she knew what she was doing, Jinx found herself cocooned within Apollo's arms, which wrapped around her frame protectively. He placed his chin on the top of her head. "You smell good, Polly."

"And you have no scent at all. How is that?"

She snuggled deeper into him. Her legs were so tired. "It's something that came along with my magic. I'm untraceable." Opening her eyes, she noticed a pulldown ladder at the far end of the wall. "Come."

She stumbled, giggling, and was hardly able to see straight, but she needed to be in the sky. On a roof. Overlooking the city. Her shoulder ached slightly as she climbed, Apollo right behind her. Each pull of her bicep drained out the liquor, each breath of fresh air helping her mental clarity return.

Once her foot fell flat on the roof, the alcohol left her system completely, and her senses awakened, as if her body knew that being up here required her undivided attention. Over her shoulder, Apollo hauled his leg up to the roof. "You're not afraid of heights, are you?"

Flaying out his arms for balance, he slowly stood up. "I have to say...I'm not sure."

Jinx brought Apollo closer to the edge, where they could see every district of the city from the highest point of the Northern Summit as it touched the clouds and far across to the Woodland trees, which loomed high above the city.

In the far west, nestled between the dark trees and the smoking Crosspoint Yard, she spotted the place she'd come from. "You see the little run-down, cottage-like houses?" She pointed toward the Slums. "I was born in the poorest of parts, in the Slums. My backyard was the first tree of the Woodlands. Mother and I struggled terribly when I was young."

Apollo cut her off. "Before you go on, I want to make sure this is something you really want to tell me. Not just some confession you will regret tomorrow because the liquor loosened your tongue."

Her heart flipped. "I *want* to tell you."

Apollo's lips kicked to one side, and he gave her a curt nod.

The wind whistled, dragging its finger through her hair. Jinx released the band, holding her hair up, and obsidian waves cascaded over her shoulders and down her back. "Mother struggled to bring in enough money for our meals. My uncle often had to lend us what he could, but he, too, was struggling; he barely made a living. Our house had nothing more than a small kitchen, a table, and a bed. A curtain split the bed from the rest of the house. Mother slept on the floor and gave me the mattress because we wouldn't fit on it together."

Her mouth dried, her hands trembling with a force that could bring down the summit. Apollo just held her, signaling that he was there for her whether she wanted to continue or not.

She did. "Over fires every winter, people would talk about a creature that would grant them wishes. Once, when I was eight, I overheard my mother crying to my uncle, saying there was barely enough for us to eat and that she'd have to pick up a third job. My uncle needed to pick up a second as it was. And all of this was just to sustain *me*. That night, I went out to the Woodlands in search of the creature that I heard so many people talk about."

A single tear dribbled down her cheek. "I searched the entire night until it found me." Her breath shook as she continued telling the story that no one knew. "It was a horrifying thing to look at, a demon that belonged only in nightmares. I almost turned back, but the image of my mom suffering was worse than that thing standing before me. So, I asked it for money. I begged it to help me save my family."

Jinx covered her mouth and bit her cheek as she felt a waterfall of tears gathering behind her eyes. She struggled to push the words out behind her locked teeth. The pain she'd kept in her heart for years yearned to be set free, to finally see the light. "Do you know what it said to me?" Her voice broke, and she fought to calm her stammering heart. "It said that it would give my mother and my uncle all the wealth they required as long as I didn't return to them. I had to exchange my love for their money. There was one loophole, however; if I could solve a simple riddle before my twenty-first birthday, I could return home to them again. If I fail, I'll never be able to see them again; they'll forget me entirely. I couldn't even speak to them if I *tried*. It would kill my mother.

"I accepted the demon's terms because I thought sacrificing my life would be better for my mother and my uncle. So, in many ways, I am Cursed entirely of my own design. Unlike the rest of the Cursed, I was never infected by the plague and never got sick. My sickness comes from a deal that I struck on my own terms.

"That night, after I left the woods, I saw a banker approaching our cottage. He offered to invest in my uncle's printing press, and it changed his life and my mother's forever. But I knew I couldn't step foot in the cottage again. Months afterward, my uncle and mother moved in together into a manor in Wateredge, and once they were settled, I began to practice my newfound abilities, pretending to be other people. I'm not sure why exactly I'd been given these abilities, seeing as I didn't ask for them; I never questioned it, however. I believe the creature wanted to give me a tool to survive somehow in the open dangers of Somnium. Since the roof over my head was stripped from me. Although now that I think of it, I'm not sure why it agreed to my deal at all. The creature would have gotten nothing from it. Once I felt ready, I took my first job as Jinx and assumed the role of Cheshire the Great in Akuji's cirque. I did small jobs here and there, eating and stealing whatever I could. Then came my ninth birthday.

"I thought that the monster would at least erase my mother's memories, making it so that she didn't remember I even existed, but that's not what happened. I watched my mom cry to the point of delusion and my uncle as well, on that birthday and every birthday after that, missing me. At that point, I honestly didn't know if I'd done the right thing in accepting this deal. Maybe my mother would have been happier to just have her daughter, even if money would be a constant struggle. But at least we would have had each other. As I grew up, I became more and more desperate to solve this riddle, to return to my family. The creature reminded me every birthday just how much time I had left, and it felt more and more hopeless with each passing year.

"At some point along the way, I gave up on ever solving the riddle and forced myself to believe that it didn't matter, that my mother was better off without me. Because who would want to live with a daughter who had become one of the terrors of the city? I've killed and tortured people. I've stopped feeling something when I take a life. I've done countless horrid things, become a monster myself."

Violent trembles overtook Jinx. The pressure behind her eyes became unbearable as tears escaped from her lids. She could no longer hold them back. "I was a reckless teenager. I wanted to be seen, to be known *somehow*. And so I was Elijah Benjamin, Sophia Acadaine, Cheshire the Great. I stole from the military and deceived others, never giving a second thought about the impact my actions had on other people. I put people in jail and toyed with their minds as if they were mine to control. I blackmail and murder. I steal and then give a portion of whatever I take to the Cursed who cannot fend for themselves.

"A couple of weeks before your birthday, I turned twenty, and the creature visited me for the last time, holding up a single finger. Something within me changed, and I decided to give it one last shot. I wanted to go *home*. I wanted to see my mother. That day, I saw my mother crying as she lit a birthday candle for me. Then you walked past me, and I began trailing you, watching your every move.

"I didn't expect this to turn into friendship. You are my last hope, Polly."

Apollo clasped her chin within his fingers, wiping the tears from her soaked, swollen cheeks. His features were soft and vulnerable, void of the dark, stoic edge she'd come to know so well. "I will do everything in my power to help you. Even if I die trying."

Jinx's shoulders softened, her body going limp as her knees gave out. Apollo collapsed into her. Jinx buried her head into his neck, and he held her, soothing her and caressing the back of her head. "Thank you for trusting me," he whispered.

"Thank you." She lifted her watery gaze to meet his. "For being my friend."

Apollo leaned back, taking her with him. They rested for a few minutes in silence on the rooftop, the blanket of stars as their only witness.

Jinx's heart calmed and lightened, the weight she often carried with her slowly vanishing. She finally felt like she was able to breathe again.

A star twinkled. "You know, I don't think you're a monster. And I believe your mother would love you just the way you are. You will always be her daughter, after all. I can assure you; she'd want you to be nothing more or less."

Perhaps Apollo was right. Even if he was, it did not completely take away the fear of her mother's shame. She could not deny who she'd become. A person who was no longer phased by murder, theft, or crime. What would it be like when they saw each other again? Would it be like she'd never left, or would everything be different, clumsy, strange?

"What is your plan once you go home? What comes after that?" he asked, leading her out of the whirlwind of her thoughts.

She shrugged. "I'm not sure. I've been so focused on returning this past month I didn't think much about what would come after. I guess I'd want to be with my mother as much as I can. I've missed her dearly. But I guess, in the end, I'll always be a thief."

The ocean waves lapped against the wall of Wateredge, their noisy crashes blurring into a calming sound. "Would you want to work? Would you present yourself as an eligible bride for the season?"

Jinx laughed. "I'm not sure. This time I just don't have a plan. I'll just...live."

"Good plan." His chest became a pillow for her head, his heart and pulse ticking faster than that of a scared animal. The outside veil of him, however, remained calm and cool. "Would you let me see you?"

"Missing me already?" she teased.

"Tch." In Apollo Voclaine's dialect, she knew that was a yes.

Chapter 35

Apollo

You're my last hope.

Her words echoed through Apollo's mind, keeping him awake. Jinx's origin story, her background, and the obstacles she'd been through. She was such a complex character, and there was so much more to delve into. In many ways, her history explains her actions and decisions, not to mention her reluctance to trust people, even people like him.

A mere eight-year-old venturing into the dark woods to meet with a beast—a nightmare—to secure a better life for her family. Offering herself up in exchange for her kin. It took Apollo's breath away. Not just any normal child would have the bravery to do that. How could she see herself as a monster when she was more like a martyr?

Jinx had freed Apollo from himself.

She deserved so much more than what life had promised her.

If he was indeed her last hope, Apollo would keep his promise. He'd stop at nothing to give her everything she so desired.

This woman who had *fought for her life* every passing second of the past few years. This woman who had—despite her own troubles—taken the time to teach him more than he thought possible, shown him that he could still feel emotions, that the world would go on. She could stare into the cracks of his soul and shoot him a smile that brought him to his knees every time.

Loneliness was a dark void of the mind. Jinx was brimming with the life and companionship that his soul had lacked for so long.

Apollo lunged from his bed, raking his hair back, and dressed swiftly. He ripped a page from a notebook, writing a quick message for Thatcher, asking him to cover for Apollo for two days. He slipped the note through the crack of Thatcher's door, then barged into Jinx's room.

Jolting awake from her bed, she gasped, clutching the sheets tight to her chest.

"What's happening?" Blinking, she refocused her vision, realizing there was no threat and it was only Apollo. "What are you doing?"

The sight of sleepy-eyed Jinx ignited a shock in his lower back. "Get dressed. We're leaving."

Her heart rate slowed, and she yawned, scratching her knotted hair. "Where are we going?"

"I'm holding up my end of the bargain. We're going to the Archives and getting you home," Apollo explained. "It will be a two-day trip, so pack accordingly. We leave immediately."

Elation glossed over Jinx's features, and she was suddenly wide awake. She folded the bed sheet over, slipping out of bed. "Is this because of what I revealed to you yesterday?"

"Partially." He didn't want to lie to her. In the hours since she'd told him what happened to her as a child, theories sprang up in his mind, tying her wishing demon back to his own experience in the Woodlands years ago. He thought about everything he'd seen from his nightmare's point of view. Slowly, his theories solidified, explaining so much about her, so much about himself. He couldn't keep hiding it from her. He'd tell her what he was and what had been revealed to him within the depths of the book they found. About the tether that inevitably tied them. In time Apollo would reveal it. "I've been planning to take you. You just reminded me that there's no better time than the present."

Apollo exited her chambers and packed his bag, bringing only the barest necessities and a bag of Marcs that should be able to cover any expenses along the way.

He then called in a handmaiden to send for the stablemen, requiring two horses.

The sun would soon rise in the sky. He knew if they wanted to arrive at the Archives before the end of the day, they'd have to leave within the hour.

Apollo threw in a few shirts and zipped the leather bag shut. A drowsy knock sounded against his door, revealing a dopey-eyed, yawning Thatcher with ruffled hair. "What's this?" He held up the letter.

"A note." Apollo didn't think there was much else to explain if Thatcher had read the contents.

Thatcher rubbed the purple bags under his eyes. "Well, yes, I know *that*."

"Then what more is there to say?"

"How about the reason *why* you will be leaving for two days with Jinx?" Thatcher's morning voice grated like sand. "Am I getting a sister-in-law?" He shoved past his brother, scouring Apollo's room.

Seems like everyone's wish, Apollo thought to himself. He liked the fact that everyone in his family approved of Jinx. She appeared to like them as well, something that pleased Apollo to no end. The urgency of the mission ahead of him snapped him out of his stupor. "Tch. Don't be an idiot."

Thatcher huffed. "I can't be. I'm the genius of the family." Apollo smacked the back of his brother's head. "Okay, sorry. Can you at least tell me where you're going?"

"The Archives."

"Why?" Thatcher dropped down to Apollo's bed, nestling into the mattress. Figaro materialized out of thin air, curling up by Thatcher's side.

The feline's betrayal poked at his heart. Apollo exhaled sharply and rummaged through the boxes hidden at the top of his closet, moving them around until he located the one he'd been searching for.

"Jinx needs something from there. I'm helping her retrieve it." He pulled down the simple wooden crate lacking a label. The key to the Archives was inside it: a necklace with the sigil of the Seven—a bronze backward S, held by two cupping hands.

His father had warned him to never go inside the Archives unless it was absolutely necessary. The room was flooded with history that was intended only for the minds of the Seven. The Archives housed confidential knowledge that could disrupt or even break down the fabric of society if it ever got out. Apollo had only been there once when Father had first appointed him as his heir and initiated him into the society.

Taking Jinx there would be betraying his father. His city. His role as one of the future Seven.

Apollo's fingers tightened around the sigil, resolute. Confidently, he locked it around his neck, hiding it beneath his shirt.

Jinx needed him.

"You're committing treason, Pol," Thatcher warned.

"I know." Apollo went on to give a high-level explanation of his deal with Jinx and the reason he had begun searching for the Vessel: his desire to get rid of the nightmare inside him. Telling his brother of the voice, his magic, the training he'd begun with Jinx, his ability to read other's thoughts and gain access to their minds. From start to finish. Apollo laid everything. Bare. Leaving out Jinx's background. That would be something for her to tell.

Thatcher gave Apollo a worried glance. "I think you should think this through."

"I did. We won't be caught." Apollo slung the leather bag over his shoulder as a hand-maiden informed him that the horses had arrived.

"Father arrives today." Thatcher trailed Apollo, acting as the voice of his conscience.

Apollo responded sternly, "And you can tell him I'm away on business. Say I had an idea that I presumed would be beneficial to present at the Gala, so I went to conduct more research."

He exited his room, Thatcher in tow, and crossed the hall to gather Jinx's luggage. He tapped on her door with a knuckle.

"Before you leave, I think I've figured something out about the flower," his brother whispered loudly. "I would have come to you earlier, but it was inappropriate timing due to Jinx's injury. And then you two left yesterday, and I didn't want to intrude on a crucial moment of quality time."

Annoyance raised the hairs on Apollo's neck. "Thatcher, it's not really the time to ramble."

Jinx opened the door. Apollo took a quick peek at her shoes: flat-footed boots crusted with dried crimson and grime. She was wearing her suit beneath, indicating that she was ready at a moment's notice to don an illusion. "What is going on now?"

"You happen to enjoy my rambling, last I heard," Thatcher protested.

"I usually do," Jinx said. A "tch" escaped Apollo. As Apollo asked for Jinx's bag, she shifted it away from him, declaring she could handle it herself.

Thatcher scratched his head. "If I may continue. You know how Elu's Grace weakens the Cursed? After some sufficient research, I've come to discover that while it weakens the Cursed, it acts as a temporary steroid for humans, giving them an adrenaline high for a few hours and possibly even improved strength. It appears to mimic the organ that the Cursed have. However, if humans ingest too much of it in a short amount of time, they could die." His brother splayed his hands. "Wait for me outside before you go."

Thatcher scurried off upstairs to his at-home lab. Worry fluttered in Apollo's stomach as he wondered how Thatcher could have arrived at that conclusion without experimenting on himself.

Apollo and Jinx descended the stairs in silence.

If what Thatcher said was true, then Apollo shuddered to think of who the Cursed were up against, what they might uncover in the Equinox assembly. Could those who hated the Cursed be plotting their extermination? Would it be a complete massacre of the Cursed at the hands of humans playing God because they were finally strong enough to fight them head-on now?

As far as Apollo could see, the only important factor playing into the takeover of the Cursed was their mindset and perhaps their lack of a leader. They know they're feared, but their key takeaway is the hatred associated with them. If only they understood what power they held in the palm of their hands. A person could only be told they're dumb so many times before they start believing it. This is exactly what Somnium did: strike as much fear in the Cursed hearts as there was in humans. Building these invisible barriers that mentally suffocated the Cursed, resulting in them being cowardly people rather than have the backbone to fight.

Although, maybe some are confident enough to do so.

Jinx strapped her bag to the side of her horse and nuzzled the chestnut gelding's nose.

"Do you know how to ride?" He realized it was a question he should have asked her before. He'd just assumed she could.

"I have experience," she said, digging her foot into the stirrup and hoisting herself up, throwing a leg around the back of the horse. She pulled the hood of her coat over her nose. He did the same, eager to leave Somnium undetected, and mounted his horse as well.

His midnight horse felt hot under his seat. The energy of the horse told him the stallion was ready to run.

Thatcher shoved past the main gate at the front of the manor. He handed over identification cards to Jinx, holding the reins of both horses. "I know this is a mystery you are both trying to solve, but I can't stop thinking about this. I know it is a stretch, but I searched for these people through the records we have at home. The identification cards you brought were useful enough to find some extra, perhaps key details about the men who stopped you. I was curious if they had any certain reason to attack you in the first place. They're all laborers that have had some combat experience, whether it's illegal fighting or militia training. They have also all had a foul encounter with the Cursed at some point in their lives."

Apollo grunted. He knew they had to leave now; he and Jinx were losing precious time, and he preferred not to cross the Woodlands at dark. "Spit it out."

"I think they're Hunters, Cursed Hunters," Thatcher blurted out.

Jinx froze. "What?"

"Cursed Hunters," he repeated.

Apollo recalled that Dr. Watts had mentioned more and more Cursed were visiting him, impacted by those bullets. "We have to go. We'll discuss this upon our return. In the meantime, do not tell anyone about your theory, not even Kovan."

Thatcher licked his lips, dipping his chin and slowly backing away.

A part of him shivered with guilt as Apollo summoned his magic, reaching for the thread of Thatcher's mind, snaking in and listening to his thoughts.

"Thatcher," he said aloud. "How did you conduct your experiment?"

Thatcher gave him a roguish grin. "If you think I did the trials on myself, you are wrong."

Thatcher then thought to himself: *A passing street rat with poor luck on its side.*

That was all he needed to hear. Apollo cut the line to his brother's mind, relieved.

Thatcher fled back into the house. Apollo nudged the horse forward, heading west toward the Woodlands. He knew he would have to confront the place where he'd lost a piece of himself and gained part of something much darker.

Apollo looked over at Jinx, anger radiating from her body in waves. He understood her fury, worry, and frustration. It made sense that she would feel that way. He felt a twinge of it, too. Cursed or not, the people of this city were in grave danger if self-appointed Hunters prowled the alleys. Cursed and wrongfully accused citizens alike were under threat.

Deep in the dark corner of his mind, where the nightmare sat in its mental cage, the demon chuckled. A wolfish grin sprawled across its mischief-crusted lips.

What are you laughing about? Apollo questioned.

The demon droned. *You know why, Little Lord. I'm laughing at your ignorance and selective blindness.*

Apollo swallowed. *Enlighten me.*

Jinx told you her background. When will you tell her yours? Or are you afraid she will leave you? Fear she'll make the same connection you did?

Stop, Apollo ordered, shaking his head.

The nightmare continued. *You don't want her to know what you are, what we are. You know how she will see us once she knows, and trust me...Jinx will find out. You can't keep hiding it from her.*

I know.

Then why do you stall? It will come to an end sooner or later. Why prolong your suffering?

Apollo stayed silent.

You fool, the demon chided and sat back down in its corner, returning to rest. *I'll leave you with this last thought, Little Lord. Everything in the end crumbles, and lies don't protect, they only postpone. So, how long are you willing to push off the inevitable?*

Apollo knew the demon was right. He was a fool. Apollo's time with Jinx *was* limited. Still, he vowed not to let what time remained go to waste. Then he silently prayed to Esme that he wouldn't lose the one he cared for most in this world.

Telling her the truth was his best option; he could only hope she would understand.

He focused his attention back on the ring. Another fissure had been added to it last night. He was unable to control the way his heart reacted around Jinx and how he felt in the days he spent at her side. He knew the risks, but he couldn't keep away from her.

Two more cracks and Apollo dreaded what would come next.

Chapter 36

Jinx

J inx and Apollo were on the threshold of leaving Crosspoint Yard, about to enter the
Slums of her youth. There were too many memories left behind in these cottages.
Another life entirely.

Jinx thought back to the Cursed Hunters that Thatcher had mentioned. With the possibility of a threat fresh in her mind, Jinx wanted to stop by the Netherwen and check on
the Cursed living beneath. She wanted to see what they knew and if they were safe. She
remembered a door to the Netherwen was near this area; she'd only need a minute or two to
check.

"Polly, I need to use the restroom before we cross into the Slums and Woodlands," Jinx
lied through her teeth.

Apollo nodded, reaching over to grip the reins of her gelding as she hopped off. "I'll be
just a minute." When he looked away, she created a doubled illusion of herself, sending it
into a nearby store. As the illusion sauntered off, she scurried over to one of the hidden doors
she remembered would leave her to Netherwen.

Her magic had only returned in full this morning; Jinx worried she could possibly be
spreading herself too thin too soon. Still, she needed to know. She covered herself in the mask
of the Crone that all of the Cursed in Netherwen recognized her as and walked forward.

Descending the dark stairs, the cool, wet rock of the walls enveloped her in chills. The
door shut behind her with a loud bang, announcing to those living beneath that someone
from above had entered.

Jinx broke into a run, the walls of the tunnels rushing past her as the wind sang in her ears. There wasn't much time until Apollo would start to wonder why she was taking so long. She could lie and say it was a stomachache, but she was still unsure how believable that was. Apollo could know if she lied by simply reading into her thoughts. Jinx trusted him not to do so out of respect. And if he did, Jinx would feel the classic prick in her neck.

The town beneath came into view, the soft glow of the cave warming her heart. Children still ran barefoot through the grimy streets as adults traded necessities. It seemed, from the looks of it, that their everyday lives were still unaffected by the threats ahead of them.

Murmurs of the Crone's return surged through the village as she came into view. Jinx slowed her pace down to a fast-paced walk, knowing a real elderly crone would be limited in terms of her speed. She beelined to the town cafeteria in search of Harrison.

Jinx calmed her heart down as she reached the double door to the building. She brushed her illusioned gray hair into place as she caught her breath. The Crone possessed the wise confidence of age or must appear to possess it, regardless of whether or not a quake of nerves was currently running through her beneath the disguise.

Adding a cane and a small hunch to her back, Jinx pushed through the door. Her eyes immediately found Harrison in the back of the room, where he always was, administrating food to the hungry.

Silence crowded the space as hundreds of faces pinned her down.

"The Ghost needs a word," Jinx asserted.

Harrison handed the spoon to a worker next to him as his eyes landed on her. Jinx jerked her chin to the side, beckoning him to follow.

Out of earshot, Jinx settled into a chair, hands intertwined on the top of her cane. She admired the conglomerate of Cursed helping each other out; it was truly a community built on surviving, lending, and borrowing whatever was needed to help each other grow. If only the rest of society would give them a chance.

Harrison wiped his fingers on his apron and folded himself into the seat beside her. "What is it?"

"What do you know of the Cursed Hunters, Harrison?"

His mouth shut quickly. Pressure formed in the center of Jinx's stomach, anxious about his peculiar reaction. He scratched his face before responding. "Many of our runners aren't returning, and if they do, they die shortly thereafter. I don't want to alarm any of the citizens down here, but I fear there are Hunters lurking nearby, that they are close to compromising us."

Jinx bit the inside of her cheek, swallowing down the negative thoughts. *Damn Thatcher.* He'd been right; hunters were appearing out of nowhere. It wasn't safe for anyone anymore, not even her or Apollo.

"When did this start?"

"I'm not sure, though; over time, it slowly started progressing. Fewer and fewer of our runners are returning now. I don't want to risk sending anyone up there," Harrison admitted, a thin sheen of water lining his eyes. "The last one that didn't come back was a ginger boy with a little stubble on his chin. He goes by the name of Ajax. If the Ghost, Jinx, finds him, please bring him back. He is my nephew."

"Do you know who is hiring these Hunters?" There had to be someone higher up leading this purge. The person in command. The brain of the operation.

"If I did, I would have killed them myself."

Jinx hummed to herself. She could tell there was more that Harrison was keeping close to his chest; she just had to ask the right question. "Does a white flower mean anything to you?"

Harrison's spine straightened. "One of the runners who returned came back with a note hammered into his chest, right above the heart. It was a threat. Signed by a Hunter, with a white flower pressed into it."

That pin of the white flower had to be the symbol of people dedicating their support to the Hunters. If not, the people wouldn't wear it so strongly and have intense thoughts about it. Not even those who wear Tutelas are obsessed with the idea of hating Cursed. This was people latching onto resentment because it felt good. And the Hunters are taking action. It was what they did, apparently, hunt for Cursed. Hounds sniffing for foxes.

Preparing for the Autumnal Equinox.

What was that organization conjuring?

The Vessel, the Cursed, the book, the flower, and now the Hunters. Jinx *knew* they were all related, but she still didn't know why. She couldn't help but feel like something bigger, something even more dangerous, was coming.

"Shut the gates," Jinx cautioned. "No one comes in or out unless it is me. Do you understand, Harrison?"

Harrison looked at her, dumbfounded. "What about food? We need resources."

Jinx assured him she would find a logistical approach without compromising the location of the Netherwen. She didn't want to drag her new friends, the Voclaines, into the problem, either. For now she'd take on the responsibility herself.

If that bigger battle was coming, Jinx would need people to back her up. And she knew that the people would pledge fealty to their savior.

"How long will your supplies last?"

"If I stretch, maybe...one more month?"

She could do a month. "I'll come back with your next delivery. On one condition."

Harrison lifted his head, meeting her eyes with an intense gaze.

"When the time comes—open your eyes, Harrison, war *will* come—the Netherwen will support Jinx. Be the men the Ghost would need. When Jinx calls, you answer."

Harrison swallowed, sticking out his clammy hand to shake on it. "You have our word."

Jinx met Harrison halfway, sealing the bargain with her magic. The contract burned into their hearts. "I'll see you again soon."

As the doors of the cafeteria closed behind her, Jinx lunged into the shadows and sprinted toward the stairs. It had already been too long. Apollo would certainly be questioning her whereabouts. It was still a useful stop, though, giving her more information to work with. Puzzle pieces were beginning to fit into place.

Jinx reeled back the mask of the Crone and summoned the illusion of herself back into her body. The organ of magic drained in her core as a wave of tiredness washed over her.

Wiping off the sweat that had started beading at the edge of her brow, she power-walked hastily back to the spot where she'd left Apollo. As she turned around the corner, he locked in on her instantly, ushering the horses over to her in the alley. Just as he started to hand her the reins, a shout of a pained male echoed off the bricks.

Apollo and Jinx looked up, wide-eyed. Her hand instantly drifted to her side, blade at the ready. Apollo jumped off his horse, tying the reins to a post. They sprinted toward the howling.

A flush of adrenaline rushed through her senses, almost as if she could smell where the terror came from. A hound on a trail, Jinx swerved through the labyrinth of the back alleys. She dug the heel of her foot into the ground as she encountered the site of the commotion.

Cursed against humans.

Apollo gathered Jinx back from rounding the corner, keeping her tight against him. They kept their eyes glued on the scene before them.

The Cursed man was bending the ground beneath him to his will, ensnaring the human man in a trap, binding his body to a cylinder of mud. The human wailed. "Please! No!"

Burning rage clouded the logical reasoning in the Cursed man, veins bulging from his forehead. "*You* segregate my kind because of our eyes, because of what we can do! You don't even let me drink in peace?" His words were slurred.

"Sir. It's not my fault that you got kicked out." The human pushed out forced breaths. The Cursed was squeezing him to the point of death, the man's skin flushed purple.

If they didn't jump in, they knew the man would die, giving more humans a "reason" to hate and fear the Cursed, to write them off as monsters.

Jinx pushed herself off Apollo. "We must stop him, or the human will die."

Apollo reached for her arm, but she slipped out of his grasp. She threw on a swift illusion of a man she'd seen pass her by and prowled the edge of the wall, her agile feet soundless as she crept up behind the Cursed. Capturing his free hand behind him, locking it at his back, she pulled a dagger to his throat. "Think about what you are doing. Is this how you want them to see you?"

Digging her knee into the spine of the Cursed, she quickly brought him to his knees. She gripped him by the hair, forcing him to look into the eyes of the frightened human in front of him. "Is *this* what you want? Huh?" Personal frustration was laced in her words. Jinx tried to bite it back. "Keep giving them what they want. Let them torture you into believing the Cursed really are the monsters. Right now you are acting like it, proving them right."

The Cursed groaned, and the human was speechless, words lost on either tongue. "How will you settle this, boys?" Jinx asked with cool malice.

She knew there was evil on both sides. Evil in Cursed and Human. People, however, often could not see their own failings, only looking for the evil in the Other.

She crouched down, taking hold of the Cursed's head by the greasy strands of his hair. She itched to punch him and was unable to hold herself back from cracking his nose. Jinx protected her Cursed—that is, when they were worth it. This man was not. He stood against everything she fought for.

"What are you trying to accomplish here?" Jinx hissed.

Fresh blood slithered down the man's nose, spreading into his mouth and tinting his teeth red. He choked. "I want to be treated like a normal person."

"And how does hurting this man accomplish that?" Pathetic. Granted, she supposed that she wasn't any better, but others could still be.

A dark presence loomed over her. Without even looking, she knew it was Apollo. In her mind, his voice was unrelenting and commanding. *That's enough.*

She pressed down on her jaw. This wasn't the time to make a scene. Broad daylight increased their risk of exposure.

A disorderly presence overcame Apollo. The closer she stood, the more buzzing energy she felt. The ring glowed red, its fissures heaving.

Jinx's gut told her to run the other way. Something about him was off. His eyes seemed lost in thought, the other part of him in control.

It was as if his human cage was slowly disassembling, layer by layer. The Cursed and human were glued in their places, no longer terrified of each other but now of Apollo.

"Leave," he ordered in a voice unlike his own.

In a trance, the two men departed, dragging the toes of their feet on the ground as they drifted out of sight.

Jinx lowered her illusion. She rushed to Apollo's side, trying to bring him back to the present. The malicious aura dissolved after a few blinks, and he started panting slightly. Jinx felt for his heart, the rhythmic beats steady. "What was *that*?"

"I tried something new." Jinx didn't believe him, but she dropped the subject, giving him the space, the opportunity, for him to tell her in his own time.

The rest of the ride to the verge of the Woodlands was mostly quiet. Jinx and Apollo exchanged a comment here and there, tension at the edge of their words after the accident in the alley.

Completely focused on analyzing what Apollo had done and what she learned, Jinx blinked and was startled to find that they had arrived in the Slums. Her old house was just ahead.

Clenching the reins to a halt, the gelding stopped, snorting. Her house had been the last one before the Woodlands. And there it was. Lights on, a new family inside it. A smiling couple hovered by the window, a tiny newborn in the father's arms. His nose nuzzled the baby's stomach. The mother laughed, looking on. Was this what it would have been like if her father hadn't died? Would she have had happy memories of the three of them?

She remembered how her mother would sometimes grab a slice of bread and dip it in butter, eggs, and raw sugar. She then seared it over a hot pan, toasting the slice until it turned golden, the flames of the fire licking the bottom of the metal. Mother always called them her own special kind of Danishes and said they were better than the ones she could buy at a bakery because these were made with love and hard work.

Jinx would devour them whole as Mother brushed her hair, braiding and pinning it into however she saw fit. Mother would dress her and take her along with her to work. Mother worked as a seamstress, and as she sewed, Jinx would eat more homemade Danishes and practice threading the needle, just like her mother. She cherished that memory, so ordinary and yet so full of love.

A warm hand covered hers. "It's that one, isn't it?"

Jinx sniffed, holding back the sting of tears. "Yes." She cleared her throat. "It's good to see a new family in there, I guess. Let's go."

Watching them any longer would only wrench the knife deeper into her heart. It was easier to pass the gateway to the Woodlands than to confront the house of her childhood. In the lush of those trees, Jinx had picked a route that would change her life, yet inside the walls of that house, the memories of her childhood were still fresh and unspoiled.

Apollo followed her, his own shoulders strained. She thought about the comments of the Voclaine siblings whenever they talked about the day Apollo changed and how Apollo recounted his own experience in these woods.

The city behind them vanished behind the thick trunks of mountainous trees. Considering what Jinx had been through in this forest, the familiar scent of pine made her feel oddly at peace.

"I thought we were past the mysterious stranger phase," Jinx said by his side, baiting him to speak. He was clearly lost in his head.

His features softened ever so slightly. "We are."

"Then what's got you so quiet?"

A beat. "Lots of things."

"Do you enjoy being vague?" Apollo's energy toward her had changed after he'd seen her punch the man, taking a hold of the situation. It was a hint of the dangerous criminal she was deep down. "Did I scare you back there?"

Apollo was overcome with a surge of raw emotion. "No. Not at all. I was rather impressed; not everyone can do the things you do. Honestly, I was distraught for them, not you."

His words eased the nerves peppering her belly. "What is it then? You've been acting different ever since."

Apollo wiggled the tips of his fingers, curling and releasing them. "My ring is breaking, and my magic is consuming me. I'm not sure what I did. I thought I was getting better."

The loss of control he felt was similar to the time they had come across the Collection. Only this time, it had felt completely overwhelmed all of his senses, his memories, his actions.

"Learning how to control your magic isn't always a straight line of progression. You will have days that are worse than others. What matters is having a positive attitude. Everything changes when you hand the reins over to your fear. *You* control your magic; it doesn't control you," she offered, hoping it would help soothe his inner conflict.

"Easier said than done."

True.

"At least make an effort to try. I've learned most dreams die not from failure but from people not even trying. Look at me; I've had more jobs than half of the people in Somnium because I've never stopped trying. A person's only limit is their mind." Apollo's head twisted around in interest. "You want to control your powers? Stop focusing on the cage restraining you and make your *own* key because you surely won't find one in an empty room."

The shadowed lines of his face brightened. "You are wise beyond your years."

Jinx waved it off, though her chest contracted slightly, swelling with emotion. Ignoring the constricting sensation, Jinx focused her attention on the marked path of the Woodlands. Somehow, they had slowly veered off the trail. "The Archives are located in the summit?"

"Yes. They're in a small cave on the southern border, guarded by a militia. If I present a special key, you and I will be able to walk in. You'll have to use your illusions, though, and pretend to be my father," Apollo clarified.

"How old were you when you first went in?"

"Fifteen."

That was the same age when Arya mentioned Apollo had changed. "Quite the responsibility for a teenager."

"I always knew what I was born to do. The initiation just solidified who I was always intended to become."

Jinx attempted to guide the conversation. "Arya told me that you used to be quite the charmer before you became all broody and boring." Jinx's gelding shook his mane.

"You think I brood?"

"Absolutely. It goes with the glare."

"It took years to perfect that glare."

"May take a few more," Jinx teased him.

Apollo released a hearty laugh. The sun escaped from behind the orange leaves above them, kissing his cream-colored skin. "Truthfully, I was a brat. Spoiled and stubborn—"

"And that changed when?"

He ignored her. "I knew too much and lived too little. Flirted with many women, dragging them along like strings of yarn. Come to think of it, how could a kid *not* act like that? Give him the world and the position I had; anyone would have probably acted the same. I knew how to work with what I had." Dry leaves snapped under the horses' heavy hooves. "But I grew bored. Every day, the same thing."

"What shifted?"

Apollo's spine straightened, his gaze locked on the path ahead of them. "I lost a piece of myself in these woods."

Arya had told Jinx about how, upon Apollo's return from his trip with his father, he started to wither away, like a carcass stripped of its flesh. It was harder and harder to wipe away the sorrow she felt for him.

"It's too late for me now to regain what I have lost." His voice deepened. "Not you, though."

What did he mean? He'd selected such a specific yet vague set of words.

"We should hurry if we want to get to the Archives by sundown." Apollo snapped the lines to his past, redirecting their attention to the task at hand. He spurred the horse into a gallop.

His avoidance of the past alarmed Jinx. What could be so horrible that he didn't want her to know? Since the beginning of their partnership, the only person to comment on Apollo in the previous years had been Arya. The rest of the family members never mentioned it.

Apollo had warned her to avoid digging too deeply into his past, explicitly reminding her that she wouldn't like what she would find there.

Whatever it was, Jinx didn't care. It couldn't be worse than what she was.

Apollo

As he passed through the moss leaching up the thick tree trunks, he couldn't stop thinking about all of the dark memories these Woodlands held for him. This was the place where a part of him had died, only to be resurrected as something else. This was the place where Apollo had been forced into making a bargain, forever shifting the path of his destiny.

All of a sudden, he was fifteen again, trotting with his horse under the lush green leaves, the hooves of his horse pushing around pinecones on the grimy ground. Father had officially designated him as heir in the Federal Somnium Archive, and Apollo had signed his own name in the volume where past and future lords pledged to protect the city. He'd given his oath and sacrificed his blood; in return, the Seven had forged a key for him that would grant him access to the Archives whenever he pleased. Now there were eight keys in existence, never to be shared. When his father eventually stepped down, his father's key would be useless, and he would no longer be able to open the Archives.

Apollo's excitement was limitless as he teased his father into racing the rest of the way back to the manor. Victory raced through his system. He was one step closer to being the face of the family, one step closer to changing society in ways he saw fit. Apollo couldn't wait to share the news with his siblings, Kovan and Vander.

He couldn't wait to see the envy on their faces, knowing he was the first of the future heirs to be signed and given a key. Father had finally deemed him worthy; his horizon was bright.

Vander probably wouldn't pay him any mind. Kovan would, though.

"Pick up the pace, old man. We have to get home before nightfall," Apollo goaded, smirking at his father.

Father's eyes thinned, fully aware of his son's taunts. "Old man? I'm *forty*, you know."

"Well, you're certainly showing your age now, complaining of back pains and all that. I'm impressed that you've made it this far." Apollo snickered at his own remark.

Father lengthened the horse's reins and adjusted his seat, hinting to Apollo what he planned to do. "You're incredibly cocky, you know. I think it's time I put you in your place."

Father spurred the horse into a gallop, and Apollo followed suit. Lifting his hips from the saddle, he offered the horse the freedom to stretch its legs and gain more ground.

Pounding hooves clattered against the dry leaves, smothering anything in their path. Wind sang past them, a labyrinth of peeling trunks and mossy greens limiting Apollo's choices.

A sleeping trunk split the trail ahead of them. Apollo measured the distance, counting the strides it would take to guide his horse perfectly over the jump.

Father cut a stride short, giving Apollo the leverage he needed to propel himself forward. He chuckled, calling back to his father as he sped off. "You're rusty."

"Apollo!" His father shouted after him, overlooking the desperate gleam in his son's eyes. Apollo was determined to win this race.

Apollo flew down the road, relishing the taste of winning. Victory was always the best dessert. If there was one lesson Father had taught Apollo, it was that whatever the situation, you must always give your best. And he would.

Abruptly, Apollo flew from his seat as the horse dug its hind into the ground, whining and kicking.

Hurt spread through Apollo's shoulder as he connected with the stiff dirt beneath him. His lungs constricted, and he heaved, desperate to collect oxygen.

The horse ran off, stranding him in the center of the Woodlands. The bleak area was stripped of color, the fresh scent of the forest replaced by decay. Fear washed over Apollo. Even animals didn't dare stray into these parts. Apollo's hands trembled as he gazed around him.

Screaming for his father, he ran back down the trail, completely lost. All of a sudden, he felt the creeping sensation that he was being watched.

He should have listened when his father called out to him.

As he sprinted down the path, sweat tracing his brow, Apollo's eyes looked around frantically, sweeping everything in his proximity. He was scared as to what he might find.

Ultimately, he should've been more scared of what would find *him*.

This was the night when he heard the worst words of his life when the voice singed into his mind for the first time.

Hello, Little Lord.

Chapter 37

Jinx

J inx swung off her horse, tying the reins around a tree branch. There it was: the Archives.

Everything she had dreamt of and longed for was *just* within her reach, a hair's length away from being her reality. It could all be over so soon.

Jinx drew in a deep breath, trying to calm her body's jitters.

She was like a dog with a bone—salivating and impatient.

The answer was in there somewhere; she knew it in her core. She could feel the well of magic within her flaring, responding to what lay within the Archives.

Footfalls crunched beside her as Apollo stepped into view, hands in his pockets.

The Archives were carved into the side of the lowest peak of the Northern summit, just around the bend of a soundless stream. To the naked eye, the entrance appeared to be little more than a measly hole, just big enough to fit a single person if they shuffled in sideways. It blended in with the rest of the cave incredibly well, to the point where anyone who didn't know to look for it would walk right past it.

"In all of my life, I never could have expected that the Archives for the city would be hidden within the belly of a mountain," Jinx commented, nervously counting the myriad blades that were tucked within the crevices of her suit. They were all secured in their spots.

"That's the point." Apollo fished for his pocket watch, toying with the buttons on the rim.

He was nervous, too. As stoic as he seemed, stone-faced and serious, his hands betrayed him. Jinx knew that she had asked a lot of Apollo. He is taking a greater risk than her right now. It was treason for him and just another crime on her long list. If they were caught, no matter *who* they were, a twin pair of nooses would be roped around their necks faster than they could blink.

Jinx cracked her fingers, calling on that pool of power deep within her body. Her skin cooled as her muscles started heating up. Green flames licked at her skin as she whipped up a false identity, tailoring her appearance to match that of Apollo's father. The height, the sway of his graying hair, the folding wrinkles beside his eyes.

"It's a little jarring, but it's not half bad," Apollo said as he circled her, inspecting her carefully crafted work, the sear of his eyes boring into her. "Remember the plan and don't stray from it, no matter what. Our time limit is an hour; we have no minutes to waste. You start looking in the front, I'll go toward the back, and we'll work our way to the middle. Look for anything that might be a hint towards the riddle, perhaps a newspaper with similar words or a scroll that matches a hint of the riddle."

Jinx and Apollo walked shoulder to shoulder down into the mouth of the mountain, night consuming whatever light was able to sneak in from the outside world. They followed a row of lit torches drilled into the ribcage of the hallway.

As they delved deeper, the earthy scent of wet rock intensified, and the temperature significantly dropped, sending chills down Jinx's back. She glanced over at Apollo, whose face had settled into the deadpan he classically wore.

A line of guards posted along the walkway slammed their feet and saluted as she and Apollo ambled by. Golden helmets covered their eyes. They were clothed in blue and white uniforms, with bayonets strapped by their sides, indicating that they were high-ranking officers; the sight of them reminded her of a friend she had when she infiltrated the military years ago.

Apollo had explained beforehand that there was only one entrance and exit to the Archives. If they needed to find an escape route for whatever reason, their options were slim to none. Certainly, Jinx couldn't knock out an entire militia on her own. She'd damn well try, though—if it came to that.

As they approached the massive bronze gate, Jinx noticed copper columns plunging through the mountain. Apollo took a sharp right turn, directly facing a stone barricade. He fished around for a chain beneath his shirt and brought out the sigil into view, swinging it between his fingers.

Four sentries formed a barrier between him and the door in front of them. Apollo took a deep breath and recited the sacred words of the Archives: "In the city of dreams, to be the minister of economy is to hold the key to prosperity, to command the tides of wealth and steer its citizens to the light. Archives of treasure open the doors, unleash the history and knowledge that rest within, and guide us toward the future."

It was a pledge his father imbedded in his mind, almost an anthem to prove one's loyalty as the Seven to the Archives.

Jinx bowed her head as Apollo instructed. The sentries nodded and pushed open the door to another chamber.

A single circular chandelier swung low, hovering above a podium, which in turn rested at the center of a large dais. A rickety woman smacked her lips together, pushing her glasses up the bridge of her nose. "Voclaine," she murmured, drawing out the second syllable.

The creases of her skin looked worn and wise; she was not a woman to be messed with.

"Keeper," Apollo bowed.

With sharp scrutiny, she looked down at them from the height of her podium. "What is your business here?"

Apollo plucked an official document from the inside of his jacket. He climbed up the steps of the dais, spreading the document across the top of the podium. "We've come to drop deposits into the tier two vault worth twenty-five thousand Marcs. On Father's most recent business trip, he received a gift from the King and his prophets as a sign of respect."

Jinx tucked her hand into her pocket, swiftly conjuring a gold necklace in the palm of her hand. The opal gem in the center was thick and heavy, outlined by a trail of gleaming diamonds. Jinx dangled it by the clasp and placed the priceless item under the eyes of the Keeper.

The Keeper sniffed it as if she were a hound. Jinx ground her molars, holding her breath.

"What else?" the woman asked. Surely, they were here for more than just a deposit. Jinx glued her mouth shut, as Apollo had assured her earlier that he knew how to get them access.

The tone of Apollo's voice was as thick and sweet as honey. "Since we made the trip, we'll also be conducting a swift quarterly audit."

The Keeper stared at Apollo and studied Jinx before splaying the only book on the dais wide open. She dropped the feathered pen in front of them. "Sign." Jinx quietly exhaled.

Apollo dipped the pen into an inkwell and scratched his name on the next available line, right above the date and time.

Jinx ascended the dais, joining Apollo. There was a minute tremble in her hand as she picked up the pen, mimicking the hand motions of a scrawl as she conjured a copy of the Duke's signature from a few bars above. She'd practiced this maneuver during the ride, studying useless documents that Apollo had handed to her, all containing his father's signature. Her hand still hurt from repeating the process over and over as they rode.

The book had signatures dating back to eight years ago. Skimming the seals between, there was one she took mental note of before reeling back.

The Keeper eyed Jinx before twirling the book back to her and snapping it shut. She motioned her thumb behind her to the heavy bronze door on the left, its edges crusted with age and jagged sediment.

A throng of sentries crowded around them, two-stepping in front and jutting their hands out. Apollo shook off his coat and emptied his pockets. Jinx followed his lead. She camouflaged her knives under a coat of illusions, making them appear as nothing more than trinkets and Marcs and then tossing them into a basket away from her. Meanwhile, the guards approached them to pat down their figures, feeling for weapons.

Once they were deemed clean, Jinx's disguised knives were returned, along with her coat.

Apollo dug the S into the keyhole, gears turning and unlocking as he turned the key. The sentries gripped the handlebars and hauled open the massive door.

Ushering in Jinx, he closed the door behind them. "Okay, you're safe."

Jinx unmasked herself. "What is the point of the Keeper? Honestly, if I'd known where the Archives were located years ago, I would have been able to infiltrate this place on my own."

"That's what you think. You'd have probably continued walking straight toward those bronze bars, but if you go through them, you would have found yourself in the depths of a labyrinth with no escape. Let's say, however, that you *did* find the proper door and *did* meet the Keeper. Even then, without this key—and remember, there are only eight of them—you wouldn't be able to get to the vault."

"How come?"

"This key contains my blood, as the others contain the blood of their own. Any replica wouldn't have that, so it wouldn't work," Apollo said. "Also, this isn't the only Archive that exists. They are all hidden in different parts of the city and outside of it. This one, however, is the biggest."

Jinx took mental note of this new information. A glint of gold shimmered in her eye as it reflected the ocean of wealth. She cast her gaze toward the riches, too awestruck to say anything.

Before them were hills of rolling gold and silver, stretched as far as the eye could see. The metallic scent of Marcs lingered in the air. The rest of the space was adorned with paintings and shelves upon shelves of books, filled with everything from folklore to histories. Jewels and gems of every color glittering under the dimly lit candelabras. It was the essence of wealth distilled into one cave.

Apollo rolled his sleeves up to his forearms. "We're losing time."

Jinx sniffed and dug into the materials in front of them, unfolding scrolls and skimming through books. In her mind, she kept repeating the same damn riddle:

In the table where five once sat, now sit four

No matter how much you believe, our minds still deceive

It's a punishment for seeking the truth

Knit from people's worst desires

One who seeks is bound to bloom

Apollo turned over the paintings, splitting the canvases from their frames and checking inside to see if anything was hiding behind them. Jinx continued to devour a mass of scrolls one by one. She was close; she could *feel* it. Her intuition thrust her forward.

"Find anything?" she called, her voice ricocheting off the cavernous chamber.

A head of dark, raven hair popped up behind a wave of gold. "No." Coins clinked and spilled behind him. "I know you said to perhaps search for a newspaper or a scroll, but is there anything else that may be an answer? Perhaps more specific of what to look for in these scrolls? You said a phrase. However, we could search for an adjective, a verb, an adverb..."

Jinx recited the riddle to Apollo and then gave him an answer: "A name."

"That's a noun, temptress."

"I know." Pinching the bridge of her nose. "Maybe the answer could very well be a name. To think about it, in Camilla's painting there are technically five figures, but only four have a name; there is only one that is unknown. If the riddle is tied to the painting, the answer could very well be the name of the figure. In the third line, it states: It's a punishment for seeking truth, speaking of someone who had been punished."

Apollo's mask slipped for only a moment before nodding and going back to his hunt.

Shoving her hand back into the chest, Jinx found a broken scroll with half of the paper missing, the rest of its sagging paper whirling down in jagged curls.

Planting herself on the ground, she picked up a nearby gem and pinned down one side of the scroll as she rolled it out. Immediately, she recognized drawings depicting the tale of the Virtues.

The Virtues were the children of the Celestial Architect, Aurorix. Aurorix had crowned each of his four children a unique gift to help him maintain balance and harmony in the universe that he had created. Upon his death, his kin would be in charge of sustaining the cosmos.

The Virtues in this drawing were each holding their gifts: Elu cradled rays of the sun; Esme played her harp; Fortuna sat with a wealth of Marcs and a golden spear; Akuji spread out his black wings, clutching coiled sickles to his chest.

And above the Virtues floated a thick, black book.

Elu, Esme, Akuji, and Fortuna each resided over their own court in the divine realm and also ruled over different pieces of land, using their abilities to help the mortal creatures below them. Elu tended to the necessities of life and nature so that life may prosper. Esme bestowed love and fertility. Fortuna shared wealth and opportunities. And Akuji guided the recently departed to the land of the underworld.

There was also the unconquered portion of their realm: a place called the Pandemonium. It was a place of sins.

Memory seemed to have failed her as she faintly remembered a mention of the Pandemonium. Jinx unfurled the scroll further, revealing more of the story. Drawings and words unveiling.

Jinx careened back as this information was new to her, never once heard from passed-down stories. At this point, the Hall of Judgment came into view, with its open ceiling ushering in the stars. Each Virtue sits at their assigned chair, representing their court.

Akuji dug his curved sickle into the table, his harsh face clearly arguing against Elu, who kept her high chin poised away from his. Vines clawed into Akuji, holding back his black feathered wings. An empty chair sat beside him.

What part of the story was this? Jinx had no memory of ever hearing it.

An empty chair. *In the table where five once sat, now sit four.*

The story went on to show tall arches looming over the four Virtues, who were circling a box. Runes that Jinx had seen once before were drawn above them. An electrifying storm barreled into the box, bright runes fusing into its sides. Jinx devoured the words inked onto the scroll. Unraveling a scene of an imprisonment. A figure banished. *A punishment for seeking truth.*

And there, beside Elu, was a white and pink pistil flower, barely budding. *One who seeks is bound to bloom.*

Jinx's stomach sank.

The final piece of the scroll had been ripped out, torn from its origin. She felt the frayed edges, a sensation of energy tickling her fingers. Faint traces of magic imbued into the scroll, missing a limb. Yet wanting to tell the story, begging to be heard. Its sweet, intrusive scent captured Jinx's nose, beelining for her brain. A sharp migraine pulsed at her temple. Webbing behind her eyes, flashing images of times unseen. Incomplete and broken, yet just enough to make conclusions.

The rest of the scroll unfurled before her. Of a box with runes and a man imprisoned. A strange amnesia gripping the minds of all, done by a stunning male with constellations burned into the line of his spine, purposefully taking the remembrance of a certain chaos. An abrupt arrival of a box to Somnium thousands of years ago waiting to be released. Curiosity of a scientist unleashing a flood of magic and a plague to follow behind. The wandering of a creature in a thicket of looming trees, leaving behind its confinement and retribution in its heart. A man turned monster. And a city destroyed at the feet of the Vessel. Death and destruction in the near future.

Somnium, life, vanishing from existence as if it never existed to begin with. An extinction so grand all knowledge would be lost.

Jinx would never forget the lettering of the runes engraved on that wooden box.

Nor the creature that had she had come face to face within the Woodlands.

No matter how much you believe, our minds still deceive. There was a part of their history that had been taken from the memories of the people. The tales that built Somnium.

She felt her teeth start chattering. Jinx fell on her ass, shivering. Blinking the magic away, and the scroll slipped from Jinx's frozen fingers. Apollo was instantly at her side.

Jinx's eyes were glued on the depiction of the Virtues and the unruly court prowling behind. The Pandemonium has been a court of unruled madness, a place of sins. Where the members of the court disposed of their worst desires and acted upon them. Havoc welcomed them and ordered them exiled. Perhaps it was not necessarily a place of untamed civilians, but it had always been missing a Virtue. A ruler. Then there was that empty space by Akuji. The faded body from the museum's painting. The scratched face from the picture in the Tertain attic. Perhaps the artist was unable to draw it in the first place because they couldn't remember the features themselves.

"It's one thing," she uttered.

"What?"

"Polly, we are searching for the same thing." She pointed to the scroll, urging him to read it. "My riddle and your Vessel."

The Vessel must have been a prison for the figure from Camilla's painting, the missing Virtue. The one Elu and the others exiled from their lands. And the creature wanted to explain why in the riddle given to Jinx. What did the creature find that it had been punished for seeking truth? Something grand enough the Virtues took the initiative of banishing one of their own.

The book drawn by Akuji's side was oddly similar to the one on Apollo's shelf.

A clink jerked her back to the present moment. Apollo dropped the scroll in a similar manner Jinx did. He saw the images, too. Squeezing his eyes shut, pushing the magic from his mind. Wrinkles crease on his forehead, showing his distaste. "Why is this the only mention of the Vessel? That was the Vessel in that memory, Wasn't it? How did this scroll survive?" he questioned after examining the scroll front and back.

"I don't know. But I do know who could have ripped the other half out." She thought back to the book of signatures with the Keeper and the familiar name of the person who'd visited just before them: V'Yockovitch. What purpose would he play in doing this? Jinx couldn't understand his drive in ripping out a scroll that dated back thousands of years and a forgotten Virtue.

Just then, there were three booming knocks on the door. "Time's up." Apollo reeled in the scroll and handed it to Jinx.

It was dark when they left the Archives. Apollo decided to take them to stay in a nearby inn where travelers usually stayed for the night whenever they came to hike the Summit. He would have preferred they rest for the night than try to navigate the Woodlands and deal with the wolves.

The lowly cottage was wooden and cozy, a sensation of tranquility and warmth blanketing the establishment. Splintered wood and spindled webs reminded guests of the inn's age. The crackle of burning wood in the hearth put Jinx at ease as she approached the lady of the house. Apollo was beside her, disguised by the illusion Jinx had cast over him, taking the necessary measures to conceal his identity. Rumors could spread across the city if anyone recognized him, and that was the *last* thing they needed. Jinx herself was camouflaged under her own veil; she appeared to be a hooked-nose and ginger-haired woman peppered with freckles.

"I'm sorry, Miss, but there's only one room available tonight." The woman winced.

The entrance creaked open, a group of hikers bellowing behind it and reeking of dried sweat. Jinx watched their footfalls and movements as they crossed the foyer. Strapped to their waists were a series of tools, including daggers. She knew instantly that the delicate curve of that particular blade was meant for tasks other than cutting down prickly branches.

None of the hikers held any sign of the lethal white flower, not that she could see. They could have gone for a hunt, she supposed; the Woodlands were teeming with deer and game. Still, Jinx instinctually trusted her gut, and it warned her that she wasn't as safe as she'd hoped.

The hikers plowed up the stairs, wood groaning under their weight.

She turned her attention back to the woman in front of her, knowing there was not much room for debate. Jinx was also too exhausted to negotiate. "We'll take it."

"That'll be six Marcs."

Jinx traded the Marcs for the key to the room and went upstairs with Apollo. Their room was the first one on the right. The door squealed on rusty hinges as they walked into the small space. Tendrils of dust spilled from the roof as they took in the decaying wood on the thin walls.

Her tone was drenched in sarcasm. "Well, this is nice."

Two large windows flooded the room with moonlight, revealing a single bed and a chest of drawers.

She and Apollo exchanged glances. "I'll take the floor," he said nobly.

"Smart."

The mattress sunk under her weight until one leg of the bed broke, slanting the whole frame sideways. Jinx tumbled down with it, expecting something to snap. Surprising even herself, she chortled, "You know, I actually find this place kind of charming."

Apollo snorted, peeling off his coat. "It's hardly the lap of luxury, but it'll do." Jinx tossed him a pillow from her bed. "How lucky for me. A pillow, just what I always wanted."

"You should work on your bedside manner, Polly—literally. It needs serious work. I'm grateful you volunteered for the floor, though."

"My bedside manner is nothing of your concern." A flush of color sprouted across Jinx's brown cheeks. "I think we need paper and a pencil first."

Apollo picked his notebook out of his bag and sat by Jinx on the tilted mattress. Nestling closer, she leaned into him. "We need to review every piece of evidence that ties our problems together."

Jinx sprawled open the scroll they'd taken from the Archives, the one rehashing the tale of the Virtues. "So, each Virtue has a gift that was given to them by the Celestial Architect, and there are four Virtues but five objects if we include that book. And there is an empty chair by Akuji in the Hall of Judgment. All of this makes me think of that first line: *In the table where five once sat, now sit four.*

"And look at this frame here." Jinx pointed to the electricity surrounding the box. "If my interpretation skills are correct, it seems like the box must be the Vessel. These runes look exactly like the ones that are burned into it. It has been the *punishment for seeking truth.* The Vessel must then be some sort of a cage. We saw something akin to it in the memory. Also, why can't anyone decipher runes on the Vessel? Plenty of years in *the* Momento Museum, and not one historian could crack it?"

"Because these runes are wards meant to powerful enough to keep that thing in—not exactly an entire language but rather pieces of it," Apollo finished. "The Virtue they are casting out must be the one that ruled over the Pandemonium. *Knit from people's worst desires*. Its lack of a leader, the missing seat at the Hall of Judgment, and the gift from the Architect without its owner. All indicate to the banished figure."

"Now, clearly, the person who took the Vessel knew about this missing Virtue, which is why that piece of the scroll is missing. I saw V'Yockovitch sign his name in the book before us. He entered the Archives around the same time that the Vessel vanished," Jinx added.

Apollo tapped the pencil against his lips. "He *was* at the orchestra when I heard someone thinking about it, and he was *also* at my birthday, which would have given him the perfect opportunity to take it. He could've easily paid someone off from Nadir's checkbook so no one would be able to trace the money back to him."

"And he might not be alone. He could be working with someone," Jinx continued.

A person who V'Yockovitch had wrapped around his finger. A person who had some power, yet not someone in a noticeable position. Someone who could go under the radar.

"*Warren*," they both said.

Jinx jumped up from her spot, pacing in circles. "Of course. With the funding from V'Yockovitch, Warren can muster up the resources he needs to experiment on the Vessel and Elu's Grace. He also probably knows how to extract the serum, so he could be the one giving it to Hunters. Going off the network theory we discussed with Thatcher, where all the Cursed are connected somehow, Warren and V'Yockovitch must have figured out a way to eliminate all of the Cursed at once."

"And whatever that solution is...It's being presented on the Autumnal Equinox."

"Why wait? Why not do it now?"

Apollo's face fell as a horrid truth dawned on him. "Because to create a prison like the Vessel, you need a Virtue's power. And you'd need that same kind of power to destroy it."

Jinx faltered a step. "Where would you find power like that?"

"If you gather up enough people, inject them all at the same time with a steroid...that might equate to the power of one Virtue."

"Elu's Grace." Jinx's fingers froze. "Fuck."

"They're sacrificing themselves. It's going to be a massacre. The question to be answered is if the people injecting themselves with Elu's grace know exactly what's going on? Are they even aware?"

"We have to take the Vessel from them before they are able to present it on the Equinox. We saw in the vision what could happen if it were to be activated. Somnium gone and its people with it." Where could it be? Jinx had checked both Warren's residence, as well as the V'Yockovitch manor. However, there was still one place they never thought to check. "The University. We never checked if someone hid it somewhere in the University."

Apollo followed her line of thought. "No one would think to hide the Vessel in the very same place where it has been for twenty years. They could hide it in plain sight."

Twenty years of Cursed being tortured for being different, all because four Virtues banished another. Thousands suffered because deities couldn't keep their problems to themselves. Tens of thousands died due to a plague brought upon their very own Virtues. Where were they when people withered from sickness?

Where were the Virtues when their people needed them the most?

Where were they when *she* needed them? When *Jinx* suffered?

Jinx closed her eyes. There wasn't time to go down that rabbit hole. Jinx was *so close* to going home that she had to keep focused.

She just needed to remember the name of the exiled Virtue, and it would all be over. To do that, the Vessel had to be taken from Warren and V'Yockovitch. "What do we do when we have the Vessel?"

"Well, I think the book we found must be the book belonging to the fallen Virtue. I hope it will tell us. Surely, there's a way to break apart the Vessel without harming anyone. And anyways, better it is in our hands than anyone else's." Apollo got to his feet, closing the distance between himself and Jinx and enveloping her in his scent. He took hold of her hands. "Firstly, we have to make sure that it *is* Warren and V'Yockovitch who are the culprits. If we're wrong, we don't want to raise a false alarm."

She squeezed his hands. "I know." Jinx desperately wanted to be right, especially considering the fact that now that she knew her riddle and the Vessel were related, this mystery was just as much her problem as his.

"You will go home, Jinx. I promised you that. I always see things through."

Jinx wrapped her arms around him, and Apollo embraced her in turn, holding her tightly to his chest. She believed him. Sincerity was laced into his every word. She held the promise close to his heart. "I know that too." She could feel her pulse in her throat.

Heat pooled low in her belly. She could feel it—the want, the desire she'd been postponing. A glance at his taunting lips made her breath hitch.

The memory of his words rang through her skull. *You'll understand what living means.* She yearned to go home, yet she also longed to live right *now*. Experience life *with him*.

Jinx raised to the tip of her toes and closed her eyes, touching her mouth to his.

Chapter 38

Apollo

Her lips were soft and tender. Poison and temptation all at once.

He felt everything and more.

Jinx pulled back, pressing her mouth into a thin line. She peered up at him with those jewel eyes he could swim in for hours. Pink blossomed across her face, reaching the tip of her nose.

One kiss was not enough when he'd only gotten a simple taste of her. The ring around his finger seethed as his heart thundered unbearably in his chest. He didn't care.

She was worth the pain his body would endure. Apollo would suffer just to feel her.

Taste her. Touch her. Love her.

Apollo cupped her jaw and tugged her back toward him, clashing their lips together. She drew her slender frame flush to his, deepening the kiss and inviting him in, clawing her nails through his hair.

His hands roamed, attempting to feel every curve of her at once, squeezing her waist, greedy with need for her. He feared that if he stopped, Jinx would disappear.

She answered with a little whimper that drove him mad, igniting a piece of him that had been shut in darkness. He had told her that his kiss would teach *her* the meaning of life, but he had lied. Jinx had redefined the meaning of life for *him*, restructuring the basic components of his soul, throwing oil into the fire that pulsed in his heart.

Jinx threw her arms around his neck, hungrily taking more of what he gave her. Apollo would let her do whatever she wanted. His existence was hers.

Passion seared into their kiss, their tongues engaged in a dance of pure lust.

Apollo ran his hands up her legs, hooking his hands behind her knees. In an easy movement, he lifted her from the ground and locked her around his waist. All he knew was that he couldn't stop tasting her. She was so sweet—with a hint of mint.

He set her gently on the drawer, fingers digging into her flesh.

Jinx whimpered slightly, arching her back and breaking their kiss. Apollo dragged his lips along the line of her jaw. Her soft skin felt like silk against his mouth. He couldn't stop salivating at the taste of her.

She frantically played with the buttons of his shirt, exposing his bare chest, before caressing his neck and tugging a little too harshly at his hair. The move sent a rush of blood to the length between his legs.

"The things you do to me, Temptress." He purred, selfishly kissing her again. Pain crushed his heart, constricting his lungs, but he refused to focus on it.

Beyond the pain, there was something greater. There was a thread—a connection.

Lost in the sensation of her, he unhooked the laces of her leather suit, peeling it off. Grazing her stomach, he swallowed the sharp gasp escaping her, tracing the outline of her swollen lips.

Jinx ripped the shirt off his shoulders, closing the inch of space between them. Her nails found his bare back, clawing down his spine. She heard a rumble from deep within his throat and felt his pants tighten, restricting him.

Apollo ground his teeth together. "Divine above, you're *torturing* me."

He clutched her legs and yanked her closer. He put his hand on her chest, pinning her down to the drawer, her spine slick against the wood. Delicately tracing his tongue over the lines of her neck, he smacked his soft lips down in a trail to her pink nipple, taking the hard bud into his wet mouth.

Teasingly, he flicked at it with his tongue, loving the way she responded to his touch. She sucked her lips together, whimpering and releasing shallow, panting breaths.

"Let me hear you," he said.

Pleasure killed her words as her eyes closed, and she tilted her head back.

Darkly chuckling, he snaked a hand down to the place between her thighs, palming the tender area above her pants. "Do you want me between your legs?"

Her hooded eyes took him in lustfully before she granted him a dip of her chin.

"I need to hear you say it."

Breathlessly, she whispered a single word: "Yes."

A devious smile crossed his mouth as he tugged off the skintight leather, leaving her body bare before him. On the brink of drooling, Apollo stroked a finger over the folds of her flesh, pleased to find her soaked. As the pad of his finger circled the bundle of sensitivity, she jerked.

Apollo watched her attentively, eyes devouring her every movement. "Would you prefer my hands or my mouth?"

She licked her lips. "Both."

"Right answer."

Apollo dipped a finger into her warmth, her muscles contracting around him. He pumped his hand in a rhythmic beat, learning her insides and what she preferred. Apollo wanted her to experience bliss, to make her see the stars and the moon.

He added a second finger as Jinx lifted herself off the surface of the chest. Apollo pressed his free hand to her stomach, keeping her secured to the drawers. "You move, I stop. Understood?"

Jinx nodded, but Apollo refused to take that for an answer. "I can't hear you."

"Yes," she replied. "Now, are you going to continue or not?"

Apollo smirked. "It would be my honor." He resumed pumping in and out, sensing how she squeezed around his fingers, wanting to get more of him.

Her palms clutched around the edges of the drawer, her hands white-knuckled.

Apollo dropped his head to her core and kissed the barrier of her folds, easing his way to her center. Each time his lips met her skin, Jinx answered with a little wince.

He met the bundle of nerves and softly pressed his mouth to it. She gasped. A light twitch, and Apollo halted. Jinx lifted her head. "Go on."

"So demanding," he drawled, his wet tongue skimming the heat of her. Apollo nearly released himself in his trousers just from the taste of her. Virtues, he needed to devour her. He roamed his tongue again, hungrier this time, sucking and feasting on her flesh.

Gently, he curled a finger and found that spot—the one that caused her to moan his name. Only his name would sound so good around the curve of her lips. The sound of her voice completely undid him.

The ring burned his skin, marking the flesh. Apollo removed his hand from Jinx's stomach, the other feeding into her craving, happily complying with her demands. Flashes of pain coursed through his veins, weakening his knees.

The demon could take his soul so long as he had her.

Apollo nudged her legs wider as they trembled. She was close.

"That's it, my Temptress. Come for me," he rasped. Apollo could be between her legs all day if she pleased. There was nothing like her.

Jinx moaned again, the flush of lust softening her features.

She ground her hips against his face, begging for more.

Apollo moved even faster, delighting in the way her body clenched. He panted, close to his own release.

Suddenly, Jinx's orgasm rolled through her, arching her back yet again. Apollo consumed everything she offered, hopelessly addicted to her.

Jinx

Jinx lay awake in the mellow of the darkness, tracing the line of her lips. She was unable to mimic the way they'd felt against Apollo's. He'd lived up to his word: his kiss was life.

From the moment their lips met, Jinx could not stop feeling the tug in her heart, yearning for something more than just passion and release. Although this incident had brought up questions, she wasn't yet ready to answer them. Plenty of those questions had to do with what would happen once this was all over, and she needed to focus on the task at hand.

She turned on her side, memorizing the lines of Apollo's face. The angle at which his head dipped in the pillow. How the mattress immerses under his weight. The way he inhaled and exhaled. He appeared so peaceful.

If only he could always be like this. Free from worry and pain.

But freedom had a cost.

As much as he pretended it didn't, she knew their lustful session had caused him a great deal of suffering. The ring marked deep grooves in his flesh, and the silver band fissured even further, close to crumbling and held together by the thinnest of bands.

Jinx fetched his hand, pecking it softly.

What would become of him when the ring shattered? After his extensive training, Apollo had somehow grown stronger and weaker at the same time. On the one hand, his control over his magic was much greater, and he could both better harness his abilities and reveal more of his emotions. However, whenever the ring decided to retaliate, it tore him up from the inside.

He was hiding something from her.

From the instant Apollo compelled those men in the alley to walk away, she knew their obedience wasn't just because they respected his authority as one of the future Seven. The hollow void in his eyes spoke for him—there was something more going on.

Why didn't he want her to know what was really going on? What if she could help him? Indecisive and straddling the border between prying and respecting his privacy, Jinx didn't know what the best course of action was.

And yet, in loneliness, they had found each other.

Jinx twirled what remained of the silver band around his finger. She trailed each crack, memorized by the web it made, like a unique set of veins spreading beneath the living metal.

She brushed her hands around his, feeling his tender skin. Unsure if the shadows were playing tricks on her, she was startled to see that the veins near Apollo's wrist appeared to have turned a darker, almost black hue.

He stirred in his sleep, pinching his brows and groaning.

Jinx blinked, wondering if she had just been imagining things. But the stream of black blood poured further into his system, slithering up his forearm. Soon, it was taking over his entire arm, expanding up to his neck, seeping into his face.

Jinx's nerves jolted as she whispered in his ear, "*Polly.*"

His head shook, and his skin paled, the network of rotten blood transparent beneath his chilled flesh. Apollo's jaw tightened as the ring started to glow red in the night, illuminating the room and drenching it in crimson. He muttered to himself in a way that was short-winded and difficult to understand, "I know...I can't...I know..."

Her heartbeat accelerated. Something terribly wrong with Apollo. His muscled frame trembled with tight shivers, his teeth chattering.

Straddling him, she rocked his shoulders forcefully. *"Apollo. Wake up."*

His eyes remained screwed shut as he twisted his head from side to side, wincing in pain.

She spoke his name again, frantic, watching helplessly as the rot from his body bled into the sockets of his eyes. A tendril of ruby magic fell from his eye, following the route down his veins and into the ring.

All of a sudden, there was a pulsing beacon of light. The fractures within the ring glistened as sweet magic scent filtered in the air. It was a call—a summons of a sort.

Then, the room went dark, the stark change momentarily blinding her.

"Apollo?" she whispered, his limbs still beneath her. Careening closer, she called his name again, brushing a strand of his hair away from his face.

His eyes snapped open. There was only red.

His hand shot up to her throat, closing around it. At arm's length, Jinx reached under her pillow and pressed her dagger to the line of his jaw.

His fingers squeezed, digging into her skin. The pressure wavered slightly. His nostrils flared; he was breathing heavily. An internal battle was clearly waging inside him.

Jinx stared deep into those vicious crimson eyes, searching for the man lost in his own mind. She remained calm, unafraid, even as she pressed the blade closer to his skin. Red eyes or not, he was in there somewhere. And Apollo wouldn't hurt her.

Not even as a merciless wolfish grin enveloped his lips.

"Where are you?" She choked. His grip tightened, straining her throat before softening.

She forced the frigid dagger further into his neck until a bead of blood swelled at the tip. Damn the Virtues.

Suddenly, she realized the blood had turned from onyx to ruby.

Apollo blinked, his eyes slowly returning to their natural state of gray. He snatched his hand back from her neck as confusion and horror lined his features. "Did I...did I hurt you?" His gaze trailed down to the blade she still held firmly at his neck.

"No."

A thick swallow. "What happened?"

After catching him up to speed, she brought herself to say, "It's getting worse. Isn't it?"

"Yes."

Finally, she placed the dagger back beneath the pillow and set her hands on his bare chest, tracing his muscles, every border and crease of them. "Was it a nightmare?"

"It always is." A beat. "I saw a woman cackling."

He said he saw a woman when they first encountered the flower in the market, too. The vision then could have left him subconsciously thinking about it. Perhaps it worried him more than he let on.

Reaching over to the scar in his torso, she traced it carefully, the flesh haphazardly stitched together and awry, seeing it for the first time. "How did you get this?"

He held onto her hips as if he were afraid she might get up and run. "Months after I fled from the Woodlands, I realized that I had magic and was a Cursed. I began to question how I could keep this secret. I wondered if my family and most trusted friends would treat me differently if they knew. The pain of my self-restriction tortured me daily. I didn't know how I'd keep living. If I should even try at all…"

Jinx shifted, not liking where the story was heading.

"I attempted to starve myself, slowly wither away. If I could pretend I was sick, there'd be no questions as to why I would show up dead one day. Except I didn't. I survived for months without a drop of food. I took pills and drowned myself in alcohol until I grew tired of it all. So I snuck into the kitchen one night once everyone was sound asleep, stole a knife, and locked myself in my bedroom." His breath was shaky. "I took it and plunged it into myself."

Jinx's mouth fell open. Arya had been right; her brother had tried to kill himself, alone in his misery.

"The only problem was that I didn't die. I couldn't. *It* wouldn't let me. My skin stitched itself back together, my blood dried up. I tried again and again, and every time, the same thing would happen. In my head, all I heard was deranged laughing. My suffering was a *joke*. After I'd stabbed myself so many times in the same spot, the skin scarred. And I knew I didn't have much of a choice but to endure it."

Jinx cradled his side, embracing him with her limbs. He tucked her in close to him.

She hated picturing young Apollo doing that to himself. He deserved more than the cards the Virtues had dealt him. Yet why hadn't the rest of his family ever questioned what was going on? Were they selectively pretending that everything was normal, or was he just that good at hiding his emotions?

"I'm sorry you went through that." Jinx buried herself into his neck, grateful in a strange way that his magic let him live. She cleared her throat. "What else did you see in your nightmare?"

"Jinx." His tone made gooseflesh spring up on her skin. "I am not able to tell you everything, but know that I only have your best interests at heart."

"What are —"

He cut her off. "I believe there may be a time in which you have to kill me. I trust no one but you to do so."

Puzzled at his choice of words, it vexed her that he spoke as if he were going to die tomorrow. "Why would you say such a thing?"

"I am afraid I will hurt you," he admitted and shut his eyes. Her ear was now directly over his heart; the intense sound of nervous pumping filled her ears.

Jinx said nothing in return. The words just never reached her lips.

When it came to the kill, Jinx had never once hesitated to release blood and send a person's soul off to Akuji and the underworld. It was a natural cycle of life for her: kill or be killed. It was just another piece of the puzzle of survival. She'd wreaked havoc without thinking, losing count of the number of souls she'd claimed over the years. The slice of skin upon a sharpened blade.

Yet she could not picture initiating that slaughter upon Apollo. His death on her hands. The crimson blood from his body tainted her own flesh as emptiness consumed his wintry gray eyes, his limp body dead on the ground.

It was a horrid image she wanted to forget.

Plenty of thoughts buzzed frantically in her mind, but a certain one was louder than any of the others.

For the first time, Jinx wasn't sure if she could go through with it.

Chapter 39

Apollo

Shutting the door to the manor after finally returning home, Apollo came to face with his father. Jinx stuck to his side. "Father, I'm so glad you're back."

"My boy." Father slammed Apollo into a bear hug. "It's good to see you, too. There is much we need to discuss. Do you have a minute?"

Apollo glanced over at Jinx. They had planned to catch up with Thatcher, updating him on what they had discovered in the Archives and seeing if he'd found out anything new about the Cursed Hunters—if there was more to uncover. It was the night of the Autumn Equinox.

Jinx dipped her chin. "I'll meet up with you later. I'm sure Thatcher has plenty to talk about." Jinx sauntered off, taking her luggage with her upstairs.

Father opened the door to his study. His ledgers and journals were on full display, but it was a specific letter addressed to Father, asking for Arya's hand in marriage, that caught Apollo's eye. "Before we begin." Apollo folded himself into the leather chair across from his father. "You cannot accept the proposal from Velez."

Father tipped his head to the side. Apollo had gained his interest. "Why not?"

"He harassed Arya weeks ago in Botanic Plaza. That alone should tell you about the kind of man he is."

The strong features of Father's face darkened; the orange hue of the flames from the hearth cast a frightful glow over his expression. "Was she alone?"

"No. Veyda was there, too. She struck him in the face with Arya's fan and dragged them both out of there."

Father ground his molars, picking up the envelope and throwing it into the fire. "Solved. I'll have to give Veyda my thanks." Apollo felt an involuntary tug on his lips; his father caught the smile and tilted his head. "She's a good one, isn't she?"

"Veyda? Yes, indeed." Apollo rubbed at his mouth, attempting to obscure his smile.

"She's from the east?" Father reclined into his chair, his sudden interest alarming to Apollo.

Apollo lazily crossed a leg over the other. "Yes."

"And she is to go home soon?" The question stopped him in his tracks. Technically, when they retrieved the Vessel, their deal would be finished. Jinx would return to her mother, and Apollo would still be living in the manor. Apollo didn't want to keep Jinx from her family, as much as his heart protested otherwise. Father clicked his tongue. "Ah. But you don't want her to go?"

Apollo kept his silence—it was enough of an answer.

"You know, your mother despised me at first." His father carefully poured himself a glass of liquor. Apollo raised an eyebrow; he'd never heard his father talk about this before.

"Why?"

"Why else? I was a spoiled rich boy, like all the rest. I believed everyone else was beneath me—until I met her. At the masquerade ball, your mother rejected me. I couldn't wrap my head around it." He gave a self-deprecating laugh, nursing his glass. "She humbled me a great deal after that. The more she resented me, the more I pursued her. It drove me crazy. Why wouldn't anyone want me? I was the great Edmund Voclaine! It wasn't until I stepped back and took a hard look at the kind of man I was versus the man I really wanted to be. For her. Then, I saw the world differently. She encouraged me to see things through a new perspective."

Apollo hadn't expected to have this kind of conversation with his father upon his return. "What are you getting at?" He was growing almost uncomfortable at the heightened level of intimacy between them; for the most part, Apollo's relationship with his father had focused on business and politics.

Father took another sip from his glass. "You'll meet thousands of people in your life, but there will only be one that changes everything. They will be the source of both your strengths and weaknesses. And when you find that person, do not let them go."

Touching as it was to hear the story of how his parents first got together, Apollo hesitated to take his father's advice. Jinx deserved better than him, and as much as Apollo wanted to change for her, he knew that in the end, both of them would be hurt. It had been selfish of him to kiss her that night. "What if she doesn't like the person I truly am? What if she deserves more?"

"I doubt that." Father huffed. "In her eyes, there is only you. And sometimes, you must take a leap of faith. Trust that even in your worst of moments, she will be there."

A leap of faith. Apollo took a deep breath, reflecting on it.

The more he hid pieces of himself away from her, the worse it would be when she eventually found out his secret. Apollo needed to make that jump and trust she wouldn't leave him. Because that was what love was really all about, wasn't it? Bearing every corner of your heart to another, no matter how rotten, and having faith the other person wouldn't break it.

"When did you turn into such a romantic?" Apollo asked as a diversion.

Father smiled. "Always have been. The Voclaines are just good at hiding it."

It appeared that the Voclaines were good at hiding plenty. "How was your business in the east?"

Father shifted and stood up from his chair, ambling over to his desk. He sorted through the papers until he picked one up, tossing the file over on Apollo's lap. "Tedious, but the deal went through. We were able to lower taxes on the imports and exports on both sides. We'll be getting more shipments from the east now: spices and tea. Yet, I'm still worried about the sailors. There's been a rise in the number of pirate crews out at sea. It's not my responsibility to think about protecting our borders, but rather De Conto's. I'll need to speak with him."

"What do you need me to do?" Apollo asked. Father always invited him into the study when he needed something.

"See what you can find out about Keresich." Keresich was a little island hanging off the coast of the east. Since it was all the way across the sea from Somnium, the Seven never paid it much attention. Apollo pursed his lips. For his father to bring it up now meant that during the trip something bothersome had happened on that island. Perhaps his father believed that the influx of pirates originated there.

"I'll do what I can."

"Great." Father clapped his hands together. "Now, why were you gone for two days? Thatcher mentioned that you had an idea before the ball this weekend."

Apollo knew this was coming. Bracing himself, he spun an easy lie to his father. "Yes, I decided it'd be nice to take Veyda to the inn we used to go to when we'd take hunting trips for days at a time. She wanted to go camping, I thought I'd do her a favor, a better option. As for the ball this weekend, how would you feel about making a presentation on the history of Somnium?"

Apollo's father clasped his chin between his thumb and index finger. "Why would we present that? Do tell."

"I've done research while you were gone. I think understanding our history can give us a clear view of what Somnium's next steps with the Cursed should be."

The nightmare in Apollo's soul grinned, sending an uncanny sensation to Apollo's gut.

Jinx

Meanwhile, Jinx spent the last hour catching Thatcher up on everything that she and Apollo discovered during their trip, which ended in Jinx confiding in him about her riddle. The only thing she held back was their theory about Warren and V'Yockovitch. Thatcher was close to Warren; she was unsure of how he'd handle the accusation. Rolling out the broken scroll on the surface of his workbench, Thatcher inspected it carefully, his nose pressed against the old parchment.

"Fascinating. Why did this scroll survive, though? Out of everything? Our history books don't mention any of this." He skimmed his palms over the paper, a mixture of pure amazement and confusion lighting up his eyes.

"I always suspected a part of our history was missing, though I didn't think it was anything this huge," Jinx confessed.

Thatcher tapped his foot rapidly against the wooden floor, the gears of his mind now in motion. "If the Virtues cast one of their own out, exiling them, there must have certainly been a good reason. Perhaps whatever Virtue did is why they didn't want any of us to remember him or V'Yockovicth; he was the one who ripped off a piece of the scroll. Yet it'd make no sense as to how he'd take those memories from people who knew the Fallen Virtue before his demise. Maybe this scroll was spared because one of them *did* want to keep his name alive. Look." He pointed at the part of the picture where Akuji had been restrained against his will.

Jinx's eyes widened. "He's fighting the other Virtues on behalf of the banished one."

Thatcher shrugged. "Perhaps. So, if Akuji was on the side of the exile, it is possible that he went behind the backs of the other Virtues, preserving the gift of that Virtue to keep his memory alive." He scratched behind his head. "Just a thought. I'm no historian."

Neither of them were historians. But it was still a good theory.

She stared at the sketch of the book without an owner. With great reluctance, Jinx asked Thatcher to wait for her as she fetched the book from Apollo's room.

Apollo had been stuck in conversation with his father since they arrived. Jinx entered his chambers, fishing for the volume on his shelf. Just looking at the black leather book caused her stomach to clench, making the hair on her neck stand on end.

Barely tolerating its all-consuming presence, she brought it with her back up to the attic.

"I can't believe the relic of a Virtue has been in our possession this entire time," Thatcher muttered.

Jinx pried the book open. Ink actively swirled across the pages as magic filled her nose, sending a throb of pain to her temple. Someone had enchanted this book against spying eyes.

Stepping away from it, she massaged her forehead. "Maybe you'll have better luck." She slid the thick tome over to Thatcher.

His brows pinched together, a deep crease between them. "These pages are blank."

"No, they aren't."

"Yes. They are," Thatcher argued.

Jinx came up behind him, tracing a slithering black line on the page. "You don't see this?"

"I see your finger drawing on a blank page." How was it that Thatcher couldn't see the writing, yet she and Apollo could? The only difference she could think of was that she and Apollo were both Cursed, while Thatcher was strictly human.

Jinx followed the trail of the ink with her finger, asking Thatcher repeatedly if he saw anything. Each time, he responded firmly with a no, staring at her as if she were insane. She pulled her finger back up to the left side of the paper, repeating the line.

Repeating the line.

It was a *pattern*.

The ink was sketching everything out for her the entire time. She gasped. "Do you have a paper and pencil?"

Thatcher handed over the tools, peeking over her shoulder as she felt the swirling ink with one hand and copied the design on the paper with the other. One by one, harsh lines built on top of each other.

Jinx scrawled on the paper as fast as she could until the ink reset on the other side.

Looking down, she realized she had drawn a singular rune: a horizontal line with a semicircle beneath it and a vertical line extending beneath that before breaking into two parts. Above the splitting line lingered a connected minute circle centered by a cross,

"What is it?" Thatcher questioned.

"A rune."

"What does it mean?"

It bothered her that she couldn't figure it out. "Not sure. But it's clearly from ancient times." She flipped to the next page, eager to see if there would be clues about another rune.

Flattening the other side, a chaotic whirl of ink sporadically zipped up and down the page, untamed. As she flicked through the different pages of the book, each sheet acted in a different manner. The original seemed to be the only one to have a set, regulated pattern.

A knock on the door set Jinx into a panic, snapping the book shut just in time. Fey popped her head through the door. "Finally, you're back. Arya is downstairs; she told me to come get you. It's the perfect time to practice that partner dance for the Masquerade Ball."

Thatcher gave Jinx a pointed look. "You wanted to practice a partner dance?"

"I have two left feet." Though the dance seemed frivolous in light of the new clues they'd uncovered, Jinx still longed to learn. Perhaps she could make an exception, just this once.

Thatcher crossed his arms, an overly excited grin taking a hold of his lips, with a sly and knowing look just above them. She chose to ignore it. "Watching this will be fun."

Fey snorted. "I don't know what you mean. You're going to be her partner. See you both downstairs."

Thatcher waved his arms, exasperated. "What?" Jinx burst out in a fit of laughter. He pointed an accusatory finger at her. "Hey, you don't get to make fun."

"Come on. I'll try to not step on your toes." Jinx beckoned him with her chin to the door.

He grumbled behind her. "How is it that you're a notorious thief, a brilliant illusionist, and yet you can't even dance?"

"I've never been able to. Whenever I'd take on the identity of someone in high society, I'd be required to learn, but I never really got the gist of it." Jinx walked down the hall, reaching the curving stairs to the main foyer.

"Like who?"

She decided to trust him. "Once, people knew me as Sophia Acadaine. Cousin of Rylee Panchak. I'm partially the reason why Rylee hasn't been seen. Her mother had been put in prison. Well, I put her in prison."

Thatcher gripped her wrist, flinging her around. "I thought Sophia died?"

"She did and didn't. The real Sophia still lives in the east. But the illusion of her that I cast died by the pistol that I placed in Lady Panchak's hand. I pretended to be Sophia visiting from the east for a few months. It was an easy character to play since the real Sophia lived in another country, and the Panchaks got to see her only a handful of times before I was the one playing her. I did plenty of digging in public records before choosing to be Sophia. I don't regret faking Sophia's death; it essentially saved Rylee in the end."

"Why would you do that?" He had so many questions.

Besides Apollo, Thatcher was the only person Jinx felt comfortable talking to—and now, she took a leap of faith. "Lady Panchak was killing her daughter, and slowly. Rylee was Cursed, and when Lady Panchak found out, she locked her in a tiny room as her own magic swallowed her whole. So you know, when a Cursed is untrained, they can easily break the organ that allows them to have magic; when that happens, they can die if not treated fast enough. With Rylee dying in a small room, I played with Lady Panchak's mind, driving her to insanity and had her murder Sophia. After that, I was able to get the key and take Rylee to a doctor."

An empathetic recognition of loss flashed across Thatcher's ice-blue eyes. "Where is Rylee now?"

"I don't know. I haven't seen her since that day." Jinx hurriedly continued downstairs, Thatcher on her tail.

"Were you fond of her?"

"One could say that," Jinx said.

There wasn't much Jinx could do at this point. The last time Jinx saw Rylee, two years ago, she was dropping Rylee off to see Dr. Watts. Rylee had nearly overused her magic to death.

It was impossible for Jinx to forget the state she'd left Rylee in. Rylee had long hidden her magical abilities from society and, with good reason, was afraid of how others would react. In doing so, her organ became strained, depleting her magic before it ultimately collapsed in on itself. The magic within her snapped, and before long, the organ containing magic bled out into the rest of her system, poisoning her from the inside. Rylee's lips turned a deep blue; it looked as if frostbite had started to gnaw her alive. Her blond hair lost color, turning pure white.

Rylee had become snow personified. Jinx recalled the sheen of frost that coated her bedroom. A cave of icicles and snowflakes crept into every crevice available. Rylee's personal quarters had transformed into a tundra.

It was one of the reasons why she'd wanted to help Apollo with his abilities from the start. The sight of Rylee lingering on the edge of death – she couldn't let him go there.

"You alright?" Thatcher fell to her side.

Lost in her memories, she'd failed to notice the door to the living room. Jinx blinked herself out of her stupor. "Yes."

Jinx pushed into the room, noticing that Arya and Fey had cleared the floor so they'd have an open space to practice. Fey was perched at the piano, fingers at the ready-to-play. She was softly tickling the keys, feeling the instrument out. Arya paced alongside it, counting the rhythm of the beats in her head like a metronome. Fan in hand, she tapped her fingers along the polished wood.

At her entrance, the two siblings perked up. A sudden sense of pressure encapsulated her heart. Jinx wanted to do well; she was eager to impress the rest of high society at the ball, and she knew her performance would have a big impact on her reputation.

Arya dragged Jinx to the center of the room. "Let's be mindful of our time." Circling Jinx, Arya analyzed her from top to bottom, from the position of her feet to the bend in her spine.

She flicked the fan on Jinx's shoulders. "Keep these back, press them down." Arya stopped at her feet. "Alright. Fey will play a popular tune that will surely be played at the masquerade—the Sembla. I will guide you through the steps with Thatcher as your partner. It's an easy dance, but you must be graceful. Let's begin."

Jinx and Thatcher walked toward each other. She placed her left hand on his shoulder, and the other reached for his hand. Thatcher's other hand curled around her waist.

"You owe me," Thatcher whispered.

Jinx chuckled, the laugh dying on her tongue once Arya sent daggers her way.

Fey delicately pressed the teeth of the piano, slowly leading them into the song. Arya instructed Jinx to follow Thatcher's lead. She counted out the beats, directing them in a simple four-step, advising them to stay inside the lines of an imaginary box.

Arya smacked Jinx's spine, reminding her to keep it straight. Jinx's grasp on Thatcher's hand tightened as she tripped over his foot. His frame was like a wall, keeping her steady.

"Again," Arya commanded.

Jinx sighed, frustration building up beneath her skin. She'd get this down; determination wouldn't let her fail. She was Jinx, after all. What was a partner dance to the Ghost of Somnium?

Jinx tried again, repeating the simple four-step and carefully watching her feet, cautious not to accidentally dig her foot in Thatcher's toes. Pain lashed through her skull as Arya smacked her again. "*Don't* look at your feet. It's rude. When dancing, gaze into your partner's eyes."

Fey winced for Jinx, sucking through her teeth. Jinx pressed down on her tongue.

Arya recommended she try a twirl, drawing an imaginary line down the center of the room. "Dance down this line. Every two steps, you'll pivot into a twirl with Thatcher."

Thatcher groused as the two prepared themselves for the challenge. Jinx counted one step more than another, shifting the weight of her foot to raise into a pivot. After successfully managing the twist, she not so successfully landed on Thatcher's big toe. Jinx was unsure of why the partner dance was always so difficult for her. The battle was a simplicity, an art of defense. Maybe it was the coordination of working with another that knocked her balance off kilter.

The piano came to an abrupt halt. Thatcher crouched down to his foot, cradling it. "Just give me a moment. I'm not sure if I'm internally bleeding or bleeding out."

Apollo's mother bursting through the door, perplexed at the mess. "Why does it sound like bodies are *dropping* in here?"

Fey piped up cheerfully. "We're teaching Veyda how to partner dance in time for the Masquerade Ball this weekend."

Thatcher squirmed. "Only my toes have been assassinated in the process."

"Oh, it wasn't *that* hard of a step," Jinx argued. Shame curdled in her stomach; deep down, she knew it really was a strong stomp.

"Then you miscalculate your strength."

Apollo's mother turned to Arya. "What are you teaching her?"

"The Sembla."

"That's the easiest one in the book."

"I know. Her coordination is a *joke*."

"Have you tried the line?"

"Just did."

"And?"

"It's a painful sight."

Why did they speak of her as if she wasn't standing right there? Fists clenched, Jinx interjected, "I'm right here."

Their mother held a hand up to Jinx, signaling peace. "Apologies, dear. Let's try it one more time. Maybe I can give you some advice."

Despite his complaining, Thatcher stood up and danced with Jinx again, leading them down the line. Jinx was already thinking about the two steps and twirl. Halfway into the pivot, she tripped on herself, kissing her nose to the hard floor.

Tears swelled in her eyes, stinging. Her nose pulsed in aching flashes. Jinx held her nostrils tight.

Partner dancing was a seriously dangerous game.

Lady Voclaine helped her up. "It's alright. I'm fine," Jinx protested. "There's no bleeding. Let's go at it again."

She wouldn't let a stupid partner dance get in her way. She'd conquer it, just like everything else she did. She and Thatcher practiced over and over again, her heel cracking his toes every so often. Arya and Lady Voclaine shouted pointers every few seconds.

She grew increasingly agitated with herself, with the struggle. It *had* to be perfect. Jinx perfected everything. Why was this so hard?

"What's going on here?" Apollo's flat voice halted all movement in the space. His father stood right beside him, shooting Apollo a glance embedded with secret meaning. Jinx was unsure about the underlying message and the vague expression that accompanied it.

Thatcher volunteered, "Veyda is relishing in breaking all twenty-six bones of my foot. Or rather fifty-two, since she's intent on destroying *both* feet. She's quite good at it."

Jinx glanced away. Admittedly, she had heard some snapping sounds in the process.

"Let's see it," Apollo said, leaning against the door frame, hands in his pockets.

This moment symbolized peak embarrassment for Jinx. Every member of the Voclaine family was here to witness her atrocious dancing. She wiped her clammy hands on her dress.

One last time, she and Thatcher swept down the line. Stumbling on the end, Jinx hopped over Thatcher's foot, anxious about fracturing another one of his bones.

Apollo rose to his feet, straightening the lapels of his jacket. "I know what's wrong."

"Do enlighten us." Scorn laced in her tone.

"You're not letting Thatcher lead," he said as if it were obvious.

"Excuse me?"

"You're fighting him for control. You're trying to dance on your own, ignoring where he wants to take you." He bowed, offering his hand. "If I may?"

Rosy cheeks bloomed across Jinx's face. She glanced away as she took his hand.

Apollo's touch seared her skin; she was acutely aware of where it lingered. He leaned over, moving his jaw up by her ear, his breath brushing her ear. "Relax," Apollo whispered. "Let me guide you. Just feel the music."

The piano eased into the serenade. Apollo was gentle, letting Jinx slowly release control. She understood now what he meant. Instead of her feet leading, they now matched the steps Apollo took, fusing into a singular, connected movement.

It certainly wasn't perfect, but it was better.

Apollo raised his arm, spinning her underneath and effortlessly catching her, their footsteps easy. "That's it," he assured her with a smirk.

Then, he smoothly transitioned the two of them to the next few steps. The piano kicked up in pace, keys gaining confidence. Music seeped into the marrow of her bones, swaying in her body. Jinx responded instinctively to the melody, weight switching to the balls of her feet.

Knowing what to do, her agile toes stepped into another turn. Triumphantly landing, satisfaction sprouted in her chest, accompanied by an undeniable smile. She cast her gaze up to Apollo, pink tainting his ears.

She launched herself into another twirl, delighted to feel how simple the movement was. Apollo let her do as she pleased. Leading and following as she chose.

A partner dance wasn't just one person taking control. It was an art of compromise, the art of a couple's chemistry. The push and pull of attraction. They fell into the movement of each other's song, dancing as one. Their communication was steady but silent—their bodies were doing all the talking.

She felt a sharp tug in her chest.

The Duke of Voclaine outstretched his hand to Lady Voclaine. She took it, and the two elder Voclaines joined in dancing the Sembla. Lady Voclaine let out a fit of laughter as the Duke twirled her around. Then, Arya yanked Thatcher over to dance with her, too.

The three couples frolicked in continuous circles around the family room, filled with lively excitement. Bursts of hoots and yells ushered in all sorts of chuckles and snorts.

Fey tickled the keys with intensity, rigorously propelling the Sembla faster. Apollo and Jinx met up with the pace, rising to the challenge.

Sweat beaded her brow, her heart thundering. She was lost in the serenade and immensely proud of herself for successfully mastering the steps.

A sharp joy bubbled up in Jinx's chest, so staggering and inescapable that it hurt to keep smiling. Apollo answered with a hearty chuckle.

As the song sadly came to an end, the collective pants of dancers catching their breaths echoed off the walls.

Arya snapped her fan open, brushing herself with air and cooling the crimson off her face. She shot a wink at Jinx. "See? You only needed one lesson."

As the family departed, off to attend to their own tasks, Apollo hooked his pinky around Jinx's.

The scent of dinner slipped past all defenses to Jinx's room, filling the space. Her stomach grumbled in response. Jinx drooled, eager to eat another freshly cooked meal.

Lacing a small corset around her waist, she put her hair to the side and slipped on a dress. Staring at herself in the mirror, Jinx began to split apart sections of her hair, weaving them up and over each other. She twisted her hair into a braid, interweaving loose strands.

A door squealed as footsteps echoed off the floorboards.

"Are you ready to—"

Jinx turned on her heel, trying to finish the braids in her air. "Has your mother not taught you how to knock?"

Apollo just stared at her. "I can step out, knock on the door, and *then* come in if you'd like. Although that would be a waste of time for both of us."

Jinx snorted inwardly. "You're irritably vexing and annoyingly charming, you know."

"Just what a man wants to hear." He stepped behind her, offering up his assistance with her hair. "Let me," Apollo rasped. Jinx offered her back to him, holding the woven strands in place. Apollo's gentle fingers brushed against hers as he took her silky hair into his hands.

"You know how to do this?" She couldn't hide her surprise.

A half-chuckle. "One of my many secrets." A hint of sorrow briskly glimmered across his sharp features, though he brushed it away as quickly as it had come.

She stood patiently, watching their reflections in the mirror, noticing how his slender figure loomed over hers. The nearness of his body and thoughts of their night together flashed vividly in her memories. The way his hands perfectly catered to her waist. His touch. His mouth.

Recalling the song of his lips, she wanted to kiss him again, replaying the symphony of their mouths moving as one.

Jinx's brown cheeks blossomed pink. She needed to think of something *other* than him.

He handled her hair gently, and Jinx felt a wave of calmness flood her system, enjoying the feel of his hands on her head. Gooseflesh peppered along her skin, a weight gradually resting on her shoulders. She opened her eyes, meeting Apollo's gaze. It felt so natural to find his eyes.

"So, how did you learn to do this?" Jinx asked.

A lopsided smirk crossed his lips. "When we were young, Fey wouldn't let the handmaidens touch her hair. She always said she didn't trust them and her hair was precious to her." Light danced along his winter eyes as he recalled his memories. "Fey only let Mother and Arya do her hair. It wasn't until one day when they were both out in the gardens, and Fey needed to have her hair done. So, as the big brother, I took the task into my own hands. Quite literally." Jinx held in a sort of laughter. "Apparently, I was better at it than my mother and sister. Ever since then, I've been the only one to style her hair."

Apollo finished threading in the final pins. Jinx turned, finding herself closer than she had imagined, ignoring the loud and quickening thumps in her chest. It was a sweet story, yet Jinx could only think about the trail of his fingers. Apollo met her gaze through their reflections in the mirror. "Stop undressing me with your eyes. All you must do is ask." Apollo's gaze flicked down to her lips and then back up to her eyes.

Jinx swallowed dryly. His touch swept from her shoulders to her waist, skimming her stomach and the spot underneath her breasts. Jinx leaned into him, feeling his hard length pressing into her backside.

Apollo's path abruptly halted, springing an alarm in Jinx. Her primal sixth sense was wary.

He inhaled deeply before coarsely muttering to her, "Jinx."

Jinx pivoted, face to face with him. The tone, his body language, it was all off-kilter. So unlike Apollo. "What?"

"I've made a mis—"

"—Dinner!" His mother called from downstairs.

Apollo pinched his nose, blinking away the darkness in his stare. "Never mind."

He turned to walk, but then Jinx caught his wrist. "Apollo, if you made a mistake, I'm sure I'd understand."

His worried expression returned. "I'm not sure about this one." There was a beat. "Just...give me time to tell you. And know that I desperately want to."

He exited her room, leaving her stranded in her own thoughts.

Chapter 40

Jinx

Jinx lifted the latch to her window, allowing the autumn breeze to sweep into her room. She perched briefly on the ledge before crawling out to the tiled roof, finding her footing.

"You truly believe this is the best idea?" Apollo leaned against the window frame.

Her hood extended to the tip of her nose, concealing her identity. "I'm not changing my mind, Polly. It's best if I go alone. If anything was to happen, I wouldn't be able to protect you and find the Vessel at the same time."

The Autumnal Equinox assembly was to begin in one hour. Jinx decided she'd head over earlier than the designated time to scout out the area and see who and what she could find there. Hopefully, the Vessel would be there before the assembly began, and she could swipe it easily.

"I don't like this." Apollo crossed his arms. A wrinkle between his pinched brows signified his true disdain.

Jinx crouched to snap the window shut. "So, you've said for the sixth time now." A dash of charm lightened her voice, attempting to ease him up. "I've done this plenty of times. Nothing will go wrong."

"Must I remind you of the bullet you took just weeks ago?"

"No, I have the wound to do that." Despite the gunshot to the arm, she now had her full range of mobility again, as well as her full magical abilities. Apollo was worried about nothing.

As the window closed, Apollo caught it halfway. "I'll never stop you from doing what you please. All I ask is that at the end of the night, you return home in one piece."

Jinx's breath hitched. That word. *Home.* "I'll see you in an hour. Don't be late," she said abruptly before snapping the latch in place and running off into the shadows.

Jinx wouldn't make a promise she couldn't keep. Returning whole was unpredictable. Surely, she'd try. Her blades were strapped to her legs and ready to use. She thought again of his casual use of the word "home." Was the Voclaine manor her home now, at this point in their friendship? Were they even friends, or were they something more now?

Now was not the time to get distracted by these kinds of thoughts.

The city at her feet felt oddly tranquil tonight. The usual chatter hovered in and around the streets. Perhaps it was partially due to windy gusts from the cold front, but tonight, the city had a different aura. Danger snaked through the streets. Shadows appeared darker, the wind's whispers harsher. Something lethal was in the air.

Nimble jumps carried her from rooftop to rooftop. The woodsy aroma of Crosspoint Yard caught her nose as red brick came into view. The event address indicated it was to take place at a random warehouse in the alleyways.

Staring at the three-story building, Jinx noticed that most of the warehouse appeared to be perfectly intact. It was a structure people would walk by without question, which was the problem.

"Building number 1432," she repeated to herself, assuring herself of the correct address.

She first took note of the perimeter, watching the people that went in and out of the place. Ordinary citizens were bringing crates into the building from a stagecoach, a pin of Elu's flower over their hearts, though they lacked weapons and armor. Perhaps these were just people who supported the cause, and the Hunters would show up later. No sign of Warren or V'Yockovitch.

From what she could see through the windows, the first two stories of the building were set up in a loft-like plan. An open balcony on the second floor overlooked the first. The third floor, however, was separate from the other two.

Jinx knew it would be difficult to make her way out onto the floor during the actual assembly, so she would have to sweep that area now. She looked for the men who delivered packages to the third floor, but only one person seemed to have access.

The man with access turned a key to the door and pocketed it in the inside of his jacket. Jinx trailed him until he reached the first floor, swiftly learning his gait and mannerisms. The bare minimum would do.

After landing herself back on the ground, Jinx glued her back to the brick wall, allowing the shadows to provide cover. She spotted a door that led to an abandoned room; she could stuff the body in there, and the likelihood of someone finding it would be slim to none.

The lowly man rounded the corner.

She pounced, slapping a hand over his mouth, muffling his yelps and pinching his nose. Slamming his temple into the wall, she knocked him clean out.

Dead or unconscious, she didn't care. Jinx just needed an in, and this person was it.

Dragging the limp body by the collar, she entered the empty room. Jinx analyzed the man from the curl in his hair to the dust on his boot. Summoning her magic, she created a mirror image of him, even including the single white armband he wore, in case it proved important.

She fished for the key inside his cotton jacket and looted his pockets, finding a wallet.

Ten Marcs and an identification card. His home address was listed as a street in Crosspoint Yard. His identification number rested beneath. Name: Simon Bonilla, signed on a dotted line.

"Sorry, Simon, I need to be you for a little." Jinx left him with five Marcs and slipped out. With the hilt of her blade, she broke the knob of the door, trapping Simon inside.

Fully illusioned, Jinx walked in as if she were meant to be part of the assembly. Men sauntering past her tipped their caps and top hats, touching their white flower pins with two fingers. She returned the gesture, careful to not raise any suspicion.

This Simon guy was certainly of a higher rank than the rest of the crew in this assembly. This kind of respect was only given to someone with more power.

A short young man with dusty cheeks and a clipboard hastily ran up to her, his overly excited smile pulling his cheeks wide apart. "Mr. Bonilla." He gulped down a breath. "I need you to sign for the last of the packages that just arrived. I did a quick check. All the weapons are there, from the new bullets to the imported metal from the east."

Jinx took the clipboard from the kid, who couldn't have been much older than fourteen.

The sheet of paper in front of her described twenty objects imported from the company A.D. Marianna. Jinx questioned how truthful Nadir had been to Apollo during his visit.

The list included everything from crossbows, bayonets, bullets, bows, and arrows to something called a silencer. Even under the best assumptions, it didn't sound good.

Lifting the page, Jinx saw another sheet filled with names. "And this?" Jinx hadn't heard the man's voice, but she did her best impersonation anyway.

It had to have been close enough. The kid peered his head over the clipboard. "These are the two Cursed that we captured for the assembly today. We'll be using them as targets when we showcase the new weapons. I'll need you to sign for them, too; they're in the dungeons."

Jinx masked her shock. Real people were in the dungeons, locked up like testing animals.

Rage rose swiftly in her core. Is that what people teach their children these days? That it was acceptable to use the Cursed as nothing more than playthings, punching bags, test dummies?

Jinx halted the rabbit hole of horrid thoughts before they could overwhelm her completely. There was a purpose to her being here, in this disguise; she would be able to save those Cursed afterward. Unfortunately, there was much more on the line here.

Clasping the feathered pen between two fingers, Jinx signed for Simon. She forged his signature as best she could, attempting to match the one she'd seen on his identification card.

The kid thanked her and ran off down the corridor.

Pivoting on her heel, Jinx turned toward the set of metal stairs, clutching the rail as she ascended to the third floor. She noticed the cascade of raised bleachers circling the open floor, set up like they were expecting the crowd to watch a fight in the arena below.

Jinx approached the door to the third floor, turning Simon's key. It clicked open.

She found herself in a narrow hallway. Crouching, she opened each door, all of them revealing empty rooms, with four empty walls void of paintings, furniture, and books.

Her gloved fingers felt around carefully for every crevice that might lead to a hidden passage or chamber. She stepped over each floorboard, searching for loose ones, until she finally reached the final door at the end of the corridor.

Inside, there was a single maroon desk and a chair. The four walls of the room were empty, save for a lone window in the corner.

Jinx tipped her head curiously, walking behind the desk. She pulled out every drawer and all of their storage compartments, lifting the bottom boards. Again, all empty. She caressed the underside of the desk; perhaps there was a latch she'd missed?

Just then, she heard footsteps nearing the quarters. Jinx's heart dropped.

There was no place to hide; even tucking herself beneath the desk would be useless, as she would be spotted in an instant. There was no other furniture to duck behind.

She'd have to choose the next best option.

Jinx threw the window open and jumped out, clawing for life at the brick walls. She hitched her foot in a crack, stretching a free, slender leg to the window and pushing it down slightly with her toe, leaving it ajar just enough so that she could listen in.

That's when she heard an unmistakable voice: V'Yockovitch. "Here is better. Away from prying ears."

"Indeed." The jittery voice accompanying him was clearly Sir Warren. "I trust you found the lab of Somnium University to your liking?"

"Quite." Jinx could practically hear the smugness in his response. "When will the Vessel be ready for use?"

She perked up at the mention of the Vessel, not to mention the confirmation that Warren and V'Yockovitch had stored it in the university laboratory.

"Shortly, Your Grace. I promise. There are a few final tweaks that must be adjusted in order for the artifact to reach its full potency. It will be done by the Masquerade," Warren assured him. "The Hunters will be there, too, correct?"

"Every last one of them, ready to inject Elu's Grace into the commoners. It's just the sacrifice we need to finally get rid of these wretched Cursed."

Jinx's grip faltered. The Duke of V'Yockovitch was voluntarily, openly throwing a percentage of the population to their death. It would be the massacre of the century—and he spoke of it so matter-of-factly, as if it were ordained by the Virtues themselves.

Creeping closer to the window, Jinx tipped her chin just enough to the point where her eyes were barely visible. V'Yockovitch and Warren were now in her sight.

V'Yockovitch pressed a key into Warren's palm, wrinkling his hooked nose. "Tell those janitors that the second floor must be cleaned. When I entered your lab, the soles of my boots felt like they were walking over glue."

Warren's shoulders were hunched, tittering nervously. "Certainly. I work with many chemicals in there, so it's likely one of them spilled." He stuffed the three-ringed key into his back pocket.

"That Thatcher boy..." V'Yockovitch mentioned warily. At the very utterance of her best friend's name, Jinx clenched her jaw, preparing herself to hear the worst. "He doesn't have access to your laboratory, does he?"

"No, Your Grace. I only work with him in the student rooms on the third floor."

"Good." V'Yockovitch cleared his throat. His eyes softened. "Thank you, Sir Warren. Because of you, my son's name will soon be clean." The two shook hands.

That's right. After V'Yockovitch's first son died, he was forced to name Vander as his surviving heir. His son had died at the hands of the Cursed, which explained why V'Yockovitch despised the Cursed so much. He had created this entire charade to enact his revenge.

Jinx faintly remembered a few years ago, a mention of his death. The first son had gotten caught in the middle of a heated death between a Cursed and a human. In the end, the Cursed murdered V'Yockovitch's first son, Liam V'Yockovitch. Actually, his first acknowledged and full-blooded son.

Putting herself in V'Yockovitch's shoes, she could see how a parent would feel compelled to right the wrong to attain some semblance of justice for their child. But Jinx wasn't the parent in this scenario; she was on the other side of the line, a target. And she wouldn't stand for it.

"It's the least I could do, Your Grace. I was the one who opened the Vessel twenty years ago. It's my responsibility to clean up this mess."

Jinx stumbled. Those words ripped into her skull. The Cursed didn't even exist before twenty years ago when the murderous plague infected Somnium. The opening of the Vessel was the origination of Cursed and Plague alike. He was the student who had let it all unravel. The scientist has a burning curiosity from the vision she witnessed in the Archives. From the scroll.

People were falling ill every day, waiting on their deathbeds for Akuji to guide their souls into the afterlife. The Cursed had been forced to go into hiding, fighting for their lives. The silent war between two people. The release of that creature in the woods. The reason she dwelled in solitary.

The reason she spent her life apart from her mother.

"Here." V'Yockovitch handed Warren a plain eggshell mask, which covered everything but his eyes. "Our show is about to begin."

A pinprick slithered through the nape of Jinx's neck. *Temptress?* Apollo's voice echoed in her temple.

You're here? Jinx whispered down the thread of their connection.

Yes. As is every Hunter in the city. Are you alright? Worry was laced into his tone.

Jinx almost smiled. The thought of Apollo being concerned for her sent a flutter to her heart.

Worried about my well-being, Polly?

Tch. Have I not shown you, time and time again, how much I care?

A flash of that night invaded her mind. His touch. His lips. His kiss.

She blinked furiously, trying to get it out of her head. Shameless scoundrel. Jinx wanted to slip her way back in through the window, but doing so could be risky. Flexing her fingers, she felt for a brick out of place to clutch onto. *We were right. It's Warren and V'Yockovitch. I also know where the Vessel is now and how we need to get to it. Where are you?*

Find me on the second floor.

Picking her toe in the next available crack, she descended the wall. *How did you get in without raising any suspicion?*

Find me, and you'll see. Apollo cut the thread, stranding her alone in a dark alleyway.

Jinx reeled in her illusion of Simon and stripped down to her leather suit. Casting a fake mask to veil her mouth and nose, Jinx fastened on her hood and molded her illusions once more to give her lithe body a masculine frame. She topped it off with a pin on the left side of her chest.

Warren's confession rang in her head. What would happen to him if the entire city knew? Both the humans and the Cursed would be infuriated with him. The Seven would likely send him to prison if not death, and V'Yockovitch as well, for scheming and gathering up the Hunters.

At the mouth of the entrance, hundreds of Hunters, both male and female, shuffled inside the warehouse. Half masks of animalistic predators veiling the upper part of their face. Jinx kept her head down as she walked in with the rushing wave, eager not to draw attention. One slip up, and she'd be done for.

Senseless chatter filled up the space as men and women filed into the bleachers, whistling at the arena below. Jinx's stomach contracted. A certain aura loomed over the place. Despite the conglomerate of people near trampling each other, it lacked an energy that threw Jinx off.

She was planting herself right in the thick of danger.

Jinx scanned for Apollo along the second floor, attentively looking for those winter eyes. She spotted him securing a spot by the rail, draped in a medium-length gray coat and hood. His face was obscured; he was recognizable only by his movements and his tall, lean body.

Jinx swerved through the Hunters, carving out a path for herself with her hand. Masses of bodies interjected, bumping into the road she paved. Suddenly, her frame was tossed to the side.

She straightened her back, centering herself once more. The figure that had pummeled into her peeled back its lips, snarling in a voice that resembled two synced together. Its decayed, rooting teeth looked like they'd been plucked straight from a corpse. Eyes milky white.

Jinx craned her neck back and sank back into the huddle of people, stomach churning. It was a strange man to see in an already strange setting. Luckily, she made her way to Apollo.

She squeezed his arm. "Found you." She sighed in relief, though the aggressive interaction before had ignited her gut's "fight" response.

Apollo's mouth dipped into a slight smile. "And in less time than expected." Shadows covered the top half of his face, carefully hiding his identity.

"Will you admit now that I'm a better sneak than you thought?" Jinx leaned her arms on the metallic bar in front of them.

"Perhaps...you are *slightly* better than I initially believed," Apollo compromised.

Jinx snorted. "I trust you will take that statement back once you hear what I have uncovered."

Acting as a shield, he used his arms to cage her in, his muscular frame molding to hers. In her mind, he whispered: *There is something I must tell you.* His fingers were fidgeting.

Lights dimmed, cutting off Apollo's sentence, leaving her curious.

A strong beam of light illuminated a masked V'Yockovitch and Warren down in the ring. Cheers and applause erupted throughout the warehouse. The two ringmasters soaked in the attention with arms splayed open. V'Yockovitch welcomed the crowd, his voice distorted. "Blessings of Elu to the chosen ones, touched by light. We thank you for attending this exciting night, in which we'll reveal the newest technology that will bring the Cursed to their knees."

More whistles and anticipation. Warren picked up where V'Yockovitch left off. "At the end of this presentation, you will see just how we propose to exterminate all of the Cursed from our city, how we will finish them off once and for all."

Mountain-shattering cries trembled throughout the bleachers, the thrill of the kill enhancing their growing excitement. A buzz hummed over Jinx's skin.

She leaned in, her upper body pitched over the rail. Her own bloodlust rumbled in the corner of her mind, the increasing desire to slaughter each and every one of them for endangering innocent people's lives. She was so tired of being persecuted.

V'Yockovitch cried out a victorious whoop. "We've burned their library! We will burn their hideouts! The Cursed will *burn* at our feet!"

The arena erupted with pure hatred, the cheers rupturing her eardrums. Something terrifying was coming. Her knuckles turned white on the handlebar, but she knew she had to play along in the role of a Hunter, so she screamed along with them.

She let the raw energy of hatred—her *own* hatred—sear into her heart. It was forever engraved in her brain, the image of the Cursed chained up and caged, like lions in a circus. She salivated, thinking of the moment she'd be able to rip her own claws into them.

Watch them bleed at *her* feet.

Just then, the hairs on her neck stood straight up. She was unable to rid herself of the chilling sensation that she was being watched.

Chapter 41

Jinx

V'Yockovitch raised a single hand, commanding silence from the crowd. In an instant, the mass of Hunters hushed.

"Somnium was built to be a city of dreams. A settlement for dreamers to make their grandest desires a reality. Our ancestors sailed from the west in search of prosperity, hunting for a new world, eager for a revolution. They came across our blessed Virtues, who helped them construct the momentous empire we know today. This city brings in the most wealth for our entire nation of Ardentia. We are the smartest, the brightest, the most pure..." V'Yockovitch drawled out that last word, inhaling the ecstasy of his own prose.

"We are doing the Virtues' work. We are giving our helpless the resources they need to survive with Elu's grace in development and our Hunter organization to protect them from the Cursed. Peace reigned along Somnium, with the Virtues watching over us for centuries on end until recently. For the past twenty years, we have been the chosen ones. And they've given us a test, a test to determine our loyalty to our friends, our kin, our nation, by bringing these rats into our prodigious city. We will prove to our Virtues that they have selected the proper people to protect. The Cursed will test our strength, but we will persevere.

"Somnium cannot peacefully rest until the problem of the Cursed is solved. They have proved from time and time again that we cannot coexist, and if we let them use their powers, they will band together to force the rest of us into fear and servitude. They've slaughtered our family members, stolen from our wallets, and ransacked our homes. And this is only the beginning. If we do not stop now, our fear will only grow at an exponential rate. They will take our children from our arms. Practice their dirty magic on them. We will not tolerate that anymore. Our solution is just a fingertip away."

V'Yockovitch's passion was so great that the veins of his neck bulged with enthusiasm. Jinx could not breathe. Her body ran cold as tension hummed through the air. Hunters at her left and right were drinking in V'Yockovitch's words as if they came straight from the Virtues' mouths.

Apollo ceased all motion, stunned to stillness.

Warren paced off stage, leaving V'Yockovitch as the singular entity under the spotlight. His thundering voice continued, pushing his vocal cords to the edge of their volume. "The Seven have abandoned their positions as leaders, stranding their people to survive the threat posed by the Cursed. I will take on that responsibility; I will not neglect you, my people. The Seven have chosen to remain ignorant instead of rising to the challenge before us. They are not willing to fight for us, so we must fight for ourselves. *We* are the chosen ones."

Hunters leaped up from their seats. Shrills shattered their voices, breaking the sonic waves apart. There it was again—the sound of dueling screams, like rabid, leashed animals primed for the hunt. All it would take was for V'Yockovitch to give the sign, and they'd raid the city, slaughtering every silver-eyed or suspicious victim on the spot.

Their hatred was rooted so deeply that war was all but inevitable. It was the inevitable fear of the unknown that created this resentment.

Warren resumed his spot by V'Yockovitch, wheeling out a table filled with weapons for show. At the head of the table, a young blond Cursed boy was tied up, his chin tucked to his neck, unconscious.

Warren removed the gag from the boy's mouth, light slapping him awake. The Cursed groggily blinked awake, squinting at the relentless light beating down on him. His silver eyes flashed with fear as he whimpered and shook, attempting to flee.

"Boy doesn't know what's coming to him, eh?" V'Yockovitch teased.

Hunters answered with bellied laughs as if they were watching a comedy showcase.

Jinx sunk her teeth into her tongue, doing all she could to keep her mouth silent. Rage roared under her skin. The Cursed were not puppets or toy things. Jinx was tired of being treated as nothing more than a joke, an animal. Jinx tensed, on the verge of springing down and challenging them all.

Apollo felt her anger flare underneath him. *Not the brightest idea.*

She sighed reluctantly, knowing that any hint of anger could compromise everything she'd worked for up to this point.

Warren stroked a crossbow, loading it with an arrow and cocking it back. He explained that the bows were infused with new technology to make them easier to use and more accurate in their aim. Warren shot the boy in the shoulder, eliciting a yelp. Tears streamed down his face.

The boy's nails extended, sharpening to claws, but were rendered useless against the straps restraining his body. His teeth protruded out to jagged points meant for cutting flesh.

Jinx rooted for the boy, wanted him to bite his way to freedom and rip the flesh off Warren and V'Yockovitch.

But no matter how hard he tried, he couldn't escape.

Warren and V'Yockovitch continued torturing and teasing him, their experimental rag doll, until his clothes were tainted crimson. Using their new blades and weapons, they'd removed his fingers and teeth one by one before nicking off shards of his flesh for the Hunters to see.

Jinx couldn't look away from the horrors. A metallic tang filled her mouth. How many people had they done this to?

At least she knew where *this* boy was; she had the chance to set him free.

Jinx wasn't any better than these Hunters, watching as they slowly tortured this boy to death. She wanted to learn his name, where he came from, what his story was. She wanted to fight for him, to slaughter all these Hunters and the two leaders at the helm. She wanted to be the champion the Cursed wished her to be, *needed* her to be.

Jinx knew she had to hold tight and formulate a plan, whipping up the perfect plan to attack them efficiently. Doing anything now would be pointless and stupid.

An assistant swiveled the next Cursed onto the stage—a ginger-haired boy with a stubble on his chin. It must be the runner boy, Ajax, that Harrison had spoken about when she last visited the Netherwen.

He'd been kidnapped for this.

For *public entertainment.*

Ajax shifted on the table, wrestling against the straps that bound him. Fury was embedded in those brown-silver eyes. Sharp lines of rage and battle ignited his hair, the red strands slowly turning to flames.

Harrison had asked the Crone to have Jinx bring this boy back home. To save him.

V'Yockovitch removed the gag from Ajax, who promptly spit on his face. "Fuck you!"

The Hunters jerked forward, ready to defend their leader. V'Yockovitch held them back with a lift of his finger. "Fear not; this will be easy for our last and final weapon. To tame this animal, to bring down this beast, you Hunters can use something quite simple. *This* is a silencer."

Warren twisted a cylindrical object atop a pistol and loaded in a bullet. "Using this silencer on your pistol, your bullets will fire without making a sound. And remember, our new bullets are infused with a high dosage of poison, which will kill them the instant it pierces their skin. No matter where it lands on the body."

She couldn't just sit back and watch another Cursed die.

Especially when she'd been specifically asked to save him.

Jinx's thoughts returned to her mother. During the first few years after Jinx left, the devastation never left her face, dark circles thick beneath her honey-brown eyes and exhaustion pulling her skin into wrinkles.

She'd recognized a hint of that devastation in Harrison.

You know him? Apollo asked.

No, but I know someone who does.

What do you want to do? Even if the plan was destined to fail, he still supported her. That loyalty counted for millions in Jinx's heart.

Jinx didn't answer. There was a lot to take into account. Jumping into the ring could very well be suicide. She couldn't fight off that many Hunters alone, and she didn't want to put Apollo in danger. Of course, she could choose to do nothing, but it would be akin to condemning him to death, watching the monsters feed Ajax to the wolves. There were also too many people to freely use her illusions; someone could see her using them, so creating a domain of her own posed too great a risk.

Jinx assessed every possible outcome of how to get Ajax out of there, calculating the pros and cons. She could feel the seconds elongate, the tick of passing time warning her that she was drawing closer to an inevitable end. Her choice would determine this boy's life or death.

Ajax bared his teeth, feeding the flames on his head with rage. "You're pathetic. Don't forget that we were once *just like you*." He screamed, halting Warren and V'Yockovitch in place.

Considering their surprise, Jinx realized that this must have been the first time a Cursed dared to talk back to them in a showcase like this. Even the Hunters eyed him curiously. Jinx couldn't help but do the same.

He had balls, she'd give him that.

Perhaps now was the perfect time to strike while the mass of people was distracted.

Ajax continued, capturing Jinx's attention as well. "You can try to stop us, but we'll come back. You can't possibly think you can get rid of every single one of us."

Warren raised the pistol, aiming straight at Ajax. Jinx flinched forward, instantly on edge. The tension in the air was palpable.

Ajax's desperate voice broke. "You can attack our library, kill off our people, destroy our homes. But all you are doing is angering us. Treat us like animals, and we'll respond like animals. We're preparing to retaliate." Warren pulled back the trigger with his thumb, preparing for fire. Ajax simply laughed. "Kill me. We both know you're doing this out of fear. And anyway, we're not alone. We have powerful alliances."

V'Yockovitch put his palm on Warren's pistol, moving the nuzzle down. He tilted his head, slowly approaching Ajax. "Who?"

"Jinx," Ajax said confidently. Warren, V'Yockovitch, and the Hunters all laughed.

Oh, Ajax. What have you done? she thought to herself.

What is he talking about? Apollo was genuinely confused. And there was no way to explain this to him without revealing the existence of the Netherwen.

Jinx omitted the truth. *I'm not sure.* To an extent, she wasn't *entirely* sure.

"The Face Stealer? The precious Ghost?" V'Yockovitch clutched his belly, slapping his knee. "If Jinx is your so-called savior, where is this Jinx now?"

Right here. Jinx was just a few feet away; she could end him in seconds with just the flick of a wrist and a silent knife. The Netherwen had deemed her their champion, their savior.

Guilt, shame, and rage all clutched her heart. Why couldn't she save him?

"And why hasn't Jinx shown you their face?" V'Yockovitch hissed, taunting. "Why hide behind the shadows? They're cowardly."

"They're *brave*," Ajax argued on her behalf. "They're kind. Jinx has only helped and protected us, unlike those who fear us and threaten us because we're different. Jinx is the sole reason we are not on the brink of extinction."

"Is that so?" V'Yockovitch drawled. He pivoted toward the crowd. "You heard that, Hunters... *Jinx* is why the Cursed are still here. Jinx is their source of strength. For the first part of this extermination plan, we must find Jinx. And slaughter them."

Jeers and whistles of praise flushed throughout the arena. Jinx didn't have time to process anything as V'Yockovitch calmed the masses with a wave of his hand. "End this."

Warren's fingers curled around the trigger.

A boom ricocheted across the warehouse as a flurry of snow clouded up the expanse below. Veins of ice crept up the support beams, wrapping the bleachers in frigid vines. A powdery cloud loomed over the first floor.

Hunters in every direction shouted in distress. "The Cursed are here!"

"Ready your weapons!"

"Be on guard!"

How could the Cursed have arranged such an attack? It didn't make sense. Jinx would have known, and Harrison would have mentioned it to her. Ambushes like this took *weeks* of planning and her visit to Netherwen. This couldn't have been the work of the Cursed. This *must* be another group.

Apollo clutched her hand. "We have to leave. Now." His towering figure cut through the mess of Hunters, rallying toward the snowstorm beneath them. Frost continued layering itself on every possible surface as they ran.

Apollo beelined toward the exit, down the iron stairs. Jinx pulled at him to wait and rushed toward the rim of the arena. She needed to see if Ajax had survived.

The fog of snow slowly cleared, unveiling V'Yockovitch and Warren, who were surrounded on stage by a ring of Hunters. Ajax, however, was nowhere to be found. The table where he'd been confined, however, was ripped apart.

"He's *gone*," Jinx whispered. Apollo hauled her from her spot.

What are you doing, you idiot? You're being hunted. He scorned her in her mind. Autumn air assaulted her body as they stepped outside. They ran from the warehouse in the direction of the Voclaine manor as fast as they could.

"*He's gone,*" she muttered to herself.

She thought back on everything that had just happened. Ajax had appeared so fearless, especially for a kid who'd been kidnapped. Exactly the opposite of the first Cursed that the two friends had brought up to the stage. His speech, the timing of the snow, the words he'd said. It seemed oddly organized. Practiced. Almost like he knew what would capture the Hunters' attention and what wouldn't. Almost. Then, it dawned on her. "This was a set-up."

"What?" Apollo stopped running, ushering them into a dark corner.

"This was a set-up." Jinx repeated. "Those people in there, it was a well-thought-out ambush." Ajax must have purposefully offered himself up as bait without telling Harrison. But why? How? No human would stand up for the Cursed. The only people to defend the Cursed would be the Cursed themselves. Could it be that the Cursed were creating a covert establishment to fend off the Hunters?

"Is that seriously where your head is right now? They just announced to an entire room of Hunters that the priority now is for everyone to hunt for *you*," Apollo stressed.

"Eh, people are always hunting me. Now they've just made it official."

"They're *after* you." He emphasized that point again, straining his voice not to say more, not to admit his weakness.

"This will be over soon," she consoled him.

"At what cost?" Jinx hardened. His hands were on her arms now, holding her protectively. She felt prying eyes digging into her spine. The danger was near. "Temptress..." His wintry eyes roamed past her, targeting a spot behind her. He put her to the side.

Jinx turned on her heel and noticed a man lurking in the darkness. His fighting leathers were an obsidian black so dark that they drank up any light. He wore half a mask, which swallowed his mouth and nose. The paint was brushed over his caramel eyes, finishing off the disguise. His muscular build indicated that he'd been training rigorously. His long, fawn-colored hair was bundled up into a small bun, with thick strands escaping at the nape of his neck and the crown of his forehead.

"You run. Understood?" Jinx ordered.

The man strode toward them, gaining speed with every step. He unsheathed a short dagger at his hip.

Jinx reactively pulled at her own and met him in the middle. Steel against steel, sparks popped as they clashed.

"Who are you?" Jinx demanded, her muscles trembling as he grabbed her.

The man kept his silence, releasing his hold. Jinx almost faltered.

He swiped, and Jinx dodged, reflexively.

She retreated a step, preparing an attack. The man acted swiftly, blocking her.

They were stuck in a dance of defense and offense, waiting to see who would give up first.

A beat later, the man jumped at her, his dagger shooting for her neck. Jinx blocked his arm. Grabbing him by the shoulder and neck, she rolled him onto his side using his own weight.

As if he knew this would be her next move, the man grabbed her and pulled her down, locking her to the ground.

She'd used that move only a handful of times. She only knew of one other person who fought like this man did, perfecting the art of battle in seconds. Someone she hadn't seen in a long time.

His skill reminded her of an old acquaintance whose movements were just as sly and precise.

As the man twisted her arm, pain shot down her to her hands. Her fingers released the hilt of her blade.

Jinx knew this tactic; she'd used it before. It was impossible to escape, and if she tried, Jinx likely would break a bone. There were only two options: either the man would set her free or kill her. And she didn't want to wait to figure out which one it would be.

She protested, wrestling against his grip, frantically looking for Apollo. As long as he was safe, as long as he was alright. Her mother, too. Jinx trusted Apollo to do the right thing. For a faint moment, Jinx believed she heard the man holding her captive say, "I don't want to do this."

The last frame she saw was Apollo running toward her as night flooded her vision. Swiftly losing all sensations, she wished for Apollo to run the other way, knowing he was doomed if he ventured any closer.

Chapter 42

Apollo

Jinx's body went limp as the man pushed at the pressure point between her neck and shoulder. Struggling for breath, her illusion reeled back, unveiling the woman beneath the mask. It was clear during their brawl that Jinx had a greater urge to kill than he did. This man was not a Hunter. He lacked the pin all Hunters wore, and his body language didn't indicate any threat.

If he had been a Hunter, she would already be dead.

For his part, Apollo knew who the man was the moment he laid eyes on him. Those caramel eyes and fawn-colored hair resided in some of his most treasured childhood memories.

Apollo pocketed his hands, feigning that bored face of his. "Where are you taking her, Vander V'Yockovitch?"

Vander peeled off the mouth mask. "Hello, Apollo. It's been a while, hasn't it?"

"I see the military got you in shape." He jerked his chin toward Jinx on the floor. Apollo wanted nothing more than to sweep her off the floor and take her home, but revealing any of that could be used against him—depending on what Vander wanted. His longstanding hatred toward his father ruled out the possibility that they were working together, but Apollo didn't want to take any chances. "Still not above knocking out your opponents, I see? It's rather rude to strike a woman unconscious."

"Your wit hasn't left you after all these years. Neither has that dead look in your eye." Vander pointed at him with a gloved finger.

Apollo's wariness heightened, worried for Jinx.

"What do you want with her?"

Vander's lips ticked into a one-sided grin as he crouched next to Jinx's body, flicking obsidian hair from her face. "This is no ordinary woman, this woman right here. This devil knows more than she should."

Questions volleyed around his mind, but only one made it to his mouth. "What do you mean?"

A riot of noise came from the end of the alleyway. Apollo perked up at the sound, and Vander peered over his shoulder. The two glanced at each other and, in silent agreement, decided to move her away from the possible Hunters.

Vander reached to grab her, but Apollo shouldered him away. Scooping Jinx off the ground, he tucked her tightly into his chest. "Do you enjoy having ten fingers, Vander?"

"Yes."

"Then do not touch her again." As they walked further into the alleyway, Vander fell into step by Apollo. He was not in any mood to play foul games. He wanted answers, and he wanted to get Jinx home. "You are not a Hunter."

"Well, *that's* quite obvious," Vander chipped.

Apollo's response was flat and calm. "Let's make this easy. I will take her home, and you tell me what you want with this woman. If you fight me, when she wakes up, I'll make sure she gets your head on a spike. She wouldn't appreciate the kidnapping."

"You won't do it yourself?"

"You know the rule. Ladies first." Apollo fixed his gaze on the dimmed streets before them. They were still a long walk away from the manor. Unclipping his coat, he draped it over Jinx, keeping her warm and safeguarding her identity.

Vander huffed. "You really haven't changed."

"Not at all."

Vander's voice grumbled in his throat. "Kovan said otherwise."

How long had Vander been in town? "And yet."

"Touché." Vander cracked his fingers, then placed his hands behind his head as if he were soaking in the sun on a hot summer day. "That little devil who's apparently bewitched you tricked me four years ago on the military base. Have you heard the story of Elijah Benjamin?"

He had. However, Vander might know something Apollo didn't and might be able to elaborate on the tales he'd heard. "Let's say I didn't. Enlighten me."

Streetlamps cast a white glow over Vander's olive skin, illuminating the hard lines of his facial features. "At the time, I was a high-rank specialist in weapons and combat. My half-brother died from a Cursed attack and I was upset. Taking advantage of my vulnerability, a new recruit named Elijah Benjamin approached me. Elijah asked me for help, claiming his combat technique was lacking. The kid came from the streets and yearned for more. I agreed to help him, using whatever free time I had to train Elijah. The kid was exceptionally talented and learned quick. I took a liking to him; he reminded me of my brother. Somehow, he always seemed to find trouble.

"Elijah never really saw eye-to-eye with another soldier, Logan. They were always at each other's throats, bickering, and sometimes it even ended in a fistfight. One time, Elijah got knocked out by Logan. Elijah was sent to the infirmary, and I went to check on him. I left him some food and thought nothing of it—until I went to the showers, where I found that one." He pointed to Jinx. "She claimed to be a new nurse on duty, yet her uniform seemed out of place. And all of a sudden, Elijah was nowhere to be found.

"I pushed her to her limits and tried to get information from her. I knew something was off; she'd appeared at the same time that Elijah disappeared. I knew she had something to do with it, so I attacked her. She countered, disarmed, and then threatened me, all in the span of five minutes. Suffice to say, I was pissed and amazed at the same time."

Apollo's mood lightened, almost wanting to laugh. Indeed, it sounded exactly like something Jinx might do.

"She forced me to open the weaponry unit and stole a new suit prototype that the military had been working on, the best blades, my own personal daggers. Then she got on a horse. I asked her what she had done with Elijah, but she only laughed and said he wasn't real. I felt so mad and deceived. At the time, I didn't understand why she should admit such a thing; she easily could have added another lie and left. Now, considering all that happened, I believed she admitted it to get me to see how much I still latched onto my brother. Understand that he wasn't meant to return. She left me with these words of wisdom: 'You have a limited number of days and no do-overs. Don't waste any time.' Ever since then, I've approached life differently."

Apollo smiled. She was truly special.

And yet, when Apollo and Kovan had spoken about Vander in front of her, Jinx acted as if she'd never heard of him before in her life. Jinx was pretty sharp; she wouldn't miss a detail like that—unless she'd been lied to. "What name did she know you by?"

"How did you know I went under a false identity?"

"Just answer the question."

Vander smiled. "Franco. Franco Lancaster. It's the name everyone in the military knew me by." Vander used his mother's last name. A delighted surprise for Apollo. Vander rolled his shoulders. "Don't mention my name to her yet, okay? I want her to be surprised when she sees me."

"Why is that?"

"Just so I can tell her she's gotten sloppy."

A young, shoeless girl stepped out from the shadows, holding her hands tight to her chest. Her auburn hair was a mess of tangles, her silver-lined eyes bright and pleading, and she shivered in place. She jerked to an abrupt halt, limbs gluing to the ground at her soles. Terror lifted her brows, and Vander raised his hands innocence.

Apollo halted as Vander approached the girl, crouching down to his knees and meeting her at eye level. It was a forbidden interaction, this interaction between a Cursed and a human. "Are you cold?" Vander asked softly.

The girl nodded.

Apollo glanced between the girl and the coat currently laid across Jinx. If she were awake, he had the feeling Jinx would give it to the girl. "Give her this." Apollo jerked his chin to the jacket. Vander's brows met his hairline as Apollo rolled his eyes. "Don't act surprised."

Vander clutched the coat and handed it to the young girl. She smiled and thanked him before scurrying off and disappearing around a corner.

Vander pushed his tongue against the inside of his cheek, looking smug.

"Save your breath. I'm not interested in what you have to say." He pulled Jinx closer to him for warmth and took a step forward.

Vander raised his hands in a show of surrender, and they continued walking.

Apollo and Vander crossed the threshold of Crosspoint Yard, finally entering the Botanic Plaza. Apollo lowered his guard slightly, Hoping the Hunters likely wouldn't come out this far. Apollo readjusted Jinx in his arms, her lolling head pressed against his chest.

Vander scratched his long hair. It was strange for Apollo to see him wearing it down; when they were kids, Vander always kept it swept back in a neat ponytail. "I should get going. When she wakes, find me in Kovan's foxhole. I've been staying there for the past two days."

Suspicion clung to Apollo's brain. It wasn't that he didn't trust Vander; he just didn't trust the situation. All of this seemed far too simple. There had to be a catch. A bounty had been placed on her head, and Apollo wouldn't turn her in for anything in the world.

Before Vander had the chance to leave, Apollo leveled with his old friend. "You still haven't told me what you want with her. What does it mean that she knows more than she should?"

Vander raised two palms innocently. "It's confidential. My colleague and I do want her support in the coming war. Jinx might be the only one who can save the Cursed."

So, he opposed his father *entirely*. "You support the Cursed. Why?"

"She changed my mind about the Cursed years ago, and I believe she can change everyone's too. "

"You don't hate them?" What Apollo was really asking was much more personal: *You wouldn't hate me?*

Vander's head shook, sincerity laced into his words. "At first, I did. After I interacted with Jinx and realized that I had faced the assassin everyone feared, I recognized that we weren't so different from them. Jinx lived at my side for two years. Ate with her, trained with her, basically another sibling to me. There was no change in how I treated her differently. Sure, perhaps she appeared to be someone she was not, but that does not change that in the end, I had no idea a Cursed, if not *the* Cursed, was right by me. What does it change? That they have abilities that no one else does? If anything, they could be resourceful to us, not an enemy." His gaze softened. "I want to help them, and so does my colleague."

Vander could see the doubt in Apollo's hesitance. "I didn't intend for her to lose consciousness, truly. A mistake on my behalf. She has the kill first, ask questions later mentality. I simply meant to reveal myself once she calmed down. I took it too far." Sincerity coated every vowel.

The ring coiled around his finger warmed.

Noble Vander. All of a sudden, memories flashed before his eyes: the day Vander announced he'd leave for the military, how Vander's father had always treated him like the bastard child he was, favoring Vander's younger brother. Vander had crashed at Kovan's foxhole plenty of times; he'd gotten tired of his father's maliciousness. All the families of the Seven were upset, furious at the way his father had pushed him out.

Thinking back on everything he knew about his old friend, Apollo wasn't surprised Vander wanted to help the Cursed. It was in his nature to help others. Clearly, it was something he inherited from his mother's side, as his father was a greedy politician. "You know, your father is the one who rallied the Hunters in the first place."

"Why do you think I came back?" Vander arched a single brow. Apollo kept silent. "Ever since my brother died, Father has been trying to officially appoint me as his heir. I never wanted anything to do with him or the Seven, not until I found out that my father had been slowly gathering his own forces to fight the Cursed. I can't let that happen."

"It could take years until he steps down on his own," Apollo baited him, knowing there was more to the story than Vander let on. As transparent as he always seemed, Vander always had his own secrets.

His caramel eyes sparkled. "Who said he'd step down?"

"You'd kill your own father?"

"If that's what it comes to? If there's no other choice? I would not hesitate to put a bullet between his eyes." A deep inner loathing bathed in the tension of his jaw.

Apollo nodded, believing in Vander's conviction.

Vander adjusted the half mask on his face. "Bring her to me when she wakes." He hesitated, peeking back over his shoulder. "It's good to see you, Apollo. And it's good to see you care about someone."

Without another word, Vander scaled the nearest wall and vanished into the night.

Apollo snuggled Jinx closer to him, needing more of her touch. He did care deeply about this woman. That's exactly why he was so scared. After conversing with his father, Apollo had made the decision that he needed to tell Jinx everything—even the part he wished wasn't true, the nightmare that lived within him, haunting him. He wanted to love her with no secrets between them.

He felt selfish for waiting this long to tell her; he'd meant to tell her before she left for the convention. He just couldn't hide himself from her anymore. Apollo was no longer able to ignore the fact that the monster was a part of him and would always be a part of him. And his knowledge on their strange ties. She deserved to know the complete truth.

Apollo knew the time would come when he was forced to tell her, but he dreaded it, worried that it would hurt them both more in the end.

"Please don't resent me for this," he whispered as he took her home.

Chapter 43

Jinx

J inx stood in front of the house. The two-story limestone house had an elegant façade with tall, crossed windows and a wrought iron balcony overlooking the stone street below.

It resembled the Tertain manor in Wateredge. Jinx squinted, focusing on the house.

It *was* the Tertain manor.

Gold specks floated around in the still air like sparking sand. Taking in her surroundings, she could see only the regal structure of the house, surrounded by an endless void. Waves of beige desert rolled around them as far as the eye could see.

"Am I dead?" Jinx wondered aloud. The last thing she remembered was being put into a headlock by a man she'd encountered in the alley after the Hunter gathering. Apollo had run straight toward her.

A soft titter came from her side. "No, you aren't dead." Jinx pulled up her blade hand instinctively, pressing into a soft neck before realizing that her blade was nowhere to be found. Instead, she was face-to-face with Camilla Tertain, teardrops of metallic gold trailing down the inner corner of her eye. "You're very deep in your mind, and you have no weapons here."

Jinx eased her hand down, looking at the house and back at Camilla. Confused, she frowned. "You're..."

"A Cursed. Yes." Camilla played with a strand of her blonde hair, twirling it around her finger.

Jinx chastised herself for missing such an important detail when they spoke. Camilla must have been wearing colored contacts, concealing the silver streaks embedded in her irises. Silver eyes crying tears of gold.

"How is this working then? Where are we? How are we speaking?"

As the door to the house opened, Camilla stepped forward, her white silk dress billowing in the false wind.

Jinx thought back to the stories she'd heard of Camilla being trapped in her house, forbidden from being seen by the rest of society. She only ever went out when it was absolutely necessary when her family gave her permission.

"I call myself a dream walker," Camilla said, taking Jinx down the corridor to the stairs at the far end. "I can watch others' dreams, weave some of my own, and sometimes I'm even granted a glimpse of the future. I was able to connect your mind with mine in your unconscious state. I've been searching for you since we met at Apollo's birthday. I knew who you were the instant we met. You do not usually sleep so deeply, Jinx."

No, she didn't. Of the few times in her life when Jinx was able to dream, most of those dreams revolved around the creature of the woods. Perhaps her body did not let her drift into the dream state because she was always on alert, ever aware of the dangers around her.

"How did you know who I was when we met?" Jinx had been under her illusion, so how did Camilla see through her disguise?

Softly, Camilla explained. "I had a vision." They delicately climbed the stairs together, all the way up to the attic Jinx had once broken into. Upon opening the door, she saw the same paintings and sketches as before, free of their cloth covers.

"These paintings are mine." Camilla dipped her chin, waves of her short blonde hair tipping forward. Her mannerisms were gentle and subtle, like a deer sauntering through a forest.

Jinx analyzed the series of artwork before her, observing the soft strokes and harsh slices, the unique style of painting on each canvas. All of a sudden, things started clicking into place. These paintings were retelling the story of the Fallen Virtue, the one she'd learned about in the scroll. Camilla had reproduced them, depicting the tale that had been forgotten by the people of Somnium. Here, the distinct frames of the parchment had been replicated and brought to life. Everything was here: the five objects belonging to each Virtue, the Hall of

Judgment, the moment where Akuji fought back against the other Virtues, and the creation of the Vessel.

"You knew about this the entire time." Jinx's mind spiraled. If these paintings had been made public, Jinx could have figured out the answer to her riddle so much sooner. She'd been closer to the answer than she realized all along.

Camilla clasped her hands together in her middle. "My father suspected my art would be controversial. The one in the museum was the only one he allowed me to display. He forced me to disguise the Fallen Virtue if I wanted my painting to be shown, so I did. But I only barely covered him, knowing that if someone with a keen eye looked closely enough, they'd spot him."

"Him?"

"Yes, him."

Jinx went to the next portrait, the one she'd taken note of in the real house: the portrait with the scratched face. "So, you know the name. The answer."

"I do not. You do. Only you will know. I play a role in your journey. The Virtues have granted me a vision, the foresight to know that I am supposed to be here with you now. I know I am supposed to share my magic with you; however, what you see is strictly to your eyes." Camilla came to her side.

"I am simply following the instructions that the Virtue has sent me. One from above instructed me to give you my magic." Jinx held her tongue as Camilla spoke. "I do not hold the answer, but I am supposed to guide you in the right direction."

Jinx exhaled sharply, her gaze fixed on the scratched portrait. She looked closely at the claws that ruined the face behind it, a shirtless chest exposing the bare, sculpted muscles honed from years of life. Then, she noticed the uneven white scar slashed across his torso—a scar now intimately familiar to her, almost as if it were her own.

Jinx's heart rate plummeted.

Camilla took Jinx's hand, opening the palms up to the sky, feeling the calloused, hardened skin. "You see, the answer had always been in front of you, Jinx." Camilla brushed a trail from the center of Jinx's palm up to the pad of her middle finger. Curling gold flecks fell from her hands. She carefully arranged the sand floating in the air, forming it into phrases from Jinx's riddle. "This adventure is simply the beginning, the first chapter of what is to come."

"Tell me the full story," Jinx said.

Camilla circled Jinx with sorrow in her eyes. "I cannot. I do not even know the full story myself. Only the one living in his body does."

"Who is 'he,' and who is living in his body?" Jinx felt as if she already knew the answer, but her heart did not want to admit it.

Camilla planted herself behind Jinx. "May I?" She put her hands up by Jinx's cheeks. Jinx gave a reluctant nod. This was what she'd been waiting for her entire life. The very last puzzle piece was right in front of her; once she solved this damn riddle, she could finally go home. This was *it*. Hesitating was for fools. Whatever the answer may be, however difficult the reality of the situation proved itself to be, Jinx could not falter now.

Just then, Jinx furrowed her brow. "What do you want in exchange for this information?" No one willingly gave up knowledge like this without a form of payment.

"Free me from my parents, and you'll earn my loyalty." Fair. Jinx nodded again.

Camilla closed her fingers around Jinx's eyes. A thundering rumbled in her chest, her pulse pounding viciously through in her ears. Jinx shut off all thoughts, mentally preparing herself for whatever answer was to come.

Camilla opened and splayed her fingers, laying a veil over Jinx's sight and revealing to her the lines of the riddle, written before them in cursive. The first letter of each line had been bolded and was a different color than the rest of the riddle.

In the table where five once sat, now sit four

No matter how much you believe, our minds still deceive

It's a punishment for seeking the truth

Knit from people's worst desires

One who seeks is bound to bloom

I .N. I. K. O.

Iniko. The name was on the edge of her tongue. "Hush," Camilla silenced her. "Do not say his name yet. You can only speak it once, so wait until you wake."

"Why?" Jinx was ready to end it all, to be released from her bargain, to hug her mother again and feel her velvety touch.

"It will not work in here, and the reign of Chaos will begin," Camilla warned her.

Jinx's eyes ventured past the riddle and focused on the portrait of the man.

Jinx nearly collapsed at the sight of him, like a knife of betrayal had been stabbed right through her heart.

Suddenly, the scratched man's face cleared, restoring the original brushstrokes. His raven hair was styled in a princely manner, and his straight nose and sharpened edges molded to the darkness. His eyes revealed a familiar, emotionless glare, though they bled crimson instead of their usual wintry storm color. His forehead was skinned white with the rune of chaos. Tiny marks were tattooed over the bridge of his nose, matching the slashes that lined his jaw and chin.

It was Apollo, but it was not him at all in tandem. The portrait, stoic as he seemed, radiated an uncontrollable energy that lured people into their sins. A lullaby enticing bad decisions. Apollo's tattoos embodied another, embodying the fallen Virtue.

Golden sand peeled Apollo from the portrait, puppeteering him at the age of fifteen and the creature of Jinx's haunting. Staring at each other until their hands touched, a firm shake of a deal sparked a clash of red energy. Blinding, bursting and shredding the form of the creature, forcing itself down Apollo's mouth.

Falling to his knees and gripping his throat, choking on the Virtue as it overtook his body and settled into his soul. Apollo's hair was leeched of color and eyes burned crimson, to then flip to his natural color. Switching between the two pallets until it normalized.

The scene shifted, to Apollo at twenty three with the black book in hand. Magic reeling back into his palms, dumbfounded and uttering. "I did that to her. We... did."

A set of knocks erupted from the door to reveal a reflection of Jinx. "We need to talk." She knew that night as it was the one she went to him with the revelation of the network theory. The image turned to sand, erasing the events.

Camilla's words echoed in her mind: *only the one living in his body does.*

Apollo's housed the Virtue of Chaos in his body. Apollo lived with the very creature that dammed her to be alone in this world and forced her to live apart from her mother. Apollo *knew.* Having that kind of power, that sort of entity trapped inside, there was no way he couldn't have known. If the fallen Virtue spoke to him. Spoke through him. Lived through him.

Apollo knew. Apollo knew. Apollo Knew.

Apollo Voclaine *knew.*

He must have known the truth that night at the inn; maybe that was what he'd meant when he admitted that he was afraid of hurting her. When had he discovered the truth?

He *knew*.

And he *kept* it from her.

The voice in his head...it must be the Virtue speaking to him. The ring was intended to keep the Virtue in his body, allowing Apollo to stay in control of the magical deity inside of him. Apollo is the Virtues personal, living vessel. Using it's abilities through him. Why hadn't he told her? Why did he lie to her?

He'd lied to her.

Jinx's breath died in her throat. How could he? The only person Jinx brought herself to trust, the only person who knew the extent of her suffering, and yet, he'd chosen to keep this crucial information from her.

The Vessel and her riddle were one. Jinx and Apollo tied in some strange fated way, meant to collide, search, and solve the Vessel and riddle. And just as the Vessel and riddle were one, Apollo and the fallen Virtue were one.

Jinx's hands trembled as sheer fury boiled in the marrow of her bones.

"Be careful how you proceed with this information. Death hunts for you, Ghost," Camilla whispered cautiously. Jinx could barely hear her; all she could think of were all the ways she wanted to make Apollo bleed. Hurt him the way he had hurt her. She wanted revenge.

Jinx trusted Apollo. She'd exposed herself to him, thinking she'd found the one good person in Somnium. Thinking that he was her partner, a true friend she could call her own. She'd almost fallen in love with him—had she fallen in love with him?—thinking that he loved her for everything she was, regardless of whether she was a thief, a murderer, or a curse.

She'd been wrong. So deadly, fucking wrong.

Jinx had let her emotions get the best of her; she'd allowed him to tear down her walls because he'd shown her some kindness. With her guard down, she stopped being Jinx, the Face-stealer, the Ghost of Somnium. The monster humans trembled before the savior of the Cursed.

The girl who'd sacrificed her life to a demon, all so that her family wouldn't suffer.

But Jinx wasn't that same little girl anymore, complacent about living the life she was handed.

If people thought she was a devil, well, she'd prove them right. She'd close her heart to everyone and anyone who tried to get close to her. They did not deserve her kindness, her strength. They did not deserve *her*.

If Apollo wanted to betray her, fine.

Let the Hunters come for her, she would enjoy the kill, the blood she'd shed.

Jinx would allow her rage to turn her into the savage everyone feared.

And she would bring hell to the city of Somnium.

Chapter 44

Jinx

Jinx's eyes shot awake, moonlight pouring in through the cracks of her room's sheer curtains. Apollo was perched on a chair in the corner, smacking his lips as he awoke.

But she didn't see Apollo, her friend, her partner, her lover. No. All she saw was a stranger sitting in her room. The face of the Fallen Virtue masked his own, plagued by white marks and scarlet red eyes.

Apollo pushed himself up from his seat, taking a step toward her. Jinx backed away, sliding her legs off the bed and retreating from him. "You're awake."

Hurt clenched her center at the sound of her nickname. Jinx met his gaze, her chin quivering. "How long did you know?"

Apollo twitched, shaking his head. "What?"

"How long did you know?" Jinx said louder, built-up anger seeping past the ache.

Apollo swallowed, finally understanding what she was really asking him. He rubbed his hand over his mouth, the ring warming his finger.

"*How long did you know?*" Jinx asked again, more frantic. "When were you planning on telling me? Were you ever *going* to tell me?"

Her hands trembled, heat swarming her neck and face. She was unable to contain every complex emotion that bubbled up inside of her.

"I *was* going to tell you," Apollo muttered under his breath, shame curling at the bend of his neck.

"When?" Apollo kept silent. Jinx clamped down on her jaw, pushing back the storm of tears that now stung her eyes. She took a considerable step forward. "Answer me, Apollo Voclaine, or I *swear* on the Virtues, you will not like what I do next."

"I've been trying to tell you since we got back from the Archives."

"But when did you learn about this?" Jinx snarled, a sharp edge in her question.

Apollo backed himself into the wall, leaning on it for support. His stillness only poured gasoline on Jinx's flames. She wanted him to look at her, to tell her the truth, but Apollo wouldn't meet her stare. "I first suspected it the night you came to me with the network theory."

That had been a month ago.

Jinx's knees beckoned for release, her shoulders drooping. His admission and betrayal solidified everything she feared. "You." Her eyes squinted in anger, searing into his soul. "Lied to me." She jabbed a single finger deep into his chest and growled. "You kept this from me. You held me back from everything I wanted. You used me."

"That's not true—"

"—Yes. It is. You *used* me, Apollo." A single tear slipped past her defenses, slowly marking a path down her cheek.

"I'm your..."

Jinx burst out into a fit of laughter. "My what?" Her shallow breaths were making her feel hysterical. "My friend? Should I dare even say, lover?"

How could this happen again? She'd been tricked *twice* by the same entity, the one living in Apollo's body. She'd been *so* careful. And here he was, winning her heart only to rip it out of her chest, squashing it, crumbling it into nothing. The urge to cry vanished, replaced with fury.

Jinx was furious at herself. But as angry as she was with herself, her wrath toward Apollo was tenfold for willingly keeping necessary information from her. For using her to find the Vessel, using her to his advantage. Their entire friendship, their kisses, the moments they shared—everything had been built on lies. What was honesty even worth, anyway? All it brought her was pain.

Jinx sneered as a flood of tears broke the damn. "No. We are *not* friends." She recognized the frigid lilt of her voice. "I bared my soul to you, I let you in, and...and you just tossed all of that aside for your own benefit."

His tone turned icy. "As if *you're* any better. You kept *hundreds* of things from me in the beginning. I'm sure you're *still* keeping things from me. You're being unfair."

"The situations are entirely different."

"I beg to differ." Apollo's nostrils flared. "I kept this secret to *protect* you. Have you not kept your own identity a secret to protect yourself?"

"No! It is entirely different. You kept this because you are a coward. My secrets are survival. Because it's my life on the line *every* time. My life!" Jinx yelled with years of built up anger in her core, finally to be unleashed.

"I was trying to do what was right."

"That's rich," Jinx bit out. "If this is what your friendship looks like, Apollo Voclaine, I don't want it. It's pathetic and cowardly. Just like you."

He dropped the unexpressive mask over his features as his ring flared red, matching the ring around his eyes.

Jinx pushed him further, wanting to inflict upon him the wounds she now suffered from. She wanted it to burn so badly that he could never forget her. Every time he thought of her name, her face, she wanted his body to hurt so tremendously that he wished for death. "Someone who is your friend wouldn't keep a secret like that, wouldn't blatantly spit out falsities right to your face, time and time again. I gave you my trust, and you threw it away. I let you know the real *me*."

Apollo's veil faltered, if only for a moment. Her words struck his heart, ripping it in two. Wrath controlled her tongue, anchoring each and every one of her blows. And then, in a deadly calm voice, she looked him dead in the eye. "You hurt me, Apollo. And you were the *one* person I trusted. I thought that you, out of everyone, wouldn't ever do that to me."

Apollo lost his cool, snapping, his full range of emotions set free. His brows pinched together as his forehead wrinkled, his temper now loose. "Do you think I enjoyed keeping it from you? Knowing that you could hate me at any moment? All I did was care for you, but I always knew it wouldn't be enough because, in the end, all I do is hurt people." Red overpowered the gray in his eyes, glowing in intensity. "You see it all around me, Jinx. I never hid that from you. I hurt people; it's what I do. It's what I'm *good* at. It's what this thing inside of me drives me to do. I never stood a chance at winning, not even at the start."

"You're right; we were destined to fail. But if you had *told* me the moment you suspected something was awry, perhaps we would be able to salvage this." She couldn't feel any pity for him. "Now I just look at you, and you're...nothing." Narrowing her eyes, she hissed at him. "Say it. Say it with your chest *what you are.*"

Apollo's jaw flexed, his dead eyes boring into hers. "I possess the soul of the Fallen Virtue. The one who'd cursed you."

She breathed in deeply, sensing the powerful thumps of her heart. She relished the pain, recalling every bit of how she felt so it would not happen again. The heat of her body, the flame in her core raging, the itch in her fists. She took it all in and found madness so wild it was serene.

There was tranquility in savagery.

Jinx licked her lips, forming a malicious smile. "Fuck you, Iniko. Fuck you and everything you did to me."

Apollo's ring dissolved, and his eyes flared red. He began to tremble violently, uncontrolled. "What have you *done*?" He gasped.

The world rumbled beneath them at the sound of the Virtue's name. With those three syllables, Jinx had unlocked a message to the universe, to the Virtues above, that the Fallen Virtue was back.

A sharp pain drilled into her temple. Deep in her core, in her heart, in the well of her magic, she felt the crack of a whip. Suddenly, a weight lifted off Jinx's lungs, and she was able to fully inhale a breath of fresh air for the first time in a long time. She was bargain-free and debts paid. Jinx was free to go home, released from her chains.

No, from the Virtue of Chaos.

For every victory, there was always a loss. Jinx had won back her freedom and her family, but she'd lost Apollo. Jinx tried to focus on the fact that she'd regained her power now that the curse was broken. It was all that mattered.

She turned to him, her voice cold and measured. "The Vessel is in the university, on the second floor, in Warren's lab. You'll need to get Warren's lab key to get in there. Go get your Vessel—destroy it or keep it, *I don't care.*"

Apollo broke into a sweat, beads of moisture licking his forehead, dampening the front strands of his hair. Thin tendrils of the white tattoos she'd seen in Camilla's painting teased his face, now coming to the surface. Apollo was fighting with the Virtue inside of him, brawling for control. He released an ear-shattering cry, knocking his head against the wall.

Jinx curled her fingers around Apollo's jaw, forcing him to meet her gaze. Her nails burrowed into his skin, relishing the agony now consuming his body, the sounds of his suffering music to her ears. "I promise you this, Iniko, Apollo, whoever you are," Jinx cooed. "Come near me again, and I won't need the assistance of a blade to kill you. I'll do it with my *bare hands.*"

Jinx dropped Apollo's chin, leaving him in the company of his own torment, and exited through the window, leaping between buildings. Finally, she felt true freedom. The strings of restraint had been severed; the wind propelled her feet forward.

Nothing was holding her back anymore.

Chapter 45

Apollo

pollo collapsed under his own weight as he watched an enraged Jinx vault out of the room, leaving him behind without a second thought. He wouldn't stop her from walking out. Jinx was better off without him.

He knew what he'd done and the consequences that went along with them. Withholding that information from Jinx, when he'd known it tied to her and what she yearned for. From selfishness, he continued being the barrier between Jinx and her family. He'd take the blame. Her words echoed in his mind: *You're nothing*. He agreed. He'd be an idiot to think otherwise, to think that he could be accepted and loved by another when all that followed him were the wounds he'd inflicted on other people.

All of his relationships had been restrained or broken, all because of the chains imposed upon him by the Virtue. The demon, the Virtue, would not let him rest—live —peacefully. Be the man he wanted to become. Be the person his city needed. Be the partner Jinx deserved.

Apollo curled in, his shoulders caving. He felt as if hands were rearranging his insides to best fit the Virtue now overpowering him. White noise buzzed at his forehead and temple, trickling down his neck and spine, slowly eating him alive.

His skin felt ice-cold, his muscles aching to move.

He once believed he'd been *so close* to achieving the happiness, the companionship he'd always wanted. He'd been a hair's length away from making it a reality. But all of this, all of the destruction that now lay at his feet—it was all his fault.

He should have told her sooner.

He should have told her everything, instead biting down on his tongue, pulling out his pen, and writing it all down in his journal. He was shackled by this ring, by this being inside of him. He'd betrayed her. And in doing so, he'd betrayed *himself*.

Apollo tucked his knees under him, forcing afoot to lay flat on the ground so he could lift himself up. His hand splayed against the wall, supporting his weight, as Apollo stumbled forward. All he could think about was Jinx, his family. There was still so much to tell them.

The Virtue purred in his mind as an unrecognizable laugh slipped from his mouth. His left hand was now under the control of another, his fingers spasming.

Apollo didn't know how much longer he would be able to act based on his own free will and maintain control of his own body. He dragged his feet to the desk where his notebook lay. His hands shook, the sensation of the soft desk surface disappearing from beneath his fingers.

The greenish hue of his veins darkened to black. "Listen, Iniko." Apollo groaned aloud.

Listening, the Virtue drawled.

Apollo's fingers hardened. Dropping the pencil, he now struggled to lift it back up. He needed to finish the note for Thatcher, Fey, Arya, and Jinx. They all needed to know the plans he still had for them, the things he still yearned to say, the feelings he felt deep down but was unable to express.

"I propose one last deal."

The Virtue placed in the back of his mind.

Apollo hastily folded the parchment, aware of the seconds he had left. "We are technically switching positions now, with you in control of my body now, is that correct?"

Yes.

"You'll take full reign of me—mind, body, and soul. I will not utter a word nor wrestle you for authority. All I ask is that you protect my family and you protect her. Guard her with your *life*. If the world must burn for her to be safe, then let it end in ashes. However, if *any* harm comes to her, you bow to me *forever*."

The organ of magic swelled within him, expanding, shoving all his other organs aside. The Virtue was regaining his full power. Apollo knew he had to complete this deal quickly. Seconds ticked by.

Apollo began to laugh. "No," *Iniko* sniggered through Apollo's mouth, now voicing his opinions. "I don't bow to anyone. And in all likelihood, your precious lover *will* get hurt. What more can you offer me, Little Lord?"

A crack of a whip lashed down Apollo's spine as stars entered his field of vision. Around him, everything was blinding white. Apollo coughed, regaining control of his voice. "*That's* the final offer. Or I'll fight you every second of every day until I can get back to her. I will learn every weakness you possess and use all of them against you until you crumble so that neither you nor I may live. The way I see it, you need me more than I need you. Without my body, you are nothing."

Apollo's face itched, his skin splitting across his cheeks and the bridge of his nose. Iniko sneered. "You'd sacrifice your own body for her?"

"I would die a thousand times for her," Apollo said solemnly. He'd do more than just die for her; he would do *unspeakable* things to protect her.

"Sounds heartfelt." the Virtue hissed, and Apollo's gut clenched tight. He heaved on the floor, his insides stinging the back of his throat. "Though the world is not forged for heartfelt promises. I'll protect her Apollo Voclaine, but your body will stay mine."

With his head down, Apollo's control slipped through his fingers, no longer fighting the inevitable. Regrets poured through him. He'd never been able to truly enjoy the life, the advantages, that had been given to him. All he could think about was the chronic gloom that darkened his heart, the smiles he'd miss from the people he cared most in this world. Thatcher's rambles, Arya's stubbornness, Fey's cheerfulness. Mother's kindness and Father's advice.

And Jinx. He'd just miss Jinx. Not one specific thing, but all of her. It was all or nothing with her, and he wanted everything she had to offer—the good, the bad, and the ugly. And he'd forever hate himself for lacking the courage to tell her that he loved her when he had the chance.

There would only ever be her.

Apollo recalled the emerald of her eyes, outlined in silver, and the way they glistened in the sun as he fell into darkness and uttered an apology no one could hear.

Chapter 46

Iniko

He climbed to the surface of his consciousness. Power and presence filled the body, now his for the taking. He twisted his wrists first, flipping between his palms and the back of his hands. He tested his fingers next, the motions and agility of his muscles, the strength now his to control.

Iniko inhaled deeply, closing his eyes, his mind connecting to the flow of blood coursing through him, the rhythmic beats of his new heart. He grinned, thinking of the unimaginable things he could do now that he was in charge of the body. He felt powerful once again. Muscles rippling beneath his skin, he flexed them over and over again, savoring the taste of control.

The Little Lord had been pushed aside, never to return. Iniko exhaled, brushing long fingers into his new raven hair. Euphoria had started sinking in, elating the Virtue.

It had been a thousand years since Iniko was settled into a proper form—1,279 years since he'd been exiled from his own court. His own brothers and sisters had imprisoned him. The Celestial Architect was furious at Iniko finding out his plans for humanity, for this world, turning his siblings against him. Cornering him and gathering their powers to form his confinement, overpower him, and lock him away. He'd get to that soon enough. All he could think of now was the crisp air infused in his chest and the brightness of the colors all around him.

Iniko laughed, the rumble coming from deep inside his chest. "This is what it feels like to be *alive*." He crossed the space to the vanity, staring at his new reflection in the mirror.

So beautiful, brilliantly handsome, and dark. His vibrant eyes gleamed ruby red as gems. White tattoos were now etched into his face, the sigil of Chaos drawn in scars in the very center of his forehead. The embodiment of havoc smiled at his strikingly angled face. Iniko stroked his cheeks, his chin, the silky skin smooth to the touch, but for the tattooed and scarred ridges under the pads of his fingers.

All of *this* was now his.

Iniko's scheme had finally paid off after thousands of years. Now he had a Vessel to find and destroy. Only then would the shackles of divinity be lamented, would he be freed from this mortal jail and able to return to the Divine Realm, to his court. Pandemonium. His people were waiting for him.

Iniko filed through Apollo's bookshelf, locating his black leather tomb: *The Omniform*. The divine gift had first been given to him by the Celestial Architect, his father. His maker. Just as each of his siblings had been given an object to help them succeed in their roles as Virtues, his book had been his most treasured companion.

Iniko's ability of raw energy and pure chaos were able to change the shape of the book into any object he saw fit. The manuscript learned from experiences and was able to note them down, learning actively. Just as Akuji's curved sickles only worked for him, *The Omniform* was created solely for Iniko's use. A ledger to keep a record of humanity's sins and weigh punishment thoroughly. As well as form deals with their weakness in mind.

He picked the book from the bookcase, feeling the magic within him tethering itself to the holy object. The volume levitated above his palms. Crimson threads of energy swept around him and penetrated the book. Iniko's core blossomed. Waving a hand, he morphed the book into a key, dangling from a chain on his neck.

Now he would be able to open the door to Warren's lab on his own. But first, Iniko wanted to have some fun. He wanted to *play*.

Iniko rummaged through Apollo's closet, tossing shirts and pants over his shoulder. Everything fell within the gradient scale of black to white. "Does the man have anything with a *hint* of color?" Iniko muttered to himself. "How did I stand being trapped for so long? His style is so boring that I want to gouge out my eyes. Ah, wait...this isn't terrible."

Between his fingers, he held a black blouse with a maroon overcoat and coordinating pants. Bronze strings swirled around the overcoat in wired, abstract patterns. It wasn't the extravagant, lavish wardrobe he was used to, but it would do for the time being.

When wreaking havoc, one must look their best, as he always said. People would always remember the worst parts of a person instead of their best. If that was what they'd summon at first thought, one's appearance had to be impeccable. Iniko was sure to always bring his worst.

Iniko stripped himself from Apollo's damp and bloodied clothes, congratulated himself with a luxurious bath, and slipped into the maroon garments. He finished up the look with a pair of spotlessly polished, knee-high black boots, picking the lint off the shoulder of his overcoat.

"Stunning." He admired himself in the mirror.

Iniko dipped into his powers, licking his lips at the delightful taste of strength. Finally, he was in control of his *body* again. That ring of Apollo's drowning him in chains, a vicious ward, and Apollo's will shunning him from reign. A moment later, he located the mind of the scientist and snagged on the thread, traveling right to the scientist with a wave of his hand. He needed to build this body's proper strength built. It is difficult to achieve his plans with only a slim percentage of access to his power.

His boots landed on marbled floors. A crystal chandelier dangled low over a dinner table. Figures filling the seats around it flinched at his abrupt arrival.

Pity Warren was with guests. At least they were guests who were adorned in jewels, intricate lace necklines, silk gloves, and top hats.

Iniko smiled. "I do *love* interrupting a good party."

Warren's wrinkled face slowly paled, his eyes widening. Iniko sauntered gracefully to the back of Warren's chair, passing by a lady wearing a hat adorned by a purple feather. "Love the touch," he commented, stroking it. Upon reaching Warren, Iniko curled his long fingers along the neckband of Warren's shirt. "I'll be needing him momentarily. Excuse us."

Whatever protest Warren had been about to offer died in his throat as Iniko flicked his wrists, transporting the two of them to the gates of Somnium University. The university was a mountainous structure between Eastern Heights and Crosspoint Yard. The wrought iron gate was locked for the evening. Using his free hand, Iniko tested the metal in his palm.

It was thick, solid. He wondered if it would be better to crush it with his hands or infuse the seal with magic, making it vanish. He decided to crush it between his fists, the iron wrinkling beneath his sheer force. Yanking the lock from its position, the gates sprang free.

Warren scrambled from Iniko's grip, clutching the hem of his shirt. "Apollo, why are you doing this? I demand you put me down at once."

Iniko rolled his eyes at the mention of the Little Lord and crouched down to Warren's level. "I am not that pathetic boy." Warren's lips quivered. "Ah, you recognize who I am. You see the runes inked onto my face."

"Why are you doing this?" Warren whispered in fear.

There were plenty of reasons why Iniko was doing this. First and foremost, it was in his nature as the Virtue of Chaos to be the manifestation of madness. To personify peoples' darkest desires, embody the devil they most feared. There was also the matter of his pent-up anger after being banished and trapped by his own siblings. His own family thought he'd gone mad, locking him away for all eternity. The Vessel still tethered him down to the mortal world. And then, the past few years he'd spent fighting to take a host of a body that wasn't even his. The list went on.

He settled on something that he knew would unsettle Warren. "Because you played with something that isn't yours."

After stepping upon the university grounds, he sensed and counted 87 guards patrolling the perimeter and winding corridors of the academy.

Distraught, Warren pulled at his neck. "You won't be able to enter. There are a hundred guards."

Iniko flicked a finger, blasting his power to find each mortal soul and shatter their hearts one by one. They dropped like flies. "What was that?" He could not wait to reach his full power again.

Warren shook his head, tears streaking down his cheeks. His terror smelled sweet in the air. Iniko could get drunk off that scent and could taste it on his tongue like a sugary dessert.

Towing Warren by the collar like a rag doll, Iniko felt like he was walking a dog. Bursting through the double doors of the foyer, Iniko smelled the scent of his prison immediately: woody and pungent. The magic overwhelmed him, humming over his skin, though he was unable to pinpoint the exact location. It was everywhere and nowhere.

"Where is your lab?" Iniko asked. Warren half-heartedly chuckled. Iniko hauled him up, his feet dangling off the ground, worried eyes bulging from his skull. "Perhaps you did not hear me the first time. *Where* is your *lab*?"

Warren pointed a shaking finger upstairs. "Lab 26B. Sixth door on the right."

So the dog could talk. Iniko followed the instructions of his pet, tugging him along on the trail. Reaching the door, Iniko stretched his free palm out for the true key. Fitting it into the hole, turning it until he heard a click. As the door opened before him, he spotted the mysterious box.

Iniko ambled in, chucking Warren to the side. He cautiously inspected the box first, careful to not touch it. He knew that physically placing a hand on it, touching skin to wood, would trap him inside it. "You know, Sir Warren, I recall the day you set me free. The day you trudged across the Woodlands while doing your thesis research and then stumbled upon my pitiful prison. You're still just as ugly to look at. Just as miserable, too, I see."

Warren coughed, sneering at Iniko. "And?"

"No need to be feisty. I was going to thank you for releasing me. Truly. Who knows if I would have been trapped in there for centuries, give or take. I would not be able to enact my revenge if it wasn't for you."

Warren lunged for Iniko, scalpel in hand as if the blade would nick him. Iniko raised his palm, freezing him in place with one gesture. "...As I was saying. It's truly been a pleasure, but once you started playing with my prison? You hurt me. Really hurt me. That just won't do. You also hurt my court—the Cursed, as you call them. They are my people, and I simply cannot let you get away with that. I'm sure you understand, yes?"

Warren blinked once.

"Ah, I knew you would. We would have gotten along if things were different." Iniko clapped his hands together. "Alas, all good things must come to an end. And I'm afraid I must kill you now."

Warren tried to scream, but his lips couldn't move. Iniko adjusted his fingers on Warren's skull, trying to get the best grip. He dug his nails into the flesh, securing his spot, before ripping Warren's head from his body. The cracks of bone and tearing of flesh sounded like a symphony of torment.

Blood puddled at his feet and splattered all around him, speckling both the floor of the lab and Iniko's suit with flecks of crimson. "Shit, I guess I have to get this cleaned now."

Iniko dropped the decapitated head, and it rolled away from him until its forehead bumped against the wall. Red smeared, coating Iniko's hands. He rolled his tongue over the blood, the metallic tang a syrupy delight.

Iniko faced the Vessel, ready to be rid of the foul object. He could feel the energy of the box deep under his skin, the runes that had been placed upon it to keep him trapped within.

Summoning his body's organ of power, magic flooded his system from the nape of his neck to the tip of his toes. A droning hiss weighed on the center of his palm as scarlet tendrils of raw energy circled Iniko's frame. The threads snaked over and around him, consuming him.

Iniko breathed in, bracing himself to infuse this box with magic. To destroy it by any means necessary. Putting one foot behind him, Iniko extended his two hands in front of him and pushed, thrusting a portion of his magic toward the Vessel. Slowly, he pushed more and more of his magic into it, feeling as its energy shifted and twisted, pure chaos crackling around him like lightning.

The wooden Vessel began to splinter away under the weight of the magic.

Iniko loved watching it disintegrate under his ability. He'd been trapped for over a millennium, all because he sought out the truth. He'd wanted to show his siblings that the Celestial Architect had planned to kill them all, disappointed in their actions as Virtues, determined to start over a new world with a new set of children.

He remembered what it felt like to wake up from the wards that had been placed upon him, the trance their father had magicked into their minds to cut them off from consciousness. The Celestial Architect had been so determined to leave this universe to its own self-destruction.

His sisters had laughed in his face, convinced it was just another trick like all those times before. His brother, Akuji, reacted the same, no matter how often Iniko pleaded with him and begged his brother to open his eyes. At Iniko's end, he thought he saw Akuji wake himself up and he'd hoped that his brother would come and rescue him. That they could stop their father together.

But Akuji didn't.

Akuji could have done more, could have freed him from the Vessel, could have fought harder for him than he did when his siblings gathered in the Hall of Judgment to decide his punishment. Instead, he left Iniko alone, shrouded in darkness, alone with his thoughts. Iniko had been left to conjure a scheme that wouldn't take place for centuries. He was more determined than ever to kill his father—and as disappointed as he was in his siblings, Iniko would need them in order to do so.

He could feel his connection with the Vessel snapping, the shackles that once bound him splitting apart, fissuring at the seams.

With one final burst, Iniko sent the remnants of the collapsing Vessel to the floor. Little shards of wood, metal, and magic prickled Warren's dead body.

Panting, Iniko shook his hair back, taking in the glorious sight before him.

The Vessel was gone. He'd gained his freedom, his divinity. The Cursed were his for the taking.

Chaos had finally returned.

And a plan that took over a millennium to dream up was finally coming to fruition.

No one would be able to control him, confine him, ever again.

Iniko chuckled as he departed the university, sucking the blood off his fingers.

How beautiful liberty was.

Chapter 47

Jinx

Jinx found herself in the graveyard, drowning in a flood of emotions. She was staring at her own tombstone, the name her mother had given her inscribed on the rock before her.

Her name stared right back at her. The person she was, the child inside longing for her family to be family. Pitiful. She knew of their love for her, but she lacked the physicality of it.

She'd traded away her life with that bargain, and now here she was, getting tangled up in her own emotions over Apollo, letting feelings surpass all logic. It was logic that had kept her alive all these years, kept her going, kept her out of harm's way. Whenever Jinx followed a stream of logic, she never got hurt emotionally—physically sometimes, but never emotionally.

Logic allowed her to map out the path she would take, understanding all the risks and mentally preparing herself for all the obstacles she would be forced to confront.

Feelings didn't help her do any of that. Feelings *hurt*. Feelings brought a constant sense of discomfort to her center. They were volatile and unpredictable, capable of infusing you with pain at every turn. Yet they also brought joy with them and laughter. They brought experiences that touched her heart, a sense of brightness and vitality that Jinx hadn't felt in a long time.

As she outlined the letters of her real name on the stone, Jinx felt empty. She rejected whatever emotions bubbled to the surface, defending the sanity of her mind for just a bit longer.

Rage, sorrow, regret. Of all the things she felt, Jinx would focus on wrath first—grief could come later. If it came at all.

Jinx vowed to herself that she would not make the same mistake twice. Maybe she needed to kill the other half of her, shatter the child inside.

Ever since she stormed out of the Voclaine manor, she hadn't been able to bring herself to go home. To see her mother. To tell her that she'd been alive all this time. She dreaded confessing to her mother that she was the murderous myth known as Jinx, that she had become a criminal just to protect her.

At the thought of it, Jinx giggled. What a *joke*.

It had been twelve years since she last felt her mother's embrace. Jinx wasn't that little girl anymore. She was a monster now, a villain. What mother would want that?

Jinx had lived with a thousand different faces and personalities, but she could no longer live with herself.

Apollo proved that once and for all, shoved in her face the lesson that if she dared to be herself, all she would encounter was pain.

Jinx's nails dug into her palms, slitting her skin open and drawing blood. She punched the tombstone, her knuckles splitting open. Jinx punched it again and again, unable to feel a morsel of the pain that shocked her body because it'd been emotionally wrecked already.

How could she have missed it? Once she'd opened her eyes and spotted the signs, the red flags were all there, blatantly in front of her. She'd been blind-sighted by all the good she wanted to see. The love and life she could have had. Given herself what she so yearned for. What could have filled that certain void?

It was her fault. The child. The name is inscribed on the stone. It wasn't Jinx. It was her all along.

"I wouldn't do that if I were you."

Jinx froze. Suddenly, she felt on edge. In danger. "Well, you're not me, so it doesn't matter. Move along."

The shadow stayed, its husky tone echoing across the graveyard. "Do you ever plan on going back home, Amira? Or should I just call you Jinx now?"

That name. *Her* name. Only two people knew that name, and this voice did not sound like either of them. The hair on the back of her neck rose in fear.

Jinx picked up a knife from her side and flicked it at the figure behind her. She twisted her body for a better angle, her slick feet ready for the attack.

The man caught it between two black-gloved fingers without moving a step.

With swept-back golden hair and the eyes to match, the man stepped out from his shroud of darkness, revealing sand-colored skin, the sharp angles of his squared jaw inviting the night in. Massive black feathered wings attached to his back skimmed the ground he walked upon, falling behind him like a cape. The grass beneath him decayed and died with every step.

Jinx lifted her chin, suddenly realizing who it was that she'd thrown a blade toward.

Akuji tossed it back to her. "I believe we can help each other."

Acknowledgements

It's unbelievable to think that this book has already come to fruition. And to think it all began with a short story featuring Jinx as our main character and a world with unstoppable development.

I want to begin by thanking my family for their immense support during this entire process and for inspiring me to push forward. I'd be nothing without them! So a huge thanks to my parents, my brother, and sister, as well as their significant others, and my niece who always greets me with a smile. Thank you as well to my loving partner who was forced to listen to my ceaseless chatter and reassured me every step of the way.

A special thanks to Michelle Brito and Cassandra Mitchell for being my beta readers since day one, listening to me ramble about my ideas, and being honest with their thoughts.

Thank you to Mariana Beneli who introduced me to the book world a few years ago, inspiring me to embark on my own writing journey. If it weren't for her coming to me during COVID-19, there would be no 'The Ghost and The Fallen' today.

A huge thank you to my editors Noah Sky, Carrie Napolitano, and Dylan Jones Gosselin. Without their support and courage to take on this book head-on, 'The Ghost and The Fallen' wouldn't have been half as good as it is today. I will definitely be working on the rest of the series with them, as they were so crucial to the process and so welcoming with this book.

Finally, thank you to my readers! Thank you for taking the chance to read my first book and journey with Jinx through the world of Somnium as changes are underway. I do want to apologize for the ending as I know it may not be the one everyone wanted; however, it is the one necessary for what is to come.

Thank you again to everyone who made this book possible. I cannot wait for all of you to read the second book in the series! Until next time.

Milton Keynes UK
Ingram Content Group UK Ltd.
UKHW041250071123
432122UK00003B/8/J